ANGELS, DREAMS, AND PARTRIDGEBERRIES

Short Stories by:

J.C. CHANDLER

authorHOUSE®

AuthorHouse™
1663 Liberty Drive
Bloomington, IN 47403
www.authorhouse.com
Phone: 1 (800) 839-8640

Published by AuthorHouse 11/30/2018

ISBN: 978-1-5462-6238-1 (sc)
ISBN: 978-1-5462-6237-4 (e)

Library of Congress Control Number: 2018911634

Print information available on the last page.

Any people depicted in stock imagery provided by Getty Images are models,
and such images are being used for illustrative purposes only.
Certain stock imagery © *Getty Images.*

This book is printed on acid-free paper.

To my beautiful family,
my love always

CONTENTS

A FEAST

I had come to the Great Smoky Mountains to think about my life. Nearsighted, overweight, feeling unmanly at age fifty, I wanted more than the daily grind in my colorless modern office, where every object had the shape of a rectangle. Something vague and essential had never touched me, or had quietly slipped away.

In the Smokies I began each day with a stroll through the lush green valley known as Cades Cove. One morning I came upon a small, silver-haired woman wearing a baseball cap and the grim look of a battlefield commander. Her tanned, hoe-handle legs bolted out of khaki shorts into muddy hiking boots. Binoculars as long as her forearms hung to her waist. Nearby, a telescope on a tripod was aimed at the surrounding woods.

"There!" she barked, pointing at a speck darting in and out of the treetops. "Did you see it? Carolina chickadee." She checked off a box on a printed list. "Their numbers have been down, but they seem to be making a comeback."

"I don't know much about birds," I confessed, "but I'm willing to learn." The speck had temporarily vanished.

"There he is again! And there's another."

"Where?"

She followed the birds' flight with her finger. So far she had not needed the binoculars.

"Oh, yes," I agreed, wondering if I had seen two birds or just floaters, a common problem for nearsighted people.

"Lilian Templeton," she said, offering me a brusque handshake. She spoke in a gruff, masculine voice, completely inconsistent with her diminutive stature.

I introduced myself with a smile, which was not returned. Ms. Templeton now used her binoculars to scan the trees. "I keep hearing a nuthatch," she said, "but where is he?"

"What does it look like?" I passed a futile gaze over the woods.

She didn't answer. The binoculars fastened onto spot after spot in the long treeline. Ms. Templeton's mouth curved resolutely down.

"There! No. Yes. There! Hear it? Whi-whi-whi. Little rascal, where are you?"

I heard only an avian medley coming from everywhere. Ms. Templeton peered through the telescope but was disappointed.

"Follow me," she instructed.

She stepped like a Clydesdale through the high, wet, sweet-smelling grass and weeds. Only once did she pause to admire two Japanese beetles mating on a leaf. I offered to carry the telescope, but she assured me it wasn't a problem.

"Oh, look!" I cried out.

Four birds soared erratically above us. Ms. Templeton never raised her head.

"Red-eyed vireos," she muttered. "They're all over."

"Oh" I said.

She led me through a patch of weeds that rose above her head. We climbed a little knoll, from which she expected a better view, and she searched the woods again with mounting urgency. The sun had burned off the early mist. I wiped a drop of perspiration from my glasses.

"I'll find you, Mr. Nuthatch," she vowed, and plunged ahead toward the trees.

I followed obediently. Without diverting her gaze, she pointed out the small, purple flowers of spiderwort and cautioned me about a clump of poison ivy. She discovered some blackberry bushes covertly intermingled in a hundred weeds, and I took a moment to sample the ripe fruit. It was tart and delicious.

"There's the nuthatch!" she suddenly cried. She confirmed it with the binoculars. "Two of them. See them creeping down the trunk? Nuthatches can move upside-down."

She handed me the binoculars and checked off "white-breasted nuthatch" as I focused on the little birds.

"It's a male and a female," she said.

"How can you tell?"

"Look at the crowns. The male's is darker."

I studied the birds until they worked their way to the opposite side of the tree. "I couldn't tell," I said, and gave her back the binoculars.

For the first time she smiled. "It takes practice. Don't be discouraged."

"Not at all. I'm having fun."

"Let's see if we can find something easier," she said, and we pushed on through the vast meadow.

A stream, studded with rocks, flowed across our path. Ms. Templeton found a bridge---a single log four feet above the water---and she marched over it, tripod and all, without hesitation. She asked if I needed help.

"I'll do it a different way," I said. Straddling the log, I inched across on my bottom.

As we walked, she called my attention to many remarkable plants. Their small, delicate blossoms and sturdy leaves formed a rich, but reticent, canvas. I had barely noticed them on my daily strolls; seeing them now through Ms. Templeton's eyes I was surprised and delighted.

At last she stopped and spread out the tripod. She surveyed a poplar grove with the binoculars as I wiped my forehead and neck and tried to observe something novel---anything---by myself. Suddenly she whispered "Yes!" and aimed the telescope.

"Have a look," she said proudly.

I bent forward to use the telescope at her eye level. In sharp focus was an iridescent, dark-blue bird perched on a high, bare branch. It seemed to be posing just for me. Its round head turned haughtily from side to side, and it fluttered once and then settled down contentedly. "Chew-chew, chew-chew," it sang.

"Indigo bunting," Ms. Templeton boasted.

"It's beautiful! I've never seen such color."

I watched the amazing creature for aver a minute. Then Ms. Templeton studied it again. When it finally flew away, her face had softened and her eyes seemed moist.

"Sometimes I get caught up in the chase," she said, "and I forget why I do this."

"Why do you?" I asked.

"That bunting is just a tiny particle in God's infinite creation. As the psalm says, He has prepared us a table. We have only to savor the feast."

"I see," I said. And for a sweet moment I really did.

HELP IS ON THE WAY

Ten-year-old Amy's mother had forbidden her to play with her best friend, Leah, because Leah, for the second time, had contracted head lice. The girls lived only two blocks apart. They often walked to each other's house alone through a weed-infested alley in their neighborhood of tiny old houses overpopulated with children, pets, and jobless relatives who needed a place to stay.

Leah loved to sleep over at Amy's and walk to school with her the next day. One Sunday evening, while the girls were in the bedroom playing a video game, Amy's mother, a short, thickset woman nicknamed Star, discovered the lice.

"Again! What the hell is wrong at your house?"

Leah began to cry, and Star resigned herself to the wretched task of extermination. "Can't send you home, dammit! Get into the bathroom."

First she examined Amy's head but didn't see anything. In the bathroom she found the leftover Rid and the nit comb. Fortunately enough liquid was left to do the job. After three applications, latherings, rinsings, and meticulous, section-by-section combings, Star dried Leah's hair with a paper towel, picked out the last nits with toilet paper, and flushed all the trash away. She covered Leah's hair and ears with a shower cap, then returned to Amy's room.

"Did you get on the bed?" she barked at the girls.

"No, honest, we didn't," Amy tried to assure her.

She inspected the pillows and blanket anyway and rechecked the girls' heads and clothes. "Maybe we caught it in time. Tell your mother she needs to get Rid. There's a comb in the box. Damn! This has got to stop."

Leah stared at the floor, on the verge of tears. Amy followed her mother into the living-room, with Leah trailing timidly behind. Star's boyfriend, Brian, lay half-asleep on the couch. A football game blared on their plasma TV, which filled one end of the room. Atop the TV was a nameless white angel, protector of the home.

"Help me, please," Star beseeched her.

"What the fuck is going on?" Brian rasped. He always reacted irritably when anything disturbed his marijuana dreams.

Leah was afraid of him and scurried back to the bedroom. But Amy stayed to hear the adults.

"It's Leah," said Star. "The second time she comes here with lice."

"Send her home," Brian muttered.

"You know I can't do that. Her mother's probably drunk, and her boyfriend don't give a shit about the kids. He's probably drunk, too."

"Did you clean her up?"

Star took a Budweiser out of the fridge and twisted off the cap. "She's clean, for now. But I ain't doing this again. Last time I had to throw out clothes, bedding, towels, half the house. I'm sick of it."

The following Friday school was out because of a teachers' conference. In the morning Star received a phone call from her aged grandmother. The woman had broken her hip the night before and was in the hospital. Star was needed desperately.

"You'll have to watch Amy," she said to Brian. "This could take all day."

Brian, having decided earlier to take the day off, had called in sick to his warehouse job. Pallid and a bit smelly, as though he really were sick, he lay supine on the couch, gazing at the TV.

"Did you hear what I said?"

"Yeah."

Star looked into Amy's room and saw that her daughter was still asleep. Amy had stayed up to watch a family movie on her bedroom TV while the adults shared a blunt and watched an R-rated movie on the big set. Star seemed to remember Amy creeping silently into the living-room to see the last half of their movie. She and Brian had been feeling too mellow to object.

"I'm going to let her sleep," she told Brian. "Fix her breakfast when she wakes up."

He didn't answer.

"All right, Grandma, help is on the way." She hurried out the door and began the twenty-mile drive to her grandmother's village.

Around eleven, Amy emerged from her room. Her mother's absence didn't worry her because Star often went to help neighbors with their problems and might talk for an hour or more. Seeing Brian in his familiar repose, she fixed herself a bowl of Cocoa Puffs. She ate at the kitchen table, from where she could see the big TV. A black man and a white woman were shrieking at each other while the beefy, tattooed host kept inserting himself between them. Amy gathered that both partners had had sex with other persons. She knew this was a sin if you were married but wasn't sure about an unmarried couple like Brian and her mother. Brian was not her father. Star had brought him home a year ago, a few months after Amy's father had been shot by the cops.

She left the cereal bowl in the sink, then dressed herself in a pink jersey and navy jeans that lay on her bedroom floor. She surveyed her Barbie and Ken dolls, electronic games, and a messy paint-by-numbers set. Nothing sparked her interest. In the living-room she glanced at the TV but it was only the midday news.

"Brian, where's Mom?"

Brian was asleep. She asked again in a louder voice, but he still didn't move. She tugged his tee-shirt.

"When's Mommy coming back?"

He finally stirred a little. "Huh? What? What do you want?" he snapped.

"Where did Mommy go?"

"I don't know. She'll be home later."

"Can I call Leah?" Amy held up his cell phone.

"Yeah, sure." He turned away and fell asleep again.

When Leah answered, Amy heard her sniffling. "What's the matter, girl? Are you crying?"

"Mandy keeps shaking me."

"So tell your mom."

"I'm not supposed to wake her up. I hate my sister."

"You still got lice?"

"Mandy's got them now."

"Well, I know what we can do so you won't be in my house and I won't be in yours. Let's meet at Scully's Market. I got a dollar and you'll be away from Mandy."

"Cool."

Amy thought the corner grocery store was a great idea. They might be lucky and find candy on sale. After the call she whispered at Brian, "Can I hang out with Leah?" Of course, he never heard.

"I'll take that as a yes."

Her cleverness delighted her. She slipped out the door into a chilly autumn day. She had neglected to put on a jacket, but she was full of purpose now, completely oblivious to the weather. She raced down the street toward the connecting alley. When she passed Mrs. Perry's house, the woman's old mongrel barked at her. Mrs. Perry stopped raking leaves and called Amy's name.

"Honey, wait. Come here a minute."

Amy walked back impatiently, wondering what the old lady wanted now. It seemed like she always wanted something.

"I saw your mom drive away this morning. Is she coming home soon?"

"She'll be home later."

"Do you know if she got any more of them pills?"

"The Xanaxes or the Percosets?"

"Percosets. She gave me some for my headaches."

"They're in the medicine cabinet."

"Where did she go?"

"I ain't sure but she won't be home till later."

"You tell her I got extra food stamps if she wants to trade for the pills. I ain't no moocher like some around here."

"She gave food stamps to my aunt Claudia. I'll tell her." Amy started again.

"You need a sweater, honey," Mrs. Perry called after her, but Amy kept on running.

The girls met in Scully's tiny, pitted parking lot.

"See, I told you I had a dollar." Amy waved the bill in Leah's face. "You can get something, too, but I want Gummy Worms."

"I want Jujyfruits," said Leah.

"Cool."

In the dingy little store they brushed past two customers on their way to the candy aisle. They found their favorites but then decided to explore all their options. Nothing was on sale.

"I changed my mind," Amy said. "I'm getting Milk Duds, no Kit Kats, or, I don't know, maybe a Snickers."

"I can't have peanuts," said Leah.

"Do you like red licorice?"

"That's nasty. I really want these." She took a bag of Spice Drops off the rack. "We can share them."

"They're a dollar-ten. You got a dime?"

"No. I ain't got nothing."

"Then we can't afford it."

Leah gazed at the brightly colored candies. She glanced across the store at the front counter. The other customers had gone, and big Scully was nowhere in sight. Like Amy, Leah wore only a jersey and jeans. She fumbled the candy under her jersey and waited for Amy's reaction. Amy stifled a laugh.

"Are you going to sneak it?"

Leah stood on her toes and surveyed the store. "Shh! Walk in front of me."

The girls crept to the end of the candy aisle. They walked innocently toward the door, but just then Scully rose up behind the counter. He looked them over. Kids were always stealing from him.

"What you got under there?" he growled at Leah.

"Nothing."

"Oh yeah? Let me see." He tramped around the counter and grabbed Leah's arm. The candy bag fell out. "You damn kids! I'm trying to run a business here. Pick that up and get behind the counter, both of you. Sit on the floor. This time I'm calling the cops."

The girls huddled together on the floor and started sobbing.

"We were going to pay for it," Amy pleaded.

"We'll put it back," Leah added.

When Scully opened his cell phone, they both cried out, "Please, Mr. Scully, don't call the cops."

"We're sorry," said Leah.

"Here, you can have my dollar," said Amy. "We don't want the Spice Drops."

"Hey! Sit down there and shut up."

A woman came in and bought cigarettes. She exchanged pleasantries with Scully, and they smiled at each other. After she left, he appeared to have a change of heart.

"All right, I'll make a deal with you. I won't call the cops if you'll help me stock the shelves."

"Sure, I'll help," said Amy.

"Can I help?" Leah asked.

"You can both help. Come with me."

He led them back to the stock room, where a brown skinned man was arranging boxes.

"Sanjay, go watch the counter for a few minutes," Scully told him.

The brown man left. Scully led the girls around rows of cardboard boxes. The room had a stale smell but was well lit by overhead fluorescents. "See what I got here. Canned beans, tuna, spaghetti. Lots of work here. I'll bet you love spaghetti."

"Yeah, we do," the girls agreed.

"It's my favorite thing to eat. But you know what? This store takes a lot of work, and I get awful tired."

Scully was a large, bulky, intense-looking man. The hair on his head was mostly gone, but he had a scruffy salt-and-pepper beard and hair in and around his ears. When he grinned, his teeth looked like rows of com. He sat down on a pile of unopened boxes.

"So, you both cool with helping me today?"

"What do you want us to do?"

"Well, come here and we'll make a plan."

He crowded them between his legs and maneuvered them onto his thighs, facing each other. They were nervous, and even more so when he rested his meaty hands on their knees.

"Hey, nothing to be afraid of I ain't the cops, am I? Do you know I used to play Santa Claus downtown? Ho, ho, ho!"

The girls exchanged a skeptical look.

"See, we're a good team, the three of us. You can help me and we'll forget all about the stealing. The cops are bastards. We don't want them in this, do we? Hell, they'd make you spend the whole school year in juvenile detention."

He pulled them in closer. Amy lost her balance, and her hand landed next to his crotch. When he held her arm, she felt movement inside his pants.

"Yes, yes, just like that," he murmured. "Nice girls. Really nice girls."

Leah was plainly scared, but Amy was seized by curiosity. She didn't resist Scully's grip. She remembered something about male anatomy that had made people in a movie laugh.

"Yep, we're going to be good friends," Scully went on. "You're going to be my best helpers, and all my best helpers get to choose their favorite candy... Oh my God!"

He suddenly shoved the girls off his lap and sprang up. Leah fell to the floor, and Amy crashed into a stack of empty boxes.

"You little shit!" he roared at Leah. "You got fucking head lice. I saw them on your ear. Get the hell out of my store, both of you. Don't ever come back here."

The girls scrambled to their feet and fled. Scully chased them to the front door. "Go on home, you pigs! Get out of my parking lot!"

He lunged toward them, and they ran all the way to their sheltering alley.

"Do you think he'll call the cops?" Amy asked.

"He better not. That guy's a perv. If he tells on us, we can tell on him."

"I ain't never going to that store again."

They twirled around the alley, flinging clumps of weeds into the air, until their rush of energy was spent. They realized now that they were cold, although neither would admit it.

"Guess you still got lice," Amy said. "I better go home before my mom finds out about this."

Leah just kicked stones. After a minute they walked sullenly toward opposite ends of the alley.

Star returned home around dinner time with a KFC bag. Brian was awake now, watching a sitcom with Amy.

"Where were you?" Amy asked.

"At Great-grandma's." She gave Brian a reproachful look. "Didn't you tell her?"

"Yeah, I told her. She forgot, it all."

Amy could tell that her mother didn't believe him.

"Never mind," Star said. "Let's just eat. I ain't cooking nothing tonight."

She handed out the chicken dinners. Brian ate his on his lap in the living-room. Amy took hers to the kitchen table to eat with her mother.

"What's the matter with Great-grandma?"

"She's in the hospital with a broken hip. And her house is a mess and nobody's taking care of her dogs. The place stunk so bad, I had to open all the windows."

"Yuck," was Amy's only comment. She hardly knew her mother's grandmother. "I washed the dishes and cleaned up my room." She pointed to the dishes drying in the rack. "And I emptied all the ashtrays."

Brian came into the kitchen to get a beer. "Yeah, she's been working like crazy, for some reason. You got something to hide, girl?" He laughed and went back to the couch.

Star pushed away her chicken and held her head in her hands. "Damn! I don't deserve this shit. Everybody's always wanting something. It don't end, ever."

Amy remembered Mrs. Perry and the pills but decided not to mention it.

"I've got to go back tomorrow," Star moaned. "It'll take all day to clean that place up."

"I'll help you, Mommy. Can I go, too? Please?"

"Come here, baby. Give me a hug."

Amy knew what was coming. She wiped her greasy fingers and went to her mother. Star hugged her tightly, pressing her cheek into Amy's chest.

"I'm a good person," Star muttered.

"I love you, Mommy. But take me with you. I really want to help."

"Tomorrow's Saturday, ain't it? Maybe I'll take you. If nothing else, you can walk the dogs. God, I don't need another day like this one."

"My day was lousy, too," said Amy in her most empathetic voice. It always gave her pleasure to comfort her mother.

BAD NEWS

Star would rather have entered a war zone than the brick and glass building of The Metropolitan Housing Authority. She had not been given that choice, however. The letter from The Authority directed her to appear at ten o'clock in the morning before an officer investigating a complaint regarding the occupancy of her house. Three years ago, The Authority had provided the old two-story house for Star and her young daughter, and it continued to subsidize her mortgage payments. The house was located in the oldest part of town, where most of the homes were rented.

"Baby, you are an arteest," her boyfriend Brian had once pronounced. "Ain't nobody plays the system like you."

They'd laughed but he was right. Star, who had dropped out of school in the tenth grade, who hadn't read a single paragraph of anything in her whole adult life, who believed in angels, devils, ghosts, and psychic phenomena, learned about every relevant government benefit and how to get it.

Every six months the Department of Job and Family Services renewed her food card for more than its legitimate value because she falsely claimed to be the guardian of her teenage nephew. When the gas company threatened her with disconnection, she wangled a grant to cover the payments. She received a monthly disability check after her friend, Dr. Harris, listened sympathetically and then certified that bouts of vertigo rendered her unable to work. She had learned about the government subsidy for poor, first-time home buyers while having her nails done in gold stars to match the design on her necklaces. After she was accepted into the program and put on a waiting list, she told her friend Latoya about it.

"Which government is it?" Latoya asked.

"Ours, of course."

"I mean, is it federal, state, county, what?"

"Who the hell knows? What difference does it make?"

After leaving school, Star, along with her younger brother and sister, lived with their grandmother because their parents, facing drug charges, had fled the state. Star worked a series of minimum-wage jobs until she turned eighteen and went to work at Sharky's, a strip club. She was a petite, blond, fair-skinned princess with a sweet voice and an ability to charm the patrons by remembering their stories. The men adored her. In her first year she earned enough money to buy a new sports car for herself and used cars for her siblings and grandmother. She developed a passion for gold jewelry. What the men didn't give her she bought for herself, and wore everywhere. The other dancers nicknamed her "Bling."

She made friends easily with the dancers, bouncers, and managers and formed useful bonds with her most faithful regulars. One of these was Dr. Harris, a kind retired gentleman, who came in to see her every week. Another man, a well-connected lawyer, used his influence to convert prison time to probation after her third drunk-driving episode.

But her triumphant years ended as she passed her thirtieth birthday. By this time she was drinking heavily, using weed and black-marketed prescription drugs, and putting on weight. Her legs ached after prancing in spike heels until 2:30 in the morning. She was living with, and supporting, a younger black man, who claimed to be a writer of rap music but spent most of his time stoned or hanging out with his friends. One night he was killed by police while fleeing from a store robbery. A week later Star learned that she was pregnant with his child, and she finally decided to fix her life.

* * *

At The Housing Authority she entered a waiting room filled with black women. Several of them wore a head scarf Somalis, Star thought, which was how she identified any black woman in a head scarf Folks in her neighborhood viewed these immigrants with disdain. Although she was not inclined to bigotry, she had adopted the prevailing attitude in this case. Somalis had come here to get welfare benefits intended for poor Americans. Somalis couldn't be trusted, were always looking for trouble, made slaves of their women. You couldn't understand their accent, their religion, their dress. They drove old rustbuckets without insurance.

Star was the only white woman in the room. She kept discreetly apart from everyone else. For the next half-hour she made a silent speech, trusting that God would overhear. He had always guided her life with justice and compassion, she emphasized. Surely He would come to her rescue again. She felt a need to remind The Almighty of her accomplishments over the last ten years. She didn't get drunk anymore or use drugs, except for an occasional joint with Brian. She was raising a bright, happy, mixed-race daughter, so no one could accuse her of prejudice. She volunteered at Amy's school, collected for the American Heart Association, shared her food card, visited friends in the hospital, gave her change to the Salvation Army. She had cut down on cussing, gossiping, and judging less fortunate people.

She caught the eye of a worried-looking Muslim woman and smiled at her. God understands, she wanted to tell her. He won't let us down. He will get us through our unforeseen crises. Star tugged at her soaken armpits.

At last her name was called. A clerk led her to a meeting room, where she was confronted by a black woman who stood six feet and weighed at least two hundred pounds. Star's mind flashed back to Sharky's, where she had always been the smallest dancer. The woman introduced herself as Chloe, and they sat down at one end of a long table.

Chloe glanced through her papers as if to ensure that everything was in order. "This is what we received," she said in a businesslike tone and slid a sheet of paper across the table.

Star saw the words "boyfriend" and "brother" but her mind had gone blank. "I'm sorry," she finally said. "I didn't bring my reading glasses."

"Okay. Basically an anonymous person sent us an e-mail informing us that people are living in your house who shouldn't be there. I think it mentions your brother, John Townsend, and your boyfriend, Brian---I forget his last name---and your brother's son. This is what we're investigating. You understand that whenever we get this type of information, even if it's from an anonymous source, we are obligated to investigate."

Star shook her head morosely and stared at the printout.

"Did you understand the rules that were explained to you at the closing?" Chloe asked. "Guests cannot stay longer than thirty days. This informant claims that these people have lived with you since you moved in, three years ago. And we have motor vehicle records that show Brian and John at your address." She presented two more inscrutable documents.

Star was too busy fighting back tears to reply. "Never let them see you cry," Latoya had once told her friends. "That's how they know you're guilty."

Chloe stacked all her papers together. "Well, we're not going to make a final disposition today. Our purpose here is just to inform you about the investigation. We'll be scheduling a formal hearing next month, and you'll have a chance to explain things. But I have to caution you. If these charges are substantiated, you will probably lose your voucher."

"I'll lose my house," Star choked out.

"Here's another copy of the rules," said Chloe, "in case you no longer have yours." She handed over a sheaf of stapled pages and stood up to end the interview.

On her way out Star passed two of the Muslim women. She turned away and hurried to the door. She wasn't going to let a bunch of Africans see her cry.

* * *

In her driveway Star patted her wet cheeks with a tissue and tried to formulate a plan. Losing her voucher meant losing her house unless John and Brian found full-time jobs. Not likely. John still had occasional seizures because of a motorcycle accident that had killed his wife and cracked his skull. He sometimes did handyman work for neighbors or was hired as a weekend bouncer in a local bar. Brian had never held a job more than a month. He survived on his pretty-boy looks, having lived off a succession of women before finding his niche on Star's vinyl sofa.

Her nephew Timmy, John's son, mowed lawns, shoveled snow, washed cars, and usually earned more money than both adult men.

Maybe she needed a lawyer. Would her old friend Daniel, one of her regulars at Sharky's, remember her after ten years? Would he save her again at no charge? It might be worth a try.

The sun had come out. The daffodils near the front stoop gleamed in response. Since moving into this house---her own home!---Star had learned how to plant and nurture a garden. The daffodils were only the beginning. Next, the forsythia and fragrant, lavender lilacs would frame the sides of the yard. Lush stands of peonies would greet her visitors in May. Then, as summer advanced, her climbing roses would swarm over the trellis that John had erected out back. When fall arrived, the crimson firebush hedge and multicolored chrysanthemum bed always made the neighbors pause as they walked their dogs.

* * *

But one of those neighbors had betrayed her, it seemed. For no reason at all.

Her own dog Maxie, a pit bull whose gentle nature belied the reputation of its breed, began barking at something behind the house. Star's mind, adrift on an empty sea, was jolted back to the moment. She walked up the driveway and shooed away a one eyed cat that roamed the neighborhood. Then she plopped down on the back stoop and hugged Maxie tightly.

Inside, she found John and Brian in their usual positions on the perpendicular sofa set. John always slumped on the smaller sofa, facing the TV, while Brian preferred to stretch out on the long one with pillows under his head. They were watching a game show on the plasma TV, which filled one end of the living-room.

"Hey, babe, how'd it go?" Brian asked.

"I don't know. It's crazy. I don't want to talk about it."

That satisfied him. John looked puzzled but then he, too, turned back to the show. Star knew how they cringed from even the possibility of bad news. She'd have to tell them, of course, but not right now. They would react with useless, tough-guy rants against hardass bitches or sadistic motherfuckers who didn't give a damn about poor folks. Their whining never solved anything, and she didn't want to hear it. Grabbing a Budweiser from the fridge, she went into the bedroom to be alone.

* * *

Daniel Bridgewater, Attorney at Law, had a prominent advertisement, including his handsome photograph, in the Yellow Pages. Star smiled at him, recalling his courtly manner and generous habits at Sharky's. She had seen him through his divorce, a transition period, and a year of his second marriage. She had slept with him a couple of times between marriages. She knew he had children and stepchildren in a wide range of ages.

Star called his office and made an appointment for the following week. On that day, as she was trying to decide what to wear, her phone rang. Mr. Bridgewater's secretary apologized for the inconvenience, but her boss had suddenly and urgently been summoned out of town. All his appointments had to be cancelled.

Star was confused and disappointed. "Can we reschedule?"

There was a pause on the other end. "Mr. Bridgewater isn't sure how long this case will take." Another pause. Actually he's not taking on any new clients at this time."

"Oh really?"

"I'm sorry for the misunderstanding. His case load has been quite heavy lately."

"The bastard," Star whispered. For a moment she considered an attack on his family. Did his second wife, or possibly his third, know where he liked to hang out after working hours? But those kinds of plots might lead to complications, and revenge was a waste of time. Besides, the last thing she needed now was a wealthy, influential enemy.

"Well, tell him I still think about him," she said. "I'll pray for his good health."

* * *

Star's friend Latoya and her three small children lived in the shabbiest house on the block. Although much younger than Star, she had plenty of history with social workers, police, public defenders, free medical clinics, and various charities. Street-level experience, she called it. Star and Latoya hung out together in each other's homes, shared a bottle of wine or a joint, and vented their grievances and their grief Star trusted Latoya more than her white friends, who were incurable gossips.

"I can't think who would do this to me," Star lamented. "I don't go around picking fights or snitching on people. Who the hell's been spying on me?"

"Ain't no use worrying about it," Latoya said. "It could be anybody. Someone jealous' cause the government gave you a house and you made it the nicest one in this crappy ghetto. Maybe they see all that bling-bling and wonder how you got it." She gestured at Star's necklaces.

"I worked for it."

"The Housing Authority might know who it was, but they ain't going to tell you. And it really don't matter 'cause you're fighting The Authority, not the snitch."

"Maybe it's that old couple behind me. They get pissed if Maxie barks when they're taking a nap."

"Look, you need to focus on what to do now. If it ain't already too late, that is. You got to make a choice."

Star heaved a sigh. "John can't be on his own. If I don't remind him to take his medicine, he'll have them seizures."

"Why can't he live with your sister?"

"They don't get along. She won't let him smoke in her house."

"What about him and Brian getting a place?"

Star shook her head. "Me and Brian been together eight years. I know he ain't much. Most days he don't move his ass off the couch. But he's there, you know? And he's the closest thing to a daddy Amy's ever had. He don't mind that she's half black. Sometimes he takes her to McDonald's or Dairy Queen."

"Well, you got to make a choice. You want to keep your house or your two men? If it was me, I know what I'd do. Hell, I already kicked out three deadbeats."

"It ain't easy. Not for me anyway."

"You need to be strong, Momma, 'cause you got to do this by yourself. Ain't no government agency coming to the rescue. Nobody going to bat for you on this one."

* * *

It was Sunday evening and Amy's classmate and best friend Leah was sleeping over. Star was eavesdropping on the girls, who were in Amy's room gossiping about their teachers and the other fifth-graders. Leah lived two blocks away. The girls often walked to each other's house through an alley, and after a sleepover they walked to school together in joyful harmony.

Leah and her two sisters had no father, and their mother was an alcoholic. Her mother's boyfriend turned mean when he drank, and Star worried about the three girls. She felt as if she were doing God a favor by keeping Leah safe.

From their conversation Star learned that Amy and Leah were paying attention to boys. They debated which boys were the hottest or the smartest and who were the losers. They shared stories and secrets, and Star smiled when they broke into giggles. A friendship like theirs might last a lifetime. It would be cruel to break them up.

The refrigerator and cupboards were stocked. The bills were paid. All the houseplants were watered and the carpets vacuumed. She had cleaned the chandeliers in the kitchen and living-room, her proudest acquisitions, bought, like her gardening equipment, at yard sales in the upscale parts of town. John had installed them after she agreed to let him and Timmy move in.

Outside, her seasonal parade of color had begun, and her yard would soon be the jewel of the neighborhood. This year she might plant a vegetable garden behind the garage.

It wasn't like the old days when she had money to give away, but things were stable and manageable. She had climbed a mountain and planted her flag.

Brian, John, and Timmy were spread out on the furniture in front of the TV. Her boyfriend and brother had been in the same position all afternoon. Star used the remote to turn off their movie.

"Hey! What're you doing?" Brian yelped.

"Sis, we're watching that," said John.

Star pulled a chair into their midst. "All right, boys, listen up. I'm afraid I got some bad news."

WHAT ARE FRIENDS FOR?

Marty called when I was analyzing studies on career education, specifically, which methods work best for given populations under different conditions. I was deep ln thought, searching an ocean of data for one or two golden formulas that would impress our government providers. I hadn't heard Marty's voice in twenty-five years, but I recognized it instantly.

Allie!" he cried into the phone. Allie, is that you?"

"God! Marty, this can't be you."

"It is. It's me. I'm in town for a couple of days. How'd you guess?"

How did I guess? Well, for one thing, no one else had ever called me Allie. My name is Allen. Some people start off with AI, but they always switch to Allen. Only Marty redefined me as Allie. For another thing, no voice, male or female, has ever had the same effect on me. Marty's voice was a fire alarm, overturning my thoughts and putting me on alert. Marty came on like those scary things that used to fly out of 3D movies, making us cringe and then laugh.

"Who else would call when I'm up to my ears in paper?"

He roared. The same exaggerated outburst that had always titillated me. In high school he was the closest thing I had to a friend.

"Allie, seriously. Is this a bad time?"

"After twenty-five years how could it be a bad time?"

"I mean if you're busy..."

"Of course I'm busy. When haven't I been busy?"

Another roar. "Hey, really, Allie, what are you working on?"

I could see him with his mouth open, as if anything I said would be a punch line.

"We do educational research here. Right now we're trying to get funding for a five-year project on career education. We're going at it from several new angles--longitudinal studies, results from postsecondary schools, whole new criteria. Basically, we're reevaluating the evaluation methods."

I suddenly remembered Marty's attention span. He was probably picking his teeth or inspecting his fingernails.

"Yeah, that stuff's important," he said. "Listen, I won't take your time. I just thought we could have lunch."

I sat upright and my mind raced. Hell, I decided, what harm could there be? A couple of days, he'd said. Two days and he'd be gone.

"Sounds good. When and where?"

"You choose the when. How does the Hotel Cambridge sound?"

"The Cambridge?" I reached for my wallet. The hesitation in my voice must have tipped him off.

"Hey, Allie, don't sweat it. This one's on me."

"Oh, I can handle it." Typically tactless Marty, I thought, but the twenty-dollar bill in my wallet relieved me.

"No way, buddy," he insisted. "It's my treat. What time's good for you?"

We decided on 1:30 to avoid the crowd. He said he'd meet me in the hotel lobby.

Afterwards I wondered how he had found me. Had he called Betsy at home? I'd have to tell her not to give out my office number. Maybe he'd talked to one of our classmates who still lived in town. Marty had gone to some tiny college in the South, supposedly because a relative got him in with a big donation. As far as I knew, he had never come back.

* * *

In high school I was a diligent loner, who weighed less than most of the girls. From my wary isolation I idolized and envied Marty; he was a bridge, albeit a shaky one, to my peers. In the morning he would burst into homeroom early, right after I arrived. "Hiya, Sunshine!" he'd call to me with his arms wide. Or another day it might be, "Numb-nuts! How the scooby-doo are ya?" He always had a nickname for me. It started us off with a laugh.

He would then grant me half an hour of divided attention. First he copied my homework or listened to my predictions about exam questions. If he was feeling intellectually virile, I showed him how to do math problems. Soon his head became saturated, and he would tell jokes and imitate our teachers. Kids gathered around my desk as they arrived. Marty would then delight us with tales of his escapades.

If he never excelled, Marty always exceeded. While other kids sneaked a beer from their parents' six-pack, Marty smuggled it around in kegs. He threw all-night parties whenever his parents left town. I attended one of these after lying to my mother about sleeping at a friend's house. That evening I watched in awe as Marty paraded into his kitchen with the keg tapper and applied it triumphantly before his cheering guests. He handed out paper cups like an archbishop dispensing Communion.

His pranks became part of our school's folklore. One night he injected plastic cement into the door locks and we all had a day off. The school board hired a security guard after that, but Marty would not be thwarted. He and some other boys kidnapped a sheep, led it up to the art room on the second floor, and made it sit among the sculptures, where it went unnoticed for half a day.

All the girls chased Marty. He had condoms stashed everywhere---in his wallet, locker, glove compartment; even, he demonstrated, in his math book. He tore around town in an open Jeep, always with two or three girls screaming and hanging on for dear life. Again and again he was cited for speeding, and finally they took away his license. He drove home from juvenile court that day at eighty miles an hour.

* * *

In the lobby of The Hotel Cambridge, I passed by Marty without recognizing him. He grabbed my shoulder.

"Ailie! Where ya going, old buddy?" He shoved his hand out and vise-gripped mine as if to let me know who was still boss.

I tried to link this stranger with the Marty I remembered. His tawny curls had vanished like burned-off sedge, leaving sparse ashen threads. Although he still towered over me, his beefy figure had gone to flab. His whole head was bright pink, and his eyes were bloodshot with the arteries seeming to extend outward into crow's feet. The drooping corners of his eyes, the loose flesh on his face and neck, and his rolling belly caused me to fantasize that an avalanche had occurred, exposing the pink apex of a mountain.

"Jeez, you finally came back," I said, afraid to make any comment.

"You won't believe this, Allie, but I started to call you a hundred times since I left home."

I didn't believe it and didn't ask why he hadn't. I was just glad he hadn't.

"What brings you back? Where do you live anyway?"

"Let's go in. I'll tell you all about it."

We entered the grand restaurant, hardly glancing at the chandeliers, velvet draperies, and huge paintings in ormolu frames. Marty had arranged for a window table. When we had seated ourselves, the waiter spread linen napkins on our laps and a boy poured our water.

We ordered martinis.

"Remember this place?" Marty scanned the ornate room, where a few businessmen and dowagers lingered over coffee. We'd had our senior prom here. The boys went spent all their money in the restaurant, and then we danced in the ballroom downstairs.

"What was the name of that girl you took?" he asked.

"Theresa Mayfield."

"Yeah, Theresa. I remember her. I fixed you up with her, didn't I? You weren't even going to go."

"I was pretty shy, and she was even worse. Thanks to you, we had a good time."

"Aw hell, I didn't mind helping you out. What are friends for?"

It surprised me to hear him call us friends, as if we had shared something important. In a corner of my mind a warning light flashed. But Marty asked about my family, and I relaxed. I told him about Betsy, whom I had met in graduate school, and about our teenage daughter. I described my work briefly in simple terms. Marty shook his head when I told him I had sat at the same desk for sixteen years.

"I don't know," he said. "I figured you'd be in the White House by now."

"I've been a wretched disappointment."

"Ha!" he roared, causing stately heads to turn. He leaned forward and spoke more quietly: "Listen, I have certain information that could change your luck radically. Not that you're doing so bad, but everyone can stand a little more upward mobility, if you get my drift."

"I don't think I do."

He signaled across the room to our waiter. "You want another one?" he asked, nodding at my half-full glass. I declined, and he ordered another martini for himself.

"Allie, I have recently become part of an event---an event of historical significance---that is going to make a small number of people very, very wealthy."

Red lights whirled and sirens screamed so loud that I misunderstood his next question.

"Did you ever hear of the Central America?"

"What? Panama? Nicaragua?"

"No, no. The Central America. It's a ship. See, here's the story. Back in 1857---before the Civil War, right?---this steamship was coming from San Francisco to New York with three tons of gold from the mint. It ran into a hurricane off North Carolina and sank about 200 miles out in the Atlantic. Well, this bunch of scientists knows where it is, and they're getting ready to recover the gold. Allie, do you know what that stuff is worth today? I'm talking up to a billion dollars. That's billion, with a B!"

I sneaked a look at my watch. Our research group sometimes had meetings in the afternoon. Marty would be skeptical if I told him I had a meeting at 2:30, less than an hour away. He might believe three o'clock. I'd have to fix things with our secretary in case he called again.

The waiter brought his drink. Marty raised his glass and said, "To the good life."

"I take it, you're about to become rich."

"You take it right, old buddy."

I knew I should change the subject but, with Marty looming before me, I couldn't think of a graceful maneuver. "How did you find out about this?" I asked.

"I know one of the scientists. We did some business together. Listen, Allie, I know what you're thinking, but this is not a scam. These guys are

Boy Scouts, geniuses. They don't even care about the money; they just want to recover the gold."

"They want the accomplishment, you know, like climbing a mountain. Allie, they've designed this robot submarine. It's like something out of science fiction. It can go two miles deep and it has these arms with claws that can break through the ruins of the ship. They guide it from a control ship with computers and TV screens and all that Star Wars stuff."

Marty paused to gulp his drink. I took a small sip of my own.

"It sounds like an interesting project," I said.

"Project! Allie, this isn't something you put together for science class. This is the biggest haul of treasure in history."

"Well, it's exciting. It's nice that you're in on it."

"You bet I'm in on it. That's why I'm here. It's my Job to raise the capital."

He swallowed the rest of his drink and signaled the waiter again. "You sure you don't want another one?" he asked me.

"We better order lunch," I said, looking at my watch.

"You go ahead. I had a late breakfast." He handed the waiter his glass and said "Ditto."

I wasn't sure what to do. Finally I ordered a club sandwich because it seemed to be the quickest and least expensive thing on the menu.

"Let me ask you something," Marty went on. "Does 80 to 100 on the dollar sound like a good investment?"

"Sure."

"Would you invest $12,000 if you stood to make over a million'?"

"Marty, I can't gamble with that kind of money."

"But it's not a gamble. They know where the ship is. I'm putting in every penny I've got."

"We have bills and a mortgage. We're starting to think about college for our daughter. Betsy's parents are sick."

"No problem. I know you don't have the cash in your pocket. But you've got life insurance, right? You can borrow on it. You can borrow on the equity in your house."

"We just don't do things like this."

"Allie, I'm going to be very honest with you. My life up to now has been a disaster. In high school I was the biggest asshole that ever broke wind. I flunked out of college in my freshman year, after my aunt practically bought the place. I've been married twice and divorced twice, and I don't even know my kids. All my adult life, I've been knocking around selling everything from Bibles to swimming pools. I'm sick of this life. I want to settle down in one place with a good woman and do something right for a change."

I didn't know what to say. He sounded sincere and quite desperate, but I didn't know what it all had to do with me. When the waiter brought his drink, I noticed that Marty's hand was shaking. The liquid sloshed as he raised the glass to his lips. I forced myself to look out the window.

"We were practically best friends in school," he said. "I wouldn't have graduated if you hadn't got me through. And what did I do for you? Nothing. A couple of dates maybe. Now I have a chance to pay you back royally, to show you that I really valued your friendship back then."

"You don't owe me anything."

"Just tell me one thing: How much life insurance do you have?"

"Marty, please, I'd help you lf I could."

He went through another description of the engineering marvels his partners were building. On one of his rumpled business cards he tried to draw the robot submarine. He pressed down hard to steady his hand. After that, he told me about his friend, the scientist-businessman, and what a shrewd investor he was.

When my sandwich arrived, I wolfed it down while Marty repeated everything he had just said. The other patrons had left the restaurant; we were alone in the grand dining room except for a few busboys. Marty emptied his glass a third time and looked in vain for the waiter.

"So what do you think?" he asked me.

"It sounds plausible, but I've got to get back. We have a meeting at three."

"Wait, Allie, please. Just answer one question. How much equity do you have in your house?"

"I have no idea."

The waiter finally came over, and Marty ordered another drink. I asked for the check. Marty went on talking until the waiter returned.

"Try to understand," I said. "Betsy and I, are conservative people. We don't take risks."

I got up to go, but Marty just sulked. He said nothing when I covered the check with all the bills in my wallet, and he didn't move as I stood waiting for him.

"Aren't you coming?" I asked.

"Nah."

He made a limp gesture with his arm. The hurt look on his face astonished me; I had never seen him like this. He wants me to feel guilty, I thought, and I resented the tactic. I wished he had never come back.

"Well, good luck," I said, and left him there, cradling his drink and gazing out the window.

* * *

Anyone who watches TV knows what happened eight months later. A team from Ohio, with a robot submarine, brought up the first ton of gold from the Central America. They hauled it into Norfolk, Virginia and transferred it to Brink's trucks as a band played and federal marshals stood by with automatic rifles. The leaders of the crew displayed some of the gold bars and coins while they held a news conference. Twenty to 150 million, they estimated, with lots more to come.

Many of the investors were present at the ceremony. When the camera panned over the crowd, I flew to the TV but it was impossible to distinguish individual faces. The event was on my mind the whole evening. Not that I had any deep regrets about passing up a fortune. (I'm content with my life as it is, and the thought of great wealth actually scares me.) It was Marty I was thinking about. I would have given anything to have seen him in that crowd.

When I recalled our luncheon, the desperation of his appeal struck me again. I kept seeing his trembling hand. Every time I replayed the tape. His voice sounded more like a plea for understanding than for money. I wasn't sorry that I'd turned him down, but that I'd turned him out.

One image continues to haunt me. As I left the Cambridge, I caught a last glimpse of Marty, dull-eyed and deflated, looking as if he were permanently stuck to the chair. He was all by himself in that vast, empty room. It took a long time, but eventually I understood why this loud, irrepressible clown had come to regard me as his best friend.

THE UNIVERSE

The first day we went down to the beach, I saw the driftwood sticking out of the dry sand like the twisted remains of a weird sea creature. Something about it held my attention---its unsightly appearance on the clean white beach, maybe, or its long, sharp edges that might have cut someone's foot. I would have hauled it to a trash can if there had been one around. Instead, I moved away from it as Viv and I decided where to put our chairs.

Viv didn't notice the driftwood. She was upset about the sun-block, which we'd forgotten to pack. She kept looking at the sun in the east and at the long row of hotels, apartments, and condos behind us. We were on the sixth floor of the Gulf Shores Hotel. Our terrace didn't face the ocean, but we still had a view of the beach and some tall palm trees.

"Maybe we can rent an umbrella somewhere," she said.

I pointed out that it was nine o'clock in the morning in March and that only our faces and hands were exposed.

"Still, we shouldn't stay long. The sun is stronger here than up north, and people over fifty have an increased risk."

We sat on our beach chairs and looked at the ocean. Viv tilted her straw hat to shield her face from the sun. We were both wearing Illinois sweatshirts---where our son goes to college---and jeans and tennis shoes. The breeze off the Gulf of Mexico was chilly. Viv took a roll of mints out of her bag, offered me one, and tucked the bag under her chair. We sat and sucked our mints and looked at the water.

"Maybe we should have gone to Miami," she said. "It's always warm there."

"Alabama's less crowded."

"Well, at least it's warmer than Chicago."

There were only a few people on the beach. Two sturdy-looking old men in windbreakers and shorts sat together. A young mother and her son were gathering shells. A lot of gulls were there, padding around importantly, and a speedy little bird was dodging the waves and jabbing at the sand. Two large brown birds flew by.

"Aren't those pelicans?" Viv asked.

I watched them fly down the water's edge. "They didn't have those whachamacallits."

"They were folded up, I think."

"Okay, so they're pelicans."

"Where do all these birds have their nests?" Viv asked.

I tried to think where the gulls and pelicans have nests, but I didn't have any ideas.

"I didn't see them in the palm trees," Viv said.

I thought about the palm trees off our terrace. I couldn't remember if they had nests or not. Viv was looking at me like I had the answer.

"Hey, what am I, the Audubon Society?"

"I was just asking. Are you bored already?"

"I'm trying to relax and you're grilling me about birds."

While we sat, I thought about the wallpaper in this kitchen back home. I'd just gone there, the day before we left, to give the people a quote on a new floor. The wallpaper had pictures of Japanese gardens with little bridges and flowering trees. Strange-looking colored birds sat in the trees, and other birds swam on a pond. Japanese women in kimonos were walking around with parasols. It was the prettiest design I've ever seen, and I've been in thousands of kitchens. All the time I was measuring the floor I was looking at the wallpaper.

"Maybe some day we can take a vacation in the summer," Viv said.

"It's busy season."

"Still, after twenty years. Their best salesman."

I picked up a shell, a miniature white conch with brown streaks. I took off my sunglasses to see it better. It was half the size of my thumb and perfectly formed. I cleaned out the sand and wiped it all over with my finger.

"Look at this," I said to Viv.

"It's pretty. Wonder what lives in those things."

I tried to think about the shell animal. It seemed like I ought to know something about it---what color it was or what it ate, but I didn't have a clue. I looked around for a target and spotted the driftwood about twenty feet away. Twisting in my chair, I flung the shell, and it landed between the bent branches that were sticking out of the sand.

"We should have brought a newspaper," I said.

"Why don't we go back, drive into town, and get some sun-block. We can come again this afternoon when it's warmer."

"Let's have lunch in town."

"Sounds great." We folded up our chairs and started back. "Oh, and remind me to get some postcards," Viv said.

* * *

In the afternoon we rubbed on sun-block and went down to the beach in bathing suits. This time I brought the newspaper and Viv brought her postcards. We sat in the same place. There were more people now and more kids. Only one man was in the water.

I read part of the newspaper. Then I watched the guy in the water and the kids playing at the edge. Viv was filling up her postcards. Whenever we go on vacation, she writes all her postcards on the first day. How she does it I'll never know.

"I'm going to try the water," I said.

She didn't look up. "If it's too cold, don't stay in."

I walked down to the water and stood on the wet sand until a wave slid up to my feet. It was cold, too cold for swimming. In my whole life I've been to the ocean only twice. The first time was in Okinawa when I was in the Army, the second in Miami, where we took a family vacation. I didn't like it either time. In Okinawa I got stung by a jellyfish and in Miami the water was full of tar that had to be cleaned off with Crisco.

Usually, on vacations, Viv and I stay home and work on the house. We might spend a day at Lake Michigan or a State park, or we might visit our parents in Indiana. One year we drove with the kids to Yellowstone and camped out.

On the way back from the water I noticed the driftwood again. I went over and pulled it out of the sand. A strange piece of wood, I thought. Somehow it'd been gouged into the shape of a distorted bowl, about a foot in diameter. There were extensions off the rim that looked like patches of gray clouds. Some bent branches stuck out of the rear. The wood was coated with the gray patina of driftwood except for the center of the bowl, which was still brown.

The little conch was lying at my feet. I sat down the driftwood, tossed the conch into the bowl, and went back to Viv. She smiled up at me.

"Too cold," I said.

"Well, maybe we can do some sightseeing this week. Mobile is supposed to be good for sightseeing. Even you might like it."

"Maybe it'll be hot tomorrow and the water will feel better."

* * *

As we sat, I happened to gaze at the driftwood again. Something was different---who knows what?---and I began to think about it in funny ways. First it seemed like a skewed nest put together by some cockeyed bird. Then I thought of it as a crater gouged in a flat lunar plateau. The cloud-like extensions were slivery gray, as unstained as the moon's surface might be. From my chair I couldn't see the little conch, but I imagined it in the driftwood bowl. An egg in a nest; a landing craft in a moon crater. The idea of placing many shells ln the nest-crater-bowl came to me.

Again I went over to look. The inside of the bowl was too rough, and the transition from gray to brown too abrupt. I rubbed a section of gray with a sharp rock until the natural brown returned.

"What are you doing?" Viv called.

"Nothing much."

I was glad when she shrugged me off and went back to her writing.

A whole variety of tiny saucer shells lay around me. I placed a few of them against the inner surface of the bowl. The white ones looked best, I thought, so I started collecting white ones and placing them in clusters inside the bowl. That didn't seem quite right, but then another idea hit me: a spiral radiating out from the center.

I hunted around the beach for more saucer shells. Only the tiniest would do, although there had to be a variation in size, shape, and coloration. Some had to be pure white and others had to have larger or smaller areas of brown. Also, I wanted perfect specimens with no holes or chips. I sifted through clumps of shells to find just the right ones.

Two little boys came over to watch me. Usually I talk to kids, but now I didn't want to be bothered. "Whatcha doing, mister?" the older boy said and, when I didn't answer, they both ran away.

I glanced over at Viv. She was looking at me like I'd lost my marbles. I went on sifting through clumps of shells hoping she wouldn't make a big deal about it. An elderly couple smiled at me as they walked along the beach.

My shirt pocket was bulging with shells. On the way back I picked up the driftwood and the conch.

"What are you doing?" Viv asked.

"I'm not sure yet. I have to go into town again."

"For what?"

"Supplies."

She just shook her head. Viv usually knows when I need privacy. "Here," she said, handing me a stack of postcards, "you can mail these on your way."

In town I tried to find a store that sold sandpaper. There were a thousand souvenir shops but no hardware store. I finally had to drive ten miles north to the next town, where I bought three grades of sandpaper, a forceps, glue, and a small saw.

When I got back to the hotel, Viv was taking a nap. I tiptoed out to the terrace, where I'd left the shells and driftwood. Sitting on the floor, I sawed off one of the bent branches because it spoiled the picture I had in mind. Then I sanded the inside of the bowl so that the silver-gray color on the outside gradually changed to deep brown at the bottom. Also the rings in the wood became more visible as the gray turned into brown.

Looking again at the shells, I cussed to myself. I hadn't noticed that some of them were duller than others. This meant another trip into town for some kind of oil. There was a drugstore, which ought to have baby oil, and maybe they had something to use as a solvent. I tiptoed across the room again and quietly locked the door behind me. At the drugstore I found the perfect solvent: cigarette lighter fluid.

Viv was watching TV when I returned. "Are you making something?" she asked.

"I'm still not sure."

"Don't mess up the carpet out there."

On the terrace I mixed a little baby oil with the lighter fluid in a plastic cup. I dropped in all the dull shells and let them sit while I arranged the others according to size and coloration. Then I set the oiled shells on a newspaper to dry. Viv and I went out to dinner at a seafood place. I tried to pay attention to her but all I could think about was my project.

The next day was much warmer. After breakfast in our room, Viv wanted to take a walk on the beach, but I was already on the terrace glueing shells into the driftwood bowl. At the center of the bowl I glued the conch, and right next to it I glued the tiniest of the brown-white shells in a spiral emerging outward.

"It's a gorgeous day," Viv said. "Can't you do that later?"

"You go," I said as gently as I could manage. "This afternoon we can do something together."

"I don't want to go by myself."

"What are you afraid of? It's safe here."

"I'm not afraid. I just don't want to be alone. When will you be done?"

"I don't know, for Pete's sake!"

She went inside and turned on the TV. For a moment I felt guilty; then I lost myself in the project again. With the forceps I dipped the shells into the glue and set them in place, holding each one until the glue dried. Slowly the spiral widened with the shells becoming larger and whiter toward the rim of the bowl.

"Do you want to come shopping with me?" Viv asked.

"Maybe later," I said.

"I'm going now. Goodbye." She was pretty ticked.

After she left I realized that I needed more shells. There were too many gaps in the spiral, where shells of just the right size were missing. Irritably I went down to the beach again. It seemed like everybody in town was there. Kids were running all over, teenagers were throwing a frisbee, people were flying kites and building sand castles. There were even a few swimmers. I started looking for shells, but everything that might have fit the pattern was cracked. I felt bad about Viv and about being alone.

The beach didn't interest me. I went up to the hotel lobby, bought some magazines, and looked at pictures until Viv came back. We got dressed and went to the fanciest restaurant in town. I tried hard to think of things to say, but nothing interested me very much.

That night, I didn't sleep well. All kinds of strange ideas went through my head. Ideas about God and creation and the fate of man. I couldn't sort it all out. Maybe I should've listened in church, I thought. Maybe I ought to read some of those books that Dave brought home from college.

* * *

At dawn, while Viv was still asleep, I put on a jacket and went off to find shells. It was colder and cloudy; a stiff wind was blowing off the Gulf. With the whole beach to myself I searched at the water's edge, going through every clump of washed-up debris. A wave slid up and drenched my tennis shoes. Gulls landed on the beach and faced me against the wind, like stern judges.

At the hotel Viv was in the bathroom. I went immediately to the terrace, dropped some of the shells in oil solution, and started glueing the others. When Viv came out, I was sitting cross-legged on the floor holding a shell in place.

"Are you going to do this all day?" she asked.

"I'll be done in a little while."

I opened the forceps and the shell stayed in place. I set the oiled ones out to dry.

"It's going to be cloudy today," she said. "We could go sightseeing in Mobile. When will you be done?"

"Soon."

"When?"

"Soon! Please quit bugging me about it!"

"What's come over you?"

Even as I barked at her, I felt bad about it. She went into the bathroom to wash her hair, and I went on glueing shells. The next time she came over to the terrace, she was putting on her jacket.

"I'm going into town to buy something for your parents," she said, emphasizing your. "If you can spare the time, it might be nice to do one thing together on this trip."

She slammed the door on the way out. Just another hour, I thought, noticing the windblown palm trees and the surging tide and feeling somehow connected to all that energy around me.

* * *

Viv came back around noon with tee shirts, hats, and a pair of shell earrings. I was on the terrace holding the driftwood.

"Done?" she asked.

"Done. Have a look."

She came out and I handed it her carefully. "It's nice," she said. "Very pretty."

"Look at the bowl straight on, instead of down. Like a tunnel."

"Yes, it's nice that way." She handed it back.

"Do you understand the meaning of it? Tell me the truth."

"It's a pretty design."

"But do you get what it symbolizes?"

"Symbolizes?"

"Yeah. Look at the spiral of shells going into the bowl. It might be contracting or expanding. Like the universe, you know? That's what I'm going to call it: The Universe."

"What about the shell in the middle? Is that God?"

The way she said it embarrassed me. "You can think of it like that, I suppose."

"So," she said, "a true work of art, with symbolism and everything. Well, why not?" She kissed me on the cheek.

"Do you think anyone will understand it?"

"They will if you make a title for it. But, please, not now." She started digging in her purse.

I wondered how I should add the title.

"Look at these," she said, handing me brochures. "If we drive up to Mobile, we can see Bellingrath Gardens. It's supposed to be fantastic. And there are Civil War houses in the city."

I tried to be cheerful. I figured I owed her the sightseeing.

* * *

"The Universe" now sits on my workbench in the basement. I tried to find a good place to display it, but there were always problems. The front hall was too narrow. In the dining room it clashed with the polished furniture. Viv nearly had a heart attack when she saw me holding it against the wall beside the teak buffet. We've talked about finishing the basement someday, and I'm sure I could make a place for it down there. But with the kids gone, the basement isn't a priority anymore.

Truth is, I'm not so sure I want "The Universe" on display. Down in the basement, where no one goes but me, it's kind of special, a secret. Viv doesn't know it's there; she's probably forgotten all about it. I sometimes think of it like one of those time capsules, and I imagine that centuries from now someone will find it and wonder who made it. It'll be the only evidence that I was on the earth---like the shells and driftwood are evidence. But if I bring it upstairs, it'll soon be just another thing around the house, with no more dignity than the pictures on the walls or the figurines over the fireplace. I won't be able anymore to sneak down to my dark little nest, hold "The Universe" in my lap, and think about things.

POSSESSION

"Ta da!" With fanfare Laurel burst into the apartment and announced to her roommate, Megan, that she' had just been hired as a stripper at The Purple Garter. Megan was distracted at the window, however, and didn't respond. Her friend, Allen, had pulled into the parking lot right after Laurel. He, Megan, and another couple were driving to Indianapolis, where Allen would be giving his testimony to the Midwest Evangelical Convention. A month ago, just before he and Megan met, he had surrendered his life to Jesus Christ, and on their last date he had suggested that Megan do the same.

"You're doing what, where?" Megan finally asked. She remembered that Laurel, an aspiring actress, liked to announce her new roles with a flourish. "Did you say stripper?"

Laurel thrust out her prominent chest and strutted around on her toes, belting out a raucous rhythm from old-time strip shows. She pulled off her sweatshirt, spun it on her finger, and flung it over Megan's head. As she stepped out of her jeans, Megan cried, "Laurel! I don't have time for this. You're just acting, right? Right?"

In bra and panties Laurel danced into the bathroom. Dry laughter erupted like a machine gun behind the closed door. Megan had heard that laughter before, and it scared her.

"I'll be back in a week," she called. "Don't do anything crazy." Suddenly it seemed wiser to meet Allen downstairs. She grabbed her suitcase and slipped out the door.

When she returned from Indiana, it was Laurel who was leaving in a hurry. They greeted each other on the staircase.

"Hi! I'm late," Laurel said as she squeezed by. Her purse hung from her shoulder, and she carried a gym bag. "How was your trip?"

"Wonderful! We went camping and…"

"Sorry. Gotta make money." Laurel raced down the stairs. "Watch me out the window."

Megan entered the apartment and opened the blinds. Laurel waved to her from a new black Corvette. Megan's Jaw dropped as it shrieked out of the parking lot.

After unpacking, Megan peered into Laurel's room. The usual mess of clothes, empty pop cans, paperback books, and music tapes covered every surface, but there was also an odor of cigarette smoke. Laurel had supposedly given up smoking two years ago, when they decided to live together. On a pile of dirty laundry Megan found two bikinis, one red and one yellow. In a shopping bag from a place called Lace 'n' Stuff were a sequined vest and a slit miniskirt.

She retreated to her own room and plopped down on her neatly made bed. "How can you do this?" fell spontaneously from her lips. The euphoria she had felt all week was suddenly gone, replaced by tear and bewilderment. "You can't go back to the old days," she whispered. "I won't let you." She thought about praying but couldn't find the mood.

* * *

Laurel had been Megan's best friend, often her only friend, since grade school. As children they slept in each other's beds and took piano and ballet lessons together. As young teens they swapped clothes, passed silly notes in school, prowled the malls, and stuffed themselves with junk food. Laurel, who reached puberty early, developed an aggressive interest in boys and lectured Megan on matters of sex, using an illustrated manual, which she had stolen from a neighbor's house, as source material. In middle school both girls lost their fathers to divorce. Megan's father kept in touch with her, but laurel's disappeared completely. He had once called her and her older sister "a couple of dirty-minded sluts."

In high school Megan struggled to make C's, while laurel churned out A's whenever she felt so disposed. Laurel readily made friends, or rather enlisted allies, among the more disaffected boys and girls. Under her leadership they cut and dyed their hair in outrageous ways, dressed exclusively in black, took up smoking, demonstrated against school policies, shoplifted, got into fights, destroyed property, and went to keg and marijuana parties all over town. Laurel especially favored Megan, even though she only embraced the fringes of the gang, never participating in their riskier escapades. Megan had become overweight and reclusive, a burden to her peers. But Laurel called her every week, took her to parties, and got her dates for the big school events. Once in a while, Megan was swept up by her friend's foolhardy impulses, like the time they drove out to the country, drank beer in a cornfield until they threw up, then spent the night in an abandoned barn.

In their senior year, when Laurel contracted a stubborn case of chlamydia and became a laughing stock, only Megan remained loyal to her. Their friendship continued until Laurel went off to college, a thousand miles away. Megan stayed home, went to cosmetology school, and got a job in a small hair salon.

Four years later, Laurel returned home and found work with a new theater company. One evening, after a bitter fight with her mother, she showed up at Megan's house. Megan's mother welcomed her uneasily, served tea, and went to bed. As soon as she left, the two old friend fell into each other's orbit again. Laurel told Megan about her college years, the drama classes and the roles she had played, her vacations to Mexico and Europe, and her many boyfriends. She had even been married briefly. "The guy started cheating on me," she explained, "so I did the same to him. We kept the whole neighborhood awake with our fights, and finally he just took off. It'll be a long time before I go through that again." Megan was rapt. Still timid, overweight, and friendless, she saw her life as an abyss of longing and frustration. To compete with Laurel, she had to embellish all her stories. But Laurel listened without impatience and seemed genuinely happy to be with her again. They reminisced and regaled each other until they fell asleep on the carpet. In the morning they decided to find an apartment.

* * *

Megan couldn't sleep. She lay on the bed, reliving the week in Indiana. At the convention she had declined to give herself to Jesus, as Allen had hoped, but promised to consider it seriously. "It's a big step," she told him, "and I want to feel it, not just say it." He was pleased and didn't press her.

After the convention they and the other couple went camping at a state park. They whiled away hours under the stars, sharing life histories, aspirations, jokes, and their common beliefs. Even when the men debated sports, in which she hadn't the slightest interest, Megan listened and tried to appreciate their enthusiasm. When Allen kissed her for the first time, she was delighted and surprisingly unafraid. He was a computer whiz, gangly with big ears, reassuringly unattractive. She resolved to lose weight as soon as they returned.

Now her mind kept circling back to Laurel. What catastrophe had reduced her to such degrading behavior? True, her theater company was close to folding, and she had to depend entirely on low-wage jobs that she hated. The men in her life seemed to disappear after a few dates. (Allen thought she was a "tough hombre.") Her sister had moved away, and her mother had locked her out of the house because of their violent quarrels. But would these problems drive her to expose her body to a roomful of leering perverts? Allen and his friends believed in a living, manipulating Satan, who possessed unsaved persons and led them into depravity. Could such things be true? Laurel treated all religious ideas with contempt. She didn't trust Allen and had spoken coldly to him when they met.

"Dear Jesus, help me to help her," Megan whispered. "I want to feel you in my heart."

She was still awake around 2:30 a.m., when Laurel came home. Megan heard her flop onto her bed, apparently too exhausted to put on night clothes. Talk was impossible now, but Megan had to work all day, and would they find any time this week? She tiptoed into Laurel's room. Her friend was sprawled face down, wearing sneakers, jeans, and a sweatshirt. One hand dangled beside the gym bag on the floor. The room still reeked of cigarettes. Megan threw a blanket over Laurel and opened a window. Outside she could see the Corvette, an eerie shadow in the dim light.

* * *

Sunday morning, Megan was making coffee, when Laurel, puffy and bleary-eyed, her last night's make-up a collage on her face, plodded out of her bedroom and sat down at the kitchen table. She wore only a sweatshirt and panties. The women regarded each other a moment, then Laurel lit a cigarette. Megan continued to watch the coffee drip while the color of her face and neck intensified. She wrinkled her nose at the smoke.

"Oh, all right," Laurel growled. "Your disapproval is noted." She snuffed out the cigarette on the Formica tabletop.

"I thought you quit." Megan hated the feeble sound of her own voice.

"I have to think about my figure now. Smoking keeps me from eating."

Megan brought over two cups of coffee. She noticed a dark blue mark on Laurel's thigh and recoiled, almost spilling the hot liquid.

"My God! What is that?"

"Cerberus," Laurel replied nonchalantly. She lifted her sweatshirt to display the entire tattoo---a three-headed dog, whose muzzles pointed at her crotch. "Do you like him? He's guard in the gate to hell."

"When did you get that?"

"When you were in Indiana. I guess you don't like him, huh?"

"Laurel, for Pete's sake, what is happening to you?" Megan shouted.

"What's your problem?"

"My problem! You throw away an acting career to be a stripper. You start smoking again and come home at three in the morning. You mess up your body with tattoos, and just look at your face. What is going on?"

"Nothing." Laurel wiped her face with a sleeve, making things worse. "I haven't given up acting. I'm just on a different kind of stage. One that pays big bucks for a change and doesn't go out of business. Do you know that I can make in one night what you make in a week? Sometimes more."

"But what do you have to do for it?"

"Just take my clothes off. The slobs buy you drinks, you do a few couch dances, it's nothing. They're not allowed to put a finger on you."

"How can you stand them looking at you?"

Laurel shrugged. "I don't care if they look. Hey, it's good for my self-esteem." She barked out a weird laugh, which Megan remembered from their teen years. It was a forced, harsh sound that seemed to come from someone hidden in her body. Laurel used to laugh that way after stealing or committing an act of vandalism.

"All the girls are nervous their first night," she said. "After that, you don't even think about it. You could do it yourself, Megan. Drop a few pounds and you'll be the sexiest one in the place. You'll have money running out your ears."

Megan didn't answer. She left the table and began tidying up the kitchen.

"Okay, okay. Sorry," Laurel said. "I didn't want to talk about that anyway. Listen, why don't we go downtown to the jazz festival this afternoon. It's my birthday tomorrow, but we can celebrate it today."

"I can't. Allen and I are going horseback riding."

Megan felt a jab of guilt. During the past two years, she and Laurel had spent much of their leisure time together at restaurants, bars, movie theaters, concerts, art shows, and flea markets. It was always Laurel who proposed the activity. If it happened to be something artistic, she would help Megan understand and appreciate it. Megan felt privileged to be trusted with the knowledge and opinions of her bright, talented friend.

"You're going to ride a horse?" Laurel said.

Megan laughed. "Yeah, me. Allen loves horses. I just hope I can stay on one."

Laurel's face clouded over. "How much longer are you going to date that guy?"

"I don't know. What do you mean?"

"Oh, nothing. I knew some of those religious types in college, and they give me the creeps. Underneath those righteous masks you can find big problems."

The phone rang and Megan answered. It was Allen. He'd come by in half an hour. After church they would change clothes and drive out to the farm. He told her to stop worrying, that he would show her how to ride a horse and she wouldn't fall off. They sent each other a kiss, and Megan hung up, nervous and elated.

"I'm going back to bed," Laurel muttered. "If I were you, I'd be careful of those people." She went into her room and shut the door.

* * *

The Jennings farm covered thirty-five acres and was stocked with sheep, goats, rabbits, two llamas, a coop of chickens, a peacock, several dogs and cats, and twenty horses. In summer the farm became a pricey horse-camp for suburban kids, although a few beds were always set aside for inner-city youngsters, who came on "scholarships." The campers were taught, as part of their chores, to care for all the animals.

Matt Jennings, who was thirty and ran the farm for his parents, had started the camp a few years ago. Before that, he had graduated from a one-year Bible college and spent a year abroad doing missionary work. He saw the camp as a way to instill Christian values, responsibility, and a love of animals into children.

On Sundays, Matt drove a pick-up truck into town and conducted a worship service at the small, independent church attended by Allen, Megan, and all their friends. To his congregation, and to his young campers, he conveyed an unshakable belief in the Bible as literal truth. Everyone who met him admired his friendliness, sincerity, and his movie-star looks. Allen idolized him and talked endlessly about him to Megan.

It was a bright, warm October day when Allen, Megan, and four of their friends arrived at the farm in a Volkswagen bus. Matt and his wife greeted them and led them to the corral to select horses.

"Please," Megan implored, "the tamest, kindest, nicest one for me."

"We'll put you on Angel," said Matt. "She's the oldest and slowest, but she'll give you a good ride."

Allen showed her how to strap on the saddle and bridle and helped her mount up. The group started out on a worn trail through the sheep and goats, up a grassy hill and past the reedy swimming hole. When they reached a broad meadow, Matt urged his horse to a trot, and the others did the same.

"Oh-oh-oh!" Megan cried out as the bumpy gait jolted her back. She and Allen were at the end of the line.

"Dig your knees in," he told her.

"Okay. I will. I'll try." She clutched the reins and saddle horn with both hands.

"You'll get it," he assured her. But a few minutes later, when she still seemed to be suffering, he asked if she wanted to stop.

"No, no! I think I'm getting it," she insisted.

"Try to let go of the saddle horn."

She tried a couple of times, but the feeling of instability was too frightening.

"It's okay," Allen said. "The first time is always rough."

Megan wondered how she could avoid doing this a second time. "It's not so bad," she said. "I kind of like it."

"Good. When we get to the dirt road, we're going to gallop."

"Gallop?"

"It'll actually be easier because it is a smoother motion."

He was right. When Matt and the others rake into a gallop, Angel raced after them with Megan doubled over, clutching the saddle horn with all her strength, and ready to sell her immortal soul to make them stop. But at the end of the sixty-second ride she sat up straight, beaming and panting out joyous laughter.

"All right! Way to go!" Allen shouted.

They all galloped up and down the road, and finally Megan let go of the saddle horn and rode sitting up.

"You did it!" Matt cried. He rode up and gave her the high five.

Her thrill was so intense that she had to fight back tears. Matt rode over to her also. "How you doing, tenderfoot?"

"I love it!" she blurted out, although she also hoped it would now end.

"Let's head over to those trees and we'll rest a while."

They tied up their horses in an apple orchard. Matt climbed up a tree and tossed down the best remaining fruit to the others. Allen showed Megan how to feed a horse, and she laughed as Angel took the whole apple from her hand. She stroked Angel's mane and murmured nervously affectionate words.

The tart, crunchy fruit tasted delicious to Megan. The brilliant blue sky and autumn colors made her forget the growing soreness in her thighs and back. She, Allen, and the other guests sat in a semicircle around Matt, as if they expected a sermon. Instead, they all talked and joked about inconsequential things until the subject of apartments and households came up.

"Allen mentioned your roommate might be having a problem," Matt said to Megan.

She was surprised that Laurel had even concerned them, and she worried about being linked to strippers. Everyone present seemed to know the story.

"I don't know what's got into her," Megan said. "She started smoking again, and she has this tattoo of the dog of hell."

"Cerberus?" someone asked.

"Yes, that's it."

They all looked at each other and at Matt. He meditated a moment, then asked Megan to tell them about Laurel's past. She did this reluctantly, feeling like a traitor but not wanting to displease Matt.

"Megan," he said gently. "You've heard me talk about Satan as a real presence on the earth and about his power to control us if we let him. But you might not be comfortable with that belief."

"I don't know. There's so much evil in the world. My family wasn't very religious."

"You've probably heard words like 'dysfunctional' and 'severe behavioral disorders' and so on. Those are the fashionable terms now, and I'm not knocking people who use them. But doesn't it seem to you that, whether you call it Satanic possession or dysfunctional behavior or some other psychobabble, the bottom line is the same? You have a troubled soul in danger of being wallowed up by an evil force. And good people like yourself are desperate to counteract that force."

"Yes, I've tried to talk to her."

"And she won't listen, right? As you said yourself, something's got into her. Something has a hold on her."

"It seems like that."

Matt paced thoughtfully back and forth. "Well, the good news is that people can and do free themselves from Satan. I've seen it many times in my travels. The path to salvation through Jesus Christ simply has to be illuminated."

"But if Laurel won't change, doesn't Megan have to get away from her?" Allen put in.

"Absolutely. And that's the bad news, I suppose." Matt looked sadly at Megan. "We can tell how close you've been. So we have to prevent that and we can, if Laurel will take the first step." He was pensive again, and the others watched him silently.

"Why don't we pray for Laurel," he finally suggested. All heads were lowered, as he improvised a prayer for her deliverance. "Remember," he said to Megan, "you can encourage her, but she must take the first step.

Tell her about us. Maybe invite her to a worship service. If she'll meet us half way, we'll do the rest."

* * *

When Megan got home, Laurel was dressing to go out. Sore, exhausted, and confused, Megan collapsed on the sofa. Laurel came into the living room and stood over her.

"Where does it hurt?"

"All over. It's like total body arthritis."

Laurel knelt beside her. "Poor baby. Would a backrub help?"

"I just want to die."

"I know what you need. A nice hot bath in Epsom salts. I'll get some at the supermarket."

"Oh, don't bother. Do you have a date?"

"He won't be here for a while, and it's no bother. I'll be right back."

Twenty minutes later Laurel returned, drew a bath, and poured in the Epsom salts. She helped Megan into the bathroom and tested the water.

"Be careful. It's hot." She placed Megan's blouse, jeans, and socks in the hamper and left to get herself ready. After a while she knocked on the door. "How you doing?"

"Much better. Thanks, Laurel. Who are you going out with?"

"A guy I know. We call him Gentle Ben. He's the bouncer at the club."

Megan's heart sank. There was a moment of silence on both sides of the door. Then Laurel pushed it open a crack.

"You have a problem with that?"

"I wish you'd quit that job. It's gross. It's not much better than prostitution."

"Oh, give me a break! It's nothing like prostitution. It's totally legal. Are those religious nuts feeding you their moral crapola?"

"You sell your body so you can drive around in a Corvette. That's the real crapola. You never cared about flashy cars."

"People change. You never cared about religion. We used to laugh at those windbag preachers on TV."

"My friends aren't like that. They're kind, decent people."

"And I'm not, huh? I've never been kind to you and I'm certainly not decent. I'm a slut and you can't associate with morally inferior people like me."

What are you talking about? I want to help you. If you would come to one of our worship services..."

"Oh, God! Here it comes. Open your heart to Jesus. Let the blood of the lamb wash away your sins. You too can have eternal life if you just disengage your brain. I knew this would happen, Megan! Those bastards are sucking you in. They're starting to manipulate you. Allen's doing it, isn't he? And you're too blind to see it."

"You don't know them!" Megan shouted back. "They want to help people. They care about kids and animals. They're a lot better than those perverts who drool over your naked body."

Laurel started to reply, but a knock at the front door cut her off. Megan thought she heard her mutter "You bitch" before a man's voice drifted in from the hallway. A second later the door slammed, and the apartment was completely silent.

* * *

In the wee hours Megan woke up in a fright, thinking that someone had entered the apartment. Lying frozen, she heard urgent little yelps and hard breathing sounds in the living room. There were whispers and suddenly that familiar coarse laughter, which now had a definitely evil cast to it. She wrapped her pillow around her head but couldn't block out the sound.

"Jesus, come and help me, please," she whispered. "I need you. Help me." She repeated these words over and over, like a rosary, until it occurred to her that she ought to be praying for Laurel, not herself.

* * *

"Tell you the truth, Meg," Allen said, "I knew it the day you introduced us." He and Megan had met for lunch at a fast-food place, and she had told him about the late-night episode. "When she looked at me, I could feel it. I'm sensitive to those things."

"You never said she was possessed." Megan laid a skeptical emphasis on the word.

"I did to Matt. I told him she might be. He said to wait, that if it was true, I'd know soon enough. Everything that's happened since then confirms it."

"Maybe. I don't know about things like that. But sometimes she can be really sweet."

"Anyone can be sweet. It's all part of the act. Evidently she's a good actress."

"I want to help her."

"No! You need to get out of there. Suppose Gentle Ben or one of her other boyfriends has AIDS or herpes or something. You use the same bathroom, eat the same food."

Megan started to bite into a hamburger but put it down.

"If you got a disease from her, what would that mean for your future husband?" Allen tensed as if he had said too much. To spare him embarrassment, Megan hid her surprise and kept the conversation on track.

"I don't think she has any diseases. How can you tell?"

"That's just it. Sometimes you can't. And some of those diseases can be transmitted by kissing. You can't expect me to take risks while you're waiting for her to change."

Now Megan lost her appetite completely. She rewrapped the hamburger and pushed her drink aside. Allen's face was a wall of ice.

"I'll try to speak to her," she said hoarsely.

He finished his meal while she sat motionless, staring at a fly on the table. Life without Allen---with Laurel as her only friend---seemed insufferably grim. Allen had talked about camping again, and sleigh rides in the winter. And what did he mean by "your future husband"?

"I have an idea," he said. "Let me make a phone call, and I'll get back to you this afternoon."

He came to the salon on her break, and they talked in the back room. "I called Matt," he said. "He's coming down tonight with his pick-up. We'll load your things while she's at work, and you can stay at the farm until you find another place. I told him about her latest stunt, and he agrees that you need to get out of there."

"Tonight? Just run out behind her back?"

"That way, you won't have to confront her. You can leave her a note explaining that it's best to separate because your lifestyles are so different. Tell her you'll always remember her friendship and the good old days and blah, blah. She won't be happy but she'll have time to calm down before you see her again."

"Allen, I can't do that."

"Why not? Isn't it better than a shouting match with her? She might do something spiteful or try to hurt you."

"She wouldn't do that."

"Remember, she's not in control of herself. Something's got hold of her, and you need to get away---fast. Every day you live with her means more danger for us."

He took her in his arms and kissed her forehead. When a tear rolled out, he gave her a handkerchief. "You're one of us now," he said with uncharacteristic tenderness. "I don't want to lose you. And who knows? Maybe this is just what Laurel needs."

* * *

Across the street from The Purple Garter, Megan made a phone call from a booth. It was eight o'clock and mostly quiet; the few passing cars had their lights on. As she waited, a car pulled into the club parking lot, and a group of young men emerged, laughing and tussling playfully. They went into the club below the red neon sign. After them, two cars arrived, and two lone middle-aged men walked casually into the squat little building. Each time the door was opened, Megan heard a faint crash of music.

A beefy man wearing a pony tail and a Hawaiian shirt came out and looked across the street. Megan shuddered as his eyes met hers. The man stuck his head in the door, and then Laurel came out in her familiar sweatshirt and jeans. She tossed away a cigarette and sprinted toward Megan. The big man went inside.

"Hi! What are you doing here?" Laurel asked cheerily. The sullen look on Megan's face made her smirk. "Don't tell me. You're here to save me from my evil self."

"Laurel, I don't want to do this." Megan avoided eye contact, and her voice was parched and shaky. "You've got to quit working in that place. If you don't, I'll have to move out. Tonight."

"You're giving me an ultimatum? Whose idea was this? Your sanctimonious boyfriend's?"

"Allen's concerned about me, and maybe he's right."

"About what? Does he think I'll corrupt you?"

"I heard you last night with that man. People like that might have diseases. Don't you remember what happened in high school?"

Laurel grabbed Megan by the shoulders. "Look at me, damn it! I don't have any diseases. This is Allen talking, not you, isn't it? He puts his sick ideas in your head. He wants to control you, to own you."

"If you'd only come to our church. Just once…"

"I'm not going to your fucking church!" Laurel gave her a hard shake. Megan tried to twist out of her grasp, but Laurel dug in her nails. She pinned Megan against a telephone pole. "I'm not a sheep. I don't want people telling me how to live." Laurel held on with desperate strength, then finally let her go.

Megan backed away. "Allen was right. You are possessed. Oh my God, it's in your eyes."

Laurel bore down on her as she retreated. "Possessed? Is that what he said about me? Ha! And you believe it, you dummy."

Megan raced to her car.

"Go on," Laurel cried. "Run out on me like everyone else. I'm not good enough for you and that pious wimp. I'm possessed. I'm nothing but a filthy slut!"

As Megan started to drive away, Laurel leaped onto the road, waving her arms and shouting, "Wait! I'll do it! I'll go to your church."

Megan screeched to a halt and rolled her window down part-way. Laurel curled her fingers over the glass.

"How about a deal, just between you and me?" she murmured. "I'll go to church and get saved if you come in here and strip."

Megan pressed the accelerator to the floor. She cranked up her window and screamed. But the demon laughter pursued her, taunting and battering, like punishment for a sin.

ANGELS, DREAMS, AND PARTRIDGEBERRIES

In the fall of 1975 I went camping with my father for the last time. I was ten years old and had no fear of the woods, but I dreaded these weekend trips. Father's moods, tortured, among other things, by a badly ulcerated stomach, had been unpredictable all year. Our trips in June and September had ended bitterly, with both of us tense and silent because of our different priorities.

Father announced the late-October trip in his usual way: "Get your gear together, Danny. We're heading for the trees in the morning." His tone anticipated my full approval, and I knew better than to disappoint him. He was not a man who talked things over; he made swift, precise decisions and suffered no opposition. Had I dared to protest, he would have fired off sensible arguments, then accusations of weakness and sloth, until I finally caved in.

By "the trees" Father meant the Wayne National Forest in southeastern Ohio, but not the groomed, well-trodden paths. We would roam, as he liked to quote, far from the madding crowd.

"The leaves will be fantastic now," he said in a voice too harsh and self-assured to be compatible with autumn beauty.

"Can Mom come?" I asked half-heartedly.

He ignored me and began sifting through a pile of his political leaflets. I didn't repeat the question because I already knew the answer. Father would not want Mother on the trip, and she, obligingly, would be too busy to go. My parents preferred to avoid each other. Their marriage had come apart years ago, but, instead of divorcing, they had given themselves over to radically different inspirations.

I went out the back door in sullen protest. Basser, my English sheep dog, joined me in the meadow, and we lost ourselves in high grass and wildflowers.

* * *

My parents and I lived twenty miles from Proctorville in southern Ohio. Our house was tiny, but our back yard blended into a vast, wild meadow, which flowed out to a woods. Rabbits, raccoons, foxes, deer, and a variety of harmless snakes meandered across the landscape. Bobwhites and grouses shot up before a footstep. Basser and I would roam far and wide without purpose while dozens of fantasies---childish adventures, secret devices, imaginary playmates---revolved in my head. Often I'd gaze for long minutes at an unfamiliar object until it seemed to take on a different nature. The outdoors was a relief, my daydreams a partial antidote to the tension that hovered in my home.

I had no close friends. Sometimes one of my classmates would spend an afternoon with us, but this was rare. The other boys called me "sleepwalker" and "space cadet." Their mothers had been warned by stories of my parents' peculiar interests.

My father taught biology at Proctorville High. Every day of the school year he complained about lazy students, ignorant parents, or the bigoted principal. Father was a thin man with a receding hairline, a short beard, and wire-rimmed glasses. He always seemed to be in motion. Whenever he left the house he took along a Thermos of milk to soothe his ulcer. I knew that people in the area argued about him.

He traveled a lot. After school and all through the summer he drove to coal and steel towns along the Ohio River and in Kentucky and West Virginia. He returned in the evenings after Mother and I had eaten. Barely greeting us, he descended to the basement, where he had a typewriter and mimeograph. For the next two hours I heard his index fingers tapping the keyboard and his occasional eruptions of mirthless laughter and swearing, as if a crowd of men were down there with him. I wasn't allowed downstairs while he worked, but I had seen him once at the typewriter.

He sat hunched over, eyes aflame, his head bobbing repeatedly as he scrutinized every line.

Finally he would emerge with a stack of paper in his purple-stained hands and carry it out to his station wagon. His noisy old Ford had gone through several engines. The cargo area was carpeted with leftover fact sheets, position papers, newsletters, and manifestos, all in a chaotic weave, muddy, creased, and torn. These political statements sounded like battle cries---End the war! Freedom now! Save the forests! And others meant to rally the mine workers and steel workers against their bosses. The shrill boldface print used to scare me, even when I didn't understand the conflict.

* * *

The next day, as Father and I loaded our backpacks into the station wagon, Basser padded up to me in his floppy, optimistic way. I scratched around his hairy face. I had always wanted to take him with us, but Father would not allow it. Basser suffered from a hip dysplasia. Our kind of hiking would have been impossible for him.

Father closed the tailgate and told me to get in, but I pretended not to hear. "Are you coming?" he asked impatiently.

"Dad, I was thinking. If we stayed on the trail, Basser would be all right."

"We're not going to stay on the trail. You know that."

"Just this once can we?"

Mother came around the side of the house with herbs from her garden. She fussed over my clothes and looked in my backpack to make sure I had extra socks and underwear. She gave me a long hug and promised to bake cookies for me while we were gone. Then she cast a baleful glance at Father's back.

"Don't wear him out," she warned.

He didn't bother to answer.

"Be careful, Daniel," she advised me with a look of concern, as if she, not he, were my true protector. Then, without any further communication, she trudged off to the house.

* * *

Mother was a tall, stout woman, whose hair had turned leaden gray before she was forty. Six days a week she wore loose-fitting sweatshirts, jeans, and blue canvas shoes. Sundays, when she and I went to church, she put on a green or blue dress, a fake pearl necklace, and pumps, which she dyed and redyed to match the dress. Like Father she was always busy, but in another room with her own tasks. The three of us spent most of our time in different places.

Mother worked around the house from sunrise until long after dinner, cooking, sewing, cleaning, paying the bills, doing most of the yardwork, repairing everything from squeaky drawers to leaky pipes. One summer, in 95-degree heat, she put a new roof on the house by herself.

"Your father can't be bothered with honest work," she often said under her breath.

She took no interest in Father's political activities and never read his literature. She had reading material of her own. Every week pamphlets addressed to Mother appeared in our mailbox. They came from everywhere and nowhere and ended their journeys on neat piles in her bedroom closet. There were pocket-sized Daily Devotions with flowers, birds, and sunsets on the covers. Square green Triumphs and rectangular Messengers had pictures of Jesus, the saints, and little children. Deeper inside her closet were The Candles with their unevenly printed pages, too faint in some places and smudged in others. Mother read alone in her room after putting me to bed. Even though her door was closed, I knew she was frowning in her doily-draped armchair under a yellow lamp.

Once a day she recited something called decrees. Decrees were an odd way of praying that few people knew about. Alone at the kitchen table she would call out a list of commands.

"Angelic hosts, came forth and blaze your mighty rays of light through all," she'd intone to the spotless cupboards. "Purify our hearts with your violet flame. Lift us to the light. Fill us with the light."

On the back steps, gazing over the wild grass toward the treeline, she would raise her muscular arms and cry: "In Archangel Michael's love and name, by the power of his sword, use your holy energy to raise the earth to her God-estate!"

She might repeat each decree twenty or thirty times and then begin another one. She read them from Triumph. The whole list took almost half an hour.

I was eight years old when she began reading decrees. I found her in the kitchen one day calling out to the angels of Saint Germain, repeating the same strange words over and over. Terrified, I ran out of the house and buried my face in Bosser's shaggy fur.

Later she explained it to me. "Angels are all around us," she said. "They hold the mighty power of God. If you're very quiet and listen with your heart instead of your ears, you can hear their voices. When I feel their presence, I must direct their power to bring about good things like health and peace and love. Decrees help to focus God's power on the needs of our world."

I nodded my head.

"But decrees take my full concentration," she went on. "You mustn't interrupt me."

I shook my head.

"Don't be frightened, Daniel."

"I won't."

"And one more thing. You mustn't talk to your father about this. Okay?"

"Okay." It must have seemed normal to me that adults should have their secrets. Or maybe I sensed that Father wouldn't care much about angels and decrees. At any rate I kept silent for almost two years.

I sometimes heard angels myself. At night they would enter my dreams, muttering all around me in harsh, murky voices. I couldn't see them or understand their words, but I feared they wanted to kill me. When I cried out to them in peace, they refused to listen and their senseless voices grew louder. I'd wake up in terror and run to Mother's bedside.

"Stop it! Stop it!" she'd hiss, afraid that the sound of my sobbing might penetrate Father's bedroom. "You didn't hear angels. You had a bad dream."

She would steer me back to my room and groan, "Oh Daniel, not again," when she saw that I'd wet my bed. She'd change my sheets in weary silence while I put on new pajamas. She wouldn't let me touch her. "Go to sleep," she'd say. "No more nonsense. I'm too tired."

Mother sewed my clothes, gave me haircuts, and drove me to and from school in her VW bug. She fed me balanced meals with a vitamin pill beside my plate. At bedtime she made sure I said my prayers. Somehow, though, she attended my needs without giving me much of her attention. I seemed to be one more item on her long list of chores.

* * *

As soon as I got into the station wagon, I noticed a little hole in the windshield, right between the wipers. Straight crack lines radiated from the hole in almost perfect symmetry. I stuck my finger through it as Father climbed in the driver's side.

"Danny, get away from that!"

"What did it?"

"I don't know what did it. Just leave it alone."

"Did a rock do it?"

"I told you I don't know. Yeah, maybe a rock did it."

"Did someone throw a rock at you?"

"Will you drop the matter, damn it!"

I sulked against the door. Father didn't say a word as we drove out to the highway. His surly gaze spanned a hundred miles. I had a feeling this trip would be as dreary as the others.

Father knew many places in the Wayne National Forest, which extends over eleven Ohio counties. We went south through Proctorville, where we passed our schools, and drove for an hour on narrow, hilly roads. Sometimes the Ohio River came into view. In one town we stopped at a traffic light, and Father spoke for the first time.

"Remember that building over there, the steel mill? They're laying off a hundred men."

I looked at the smoking jungle of gray structures. I counted seven tall smokestacks. One of the little cars was climbing the long track to the top of the blast furnace. It dumped its load and started down again. I imagined myself riding on the car to the top and then diving into an empty vat but never hitting bottom. The light changed and we headed out of town.

"Are you going to get laid off?" I asked.

He glanced at me sharply. "No, of course not. I'm a teacher, not a steelworker." He pulled down a veil of gloom, and I wished I hadn't blurted out such a stupid question. The steelworkers were suffering and I couldn't find anything intelligent to say. I gazed at the hole and crack lines. They kept turning into a cat's face. In my mind I asked the cat why anyone would throw a rock at our car. Before it came up with an answer we entered a yellow blur of autumn trees.

* * *

Somewhere in the forest Father turned onto a lonely dirt road. We bounced over ruts until we came to a stretch of grassy berm. Father stopped the car, and we unloaded our things and ate our bologna sandwiches. It was a clear, sunny day, but a chill was seeping into the air. I had on a black tee shirt with the peace symbol, my Pirates cap, knee-worn jeans, and hiking boots.

"You remembered to bring a sweater, right?" Father said.

I mumbled a reply. My pack contained some Mexican coins, a jackknife, extra socks and underwear, a flashlight, and two comic books. I imagined that somehow a sweater had been sucked from the floor of my closet into my pack. My sleeping bag had always kept me warm, and maybe I'd never need a sweater.

Father tied a red bandana around his forehead. He wore a khaki tee shirt, camouflage pants, and hiking boots. The treads in his boots were almost gone. After we strapped on our packs he said, "Okay, let's move out."

As we slipped through an opening in the woods I worried that Father would soon be angry with me. I tried to recall our last trip. We had camped out on the Labor Day weekend, somewhere else in the Wayne Forest. Everything was green then, and all three days were hot and muggy. At night it rained. Now the air was dry with a scent of fallen leaves, and it was turning cold. Red and gold color surrounded us. The forest had changed, and I couldn't remember Father's lessons.

I followed him through dead, viney underbrush that made me think of Halloween skeletons. We scrambled up a hill and picked our way through billowing green laurel. A fallen log was covered with patches of white fungi. I stopped to feel them. Lace doilies made of rubber, I thought, and the idea amused me.

"Danny!" Father shouted, and I ran to catch up with him.

When we emerged on a flat meadow, I remembered one of his lessons: Erosion. Trees stopped erosion. Their dead leaves kept rainwater from washing away the soil. But logging companies cut down the trees. Oil drillers knocked them down with bulldozers. Greedy people were destroying the earth.

I went over it again: Erosion. Dead leaves. Greedy logging companies and drillers. The earth would be destroyed. I hoped that Father would ask me about erosion.

We descended a gentle slope by the edge of a ravine. Below I could see the tops of evergreens. Across the chasm were outcroppings of sandstone covered with moss and ferns that looked like a green waterfall. I heard the scream of a hawk.

Father marched straight ahead with his eyes on the ground. In his khaki shirt and camouflage pants he reminded me of soldiers on TV. But he had never been in the Army; he cursed at the soldiers in Vietnam. In the woods, as at home, he seemed to know exactly what he was doing and where he was going. He'd forge ahead with a fierce glare in his eyes, the same expression he wore when he typed his papers. He avoided the trails. As he put it, "You run into everybody. Jerks with cameras, kids goofing off, old ladies rattling on about their grandchildren."

The hawk and the green waterfall caught my attention, and I fell behind again.

"Danny, for the last time, quit your daydreaming!" Father yelled.

I ran to him. No way would I be one of those goof-off kids.

He suddenly changed direction. We moved away from the ravine and into the trees. Father sat dawn on a log. "Okay, Danny, take off your pack."

He helped me squirm out of the straps. I repeated to myself: Trees stop erosion. Loggers. Drillers. The earth would be destroyed.

He looked at his watch. "I want you to find me two edible plants. You've got three minutes."

Edible plants! That was the other lesson. I glanced around the forest floor, but every shrub and weed looked the same. I stood there paralyzed, as if waiting for some plant to raise its hand.

"Two and a half minutes," said Father.

I hunted through the brush. I stooped to examine leaves, stalks, and dried-up petals.

"Two minutes."

I tore and sniffed. I touched my tongue to the tips of leaves. "One minute. Come on, now, think! What part of the plant would you eat? Think about color."

Hopelessly confused, I pulled on a long, trailing vine that was still producing white flowers. The roots came out easily. I wound the vine into a coarse spool and took it to Father.

"What's this?" he said with a look of distress. "You want to eat this?"

I shrugged and stared at the ground. He tossed the wretched plant behind him.

"I should make you eat that thing," he said. "Don't you remember anything we talked about?"

"I remember about erosion."

"That's fine but I'm talking about survival now. What if you were alone in the woods and it was a question of eating or dying? Where would you be after the first week?"

Not wanting to answer, I just scuffed my toe on the log.

"Dead as dog shit, right?" He made me stand still. "Right?" I nodded, keeping my eyes lowered.

"Can you find me one edible plant in thirty seconds?" When I made no reply he said, "Danny, what's growing two feet in back of me? Will you look, please! This is important."

A blizzard of green was all I saw through my moist eyes. Father reached behind him, yanked out an evergreen shrub, and held it under my nose. He pointed, in descending order, to four red berries. "Do you remember its name?"

I didn't.

"Partridgeberry. Say it. Partridgeberry."

I mumbled the word with him. "Here," he said, "eat one." We each chewed up and swallowed a berry. "Not much taste but it could save your life."

I hoped we were finished. I still couldn't meet his eyes.

"All right, that's one. Now study the trees around us, especially the bark."

The instant he mentioned bark, I remembered the shaggy hickory tree. I spotted one and plowed through the brush toward it. Dried husks were scattered all over the ground. I pried out the nuts and, supporting them against my chest, carried as many as I could back to Father.

"Let's crack them open," I said.

"We don't have time. Just leave them here and we'll move on."

He stood up. I let the nuts fall, and Father helped me strap on my pack. While he worked behind me I gazed sadly at the nuts. I wondered if I could really crack them open. Father might be pleased if we had them for supper.

"Let's go," he said.

I quickly stuffed two handfuls of nuts into my jeans. We continued down the slope beside the ravine. Soon I heard the hiss of moving water.

A wide stream rushed beneath a canopy of leaves. The joyful water made me laugh, as I did when Basser licked my chin after school. Father relaxed his pace, and we ambled along the bank in search of a campsite. I felt a need to talk to him but didn't know how to begin. If I didn't think of something, he would probably start another lesson.

"Dad, do you ever hear angels?"

"What?" His initial look of surprise turned into one of suspicion.

"Do angels talk to you sometimes?"

"Talk to me? No, they don't. And who's been talking to you? Your mother?"

He glowered at me. I was shocked that he knew. I had not intended to divulge Mother's secret but only to bring up the general subject of angels. Now I felt that I had betrayed her.

"Has she been filling your head with that rubbish?" Father demanded.

Again I avoided his eyes. He lowered his pack to the ground. "We'll camp here," he said crossly. "Take off your pack."

I obeyed instantly. Father paced back and forth, gathering steam. Then he stood over me while I hung my head.

"Danny, I'm going to tell you a few things and I want you to listen for once. We in America are fighting a new civil war. You remember that hole in the windshield? That wasn't a rock. It was a bullet! Yes, it shocked me too, but it shouldn't have. We're in a war against greedy, powerful men who ruin people's lives and destroy the earth. But now the little people are waking up. For years I've fought oppression and destruction, and I want you to take up the fight someday. But, Danny, you can only win if you understand what the war is about and proceed according to a sensible plan, like an army. You must learn and then act. You cannot waste time daydreaming. Gods and angels are just daydreams, Danny. They're fantasies of weak, fearful people. You've never seen an angel, and neither has anyone else. You can't survive on dreams."

When Father grew this agitated, I knew it was futile to speak. So I stood there beneath the hail of his wrath until he finished. Then I traced a circle with my toe while he set our packs under a tree, wiped his glasses, and shakily turned the pages of his field guide. Suddenly he sat down on a rock and pressed one hand into his lower chest. His attacks of ulcers began like this.

He found his Thermos, poured a little milk into the cap, and gulped it. Pressing his chest again, he breathed deeply and wiped his face and beard with his bandana. When the pain finally subsided, he looked confused and embarrassed. As I watched him from the corner of my eye, I felt relieved because the attack would redirect his thoughts.

The sky had clouded over and the temperature had dropped a few more degrees. It was late in the afternoon. We had not seen another soul for hours. Father started to unravel the tent but changed his mind.

"Let's leave this for now," he said. "I want to show you some things before it gets dark."

He led me up the bank. Every few yards he stopped to point out signs of life. He showed me the remains of larvae on the bottoms of rocks that he pulled from the stream. He talked about flies and beetles that live under water, sometimes for years, until they turn into adults. Names and facts poured out of him. Larval stages, nymphs, life cycles. Insect A was prey to insect B. Insect B lived this long as a nymph and that long as an adult. One swam on its belly, another on its back. Still another had split eyes that could see above and below the water.

Father plunged his hand into the stream and pulled out a crawdad. Holding it in the middle with his fingertips, he pointed out the antennae, claws, tail, the five pairs of legs.

"If one leg is lost, he just grows another. He can flip his tail down and swim backwards to avoid danger. The first order of business in nature is survival."

That was today's lesson: survival. Father kept repeating the word and made sure I appreciated that all the strange characteristics of these creatures were meant to support their existence.

"Humans have to survive also," he went on. We were wading in the shallow stream, ostensibly in search of more animals, but Father's attention had shifted. "We're in a never-ending war with our own species. They're already combing these forests for oil and gas. One day, if we let them, they'll turn the whole country into a desert."

They trampled on helpless people around the world. They polluted the air and water, brainwashed the citizens, fired their workers to increase their profits. We had to stop them now.

In the midst of his passion he doubled over, fell into the water, and staggered onto the bank. He began rubbing his chest and side. Grunting in pain, he started back toward the campsite and immediately dropped to his knees.

"Danny, he whispered, clutching his side. As I scrambled onto the bank, he crawled toward a massive oak tree a few yards away.

I hadn't realized how far upstream we had come. When I looked for our campsite, and Father's precious milk, I saw only a darkening landscape thick with misshapen trees and ominous foliage. The din of the water seemed to have risen up and formed a ghostly presence. The angels of my nightmares were coming for us, I thought. They were angry with me for betraying Mother, and with Father for his blasphemy.

I ran to him. He was retching violently and he waved me away. Something red and horrible fell out of his mouth. Part of it stuck to his beard, and he flung it off in disgust. Waves of pain and nausea swept through him, as if chunks of his insides were being scorched away. He tried to stand but toppled onto his side, gasping and drawing up his knees, expelling loud farts between the moans. I was scared to death. His attacks had never lasted so long, and there had never been blood. But the worst part came when he began growling, cursing, and writhing insanely. He seemed to be locked in mortal combat with an invisible opponent.

At last he collapsed against the big tree. His eyes gazed helplessly upward. I approached him slowly and noticed a change: a softer cast to his eyes, a relaxing of his facial muscles, a frail smile dappled with sweat. Had I ever seen him smile?

He was looking at me in a different way, with mildness and affection. He tried to reach out to me, but his strength was gone. A feeble hissing sound emerged from his mouth. Leaning over, I heard him repeat the words "son... son..." I wiped his face with his bandana, and he brushed his lips against my fingers. I knelt beside him. Our heads were on the same level, and I let him look at me as I stared deeply into his eyes.

He seemed to have thrown off a terrible burden. Long afterward, I imagined that the madding crowd of bosses, drillers, loggers, and soldiers---the dark angels of my father's dreams---had retreated, leaving me in the open, visible for the first time.

"I'll get the Thermos," I said, and with a resolution that astonished me I raced downstream, completely forgetting my phantom terrors. I leaped over rocks, logs, and roots and splashed in and out of the water where the bank narrowed. A cold, heavy, moonless twilight had settled in. The forest was still. I liked the reassuring feel of the chilly, calf-high water as it soaked my pants and seeped into my tightly laced boots.

I found the Thermos in Father's pack, but in my haste and exhilaration I neglected to take anything else, not even our food or a flashlight. I fled back upstream, clutching the Thermos under my shirt as if exposure to the air might spoil its contents. On the way I thought about the hickory nuts in my pockets and was proud of my foresight.

Father was barely awake. He acknowledged my triumphant return with a faint smile and a touch, the finest rewards I had ever known.

"You drink it," he whispered, as I held the cup to his lips.

"But you're sick."

He shook his head weakly. "No. You need to drink it."

At that moment, I think, I knew he was dying. But the possibility of his death was too much to dwell on, so I found a rock and cracked open the nutshells, collecting their meager fruit in my baseball cap. Again Father declined to eat.

"Good boy," he said. "Eat them all. Tomorrow maybe you can find more."

I chewed up the tasteless nuts. It was quite cold now, and I realized we should get out of our wet clothes. The ground was covered with leaves. In the final minutes of daylight I carried armloads of leaves to the oak tree, pulled off Father's boots and pants, removed my own, and buried us in a dry, crunchy blanket. I planned to fetch our gear in the morning, pitch the tent, start a fire, and cook our food. Father would direct me and I would carry out every task and not waste time daydreaming. Snuggled up against him, feeling the coarse hair of his limbs, I hardly thought of home and safety. The forest was our perfect home, and we were safe in each other's arms.

For three days he clung to life. Most of the time he lay unconscious; occasionally his breathing grew labored and his eyes fluttered open, as if he had struggled up from a chasm to make sure I was okay. He couldn't communicate. He probably never saw the tent and the fire. But when I showed him my capful of partridgeberries, which I had spent the day gathering, I caught the flicker of a smile and knew he was pleased. Now I had to survive. If I did, he and Mother would be pleased together.

That made a pleasant daydream as I kept the fire going, dried our clothes, and tried to stay warm. On the fourth day I was rescued by members of a search party who had spotted the station wagon and fanned out toward the streams. Father had died. They found me huddled against him, shivering and debilitated, murmuring to Bosser as I did at home. One man thought my mouth was bleeding, but it was only juice from the berries.

THE ESQUIRE READER

This morning I'm worried about all sorts of things I ain't never cared about before. Like being hard of hearing in my left ear and my lack of proper schooling. And my teeth. Shee-it, I'm thinking, grinning at them in the bathroom mirror, they're all yellow and black like charred popcorn that somebody tossed in the trash. Gloria been right all along, nagging at me to brush and see the dentist. I think about them commercials and I figure if my teeth are in this bad a shape my breath must stink terrible. That won't go over too good downtown. Here's an uneducated old wino, them white lawyers'll figure, and they'll send me home. That's what they done to George Pierce, a friend of mine that now calls himself Whalid Abdul.

But I ain't George Pierce. When they called me to juri-duty I made up my mind I was gonna be seated. I ain't going into no courtroom with no leather vest and beads and rings on my fingers, looking like a pimp. That used to be George's style before he joined the Brotherhood. Me, I'm a family man that's raised three daughters, never cheated on my wife, had the same job with the Department of Sanitation for thirty years, and never made a crooked dollar. I fought in Korea and the shelling made me part deaf. I'm a Christian. Gloria and I belong to First Baptist, although lately I been spending my Sundays in bed. I own a decent suit and a good pair of shoes, and I'm a mind to do my duty. Also, a few days off the truck ain't gonna break my heart.

I know Gloria's gonna howl if I use her toothbrush, so I look in the medicine chest and somebody's old one is laying there with the bristles still in good shape. Probably Roberta's since she was the last to leave and she was always so prissy about her habits. I wash it out with hot water and give my teeth a hard going-over with Crest. That don't help much, so I heap on another round and concentrate on the bad ones in front. After I rinse out I open my mouth different ways and decide it don't look too bad if the light hits right. But what about the smell? Might be smart to stop by a drugstore and get some of them breath candies they show on TV.

I put on my blue suit that Gloria pressed for me last night. I could use a new belt. The one I got is frayed and, round as I'm getting, it's about run out of holes. I find my tie clip in the drawer, but I remember Gloria saying they're out of style. Dobbs and Jameson don't wear no tie clip, she told me. They the people on the north side she cleans for on Monday and Tuesday Lawyers, one divorced, the other thinking on it. Dobbs, he wears Giv-een-chy suits, she told me, but he don't wear no tie clip. I wonder if I should. I like the look of it, my initials in gold against the black rhinestone, but, what the hell, if it ain't in style, best leave it off.

In the kitchen Gloria's in her bathrobe frying up some mush. She gives me a glance out the side of her eye and wrinkles her nose. She don't say "Morning" and I can tell what kind of mood she's in. I look down at the crack in the counter linoleum.

"See them roaches been visiting again."

"You fix them baseboards, maybe they stay out."

She knows better but I let it go. She's always after me to fix something---the hole in the screen door, the leaky faucets, the house needing paint. We know the landlord ain't gonna do it. But today I don't want to get her started cause she's already peeved. Hell, she been on the voting rolls long as me and she never been called to jury duty. She was even a precinct committeeman for the Democrats and she worked in the governor's campaign, but they still never called her. It's just like any other Monday for her, all day in Dobbs' house by herself. She shoves my breakfast at me and goes down the hall to get dressed.

The morning paper's laying on the table. Most days I just look at the headline, but today I figure, Let's see what's happening in the world. Airplane got hijacked in Italy. President says the economy's going full steam. I turn to the local section. A fire at the controls plant and they're calling it arson. Foundry's laying off some more men. Willoughby case is going to trial. Hmm, wouldn't that be a good one. I seen it on TV, his daughter accusing him of murdering his wife by putting poison in her medicine and him denying it and saying he loved her. Makes me shiver to think about that kind or thing, specially with Gloria up that end or town every day.

"Don't forget your lunch," she calls from the bathroom.

She already packed my pail. Bologna sandwich, potato chips, my thermos of coffee. But I'm thinking, How's that gonna look down there with all them high-class white folks, me eating out of a pail? I check my wallet. There's four bucks and I figure I'll use that to grab a hamburger some place. First day at least.

"What time you be home?" she calls, and I can tell she's ready to make up.

"How do I know? I ain't never done this before."

She comes into the kitchen, dressed in her blue uniform, and cleans off the table. Finally she looks at me straight on and sizes me up.

"You look real fine. Do a good job down there."

"I'm buying my lunch.

She goes "Mmm" and nods her head.

* * *

Rush hour's near over and the bus is only half full. Mostly folks heading down to the employment office. Two young guys in one seat are yapping and laughing like fools. Some older folks are sitting by themselves; they look grim. A woman sitting alone is wearing a white nurse's uniform under her coat. She's got a bandage over her eye and she just stares out the window. She must be late for work but that don't appear to bother her.

Looking at the men again, I think of George Pierce and what he's always saying about social injustice. Society got it all backwards, he says. The people who do the shit work ought to get the most pay, instead or the other way around. He says, How much you figure them north-side dudes would charge to pick up your trash? Sometimes George makes sense, but the trouble is, all his bitching don't make him any better off. I like what Reverend Smalley says: There's two ways to be rich. One is to grab more, the other to want less. I follow the second road. I take things as they come, keep the right attitude, and trust things to get better. I don't make a lot of money, but Gloria and me, we work together and live pretty good in a decent home. They made me a driver a few years back, and next year I spect to have a shot at supervisor. I got my self-respect and don't scrape to nobody. And starting today, even them white lawyers in their Giv-een-chy suits are gonna listen to me. George Pierce can't say that. All his bitching and changing his name to Whalid Abdul ain't got him one bit of respect. They sent him home before and they'd send him home today.

I leave the bus at the big new courthouse. There's a drugstore on the corner, so I pop in to buy some breath candies. The young white dude in front of me is buying cigarettes and a couple of magazines---Forbes and Esquire. He's wearing a sharp three-piece suit like the guy on the cover of Esquire. As I leave the store I chew up two of the candies and swish the juice around my mouth. I straighten my tie in a store window. Then I join the crowd crossing the flagstone plaza to the courthouse.

Inside, everything's steel, glass, and hard white plastic, all square and clean. The windows take up the whole wall, and rows of little spotlights hang down from the high ceiling. On one wall there's a double row of color pictures of the judges. People are rushing every which way. The loudest sound is the clop-clopping or high heels.

I show my juror's card to the girl at the information booth.

"Take the elevator to the sixth floor," she says. "Turn right and go down the hall to the waiting room."

The elevator fills up with men in gray and brown suits. There's a good-looking woman wearing a tan coat and carrying a briefcase. One man greets her and introduces her to another man.

"She's a social psychologist," he says. "Our edge."

The young dude from the drugstore gets on with his magazines. We all ride up, watching the numbers over the door.

The guy with the magazines gets off with me at six, and. I follow him down the hall to a room marked "Jurors Only." Turns out he's been called too. I can tell he's been through this before. He goes in casual-like, hangs up his coat, takes a seat, and lights up a cigarette. He looks back and forth from his Forbes to his Esquire. Then he puts the Forbes underneath and opens the Esquire.

The room is big with a rug, armchairs, two sofas, and some low round tables. There's a big window facing the city parking garage. Old dog-eared magazines and ashtrays are laid out, and there's a deck of cards and vending machines. Three white women are already in the room. Two of them look like north-siders, all stylish and skinny. The third is dumpy and her hair's all gussied up. She's smoking in a corner by herself. She gives me a look and then stares out the window at the parking garage.

Pretty soon a lot more people arrive. They find seats and some of them make a little small talk in quiet voices. A tall black girl comes in wearing a fro and glasses. One of them long-strap handbags the college girls carry is hanging from her shoulder. She looks like she means business. The white folks watch her tromp to the empty seat beside me. The two north-side ladies keep peeking at her, and she gives them a real glare, so they turn away. Most all these folks look fine in their good clothes, but some of the men don't look right in a suit and tie. You'd picture them in a tee shirt and jeans. I notice a spot of something on the knee of my trousers, and I cross my legs the other way. Gloria said I look fine. I know I don't look no worse than some of these white dudes. I pop in two more breath candies. Hell, they got no reason to send me home like they did George.

After a while a little bald-headed guy comes in and introduces himself. I give him my good ear. He's the Jury Commissioner, he says, and he's here to talk about the duties of a juror and the procedures of the courtroom. He says the most important thing is to listen to everything the judge and lawyers say. Watch the witnesses close, he tells us, but don't take notes. Put aside your opinions and go by the law as the judge explains it. A man's innocent till he's found guilty---that's the American way. It's our job to weigh the evidence and come up with a true verdict. Nobody has any questions about that, so he goes on to explain about courtroom procedures.

"How long do we get for lunch?" a man asks.

"It's up to the judge," says the Commissioner.

"When do we get paid?" asks another man.

"On Friday. Eight dollars a day."

Well now, that's a surprise. Nobody told me nothing about getting paid. Maybe it was in the letter but I never got that far. Eight dollars a day, forty a week, maybe eighty if I'm here two weeks. I can borrow some cash from Gloria, eat lunch in a nice restaurant, pay her back on Friday, and we'll still have. enough for a night out.

The Commissioner gives us a form and tells us to please print. The black girl next to me lets me use her pen. After that, the Commissioner hands out plastic juror tags and we pin them on. Then we take an oath to tell the truth in our interview.

"I'll be back to call individuals as they're needed," he says, and leaves the room.

An hour goes by before he comes back. He calls a name, and the dude reading Esquire rolls up his magazines, stuffs them into his coat, and follows the Commissioner out the door. About twenty minutes later the commissioner calls somebody else. This goes on the rest of the morning. Some of the people he calls don't come back, some do. The ones that do act shy, they don't look at nobody, and you can tell they been turned down. The Commissioner calls the tall black girl. Twenty minutes later she comes back a-scowling, not looking at nobody. I can't figure it. She looks neat and she's dressed good enough. I'd say she been to college. Why'd they send her back? I know one possible reason but I don't like to think about it. Makes me angry and my stomach gets upset. But why'd they send her back?

The Commissioner calls some more names. More folks get turned down. All kinds of white folks are turned down; only a few are picked. Don't make no sense to me. I'm worried cause some pretty spiffy-looking white folks don't make the grade.

At lunch time I still ain't been called. I'm just leaving the room when I notice Albert Sills down the hall at the courtroom door. Albert's an old member of our church. I forgot about him being a bailiff up here. Well, I think, maybe he can tell me what's taking so long.

"Hey, man," says Albert, "you been called, eh?"

"Well, they ain't called me yet," I says. "I been sitting around all morning."

He laughs. "And likely you be sitting around all afternoon. This the Willoughby trial."

"No! That a fact?"

"You bet. Them lawyers been going at it all morning. You be having a long wait."

"The Willoughby trial! Man! I had a feeling about that. The guy that poisoned his wife."

"Now don't you go talking like that if you want to be seated. You talk that way, they'll excuse you right off the bat. You heard about the Willoughby case?"

"Well, I saw it on the TV news. It's been in the headlines for a month. Course I didn't pay no attention."

"Yeah, that's better. You got your mind made up, you don't belong on no jury."

"I s'pose. But how they gonna know what I'm thinking?"

"Hee, hee," Albert laughs. "You just a baby, man. Them lawyers are slick. They got ways to tell which way you be voting. You wait and see."

"Hell, my mind ain't made up."

After visiting with Albert a while, I go eat, and I'm glad I didn't bring my pail cause I'd be the only soul left in the whole building. Afterwards, back in the waiting room, the Commissioner starts calling people again, one every twenty or thirty minutes. Just like in the morning, some stay and some come back. I think about them stories on TV, Willoughby's daughter's face full of rage and her voice trembling, accusing her daddy of murder. And him walking cold and stiff, refusing to say anything 'cept he loved his wife and didn't do it. Hard to believe he could love any body... Hey, some trial this gonna be. Might last a week. Wow! A whole week off the truck and forty bucks to boot. I remember what the Commissioner told us and what Albert said. On a jury you got to be impartial. That's the secret: impartial. Guess that must be a problem for lots of folks, but it sure ain't for me. Hell, for a week off the truck and forty bucks I can be impartial as a fence post.

Finally, close to quitting time, the Commissioner calls "Mr. Vernon Shaw", and I follow him down the hall.

In the courtroom I see the judge, a big jowly white man with gray hair and black robes, sitting up high like a walrus. Looks like his eyes are closed, but I can't tell for sure. There's two tables with little groups of men at each one. They got papers spread out and clipboards and briefcases. In the jury box I count eleven people, the ones that didn't come back to the waiting room. Their eyes are all glazed. The Esquire dude is there and some of the women, the stylish ones and the frumpy ones. All white folks so far. Albert Sills is standing at the door. The Commissioner gives him my form, and he climbs up to the judge, clears his throat, and sets the paper down in front of him. The judge clears his own throat.

"Mr. Vernon Shaw," he announces. "Please have a seat here in the witness chair, sir." He reads from the paper I filled out, tells everybody about my job and family. Then he explains to me about the mess Dr. Willoughby's in. He points out the doctor, who's sitting at one of the tables like a statue, but I already know him from seeing him on tv. Anybody that cold'd be hard to forget.

"Have you read or heard about this case?" the judge asks me.

I saw something about it on TV," I say. "Didn't pay much attention."

"Have you ever met the defendant or anyone in his family?"

"No, sir."

"Do you feel that you can render an impartial verdict in this case?"

"Yes, sir, I believe I can." I look over at Willoughby, who still ain't bothered to look my way. Wouldn't take much to find him guilty.

"Mr. Prosecutor," says the judge, "questions for cause?"

The two men at the other tabla gaze at me weary-eyed, like it' s been a hard day. "No, Your Honor," says one of them in a gloomy voice.

"All right, questions from defense?"

A young dude with feathered blond hair and a sharp gray suit stands up at the Willoughby table and walks over to the lectern with his clipboard. Looks like he just stepped out of a TV ad for aftershave. I remember seeing him on the elevator with that good-looking woman, and she's here too. I give him my good ear, but I keep my eye on him too.

"Mr. Shaw," he says, "my name is John Barlow. I'm with the firm of Roper, Harris and Martin. You know Dr. Willoughby and seated to his right is Mr. Martin, the senior partner of our firm." I nod at Mr. Martin and he gives me a little thin smile. On the other side of him is that woman, the psychologist or something. She's all decked out in a tweed suit and high heels, and she's looking at me over real hard.

"How are you today, sir?" John Barlow asks me.

"Fine, sir, and yourself?" I reply.

"Fine, thank you." He smiles a little uncertainly, the way lots of white folks do when they have to talk to a black man. I figure he's a mite green; like maybe this is his first big case. "Mr. Shaw, could you describe more fully what your job entails, that is, just what do you do at sanitation?"

I tell him how I was a hauler for twenty-six years and then they made me driver. I tell him I spect to be supervisor next year. He nods up and down. "Very good," he says. "You seem to be a very steady worker. We could use more like you these days."

I don't bother to answer.

"Mr. Shaw, I'd like to ask you one or two personal questions, if you don't mind, just for background. First of all, how long have you been married?"

"Thirty-five years."

He makes a face to show how impressed he is. "And you have three children?"

"Yes, sir, three girls. All grown up and left home."

"Ah, very good. And you and your family have never had...uh... problems of a legal nature...with the law, I mean."

"No, sir."

"Right, I didn't think so. Mr. Shaw, what was the extent of your formal education?"

My heart sinks when he asks me that. It takes me a minute to answer. "Well, I left school at fifteen. I had to work."

John Barlow acts embarrassed. He spends a lot of time shuffling through the papers in his clipboard. "You understand this is just for background," he says, but I figure all this background got to mean something. Strike one, I'm thinking.

"Are you active in any organizations?" he asks. "Men's clubs, church groups, political, community service, that sort of thing."

"Well, I used to be in the Y. Been a member of my church for over thirty years."

"Ah, fine, fine. Do you like sports?"

"Sure."

"Which ones do you like?"

"Oh, baseball, football, basketball. I like 'em all."

Now I'm starting to think: Men's clubs? Sports? What's all this got to do with the Willoughby case? But I don't care, really, cause he ain't asking me nothing that might keep me off the jury. 'Cept for my lack of schooling, and maybe he'll forget that. While we're talking the judge is leaning back in his chair and gazing at the ceiling. The jurors in the box are looking in my direction, but they don't appear to be seeing nothing. John Barlow's rivals at the other table are sitting still and sullen, and that cold bastard, Willoughby, still ain't moved a hair.

"Do you play any sports?" John Barlow asks me.

"Not anymore. Too much of this." I pat my stomach and he laughs.

"You're more of a spectator then. You watch sports on TV."

"Yeah, that's about it."

"You like to watch TV?"

"Oh yeah, it's relaxing. Course I try not to overdo it."

"What are your favorite shows?

"Well, let's see. I like Miami Vice and the Cosbys, you know. They're kind of fun.

"Good. Very good. Would you excuse me a moment?"

He goes over to old Mr. Martin and grins like he's pleased with me. The old man whispers something to the lady psychologist. She don't seem convinced. She whispers back to Martin, and Martin whispers to Barlow. Then Barlow comes back to the lectern.

"Uh, Mr. Shaw, I wonder if you could give me some idea of how much you read or, rather, the things you do read."

Damn that woman, whoever she is. Here we go again about my lack of proper learning. What do I say now? I could tell him I read the newspaper every day but then they'll figure I believe all that hype about Willoughby and I ain't impartial. If I tell the truth, they'll figure I'm too dumb to sit on a jury.

"Mm, let's see," I say. "I sometimes read Esquire."

"Esquire?" John Barlow says. He frowns hard at me, the way Gloria does when I tell her I'm too tired to go to church. "You read Esquire?"

"Yes, sir," I reply, but my voice don't want to go along.

He goes over to Mr. Martin again, and Martin, Barlow, and the woman whisper back and forth. Martin grabs Barlow by the arm and looks up at him, but I can't make out what they're saying. I'm afraid I put my foot in my mouth. Strike two, I'm thinking. They all give me a hard look. Then I hear the old man say "Wait, John!" and he stands up and whispers some more at him. Finally Barlow walks past the lectern and comes right over to me.

"Uh, Mr. Shaw, do you have a subscription to Esquire?"

"No, sir."

"You buy it from the newstand."

"Yes, sir, that's right." I'm starting to squirm a little.

"I see. Tell me, what's your favorite section of the magazine? Or maybe I should ask what you read it for. The articles, stories, reviews?"

"Sure, all those things."

"Can you tell me something you've read in Esquire recently?"

Oh, this dude is sharp. He's got me smack against the wall. "Can't recollect what I read lately. Nothing too important, though."

"Do you read Esquire very often?"

"Oh, now and again."

John Barlow's face slithers into a smile. "Do you read any other magazines?" he asks.

"Once in a while I pick something up."

"Any books?"

I look down and shake my head no. Shee-it, I'm thinking, now he knows I'm faking it. Strike three and I'm out. He's going to send me horne just like George Pierce.

I guess George been right all along. You ain't got money and fancy clothes and a white man's education, you don't count for nothing. Barlow goes back to his table and talks some more with Mr. Martin and the woman. She gives them a nod and then Barlow nods to the judge.

"No further questions?" says the judge.

"No, Your Honor," says Barlow.

"Okay, Mr. Shaw," says the Judge, "thank you. I believe that completes the selection of the jury except for the alternates. Let's finish up tomorrow morning."

The judge pries himself out of his chair and walks out through a back door. John Barlow grins at me. I'm still sitting in the witness seat, not sure if I missed something cause of my bad ear.

"You can go home now, Mr. Shaw," says John Barlow in a friendly way.

"Well, am I on or off?"

He laughs. "You're on! See you tomorrow, sir."

The two men at the other table are shaking their heads and stuffing papers into their briefcases. They don't look too pleased. Then I remember something George told me. Those two must have used up their challenges, so they don't have no more say. I'm gonna be seated after all. Well, how about that!

I walk out of the courtroom grinning ear to ear, and there's old Albert waiting on me.

"You made it, eh?" he says.

We laugh and he starts to give me the high five, but I figure that ain't so dignified, so I push my hand out for a handshake.

"Never a doubt," he says.

I laugh some more and pat him on the arm. He walks me to the elevator.

"Well, see you tomorrow," he says. "This ought to be some trial."

"You figure it might last the whole week?"

"Oh, at least that. More likely two or three. Rich folks have long murder trials."

I'm thinking, Hey! Three weeks off the truck, a hundred twenty bucks in my pocket. This gonna be a vacation!

I'm still mulling over the whole thing at the bus stop. Hell, I never had nothing to worry about. They seen right away I was honest and clean-living. Just shows, you live right, you get respect. And as for the trial, I mean to do my duty and be impartial all the way through. Even a fiend like Willoughby's innocent till you prove him guilty.

THE HANDS OF GOD

Professor Walter Klug lived on the wide border between chemical biophysics and physical biochemistry. In his laboratory at the university he wrote papers such as "Theoretical Absorption and Circular Dichroic Spectra of Triple Helices" and, as part 55 of his series on molecular recognition, a ten-page tour de force entitled "Computer Prediction of Reactive Sites in Enzyme Models." Teeming with Greek letters and mathematical symbols, Klug's papers looked like encyclopedias of insect parts. He sent his manuscripts to the most prestigious scientific journals, where they were published without a single editorial alteration, as if they had never been read.

Klug was a pure theoretician. In his student days at M.I.T., where the school motto is Mens et Manus, he decided he had the mind but not the hands. He hated the painstaking preparations that went into experimental research. He grew frustrated with perverse instruments and protocols that always ran into trouble. "I can destroy a $200,000 spectrometer just by looking at it," he had boasted over the years. His present lab, with almost no equipment, had an abandoned look. The only things on the workbenches were a few dust-covered petri dishes and pipets, as forgotten as bones in the desert.

No graduate student had worked for Klug in more than a decade. The ones who even bothered to interview him came away disoriented. "He's in another galaxy," they said. "He shows you six pages of equations and not a shred of data." They fled to the bubbling, humming experimental labs and their gleaming, state-of-the-art equipment. Klug remained the lone barren member of the faculty, producing no academic offspring.

A paunchy man of fifty-five, Klug had thick brown hair and eyebrows and a wide nose and mouth. From his eyes came a searing glare, from his mouth a gruff, impatient voice. When he clattered down the halls on his flat, pronated feet, people looked the otherway, as if Jehovah Himself were trampling through the vintage. On his heavy body he woe ancient, threadbare suits with ties that he might have chosen in the dark. He smoked ten cigars a day, blew smoke around with total abandon, and started fires in other people's wastebaskets.

Klug rarely spoke with his colleagues. He turned down committee work, sat by himself in seminars, and avoided all social events. The professors in the Biological Sciences building regarded him as an acerbic genius, who toiled behind some mystical barrier. When they saw him coming, they quietly shut the doors to their laboratories, lest his penetrating eyes, if not his cigars, undo their sensitive experiments.

On warm days Klug ate his lunch at Duck Pond, a little man-made body of water in the center of the campus. Students gathered here during the noon hour, spreading their books and meals amid the viburnum and willow trees, but they were gone by two o'clock, when Klug arrived. After making sure he was alone, he would set his briefcase under a tree, lower himself to the ground, pull his legs up Indian fashion, and take out his lunch and a sheaf of papers. While he pondered and wrote, he fed himself the food his housekeeper had packed, consuming each item with as much interest as he took in his breathing. His appetite coasted on energy graphs and gamboled through fields of quantum parameters. At times he would state so intently at the pond that the ducks would swim to the opposite bank.

One afternoon in September, as he pursued his analysis, he was disturbed by a youthful, pugnacious voice. He looked up into dazzling light, for the sun on the pond had blinded him. He rubbed his eyes. When he heard the voice again, he was afraid.

"You hear me, man? What you got in that briefcase?"

Klug tried to back away, but he was sitting against a willow tree. He rubbed his eyes harder.

"Gimme that thing, man."

Klug pulled the briefcase to his chest. He felt the ground blindly for his papers. A boot kicked them out of his hand.

"Who are you? What are you doing?" he demanded.

"What's that shit you're eating?" said another voice.

Klug's vision was returning. He looked at his lunch but didn't recognize it. It was a casserole of some kind, half-eaten and suppurating in a plastic dish.

"You want my lunch? Here, take it."

"I don't want your fucking lunch. I want this."

A strong black arm tried to snatch the briefcase. Klug turned his body to protect it. He felt a flurry of kicks on his arms, back, and thigh. His head was stomped against the tree. The briefcase was torn away.

"Give it back!" he cried.

As he rose clumsily to his feet, his attackers leaped outside the hanging willow branches. The one with the briefcase continued to search inside it. He threw a handful of papers into the pond.

"No!" Klug lunged forward.

He saw the briefcase sail into the air and land in the water. Something heavy struck the back of his head, and he fell into the pond, smashing his knee on the rocky bottom. Ducks flew up quacking, the attackers fled, and people came running down the paths.

* * *

Twenty-four hours later, Klug sat on a hospital bed with his right leg in a hip-to-ankle cast, elevated on a pillow. His foot, puffy and white with bent toes and irregular toenails, seemed to be oozing out a plaster tube. He wore a white hospital gown, and his head was wrapped in a white gauze bandage. His head throbbed so intensely that water ran from his eyes and nose. Any sharp movement made him gasp as if hot oil had been dropped on his skin.

His right knee had been shattered, his left calf muscle badly pulled. His arms and much of his body under the gown were covered with yellow and purple splotches.

Suddenly he moaned.

"Need help?" asked the man in the other bed.

Klug felt waves of pain from all directions filling his gut with a nauseating vortex. Unable to reach the metal pan on his table, he vomited into a half-full glass of water, which overflowed onto his sheets. His roommate signaled for a nurse.

"Are you sure you don't want something for the pain?" she said to Klug.

It was her second offer. She carefully turned him onto his left side and rolled up half of his bottom sheet. Then she turned him as far as possible onto his cast and slipped the sheet out from under him.

"I don't want your damn pills or your damn shots!" His teeth were clenched and sweat ran down his face.

In silence she gathered up the soiled linen. After she left the room, he fainted.

Now two nurses ministered to him. One shook him gently until he revived. Then she took his pulse and blood pressure while the other wiped his face with a damp towel. They worked together to insert a new sheet beneath him. Like a peevish child he scolded them and tried to squirm away until exhaustion plowed him under.

"I'll take one pill," he rasped.

* * *

Hours later he awoke in a partial delirium. His roommate had the TV news on, and a man was reporting live from a crime scene.

"...and the mayor has acted by creating the special crack unit."

"Cracked it...cell receptor theory" ...cracked the problem," mumbled Klug.

"...this raid and all the others seem to be in response to the specter of vigilante groups...

"Spectra... model proteins... next slide."

"Some people here are skeptical, though, like this resident, who's seen it before...

"It don't do no good, man. They be back tomorrow...

Hearing these words, Klug opened his eyes. On the TV he saw a crowd of black people standing behind the reporter.

"Here is how you can recognize a crack house," said the reporter. "Look for boarded-up windows, unfamiliar vehicles, lookouts with walkie-talkies or beepers, visitors coming and going at odd hours. If you become suspicious, don't take action yourself. Call the police hotline."

"Where was that place?" Klug barked at his roommate.

"Oh, you're awake. You were talking in your sleep."

"The crack house. Where was it?"

"Crack house? Oh, downtown somewhere. I wasn't listening."

"Damn!"

"Must have been downtown," said his roommate. "Why? You need to stock up?"

Gritting his teeth, Klug raised himself onto an elbow and jerked the curtain between himself and the other man.

Later in the evening, two faculty members from the Department of Biochemistry came in. Dr. Hopkins, the prim, white-haired chairman, peered around the curtain.

"Ah, Walter, there you are."

Klug started. He glared at the visitors as if they were two more medical students about to examine him. They waited until he relaxed and indicated a chair. Dr. Hopkins sat while the younger man, Dr. McBride, remained standing.

"How are you feeling?" asked Hopkins. He sat stiffly with his hands folded. As he enunciated his words, he leaned forward like the needle on a gauge.

"I'm fine," muttered Klug. "You shouldn't have bothered."

"It's a scandal. These hoodlums come right onto the campus, and Security can't stop them."

Klug grunted and looked impatiently at his table. He started to reach for something but winced in pain.

"Can I get you anything?" Hopkins rocked forward.

"Nah." Klug waved him off.

Hopkins smiled tightly. McBride looked at the floor.

"Walter," said Hopkins, "I imagine your knee could take some time to heal."

"Six to eight weeks in the cast. Another two or three on crutches."

"Oh, dear." Hopkins exchanged a glance with McBride. "Well, I don't want you to fret about your courses. Mac here has volunteered to finish 640 and, with some boning up, he feels he can handle 740 in the winter."

Klug narrowed his eyes at the younger man.

"Not with your flair, of course," McBride added.

"I'll be back by winter."

"It could be dangerous for you, getting around in winter," said Hopkins.

"I'll be back, I said."

"Yes, well, we don't have to discuss that now. The important thing is that you needn't worry about it. We want you to concentrate on you recovery. And, by the way, our long-term disability is excellent."

"I'm not a damn invalid!"

Klug surmounted the pain and opened the drawer in his table.

"Of course not, Walter. Here, let me help you."

Before Hopkins rose, Klug withdrew a cigar and lighter from the drawer. He sank back against his pillow and lit up.

"Is that allowed?" Hopkins whispered.

Klug sucked hard on his cigar and exhaled calmly in the direction of Hopkins. The latter moved his chair back a foot. Klug aimed another stream at McBride, who ambled over to the window. Then he fired a third round that enveloped both men.

"Perhaps we should let you rest," said Hopkins, getting up.

"Hang in there, Walter," said McBride.

A thick globular frog trickled out of Klug's mouth and nose. It hovered staunchly before his face, dissipating only after the visitors had gone.

* * *

During his ten days in the hospital, two more people came to see him: a salesman for a computer firm, who wanted to sell him advanced software, and a theoretical biophysicist from England, in town for a symposium. The salesman spent less than five minutes in the room. Klug received him so coldly that he never took out his brochures. The Englishman compared American and British universities and discussed his quarrel with a book publisher. When he mentioned his topic for the symposium, Klug's eyes filmed over. He slumped in his pillows and, like a dying motor, spluttered a few pointless words. The visitor never asked about his prognosis.

Klug's roommate went home. Two others came and went. He had no interest in any of them and discouraged their attempts at conversation. He was often cross with the nurses, and they avoided his room. "Thinks he's God Almighty," they muttered. For much of the day he read the newspaper and newsmagazines. He watched the TV news four times a day, irking his roommates, who wanted to sleep. Drug-related stories held his attention. Whenever he came upon one, he reread it or watched for its updated version on TV. For long intervals he digested the information, burning the walls with his ominous glare.

On the eve of his discharge, a young black man was wheeled in on a gurney. A male and female nurse lifted him onto the bed, carefully laying him on his right side, facing Klug. He was under anesthesia, and a tube protruded from his nose. While the male nurse connected the tube to an aspirator on the wall, the woman brought in an IV stand.

"Take care of this guy," said the man. "He's a hero."

"What did he do?" she asked.

"Tried to take out some crack dealers in his apartment building. They had weapons."

He left, and she started the IV. A portly black man, about Klug's age, came in and waited for her to finish. She smiled at him on her way out.

The man exchanged a nod with Klug. He pulled a chair up to the opposite side of the bed and sat down heavily. His glistening eyes settled on the back of the young man's head. His brow was knit and his head slightly cocked, as if he were trying to understand something. He wore a denim shirt and jeans, both frayed and stained. A pack of cigarettes made a square outline in his pocket.

Klug watched the man, surreptitiously at first, then more expectantly, as if he felt some affinity.

"You can sit on this side if you like," he offered.

When the man didn't move, Klug turned his attention to the unconscious patient. His mouth was open and his breathing was audible. Green fluid appeared in the tube and was slowly drawn toward the wall. Klug noticed a resemblance between the two men even though the older face was lined and anxious while the younger was as smooth and innocent as a child's.

The end of visiting hours was announced. As if programmed, the older man got to his feet with great exertion, supporting himself momentarily on the chair. He pressed in the small of his back.

"I'm sure they'll let you stay," said Klug.

The man hesitated. He looked at Klug, at the young man, at the door.

"Here, bring your chair over to this side. They won't bother you."

"Thank you," said the man.

He dragged his chair between the beds. Like a sentinel, Klug focused his eyes on the doorway. When the other man assumed his former position in the chair, Klug drew the curtain and waited.

Soon he heard the patient stirring and trying to speak. He heard the man in the chair move.

"Davy, Davy, you awake? Can you hear me, son?"

The young man seemed to be struggling.

"Hey, Davy, David, no! Don't you mess with that thing. You lay there real still, and I'll get the nurse. You're in the hospital."

Klug pressed his call button, but the man rushed out of the room. Seconds later, his heavy footsteps returned, accompanied by squeaky shoes. The chair was pulled out from between the beds.

"David?" said the nurse. "Do you know where you are? You're in a hospital room, and your father is here. You've just had surgery."

Klug could hear her rearranging things.

"Listen to me, David," she said gently. "It's very important that you don't move around. Yes, I know that tube is uncomfortable, but try not to fight with it. This other one's an IV. Can you swallow, David? Good. Now let me get a pulse."

There was silence for fifteen seconds.

"Okay," she said. "Are you thirsty?"

"Unh," came a distorted voice.

"I know. It's hard to talk around the tube. You'll get used to it pretty soon. Are you hurting anywhere?"

"Yuh."

"Inside? All over inside? I can give you something for the pain. It'll make you sleepy."

David gagged a reply.

"Okay, I'll get you something. Remember, now, don't move around."

Her shoes squeaked out of the room.

"Daddy?"

"I'm here, Davy. Don't you move. I'm right here."

"Paralyzed."

"No, no, wait. We don't know nothing yet. The doctors don't know."

"Can't move."

"Davy, boy, you listen to me. They're going to operate on you again. Nobody can tell nothing till they operate. So don't you go giving up. You ain't no quitter."

"Oh, Daddy... Daddy."

"Davy, I talked to the doctors. They're good men, the best. You're a hero, son. Everybody around here knows what you did. They're taking real good care of you."

David coughed and moaned.

"You got to trust in God, son. God won't give up on you, so don't you give up on yourself."

The nurse came in. "David, I'm going to give you a shot." There was silence while she worked. "You'll feel sleepy in a little while," she said.

After she left, neither man spoke. The lights on the floor were turned down. Time passed, and the father's breathing grew labored. Klug eased the curtain back. Seeing that both were asleep, he studied them as closely as he might have studied a page of quantum physics. Some inspiration caused his hand to move toward the man in the chair. His fingers extended almost to the man's shoulder; they were half an inch from a tear in his shirt and they could feel warmth from his body.

"We shall not be victims again," whispered Klug, as if he had found the solution.

His fingers and arm retracted. He scrutinized his hands and touched an age spot that he hadn't noticed before. He traced a finger over his prominent veins and pulled at the loose skin on his knuckles. Then he made his hands into fists. He smiled as they became taut and alive.

"We have a job to do," he said to the man asleep. "But how do we do it?"

Closing the curtain again, he waited for his own sleep to come.

In the night he awoke to their low voices. David's was clearer now, although still a little slurred. He had somehow adjusted to the tube.

"Just listen to you," his father said. "One year of college and nobody can tell you nothing. Well, you wrong, Mr. College Boy. God is real and He cares about you and He ain't going to let you down. And I'll tell you something else. He's going to rain fire on them that shot you. When God gets through, there won't be no more addicts and pushers; they're going to perish in flames."

"It won't happen, Daddy."

"It will, I tell you. I know it sure as anything."

"When? Tell me when."

"I can't tell you when or how, but I know it's coming. God will bring the fire."

"Daddy, God is... a theory. That's all it is. A theory."

"Now you be careful, boy."

"You can't wait for God. You have to make things happen with your own hands."

"Well, you fought them pushers with your own hands, but how do you know God wasn't moving them hands?"

"It's only a theory." David's voice was muddled again, and he sounded weary.

"We'll see, son," his father said. "For now, though, we ain't going to lose heart."

* * *

The house across the street couldn't possibly be occupied. No lights were on; no sound escaped it's time-worn frame. Its front door was open, and the cold November wind invaded like an enemy. On the porch, revealed by a street lamp, were two large tires and a dark shape that Klug could not make out. He squinted at the shape, for it seemed to move when the wind blew.

Klug supported himself on a mailbox, perhaps the only freshly painted object on the street. His watch read two o'clock. Above an empty lot, the great hunter, Orion, was visible in the sky. Klug puffed on a cigar. He wore a shabby coat, moth-eaten trousers, and old tennis shoes.

An old black man in an even shabbier coat strode down the sidewalk, self-absorbed, humming a tune. Klug half-crouched behind the mailbox and watched him closely. They never made eye contact. The man and his melody faded into the darkness.

"Hey, man," said Klug under his breath.

A car slowed down as it approached. Klug saw three people inside. Again he started to hide behind the mailbox, but it was too late. The car stopped, and a white man in the front passenger seat rolled down the window. He wore only a dark tee shirt; the rest of his arm was clothed in tattoos.

"You straight, gramps?"

Klug saw two women in the car. One drove, the other sat in back. He folded his arms and straightened up.

"What're you doing out this late?" said the tattooed man. "You ought to be in bed, gramps."

Klug stared into his face.

"Is he a cop?" the driver said.

"Let's get out of here," said the woman in back.

Klug turned up the intensity of his glare.

"Come on, Lenny," said the driver. "Something ain't right."

The man gestured, and she sped down the street.

"Ha!" Klug shouted, pounding the mailbox. He limped energetically up and down the sidewalk. Two more cars crept by. He watched their occupants as they searched both sides of the street. No longer did he try to hide.

He turned his attention to the house again. Tossing away his cigar, he limped across the street, his eyes fixed on the black doorway. He hobbled up two steps to a pitted walk and up three more to the porch. Between gusts of wind a faint unpleasant odor emerged from the house. Klug saw that the dark shape on the porch was a child's doll carriage. The wind made it roll a few inches back and forth. He listened at the doorway and observed that the door latch had been crushed.

Inside the house, the odor was strong and foul. The floor creaked as he stepped into a large front room. Enough light filtered through the shredded glass curtains to enable him to see a sofa, an overturned armchair, a fallen lamp, two straight-back wooden chairs, and, to his amazement, an upright piano. A line of splotchy holes ran along one plaster wall.

Klug made his way through the room, supporting his lame leg with his hand. Just ahead of him, an unseen creature scampered into the kitchen.

The odor was coming from there. When he flipped on the light, he almost lost his balance as he recoiled from a wave of cockroaches radiating from the center of the floor. Before he stabilized himself they had disappeared.

The origin of the wave was a putrescent dog, lying on a dark stain. Most of its face had been eaten away. A river of ants flowed from under the sink, across the linoleum, and up the dog's neck, splitting into tributaries over its teeth and gums and reuniting in a maelstrom on its shattered muzzle. Around the carcass lay bits of garbage and aluminum cans, each surrounded by its own pool of ants.

Klug turned off the light and limped shakily back through the front room to the hall. At the staircase he steadied himself on the bannister. He gulped the wind as it blew in the doorway.

Before him was a small study. He made out a roll-top desk and rows of wooden shelves. The shelves were empty except for a clarinet in an open case and some dog-eared sheet music. Inspecting these items in the dim light, he stepped on a plastic doll, and its cry made him jump. At his feet lay a pile of dirty clothes.

"Ah, yes," he said.

Squatting on his good knee, he gathered up a shirt and pants, shook them had, and set them on the desk. He shook out a blouse and skirt, four sweatshirts, pajamas, and two sneakers. With his arms full he limped into the front room.

"How shall we do this?" he murmured. "Ah, yes, for starters, Mr. Alpha will sit here." He arranged the shirt and pants on the middle sofa cushion behind a coffee table. "And Mr. Beta will do business here." He pulled a straight-back chair up to the coffee table, laid a sweatshirt on the seat, and kicked the sneakers underneath. "And Ms. Gamma monitors the proceedings from the piano. Yes. Perfect!" He draped a blouse and skirt over the keyboard. Then he lifted the blouse and played the first notes of Beethoven's Fifth.

"And, of course, the kids will be running around and, what the hell, the guests can make themselves at home. He flung the rest of the clothes around the room.

He took out a cigar. As he lit it, he observed his hands. They were strong and steady, the sort of hands to be trusted with a really important mission. A cloud of smoke hovered and then disappeared in a gust of wind. He held the cigar against the glass curtains until a flame wobbled into being. Then he placed the cigar on the exposed stuffing of a sofa cushion.

He limped out of the house and across the street. As he reached the sidewalk, he heard a familiar tune. It was that old man again, still humming, and returning with a plastic convenience-store bag. The bag clinked as he swung It.

"Well, looky here," he said. "What's happening, man?"

"I couldn't say," said Klug.

"Looks like a fire. You see that?"

"Yes, it does look like a fire."

"Man, I knew it'd happen sooner or later. That house was the Devil's place, you know what I mean? All kinds of things going on in there."

"The Devil's place," said Klug to himself.

Something crashed inside the house. A dog in the yard next door started barking.

"Brr, too cold to stand here," said the man. He began walking, and Klug Joined him. They glanced behind them several times.

"Don't know what it's all coming to," the man said vaguely.

"We've learned something tonight," said Klug.

"Yep, we learning."

"Dad's theory may be valid after all."

"She is. Yep." Seeing the look in Klugs' eyes, the man dropped back a step.

"And assuming it is," said Klug. "Nothing can stop us."

MY LITTLE RED SWEETHEART

I work for a guy named Teddy at a place he calls Ambrosial Ambience. It's an old two-story house on the west side of town, next to a Pay-lo gas station that went out of business months ago. From the side window, I can see the colored triangles drooping over the empty pump stands. Sometimes little kids play in the trash bin. Our customers park in a dirt alley between us and the gas station, or else they leave their cars a block away and walk here fast with their heads down.

The house is almost empty. When you walk in the front door, there's a desk at the entrance to the living room. We keep the cash box in the top drawer. In the living room, there's a couch, a coffee table, and a TV set. Down the hall is a kitchen with nothing in it but a refrigerator, where we keep pop. Upstairs are the bedrooms and the only bathroom with plumbing that works. The walls in every room are bare and crumbling. The furnace works in winter, but all we got in summer is a floor fan.

I'm here from three in the afternoon, when we open, to midnight, when we close. I get Sundays off and one more day that I work out with Cindy and Lisa. As long as two of us are here, Teddy's happy, but if someone don't show, he gets pissed and threatens to kick her off the team. That's what he calls me and Cindy and Lisa---his team. He says, "I'm the manager, you're the players, and the manager can fire the players anytime he damn well pleases. "He says this even when we show up every day, even when we have a good week, moneywise. He just likes to say lt.

Teddy's a big lard-ass with thick black hair that hangs over the sides of his face down to his shoulders. His skin is brown and smooth. If he had feathers in his hair, you'd think he was an Indian chief. Without the feathers, he looks like a flabby TV wrestler. He wears an Yves St. Laurent leather Jacket with a fur collar. He paid 850 dollars for it, so he says, but Cindy thinks it's stolen property and he bought it cheap. "Only question is whether he bought it from the thief or the cops," she says.

When Teddy comes in around closing time, the first thing he does is count the cash. Then he plops onto the couch light a cigarette, puts his feet on the coffee table, and sits there watching TV and flicking ashes off his Jacket. He likes to rub his chin on the fur collar. He stays until twelve o'clock even though we hardly ever get customers after eleven. It's just to make sure we don't leave early. Teddy figures he can't trust us and he's right.

* * *

When I was seventeen, I ran away from home because of all the fights I was having with my mother. She had one boyfriend after another---Jerks, greasers, and drunks. They got worse every time. I couldn't stand being in the house with them and seeing them look at me. One day, one of them tried to grab me, and I hit him with the frying pan. My mother locked me out of the house all night. I left the next day.

When I got to the city, a couple of women let me stay in their apartment over an Army surplus store. They were nice and didn't make me pay my share of the rent. They introduced me to the trade. "The only thing that counts is the money, they told me. "Don't think about nothing else." We used to work Franklin Avenue between the Fourth Street bridge and Pawn Shop Row. The men came from all over town---factory workers with their wedding rings still on, brainy looking guys from the suburbs, college kids with pimply faces, either babbling like idiots or afraid to open their mouths. We'd take them up to the apartment for fifteen minutes and send them on their way.

Every now and then, the cops would come by and bust some of the girls. They never got me, though, because I knew how to get away over a chain-link fence into a school bus parking lot. One night, the cops rounded up all the girls and fags on Franklin Avenue. They took over an hour to pull everybody in. Lucky for me, I saw them first and ran for the fence. I hid under a school bus until it was safe.

The cops took all the girls, including the women I was living with, to the police station and made them sit there all night. Then they told them to get out of town. They said our area was going to be made into a convention center. Then the cops started patrolling Franklin Avenue every night, and the girls left to other places. I would have gone with some of them to work the truck stops, but Teddy came along just then and said he'd find me a place to live and pay me good money. He said he was recruiting some new blood of his team.

When I started with Teddy a year ago, he had the other girls. April and Vera were almost thirty; Mavis was a black girl about twenty-five. Teddy wanted me because I was younger but mainly because I had red hair and light skin. He said he needed a balance, and April and Vera were almost as dark as Mavis. He also wanted an Oriental girl. A good Oriental girl was a gold mine, he said, but you could only find them in the big cities. "One of these days I'm going to Chicago and get one," he told me. So far, he's never done it.

April, Vera, Mavis, and I used to work at Teddy's old place downtown. He called it Pleasure Dome. After the cops made him close it, he bought the place we're in now, on the west side. He wanted us to think up a name for it so he could advertise in the Yellow Pages. Since none of us cared what he called it, he tried out some names of his own. He thought up Temple of the Love Goddess and Cupid's Retreat. He wanted a French name, but none of us knew any French. Then he met someone that told him about a place in Philadelphia called Ambrosial Ambience. Teddy liked that one. He said it sounded French. (When the phone rings, we're supposed to say, "Thank you for calling Ambrosial. How may I serve you?" We never say it, though; we just say hello.)

A month after we moved in, Mavis had a fight with April and Vera. They thought she was taking from the cash box. When they both accused her in front of Teddy, Mavis blew up and punched April in the mouth. Teddy tried to separate them, but Mavis scratched his face, ran out the door, and never came back.

The next month, April left with one of her regular customers and Vera just disappeared. Teddy got Cindy and Lisa to replace them. Now he gripes that we're all redheads with light skin, and he don't like Cindy being over thirty. He's looking for another black girl---someone classier than Mavis, he says. And of course he still talks about an Oriental girl.

* * *

On the west side of town, we get more working men and not so many college kids. The men come in wearing their work clothes and smelling of beer or chemicals from the solvent plant. They don't say much and they act cool when they pull out their seventy-five dollars, like it was nothing to them. Before we get on the bed with them, we make them take a shower. Even with a shower, I wouldn't let some of them touch me in front. When I get a real bad one I Just lay on my stomach and tell him, he can give me a massage. If he wants me to turn over I tell him, "Sorry, that's not allowed." If he says, "What am I supposed to do?" I tell him, "We only allow massages. If you want to get yourself off, that's okay." Some of them do it themselves and some move up against my help and do it. I let them do that if they're wearing a rubber.

One of our regular customers hasn't got feet. He drives up in a special car, pushes himself out, and comes up to the door on crutches. When Cindy sees him, she hides in the kitchen. She says she'll throw up if she has to look at his stumps. Lisa don't take her eyes off the TV, and he gets the message. I don't mind him, though. He's always clean when he comes in, and I don't make him wash. The only problem is waiting for him to get up and down the stairs sitting down. I hold his crutches while he pushes himself along with his huge arms. In the bedroom, he sits on the bed and takes off his clothes except for the thick white socks he wears. I set his clothes on the chair for him. Then I strip and lay on my stomach. It don't bother him that I won't let him touch me in front. He just puts on a rubber, snuggles up beside me, and does it in less than a minute.

I don't think about him while he's doing it. I don't think about any of them. The guy without feet gives me twenty dollars extra when he leaves, and that's all I think about.

* * *

Working for Teddy, I make good money. Some weeks I make almost five hundred dollars, a lot more than I made on the street. Every night Teddy collects the cash, and we give him a list of how many tricks we had.

Saturday night, he divides the money, taking sixty percent for himself. I always get more than Cindy and Lisa because I'm younger and prettier and most of the customers pick me. I get a lot of repeat customers. Cindy told me she might leave soon, hire some girls, and start an escort service.

"Twelve years of this shit is enough," she said.

"You been doing this twelve years?"

"You got it, hon. Don't it show?"

"It don't show."

But It does. Cindy's face is ash gray except for the blush. She's always tired and crabby, and some days she smells bad. Teddy thinks she's on drugs or infected. When he put it to her, she denied everything, and he told her to go to the clinic or he'd kick her off the team.

"I run a class operation," he said.

"Oh, get off it!' she yelled back. "Give us a decent split and then tell me about your class operation."

"You know I can't give you more. I got overhead."

"Yeah, yeah, we heard it all before."

Cindy settled down, swearing under her breath, and Teddy's lips curled into a smirk. "Overhead" is our private joke. When he's in a good mood, Teddy likes to kid about "overhead expenses" and "making a contribution to law enforcement." But if we ask him about it, he gets serious and tells us it's none of our business.

* * *

I had a sweetheart once. When we were downtown, I used to pass by Import Classics, where they sell Ferraris. In the showroom, they had a red convertible that I fell in love with. It was close to the window, and you could see the white seats and the dials. I'd dream about driving that car up the freeway, fast as it would go, past the farms and woods, through the little towns, up to Lake Wyandotte, where I used to go swimming when I was a kid. I'd dream about the wind rushing around me and my hair streaming. Or maybe it was night and the stars were close and clear. Just me and my little red sweetheart, going fast as Halley's Comet, so fast I could disappear off the earth.

* * *

Teddy bought all of us cars so we could get to work. They were old rust boxes that he picked up from a junk dealer. He bought me a big old Chevy that sounded like a tank and blew out smoke whenever I hit the gas. One day, I drove it down to Import Classics to see if the little convertible was still in the window. It was, so I went inside and looked at it up close. Then I talked to a salesman that reminded me of the guy that does sports on the TV news.

"How old are you?" he asked me.

"Twenty-one."

He gave me a look. "Twenty-one, eh?"

"Yeah. I just had my birthday."

"Are you employed?"

"Sure I'm employed."

"Whereabouts?"

"What do you care? I can make the payments."

He sniffed. "I'll just bet you can. Only problem is, you'd have to come up with 7500 dollars for a down payment."

I shrugged and touched the mirror on the driver's side. I looked at the white seats and the dials. God! I wanted to get in and hold the wheel. The salesman was leaning on the door and looking past me.

I asked if I could have one of the brochures on the table.

"Sure, sure, take all you want."

I took a brochure and left.

On the way home I made up my mind to start saving for that down payment. I didn't spend much on food, and the rent on my tiny apartment was cheap. What I had to do was quit buying clothes and junk, like all the dresses and jewelry I never wore and the pile of tapes I was sick of listening to. I wasn't paying insurance on the Chevy, but the repairs were costing me a fortune. So I decided to make Teddy pay for my car repairs, and every week I'd put something away for that down payment.

Then Mr. Lane Porter showed up at Ambrosial Ambience. He came in about ten o'clock, and, since I didn't hear a car in the alley, I figured he parked down the street. He was a pale, skinny man that looked like he had indigestion. His hair was gray around the sides and cut real short. And he had a little gray mustache.

"Hi! How's it going?" I said to him. I was wearing my robe over a chemise, and I let the robe hang open a little.

He nodded his head and grunted. He looked into the living room, where Cindy was half-asleep on the couch. He tried to see down the hall into the kitchen. Then he whirled around like someone was standing behind him. I knew the type.

"What do you…" he began, but his voice gave out.

"Okay, we have a basic session for fifty dollars and a deluxe for seventy-five."

"Deluxe."

When he took the bills out of his wallet, a credit card fell out, and he fumbled around trying to catch it. He snatched it off the floor and stuck it in his pants pocket. I put the money in the cash box.

"I need to see an I.D.," I told him.

"I.D.? Why do you need an I.D.?"

"So we can be sure of everything."

"Be sure of what? I'm not a cop."

"It's still required. Don't worry, we don't keep no records."

He looked annoyed. "I didn't bring an I.D."

"That credit card will do."

He peeked over at Cindy again. She was snoring now. He tried to see down the hall and up the staircase.

"Just this once, could you relax the rules?"

Teddy told us never to let them upstairs unless they show an I.D. "It's for your own protection," he told us. "Sure, we lose some business, but everything stays nice and quiet."

I thought about it. Cindy was asleep and wouldn't wake up until Teddy came by in an hour or so. I figured I could turn this trick in a few minutes and pocket the cash. We had some business earlier, so Teddy wouldn't be suspicious. The guy didn't look dangerous at all.

"It's a hundred without the I.D.," I said.

He made a face but he pulled out his wallet again. I put the extra twenty-five in the cash box. "Okay, hon, right this way."

* * *

Everything worked fine, and the next day I put my first hundred in the bank. Before going to work, I drove down to Import Classics. I parked on the street, right in front of my little red sweetheart. For half an hour, I sat there looking at it. I thought about breezing up to Lake Wyandotte with the pedal on the floor, passing all the trucks and campers, going along the country roads under the tall trees and past the horse farms. No one would know it was me. All they'd see would be a faint red streak in the air.

When I quit daydreaming, I noticed a woman in a gray suit in the showroom. She was talking to that smart-ass salesman about my little sweetie. The woman looked like an executive or a lawyer. She sat in the driver's seat and checked out the dashboard while the salesman leaned over the windshield and pointed to things. Watching them talk and laugh, I knew she was going to buy the car. I hated her because I wanted that car, not one like it, and I knew she wanted it too. Finally, she got out and looked at her watch. The salesman gave her some brochures, and she left the showroom, heading toward the business district in her gray suit and high heels.

On Friday I went to the beauty school where I get my nails done. While I was waiting, I happened to look at the newspaper on the table, and who was staring back at me but the guy without the I.D. That's when I found out his name was Lane Porter. He was in an ad for a real estate company, and next to his picture, there was a little story about him. He was in the ten million dollar club, it said. He was also in the Rotary Club and the Rosemount Booster, and he had a big family. I knew it was the same guy because of his short hair and mustache.

The girl doing my nails went on about her boyfriend and his new job and his family. She wouldn't quit talking. When she asked me a question, I'd go "Huh?" because I wasn't listening. I was thinking about Lane Porter and all the money he had and the gold credit card that fell out of his wallet. As soon as the girl finished my nails, I went back to the waiting area and looked at the picture again. It was him for sure. I tore out the ad and put it in my purse.

Saturday night, when Teddy came in to pay us, I told him about Lane Porter and showed him the picture. He smirked at it.

"Told you this was a class joint," he said.

"The guy's loaded," I said. "He lives in Rosemount."

"So?"

"So we can bleed him."

Teddy chuckled. "Nah, we're not getting into that stuff. Too risky."

"All we got to do is call him up. I'll do it myself. He'll shit in his pants when he hears my voice. He's got a wife and four kids and he's in all them clubs. He'll give us anything we want."

"I said forget it and I mean forget it."

Cindy woke up and almost fell off the couch. She stumbled over to the desk. Teddy gave her two hundred and eighty dollars.

"Try to look alive," he said, "and for Christ's sake, take a bath."

"Fuck you," she said, and went out the door.

"What's the big risk?" I said.

"Listen, you made close to five hundred this week. That's not enough for you? We got a good business here and we don't go looking for trouble."

"Are you scared of this guy?"

"I'm cautious. I'm a cautious manager. And just remember, the teams that win have cautious managers."

I didn't want to hear that crap about the team, so I put the ad in my purse and left. Teddy was counting his sixty percent for the second time.

I was too hyped to sleep. Instead of going home, I took the freeway around to the east side of town and got off at the Rosemount exit. I stopped at a gas station to look up Lane Porter's address and get directions.

His house was across the street from a golf course. In the moonlight, I could see the dark outlines of the little hills and the lighter sand traps. Porter's house looked like one of the fraternity houses at the college. It was huge and made of brick with four high columns in front, and it sat way back from the road on a half-circle driveway. The whole front was lit up by floodlights. I couldn't believe that little kids grew up in a house like that.

Since nobody else was around, I drove back and forth past the house. I thought about driving up the circle, ringing the doorbell, and watching Lane Porter croak when he opened the door. Part of me wanted to do it, but another part was scared. So what I did was drive about a hundred miles an hour around the circle with my engine louder than ten Army tanks. I raced back to the freeway howling as I Imagined the Porters leaping out of bed and running to their windows.

On Sunday morning I called him up. A boy that sounded like a teenager answered and told me his father was in church. I called again at one o'clock, and Porter's wife told me he'd gone to his office. The number was in the ad.

When he finally answered, he sounded so friendly that I almost hung up. For a moment I forgot what I was going to say.

"Lane Porter?"

"Yes, speaking."

"I just wanted to congratulate you for being in the ten million dollar club."

"Thank you. Who is this, please?"

"Don't you recognize my voice?"

"No. I'm sorry." I couldn't believe how nice he sounded.

"I'm someone who knows where you were Tuesday night." There was a pause, then, "What?"

"Tuesday night. Remember? Ambrosial Ambience."

"What are you talking about?" The bottom had dropped out of his voice.

"I'm the girl you were with."

"What girl? What do you want?"

"I don't want nothing, Lane. Unless you'd like to give me some of that ten million. I wouldn't mind that."

"Ten million? I don't have ten million dollars." He was hissing into the phone. "That's a sales figure."

"I don't mean the whole thing, Lane. Ten thousand'll do just fine."

There was another pause, longer this time.

"You still there, Lane?"

"Look, Miss, I don't know who you are but you've got the wrong person. Now, really, I'm very busy…"

"Don't hang up on me or I'll have to call your wife."

"You can't blackmail me, Miss, because we've never met. You saw my picture in the paper and thought up your little scheme. You want to call my wife, go ahead and call."

He hung up. I sat on the floor, feeling hot and confused. Then I was angry at myself for blowing it. I couldn't think what to do next. Pounding on the floor, I tried to unscramble my brains and make plans. He couldn't piss on me like this. All I wanted was ten thousand bucks from a guy in the ten million dollar club and the Rotary Club and the Booster Club, a guy that lived in a mansion. I got up and paced back and forth from my living room to my bedroom. Every time I went into the bedroom I saw the Ferrari brochure that I propped against the lamp on my nightstand. I tried to come up with a plan, but I was getting tired. My head was swimming. Finally, I just flopped onto my bed. The last thing I saw before falling asleep was my little red sweetheart.

It was six in the afternoon when I woke up. For some reason Cindy popped into my mind. Remembering how bad she smelled, I took a long bath with Calgon oil and perfumed soap. I washed my hair twice, blow-dried it, and tied it in back with a white ribbon. Then I put on my pink dress with the ruffles on the neck and sleeves. In my drawer I found my ruby earrings and the cultured pearls I'd bought months ago and never wore. With everything on, I walked out to my car with my head up and took the freeway around to Rosemount.

Lane Porter was on a green tractor mowing the lawn inside the circle. He was looking off the side to make sure he missed the flower beds. On the porch a dog was laying on its belly next to a high column. I waited at the curb for a while, watching Porter and the dog and a couple of old geezers playing golf across the street. It was getting dark and colder. Suddenly two little boys ran out the door and started screaming and chasing after the tractor. Porter yelled at them, and they ran back to the porch. They tried over and over to get the dog to fetch their ball.

I looked up and down the street. Then I drove slowly up the driveway. The boys quit playing with the dog. When Porter turned the tractor, he saw me, and I could tell he recognized me right off. He stopped and sat there watching me drive around his driveway in my noisy old rustbucket. He started to call something to the boys but changed his mind and sat down again. I could feel him sweating in the cold air; he looked like he was having a heart attack. I stared right into his face, and when I got to the other end I smiled and waved to him. Then I peeled out and headed for home.

* * *

It must have been after midnight when the knocking woke me up. I'd fallen asleep in my armchair. TV movie was still on, some old war picture with bombs going off around the soldiers.

"Who is it?" I said through the door.

"Just me." It was Teddy but he sounded strange.

"What do you want?"

"Open up. I got to see you."

The minute I opened the door, he pushed his way in, slammed the door behind him, and grabbed me by the hair. He pulled my hair back, and when I screamed and tried to get free he threw me onto the floor. He straddled my stomach, holding my arms down. I thought he was going to rape me.

"What the hell're you trying to do" he shouted.

"Nothing. I was asleep."

He squeezed both my wrists in one hand and took half of a brick out of his jacket. He jammed it into my cheek.

"I told you we don't bother the customers!"

All I could do was whimper.

"When I tell you something, you do It!" He jammed the brick in harder, and I moaned. "You gonna listen to me or do I mess your face up?"

I made the noises he wanted to hear.

"You sure about that?"

Ughh!' I cried out. He took away the brick and got off me.

I was doubled up on the floor, hiding my face and crying. Teddy went into the kitchen and came back with a can of Coke.

"Don't you have any beer?" he said.

He sat in the armchair with his Coke. Between sobs I could hear the TV movie. One of the soldiers was yelling at another one, telling him he screwed up the whole operation. The other soldier was trying to talk, but the angry one was yelling that they were all going to get clobbered. Teddy sat there watching and gulping Coke until the commercial. Then he came over to me, bent down, and touched my arm.

"Come on," he said. "Up we go." I pulled away from him and he said, "Come on. I won't hurt you."

He helped me up and put his arm around me. He steered me into the bedroom and sat down on the bed with me, keeping his arm around my shoulders. The bed sank under his weight. I was afraid to look at him. I just wanted him to take his arm away. His voice was kinder now. "Listen, you got to let this guy alone. Don't call him on the phone and, for Christ's sake, stay away from his house."

"Who told you?"

"Never mind who told me! Then he softened up again know people," he said. "Lots of people know lots of people." He moved his hand over my back, and I shuddered.

Remember when they made us close the place downtown?" he said. "If you keep after this guy, they'll close us down again. Which we don't want, right?"

I shook my head.

"Right?" he said again.

"No."

"Okay." He pressed me closer to him. "So you're gonna let this guy alone, right?"

I nodded my head. "Yeah."

"Good girl." He took his arm off me and touched my cheek where the brick had been. I jerked away. "Don't worry. It's a scratch. Tomorrow you'll still be beautiful."

For a while we sat and I looked at the floor. I could feel Teddy staring at my face, like he didn't trust me.

"Hey!" he said suddenly. "I Just got an idea. I'm gonna make you captain. "Ha!" He slapped his knee.

"I'm the manager, but we need a captain too, right? Lisa wouldn't be good, and Cindy's got an attitude problem. She's not a team player like you. I might have to retire Cindy if she don't shape up. But you, man, you'd be great captain. You're my best girl. What'd you make last week --- five hundred? Hell, that's a record!"

He rocked himself onto his feet and moved around the room, slapping his hand with his flat. I Just stared at the floor. Then he squatted down and took hold of my hands.

"You know the best part about being captain? You make more money. How about that?"

When I made a little smile, he burst out laughing.

"All right! She's interested. Well, listen to this. Starting next week, you and me are on a fifty-fifty basis. How's that suit you?"

He was squatting in front of me like a giant toad, holding my hands and trying to read my face. Even though I wasn't looking, I could still see the brick bulging out his leather jacket. I prayed for him to leave because I knew I was going to cry.

"You're a real team player," he said. 'You deserve the raise. But don't go bragging about it, now. We don't want Cindy getting all pissed off."

I nodded and kept looking away.

"Good," he said. He pushed down on my knees and stood up. "Get some sleep now. You on tomorrow night---hey, I mean tonight---you on tonight?'

I barely moved my head.

"You and Lisa? Good. Maybe I'll drop by around ten. Business is slow on Mondays."

He went out to the living room, and I heard him click off the TV. He gulped the last of his Coke. "See you tonight, Captain," he called on his way out.

I lay down on my pillow, and tears flowed over the top of my nose into the pillowcase. My temples ached. On my nightstand the Ferrari brochure was still propped against the lamp. It looked like someone was sitting in the car, but it was all so blurry that I couldn't tell for sure. I squinted, trying to get the car in focus so I could see the driver. My head was killing me. A man, I thought; then I thought it might be a woman, maybe the woman in the showroom. Maybe it was Lane Porter. Then It seemed like the car was moving toward me, and I was afraid to fall asleep. I tried and tried to stay awake so the driver wouldn't speed up. I knew that if I started to dream, the one in the car would get me.

THE PASSING OF THE GLORY

When Ed Benner turned fifty, he took his wife and younger daughter to a Ponderosa Steak House to celebrate. They went on a Thursday evening, the day after his birthday, because on Wednesday Ed's church-league softball team had a game. Twelve years ago, Ed had, by himself, organized the Trinity Methodist team, and he had missed only one game in all its history. That was the evening he had to attend a rehearsal for his older daughter's wedding. He had fumed and sulked throughout the procedure and had to be told three times where to stand and what to say.

* * *

In his high-school days, Ed's coaches considered him the finest athlete they had ever seen. He played football, basketball, and baseball, and in winter he was even allowed to wrestle if there was no conflict with basketball practice. By his senior year the whole school could recite his records and statistics. A waggish yearbook editor placed the epigram Sic transit gloria mundi beside Ed's senior-class picture. Ed asked a few friends what it meant and, when none of them knew, he thought no more about it.

The summer after graduation, since college was never a serious possibility, he signed up for an open tryout with the Flyers, the town's minor-league baseball team. He and a hundred others went through hours of tests to demonstrate their fitness and basic skills. Ed was one of only six who lasted to the final out. He was not, however, one of the two who were made offers. Returning home in despair, he flung his glove so hard at a window that the glass cracked for almost two decades the glove stiffened in an old trunk; Ed finally brought it out and oiled it when his son, Pete, began playing in Little League. By this time he had turned his former humiliation into a source of pride. He grew animated and laughed easily whenever anyone recalled that he had made it to the final out with the Flyers.

Pete had little of his father's athletic ability. Small and unattractive, he developed all kinds of solitary pastimes. At age nine he invented a game in which he set up a Monopoly board, arranged the money, and then rolled the dice again and again without moving any pieces. Sometimes he sat on his bed for hours tracing the most repulsive drawings from horror comics. He would push his dresser against the door and keep himself perfectly quiet. Ed, who wanted to teach him baseball, had to yell at him from the hall.

"Come on, you been goofing off all afternoon. You need to work on your swing."

Pete would follow him outside. They would walk, without speaking, to the high-school field where Ed had once dazzled crowds and practice till dinner.

One day, Ed and Pete faced each other in the two batter's boxes.

"Swing," Ed told him.

Pete swung the bat as hard as he could.

"Again. Keep it level."

He swung again. Ed stood there thinking.

"Dad, I just can't hit fast balls, and that's all they throw."

"You can hit anything. Don't tell me you can't hit."

Ed set the bat at a lower angle and had the boy shift more weight to his right foot. Pete froze in this position while Ed stalked to the mound. Ed took a little speed off the pitch and threw straight across the plate. Pete hit the ball solidly.

"Now, why can't you do that in a game?" Ed demanded.

Just before Pete's third year in Little League, Ed talked with Reverend Snyder about forming a softball team. The pastor, who hardly knew Ed, was enthusiastic. Ed made phone calls and in a few days he had enough men for a team. He used his old connections to get Trinity into the best of the church leagues. He collected fees, bought uniforms and equipment, and became a player-manager. That summer he stopped going to Pete's games.

* * *

Twelve years later, at Ponderosa, Ed wasn't thinking about reaching fifty. He had just led Trinity to their tenth league championship. He himself had batted over 600, as he had in every previous year. Now he looked forward to Saturday morning and the playoff against their arch-rival, Northwest Baptist, from the crosstown league. If Trinity won, it would be their fifth undefeated season. Ed reminded his wife, Louise, and daughter, Karen, of these statistics. Karen, a high-school senior, was the only one of his three children still living at home. She and her mother smiled tolerantly at Ed and never changed the subject.

While he ate, Ed occasionally worked his left shoulder in a circular motion and craned his neck to the right. He did this more frequently as he drank his after-dinner coffee. All day an odd pain had been bothering him, shifting its locus from just inside his left shoulder blade to his chest, down his left arm, and into his fingers. His movements attracted stares in the closely spaced restaurant.

"Your arm hurt?" Louise asked.

"It's just a little stiff."

But the pain kept nagging at him, and Louise grew concerned. "I'll rub in some Ben-Gay when we get home."

"It's nothing."

"It's that catch you made last night," said Karen. She had come to the game, planning to watch a few dutiful innings and jog home. But Ed had asked her to score, and she had to stay. "Mom, you should have been there. He caught it over his shoulder, running full speed."

"And about killed myself when I tripped." Ed was glad that Karen remembered the game-saving catch. He waited for her to tell Louise how his teammates mobbed him and how even the opposing manager offered a word of praise.

"Reverend Snyder was there," said Karen.

Ed looked down at his plate.

"Oh, dear" said Louise. "Ed, did he say anything to you?"

"He said congratulations."

"Is that all?" Louise was annoyed. "I've told you a dozen times. We've got to start going again."

"We'll go, we'll go," Ed mumbled.

When they got home, Louise drew a hot bath for him. Then she rubbed Ben-Gay into his back while he sat on the edge of the bed.

"Does it burn too much?"

Ed ungritted his teeth. "Doesn't bother me. Feels like it's doing some good."

Louise gripped his muscular shoulders and arms and ran her fingers caressingly through the patches of black hair all over his chest and stomach. Ed, at fifty, sagged only a bit around the middle.

"How's that make you feel?" she crooned in his ear.

"Yeah, that's nice. Thanks." He stood up, went into the living room, and turned on the TV to the baseball game. Louise put on a nightgown and sat glumly in the kitchen, writing letters.

Ed kept himself very still in his recliner. After a while, he thought the pain might really have gone, but he didn't dare move. Then he heard voices on the front porch. Michael, Karen's boyfriend from the university, had come to visit. Ed imagined him sitting with one leg on the wobbly porch railing, his shaggy red head tilted back against the pillar. Somehow he had figured out how to sit safely on the railing.

Ed didn't trust Michael. According to Karen, he was a freshman in fine arts, a sculptor. Already, one of his creations had been photographed by a national arts magazine. Karen had shown the picture to Ed and Louise.

"That's really something," they had allowed.

"But what?" Ed asked Louise the next day.

"It's kinetic. It moves."

"Bullshit!" I think they're getting too chummy. You know where the high-school kids get their drugs? From the university. If I catch him with any of that stuff around here…"

"Ed! He doesn't use drugs."

Tonight the voices on the porch annoyed him more than ever. He thought about telling Michael to get off the railing and move his Japanese oar out of the driveway. But the loose railing of the old frame house was an embarrassment; Michael came from a wealthy suburb north of town. His parents had bought him the Honda as a graduation present.

Because of the TV, Ed couldn't hear what Karen and Michael were saying. He rose to turn down the volume, and suddenly the pain stabbed him so fiercely that he sank to his knees. He grabbed the arm of his recliner with his right hand. Slowly he raised himself onto the seat. His heart was pounding and his skin was wet. He inhaled deeply. With his lungs expanded, he could feel a node of pain. In his chest or back? Was it his heart? Could you suddenly have heart trouble after years of vigorous health? Maybe he pulled something when he fell in center field. He looked at the TV but couldn't figure out what the players were doing.

Eventually Michael went home, and Karen and Louise went to bed. Ed watched the game until he grew sleepy. He rose and, to his relief, the pain did not attack him. He could feel it lurking, though, near the top of his spine. Bent forward with his neck stretched to the right, he shuffled down the hall. In their dark bedroom he eased off his pants, lowered himself beside Louise, and spent several minutes rearranging his position unobtrusively. When he was comfortable, he tried to relax.

Before he fell asleep, he thought about Pete, who now lived in California with some mysterious cult. Months ago, Pete had written a letter about his lord and teacher, an old man called Bhagava. Pete had turned over everything he owned to him.

Jesus, Ed wondered, where were his brains, falling for a scam like that?

Pete hadn't called on Father's Day. He had called on Ed's birthday, when Ed was at his game. Maybe he'd forgotten the time difference. Anyway, he hadn't tried again.

* * *

Ed entered his drab, metal-partitioned office at 8:00 a.m. and sat down at a desk cluttered with shipping invoices and recipe notebooks. Two doughnuts remained in a box from yesterday. Reaching to throw them out, he felt another intense stab of pain, just like the ones that had wakened him and caused him to leave his breakfast untouched. He dropped into his wooden swivel chair and stared desperately through the open door to the work area.

Bob and Vinny came in through the loading dock. Bob wore overalls. Vinny, the youngest employee, wore a tee shirt that read "Grab a Heine" over fat buttocks. They tossed their lunch bags onto an unowned desk, sat on piles of flour sacks, and lit cigarettes. Ed glanced through the day's orders on his desk. He rolled his left shoulder in both directions. The pain reared and hid as if it were playing in tunnels.

Ed worked for a company that sold fillers for packaged meat. It was the only job he'd had since high school. For twenty years he had carried hundred-pound sacks of flours, phosphate powder, and lactose to a great mixing vat, which emptied the product into three-hundred-pound drums. He pasted on labels, rolled the drums to the loading dock, and loaded them onto trucks. Occasionally he mixed spices, a delicate small-scale operation requiring attention to recipes and an unpleasant clean-up of sticky syrups. The aromas made him light-headed. He hated the spices.

In his twentieth year with the company he had been promoted to foreman. He supervised eight men, distributing the orders, spot-checking the product, and training new employees. Often he helped with the heavy lifting because it made him feel good and he much preferred it to paperwork and hobnobbing with the garrulous salesmen in the front office.

When all eight of his men had arrived, he walked out of his office with the day's orders. He noticed Vinny's look as he massaged his shoulder, and he stopped instantly.

"Heard you're about to collect another trophy," said Bob.

"I don't know. Northwest's a powerhouse this year."

"Aa, you always whip their ass. What'll it be, the tenth year in a row you won the thing?" Bob turned to Vinny, who was new. "Ed's got trophies up the kazoo. He plays football in the fall, basketball in winter, and softball in the summer. Every team he's on wins a trophy. He's got more trophies than socks."

"Bursitis?" Vinny asked. Ed was rubbing his arm again.

"Nah, just sore." Bursitis, he thought. Maybe that was all it was.

"Is it a sharp pain or dull?" Vinny wanted to know.

"Can't tell. It moves around."

"In your chest and back?"

"Yeah."

"You better have it looked at," said Vinny. "My uncle had the same thing and it was cancer. He lasted one year."

"What're you, a doctor?" Bob interrupted.

"I just said he should have it looked at."

Ed got the men started and went back to his office. A doctor? Where did you find a doctor? He hadn't seen one since he was a kid. Louise went to a gynecologist and an eye doctor, and the insurance never paid for anything. Insurance! What if this was serious and he had to break into their savings? Ed swiveled absently in his chair. The pain was in his left forearm now, where it was less intense. His back felt better. He stood up and went over to a pile of flour sacks in the work area. With his right arm he pulled a hundred-pound sack of soy flour onto his hip. He steadied it there for a minute, while the pain stayed in his arm. Relieved, he shoved the sack into its place. Then on the way to his office, the pain leaped into his chest, and he staggered against the door.

"Hey, man, you okay?" Vinny called from across the room.

Ed inched toward his desk, rubbing his chest with both hands. Vinny followed him into the office.

"I'm telling you, man, you better have that looked at. If I was you, I'd take the afternoon off and go to your doctor."

"I don't have a doctor." Ed's voice was dry and almost inaudible. It embarrassed him to admit to twenty-year-old Vinny that he didn't have a doctor.

"Well, go up to St. Cecilia's and check into the emergency room. If you want, I'll go with you."

"Aa, get to work. It's nothing."

* * *

Ed waited until no one was near the receptionist's desk before he approached. The woman, wearing a red tie and navy blue vest, was keying something into a terminal. He looked down at her badge and tried to read her long last name. She smiled.

"Can I help you?"

"Well, I got this pain in my back. It's probably nothing. I don't want to make a big deal out of it."

"A sharp pain?"

"Not real sharp, but sometimes it kind of jabs, you know?"

"Intermittent?"

"How's that?"

"Is it steady or on-and-off?"

"On-and-off, I'd say. It's no big deal, but I figured I ought to check."

"Any shortness of breath, sweating?"

"Nah, nothing." Suddenly Ed remembered the sweating, but he didn't change his answer.

"Are you taking any medication?"

"Me? Hell, no. I never took a pill in my life."

She asked about insurance. Ed fumbled through the dividers in his wallet and produced his insurance card. The woman tapped on her keyboard.

"You can have a seat," she said.

Ed sat in a corner of the nearly empty room. The walls were lined with white plastic chairs, and there were low tables covered with magazines. On his right a young couple sat gloomily. The man had not shaved, and his denim work clothes reeked of oil. The woman seemed on the verge of disappearing: pallid complexion, prematurely gray hair, faded print dress. Either one of them could have been the patient. Further, on, a hideously fat woman smoked and gazed at each person in turn. A toddler suddenly squealed, ran away from his mother, and began playing with the cigarettes in the fat woman's ashtray. His mother, wearing a makeshift bandage around her hand, retrieved him irritably. Ed opened a Sports Illustrated. He looked at the people from under his brows.

An hour later he was led to the examining room. He sat on the edge of a gurney while a nurse drew the curtain and helped him remove his shirt and undershirt. He could not raise his left arm above his head. The nurse took his temperature and blood pressure.

"It's probably just a pull," he said.

"No you feel it in your arm?"

"Oh, now and then it runs down my arm a little."

"Mmm" said the nurse---with too much concern, Ed thought. He wanted to ask if his heart was going bad.

"Are you comfortable?" she asked.

"Yeah, I'm fine."

"Okay, Doctor will see you in just a minute." She disappeared through the curtain.

The doctor was finishing a conversation as he arrived. Ed heard him call, "Listen, if she's invited, better add another six-pack," and a woman laughed across the room. Someone ran up to the doctor, and they whispered outside the curtain. There was more laughter, and the doctor said, "Wait for me at the desk."

He came through the curtain holding Ed's card. "Mr....uh...Benner. I'm Dr. Wall." The two men shook hands. The doctor' was a pudgy, round-faced young man with bad teeth. His eyes fell lifeless as soon as he looked at Ed.

"Tell me about this pain in your back."

"It's probably nothing. I didn't even want to come." Ed described his symptoms again. Dr. Wall scraped at a stain on the floor with his shoe.

"Any pain around your jaw?"

"No."

"Nausea? Dizziness? Sweating?"

"No. Maybe a little sweat."

He listened to Ed's chest and back. He probed around with his fingers, asking if it hurt there or there.

"No, it's in my arm now."

"Okay, Mr. Benner, I'd like you to sit back and we'll get an EKG and then a chest x-ray. Someone will be in in just a moment."

"What do you think?"

"Can't say yet" Dr. Wall was half-way out the curtain. "Let's get some data."

"Someone said it might be cancer."

The doctor turned palms up. "Might be lots of things. No sense worrying yet."

He saluted goodbye and left. Minutes later, the nurse rolled in a computerized electrocardiograph on a cart. She made Ed sit back, squirted cream on his chest and arms and around his ankles, and attached suction cups across his chest and straps on his arms and legs.

"Take a deep breath," she told him with hurried cheerfulness.

The machine hummed lightly. Ed squinted at the dials and the practiced fingers of the nurse. He had a sudden vision of himself lying helpless, at the mercy of women, with tubes and wires radiating from his head and torso. When the printer chattered, he stared at the nurse in fright. She smiled mechanically and rolled away the cart. He waited. Outside the curtain a door swung open, and feminine laughter floated in.

Twenty minutes later the doctor returned and told him his EKG was normal.

"Were you in an accident recently?"

"A car accident? Not me."

"Well, let's get an x-ray and see what we can see."

The doctor wrote out some instructions. An orderly brought over a wheelchair and started to help Ed off the gurney.

"What the hell's that for?

"It's required," said Dr. Wall. "Everybody gets a free ride."

"I can walk."

"Sure. It's just procedure."

"I'm not paralyzed, for Christ's sake."

The orderly pushed him down the hall and left him in line outside Radiology. A few minutes later he saw two nurses' aides approaching him. He turned away too late. Ann Moore, wife of the Trinity first baseman, spotted him.

"Ed! What are you doing here?" Her voice caused others in line to turn.

"Aa, some twinge in my shoulder."

"Twinge? Is that all?"

Ed glared at the old man in front of him, who had half-turned in his wheelchair. "It's nothing," he muttered. "The guy wants an x-ray just to be safe, but it is nothing."

"Think you'll play tomorrow?"

"You better believe it."

Ann Moore introduced her coworker. "This is Ed Benner. He's athletic director of our church." Ann and Ed laughed. "Listen, now," she said, "can I get you anything?"

"Nah, I'm fine. Wish this line'd move." He repressed a grimace. The pain was in his back again.

Ann scrutinized his face and frowned. "Okay, if you say so. We'll see you tomorrow." She glanced at him once more over her shoulder.

After the x-ray, Ed had to wait half an hour in his wheelchair before Dr. Wall returned.

"Jesus, I thought you ran out on me."

The doctor chuckled until he realized that Ed was not kidding. "The x-ray looks fine, Mr. Benner," he said soberly. "But I think you ought to see Dr. Shenoy in the annex. He's a physical therapist, very highly regarded."

"A what? What do you think it is?"

"Well, I'm not positive, but it might be a pinched nerve. That's why I asked you about the accident. Dr. Shenoy sees these things all the time and he can tell for sure."

"Sounds pretty bad." Actually, Ed was somewhat relieved. He even felt a surge of affection for the doctor.

"Don't jump to conclusions, now. Dr. Shenoy can tell for sure."

The appointment was made for two o'clock. Ed's spirits were on the rise, and he went to the hospital cafeteria for lunch. The bland food tasted good. He guessed he could play ball with a pinched nerve; just so it wasn't anything serious. He decided to call Louise and found a telephone booth in the main lobby. When he reached for the receiver, the pain suddenly burst through his left side. He grunted aloud. He backed out of the phone booth, made his way through the crowd at the elevators, and lowered himself onto a chair. He was breathing heavily and sweating. Now he was worried about the sweating. Maybe his heart really was going bad and that goof-off doctor didn't have sense enough to see it. For two hours Ed remained in his chair, isolated, words and half thoughts bobbing like flotsam in his brain.

Then, as his appointment neared, he made a bargain. I'll call Pete, he vowed, if this Dr. Shenoy can do something. I'll call Pete, and somehow we'll get together. We'll make up for all the bad years.

Ed was elated by the idea. He felt genuinely hopeful. He stood up carefully and inched his way toward the annex. In the corridor he radiated sympathy upon an elderly woman in a wheelchair, and he declined to look at the legs of a pretty nurse.

* * *

Dr. Shenoy was Vidyadhar K. Shenoy, a five-foot-three, boyish-looking Indian. He wore round, horn-rimmed glasses and spoke in a wet, rapid, accented tenor. His words flew at Ed like strobe flashes.

"How long have you had the pain? Does it feel like a needle is jabbing you or what? Can you tell whether the pain is localized in your shoulder or does it spread out?"

He probed around Ed's back and neck with moist fingers.

"Does it increase or decrease now? And now? Okay, press against my hand...harder...now your other hand...see, your right hand is stronger than your left." Dr. Shenoy chuckled.

Ed concentrated on the doctor's hand movements. He thought he'd left his wits back in the lobby.

"I have a videotape for you to watch," said Dr. Shenoy. "It's a bit impersonal but it saves me the trouble of explaining the same thing ten times a week. Afterwards we'll discuss the matter and you can ask any questions."

He called his nurse, and she led Ed to a tiny room with some chairs and a VCR. She inserted the casette, adjusted the picture, and left. Ed was still catatonic. He hoped no one else would come through the door.

On the videotape Dr. Shenoy presented a white plastic spinal column with red axons and blue dendrites emerging through the vertebrae. He talked about calcium deposits in the apertures. Calcium deposits caused pinching of the nerves. He described the sensations. Ed watched and listened and waited for the bottom line.

Surgery was not advisable, advised the doctor. The best treatment was a form of traction. The doctor walked over to a patient, who sat in a chair wearing a specially padded headset with a chin strap. The headset was attached to a pneumatic tube.

"Now I shall turn on the machine," said Dr. Shenoy, "and you can see how the patient's head is pulled up and up. We can use forty pounds of pressure, more than sufficient for even a thirteen-pound head. It is not at all painful, but the patient can't talk because his mouth is pulled shut."

"Jesus!" Ed muttered.

"Fifteen minutes a day," said Dr. Shenoy. "Indefinitely in many cases." He returned to the demonstration table.

Along with the traction therapy, he continued, the patient must avoid "jeopardizing situations." Dr. Shenoy repeated the phrase twice before Ed figured out the words. Jeopardizing situations were certain sleeping positions and activities in which the head might be bent backward.

"Painting ceilings is definitely out," quipped the doctor. "Also sports like basketball. One basketball game can undo months of therapy. Even baseball is dangerous, when a person looks up to catch a ball or twists around with the bat."

"You fucking monkey," Ed whispered.

"Are you telling me I can't play anything?" he roared at Dr. Shenoy in his office.

"Mr. Benner, I don't like to tell people they can't do something. I can only inform you of the risks. You have to come to your own conclusions." Dr. Shenoy leaned back in his chair and touched his fingertips together. With his horn-rimmed glasses he looked like a child prodigy.

"You said softball on the tape. Jesus, how many fly balls do you get in one game?"

"I have no idea. It's for you to decide."

"I can see basketball, but softball?"

Dr. Shenoy shrugged.

"What about my job? Sometimes I have to lift heavy bags

"It needn't be a problem if you don't overexert or bend your head back."

Ed was fuming. "All right, so where do I get this traction thing?"

"We have two of them here, but I'm afraid they're in use this afternoon. The nurse at the desk can make an appointment for you for Monday. After you learn to use it, you can buy a unit for your home. The nurse can give you the names of medical supply stores."

"What do they cost? A million bucks?"

"A small unit may run eight hundred. Do you have insurance?"

Ed didn't answer. He imagined himself being pulled up by the head while Louise and Karen melted with pity.

"Can't you just give me something for the pain?"

"Certainly, but of course it's not a cure." Dr. Shenoy wrote out a prescription. "Don't take these before you drive because they'll make you drowsy."

Ed left the doctor's office. He paused at the nurse's desk, then stormed out of the waiting room. On his way to the parking lot, he passed the pharmacy and quickened his pace. Not until he started his car did he feel the pain, mounting insidiously between his back and chest.

It was four o'clock. Ed decided to go directly home to avoid the freeway traffic. He entered the ramp just ahead of a Cadillac full of teenage boys. Both cars waited to blend into the flow, and when an opening appeared the boys pulled out too fast. Ed had to swerve violently to the right and ended up on the berm.

"Bastards! Rich fucking scum!"

When he twisted around to see the traffic, the pain tore through his left side. He turned forward. With his right hand he tried to aim the door mirror. The cars whipped by him.

"Come on, come on," he growled at their reflections. Someone finally waved him in. He spurted ahead, overshooting his lane and causing a momentary panic. He steered with his right hand; his throbbing left arm hung uselessly.

A bumper sticker in front of him read: GO JESUS. HE'S NUMBER ONE. Ed remembered his bargain to call Pete. "I would have called him," he said aloud. "I would have."

Now I'll have to call Norman, he thought. Norman was the only one left from the original Trinity team. He was Ed's age. Ed figured he could trust him to manage. But before he asked him, he'd have to listen to Norman's shock and sympathy. Norman would plague him with questions and talk about his own problems and give him lots of idiotic advice. Then Louise would put him to bed like a cripple.

"Damn it! I can't miss the game." He pounded the steering wheel.

An idea struck him. He should have made the bargain with Jesus himself, the way the preachers do. Of course! What was he, a damn atheist? He prayed. "Take his pain from my body, dear Jesus. Please take this pain, and I'll call Pete. I'll call him tonight. Hell no, I'll fly to California. I'll take the money out of our account, and Louise and I will fly out there. Oh, Jesus, we'll be a family again, the way you meant it to be. I won't criticize Pete's religion, and maybe he'll change and come back to the church. The church…yes! This is your plan, Jesus. Your plan to bring Pete back to the church."

Ed hunched forward, his right hand gripping the top of the wheel, his left dangling off the seat. He stretched his neck to the right and tucked his head in at an odd angle. In this position the pain only danced and teased. He was doing seventy-five and glaring straight ahead. "Jesus, forgive me for ignoring you so long. I've been irresponsible in many ways, but in my heart I believe in you and your church." Ed hit the brake and squealed into the exit lane.

When he got home, Michael's Honda was parked in the driveway, blocking his passage. Michael and Karen were on the porch. Michael sat on the loose railing, his hands resting on Karen's hips. Karen puckered her mouth impishly at him.

For a full minute Ed watched them. Then he blew his horn furiously. Michael swung around, and his sudden movement caused the railing to collapse. He fell into a forsythia bush. Before he could recover, Ed jumped out of the car, stormed up the driveway, and grasped the front bumper of the Honda with his right hand. He strained to lift it, to hurl the little car into the street.

"Daddy! What are you doing?" Karen screamed.

Ed grunted and swore and pushed against the hood. Michael, aghast, stood on the lawn making feeble gestures. Karen raced down the stairs and tugged at Ed's shirt. "Daddy! Stop! What's the matter with you?"

Suddenly Ed bellowed in pain. He dropped to his knees, clutching his left shoulder. Karen motioned to Michael, who dived into the car, locked the door, and backed swiftly into the street". He sped away without looking back.

"Daddy, what is it?" Karen cried. "Are you crazy?"

Ed was rocking from side to side, holding his left arm and moaning at the ground. Karen pressed her fists into her cheeks.

"Oh, my God, what's wrong with your arm?"

Ed rose clumsily and staggered toward the house. His eyes, filmy and abstracted, saw nothing. "Phone call," he murmured. Got to make a phone call."

FATHER'S LAST STAND

During World War II many Army regulars and new recruits left their homes in central Appalachia and traveled to Fort Devens in my boyhood town of Ayer, Massachusetts. The migration, which often included whole families, alarmed our drab manufacturing community. It seemed that one day we were living peacefully with people we had known for years and, the next day, forces as alien as the Germans and Japanese occupied our territory. Many of them came from coal-mining regions and hardscrabble farms. They had loaded their families and belongings onto rickety open-bed trucks and set out, sullen and fearful, to establish themselves in a more abundant place.

In two or three days they arrived in Ayer. As their trucks---piled high with furniture, bedding, pets, and children---groaned and clattered up Main Street, the men and women never turned their heads. Only the children stared wearily back at the incredulous New Englanders. The more erudite onlookers, disregarding the Kentucky and West Virginia license plates, joked that Ma and Pa Joad were moving east; the hands at the sewing-machine factory muttered that "the next thing you know, they'll be sending up the niggers."

A few families settled in Devencrest, a flat, treeless square mile of one-story clapboard houses adjacent to the base. Devencrest had been hastily thrown up during the First World War for military families, but in the intervening decades they had been replaced by civilians of modest means. My own family lived here because my father worked in town as a county personnel officer. Father was probably the only man around who had been to college, but his two years at Boston University had brought him no more wealth than he could have earned on the local assembly lines.

* * *

One chilly autumn day in 1944, when I was twelve and my brother, Bobby, ten, we stumbled on a box of jelly-filled hamantaschen, forgotten for six months in a cupboard. Father had brought them at Purim from my grandmother, who lived in Boston and cooked for all the Jewish holidays. They were stale now and Mother would never have let us eat them, so I hid the box under my coat and we casually went outdoors. We raced off to an empty field, known as Fenway Park, where kids played baseball and touch football.

Two boys, one about my age and the other a year older, were already there, batting rocks into the air with sticks.

"Jason, it's the Slades," Bobby whispered.

The boys were new at school this year. The older one was in my classroom, the younger one in Bobby's. Having seen us before we had time to change direction, they approached us with dull, immobile expressions, their long black hair hanging unevenly over their ears. They wore only light, threadbare jackets although Bobby and I shivered in our winter coats.

The older boy, Will, stared at the box in my hands. When he had come within ten feet of us, he suddenly flung a rock into the air, so far that it sailed across the field over a chain-link fence into someone's yard. I knew that I could not throw a rock half that distance.

"Hi, Will." I said. "Want some cookies?"

His eyes widened. "You got cookies in that box?"

"Yeah. You can have some if you want."

Will and Roy Slade came up to us. "Give it here," Will said. I handed him the box, and he frowned at the odd triangles. Bobby looked at me in horror.

The Slades walked over to a clump of boulders and sat down. Bobby and I followed them. They ate two of the hamantaschen.

"They're stale," Bobby said. "They taste lousy."

"My dad got them," I said.

Will and Roy ate two more. Bobby looked at me again, his face demanding action. I stepped forward, but Will stood up and half-turned his back. His shoulder was level with my eyes.

"My dad brings home cookies and stuff all the time," I said. "I'm always giving them out."

"You eat too many of them, you'll rot your teeth," Bobby warned. He tried to take the box, but Roy knocked his arm aside. The Slades shielded the box with their bodies. On the verge of tears, Bobby shoved me and ran home.

When they came to the last of the hamantaschen, Roy reached for it but checked himself. Will gobbled it up and tossed the empty box onto the ground.

"You got a football?" he asked me.

"Uh-uh." My eyes were fixed on the box.

The Slades went back to hitting stones, and after a respectable interval I trudged home.

* * *

The Slade family was the subject of endless gossip, much of it in my own house. We were the only Jews in the area, and Mother constantly spied veins of intolerance behind the patronizing smiles of our neighbors. In a way the "hillbillies" were her saviours, for they allowed her to mix common broth with the Christian women. As we lived just down the street from the Slades, she was always in a position to pour the latest news into the town cauldron.

And the Slades were so obliging. In their first month on our street the sheriff responded twice to reports of domestic violence. The incidents occurred on late-summer nights after Sergeant Slade, a career soldier in the Infantry, came home drunk and the cries of his wife jolted the neighbors out of bed. The second time, Mrs. Slade remained in the house for days. When she finally emerged, those who saw her swore to Mother that she'd be scarred for life.

During his three months at Devens Sergeant Slade, according to rumor, was reprimanded more than once for brutality to recruits. In the sewing circles and at Burke's tavern he was described as a man with warrior's blood, who degenerated in peacetime and was frustrated as a mere trainer of fighting men. In the fall of 1944 the Army transferred him to Europe, on his own appeals, it was said; and through his own negligence, the story went, his wife and three sons were left without even their full dependents' allowance.

* * *

On Thanksgiving Day Bobby and I were in our front yard when Mrs. Cavanaugh, our frail, white-haired neighbor, came down the sidewalk in great agitation. She had Bullseye, her cranky old bull terrier, on a leash and she kept pleading with him and jerking him away from his favorite telephone pole and hydrant.

"Jason, Jason dear, where's your mother?"

"Cooking the turkey," I said.

"Please, dear, I have to see her."

I ran inside and got Mother and Father. Mrs. Cavanaugh grabbed Mother's arms.

"Rose, Rose, it's horrible! Call Joe Miller. Please call him!" Joe Miller was the sheriff.

"What is it, Ruth? Your heart? Come in and sit. Arnold, get some water. Bobby, watch Bullseye."

Mrs. Cavanaugh dropped onto the sofa. "Listen," she began chokily, "I was walking Bullseye over by the field---you know, Fenway Park---and we went over to that dried-up creek bed. Suddenly he started barking at something, and when I looked behind a rock, there was little what's-his-name, the little Slade boy, the toddler..."

"Jimmy," I said.

"Yes...Jimmy." She squeezed my arm. "Jimmy found a dead possum and he's up there trying to eat it!"

"Oh God!" Mother cried in disgust.

"I yelled at him to get away from it. I tried to pull him away but he started screaming at me. He was trying to cut it open with a piece of slate. Even Bullseye's barking didn't scare him. He just kept oh...oh, dear Jesus! I'm going to be sick."

"Arnold, quick, take her arm. Ruth, come into the bathroom."

They guided Mrs. Cavanaugh down the hall but half way to the bathroom she recovered. "I think it's going away," she said. "I'll concentrate on something pleasant."

"The turkey," Mother suddenly remembered. She rushed into the kitchen and opened the oven.

"It smells good" Mrs. Cavanaugh said. "Do you put sage in the dressing?"

Father called me over to the back door. "We'll take a look," he said to Mother.

We headed toward Fenway Park. "I thought she was going to throw up on the rug," I said.

"No need to worry about that. Mrs. Cavanaugh is probably healthier today than she's been in years."

We saw no one at Fenway Park but we did find the stiff opossum. There were gashes on its belly, and a piece of slate lay nearby.

On our way home we went past the Slades' house. Their white clapboard, with its grimy, peeling paint and sagging porch, was the ugliest on the street. In the narrow driveway their old truck leaned on a flat rear tire. Apparently someone else had called the sheriff, for his car was parked in front. As we passed, on the opposite side of the street, we could hear Joe Miller shouting incomprehensibly and then the shrill fury of Mrs. Slade. The sheriff emerged, flabby and fuming. He slammed the torn screen door and tramped down the walk. Without a glance at Father and me, he squeezed behind the wheel and burst down the street in a shriek of rubber.

Father and I lingered a while, and I waited for his reaction.

"This is shameful," he murmured. I thought he meant the vulgarity of Mrs. Slade.

* * *

Sheriff Miller was not the only public official to visit the Slades. When Will and Roy didn't show up at school for a week, Miss Dora Pike, Red Cross volunteer, church organist, Girl Scout leader ex officio, and truant officer, came to call with a briefcase under her arm. The boys had been seen everywhere during school hours. Pappy Donovan had chased them out of the lumber yard, and the engineer on the Boston & Maine had actually stopped his freight five miles out of town and given them a ride back.

Miss Pike spent fifteen minutes in the Slades' house. She later reported to her friends that Mrs. Slade looked terribly haggard and her house was a shambles. The youngest child threw pots and toys at his mother and at her. "Obviously," Miss Pike declared, "the woman has no control over her children. It was unconscionable of her husband to desert them, war or no war."

The local health officer arrived at the Slades' home one afternoon. He had received an anonymous complaint that their verminous dog roamed the neighborhood menacing pets and children. The man had to make a second visit, and on that occasion Mrs. Slade lost her temper and screamed at him in such foul language that he fled in confusion. The next day, we all had a show. A burly dog catcher drove up in a panel truck, chased the animal around the house, and finally cornered it against the porch. He threw a net over it and waited for it to cease struggling. Then he lifted it, whimpering in the net, and hurled it into the truck. Mrs. Slade never came out, probably because of the crowd, but the three boys stood together watching the man do his work. As he drove away, Roy Slade wiped tears from his eyes and Will flung a rock at the truck.

Later Mrs. Cavanaugh admitted to my parents that she had called the Health Department twice.

"I had to," she insisted." That dog was a sewer. He kept sneaking into my yard and stealing Bullseye's food. Bullseye tried to catch him but thank heaven for his arthritis. Why, what if held bitten Jason or Bobby?"

"You'd think they could have tied him up" Mother reassured her. "She's the one to blame."

"The boys were crying," Father said to me. "Those tough boys." He went out for a long walk by himself.

* * *

Father, in his mid-forties, was an odd mixture of style and conscience. Slightly built, always perfectly erect with wire-rimmed glasses and a thin, smartly edged mustache, he looked much more important than he was. He dressed with assiduous propriety In the inexpensive clothes he could afford. Every morning he shined his shoes, examined his shirt collar for the right amount of starch, and arranged a fresh linen handkerchief ln his lapel pocket. He parted his hair like an open book, with a white line down the middle, and he kept it in place with Kremel, and only Kremel, hair tonic. When he needed a haircut, he drove all the way to Boston to be shorn by the only barber he trusted.

Father, who worked in the field of personnel, had once written an article on the correct way to attend a job interview. In three pages of text the word "appropriate" appeared four times. Haircuts and dark ties were appropriate; touching any part of the face was not appropriate. Mother loved to tease him. "Look at your father," she would say as he left for work. "Beau Brumme" The Second." She would kiss him on the cheek, and I would imagine myself dressed in the finest blue suit and tie, receiving the cheers of my countrymen.

Yet for all his impeccable attire and decorum, his opinions deviated scandalously from those of his peers. In 1927 he had marched through Boston holding one end of a FREE SACCO AND VANZETTI banner. He liked to open the family album and show us the newspaper photograph of him and his friends, in business suits and fedoras, of course, at the head of the parade.

"We marched twenty blocks in 95 degree weather!" he told us more than once. "The struggle for justice is never easy."

Mother would laugh to herself. "Such a radical," she'd say in a low voice.

In the Thirties, Father had joined the Communist Party because he believed that American capitalism was incompatible with social justice. He quickly dropped out because of the "slovenliness" of the comrades.

"I could understand the unemployed workers showing up in rags," he told me, "but when a fat college professor pulls out a filthy handkerchief and picks his nose in front of a whole room, well, you know people like that are not serious about peace, bread, and land."

According to Mother, Father never once spanked Bobby or me. He never had to. Even today we remember his stony look of disapproval. The power of that look was all he needed to squelch our childish misbehavior.

My parents had been raised in orthodox Jewish households, but as adults they had given up their religion. The Third Reich had made them acutely, if quietly, aware of their heritage, and Father longed to perform some uncomfortable act of solidarity with Jews other than mumbling Hebrew in a synagogue. I was sure that, had he been younger, he would have signed up to fight. And he would have been made a general, I believed, for he knew so much about fascism and communism and the history of Europe and the Far East. He knew the names of all the world leaders. He could find any place from El Alamein to the Coral Sea on ourglobe, and every day he informed us about the progress of the war. He knew all about economics and the New Deal too. There was nothing, in fact, that Father did not know, and I repeated his words wherever I went.

In the afternoons, just before dinner, he liked to take a stroll around Devencrest. ("Fresh air and exercise clear the mind," he advised us.) Sometimes he lingered at the end of our street opposite the Slades' house. I found him there once, chatting in the early darkness of December with Mr. Salvucci, who worked at the sewing-machine factory.

"It's a damn disgrace," Mr. Salvucci was saying. "This used to be a decent neighborhood. Now, with this bunch and those Coyles on Shandon Road with their---what is it?---seven kids in a four-room house and all of them running around without shoes and stealing from the stores...Hell, I can't even let my daughter out of the yard."

"You're positive you saw soldiers going in there?" Father said.

"Well, now I didn't say I saw them. My wife did. She said four of them---young kids---pulled up in a Jeep, parked right there in plain sight, and went in, uniforms and all. An hour later they came out whooping like banshees and drove away. Now you tell me what's going on in that house."

At this point Father deemed it wiser that I hear no more. He bid Mr. Salvucci good evening and we returned home. At dinner he picked at his food, and when Mother inquired he muttered something a queasy stomach. But when I flicked a spoonful of mashed potatoes at Bobby, Father gave me one of his looks, brimming with outrage, and reminded me that "we never, ever waste food in this house!" He then plunged heartily into his own meal, sopping up every trace of gravy with his bread.

The next day, he made an announcement: "This year I think we should celebrate Christmas and I think we should invite Mrs. Slade and her children to Christmas dinner."

"What!" Mother cried. "Are you crazy?"

"I'm not crazy."

"You're crazy. Christmas? With those people?"

"They're bullies" Bobby added, "and they steal."

"I don't condone their stealing," Father said, "but they're also victims. Our society takes from these people and gives them nothing in return. Perhaps if we show the way, others will treat them better, and they, in turn, will become more sociable."

Bobby appealed to Mother.

"He's kidding," she said. "Since when do we celebrate Christmas?"

"I'm not kidding."

"But we're Jewish," I said.

"Precisely why we must celebrate Christmas with the Slades."

"Explain," Mother said.

He drew a breath. "It is the duty of adults to feed hungry children, and it is the duty of Jews to honor any man fighting the Nazis." In a low voice he spoke reproachfully to Mother: "Haven't we heard the stories of what's happening in Europe? God forbid, but they might be true. So this year," he went on, "let's honor Sergeant Slade by caring for his family."

For a moment Mother was speechless. Then she counterattacked with rising vehemence.

"Ach, this is sanity: It's the duty of Jews to celebrate Christmas. And why is it up to us to care for his family? He deserted them. He volunteered to go."

"All the more reason."

"Vay iss mir! Arnold, how can we do this? The whole town's ready to run them out."

"Yes, that's what you're really concerned about, isn't it? The gossip. The anti-Semitism. You're afraid to do the right thing because of Millie Joyce and Grace Ferrell and that foolish old Ruth Cavanaugh. Well, listen, I've stood up before and I'm not afraid now!"

"Patrick Henry, spare me."

"But now that Mother had had her jibes, I knew she would give in."

"Will we get presents?" I asked.

"Presents, tree, turkey, the works!" Father proclaimed.

"Yahoo!" Bobby and I jumped up and bearhugged him.

Father was truly delighted with his idea. He knew, without Mother's reminder, that his invitation to the Slades would also be an invitation to the local scandalmongers. He may have seen that as his long desired tribulation, although he undertook the preparations with more energy and optimism than ae normally associated with sacriflce.

He borrowed a hatchet and drove Bobby and me out of town to a pinewood. When we found a tree that looked manageable, Father felt his way through the low branches and chopped furiously, wo king himself into a sweat, until the tree mercifully toppled over. We hauled it to the car, stumbling and laughing. I imagined the look on Mother's face when she saw us.

But Mother was waiting at the door with two boards and some nails. "What's that for?" Father asked.

"To support the tree. Were you planning to stand it in a corner?"

Following her instructions, he sawed off the mutilated bottom of the trunk and nailed it into the crossed boards. They were too shot and the trunk too bent. No matter how he shifted it, the tree would not stand. Finally he buttressed it with a chair and covered the chair with a blanket.

"We don't have any ornaments," I pointed out.

Mother had planned for that too. Out of nowhere she produced all sorts of construction material---paper, cardboard, fabric, wood---and the four of us spent hours cutting, folding, painting, glueing, and hanging our creations.

"Let's do this every year," Bobby proposed. "Let's convert!"

Mother and Father smiled at his big word. "Now let's not forget why we're doing this," Father said.

"Yeah," Bobby grumbled, "the Slades."

"Do we have to invite them?" I asked.

"Yes," Father answered firmly.

"But they'll spoil everything."

"They'll steal all our stuff," Bobby said.

"Maybe if we make friends with them they won't steal anything," Father said. He looked hopefully at Mother, but Mother replied, "Don't look at me. I'm going along but I think it's crazy." She got up and went into the kitchen. (By some unspoken agreement in the kitchen, under certain circumstances, was Mother's sanctuary. Her withdrawal there meant that she desired no further discussion of the matter.)

"Listen, boys," Father said, "I've been thinking about your presents. How do Schwinn bikes sound?"

"Wow! Really'?" Bobby shouted.

Mother reappeared in the doorway. "Arnold, where are you going to find bikes that we can afford?"

"Well, they'd have to be second-hand. There's a store in Boston that fixes up used bikes, and their prices aren't so high. I figured the boys could use new bikes."

"Schwinns! Yahoo!" Bobby cried. He romped through the house, turning imaginary handle bars.

My own reaction was more complex. Although I wanted a Schwinn as much as Bobby, I realized that we were being bribed. Father's ploy surprised me. Before this he had always worked his will merely by enunciating it in all of its clear-headed rectitude. Why now should he resort to tricks? He wasn't looking directly at any of us, and there was a certain irresolute mildness in his voice. I suspected he might be having second thoughts about the Slades.

"Just one thing," he said. "We'll get the bikes after Christmas. It wouldn't be fair to the Slade boys to see them standing here."

"That's okay," I said. "We can wait."

"Yeah, we can wait," Bobby agreed. "And we'll keep it a secret so we won't hurt their feelings."

Our enthusiasm brought a satisfied smile to Father's lips.

* * *

The week before Christmas vacation, we received a box of Chanukah cookies from my grandmother. Mother set out a plate of them after school, and then she put the rest in the same cupboard where we had found the hamantaschen. The memory of the humiliating incident at Fenway Park suddenly loomed in my head. Bobby had never brought it up again and had only referred to "stealing" by the Slades. Glancing at him, I was relieved that he seemed to be thinking of other things.

When Father came home, he said we ought to walk over as a family and invite the Slades.

"Will had to go to the office today," I said. "He was fighting with Johnny Ferrell and he knocked Johnny's tooth out."

"Why don't we ask them tomorrow," Mother said. "It's too dark now."

Father agreed to postpone the invitation until the weekend. On Saturday nobody mentioned the Slades, and we all avoided the subjects of Christmas, bicycles, and anything that might lead back to our original plan. Father was particularly irritable and hardly associated with the rest of us. I hoped he would find a face-saving excuse to call off the plan, for then he surely would not deny us the bikes.

But in the afternoon he strode into the room with fresh resolve. He had on his best suit and tie.

"Shall we go?" he said.

Bobby and I were playing chess on the rug. Mother was reading a magazine. "Where?" she asked without looking up.

"To the Slades", of course. We really ought to go today so it won't be a last-minute thing."

"Arnold, why make a federal case out of it? Just call her up."

"I thought they didn't have a phone."

Mother's lips tightened. "Well, take the boys with you. Tell her I'm shopping. If she wants to come, I'll speak to her tomorrow." Mother closed her magazine and stalked into the kitchen.

"Jason? Bobby?" he asked.

"We're in the middle of a game," I said.

"Now look, everybody," he demanded loud enough for Mother to hear in the kitchen, "We all agreed to perform this one little act of kindness. If you're too shy to come with me, that's all right, but if anyone is thinking we shouldn't do this, speak up now."

Bobby and I stared at the chessboard. Not a sound came from the kitchen. "Just give me one good reason," Father went on. "No? All right, I'm going." He pulled on his overcoat and gloves, adjusted his hat in the mirror, and went out the door in a flourish.

As soon as he left, Bobby and I scrambled to our feet. We watched him out the window as he marched down the walk and turned gravely in the direction of the Slades.

"Come on," I said. We grabbed our coats and went quietly out the back door. Mother was too upset to care.

We followed a little behind Father, keeping him in view from the back yards. Father's own eyes were fastened on the Slades' house, and his pace became slower as he approached it. When he reached Mr. Salvucci's house, he paused, looked right and left several times, and studied some of the other houses as if he expected that people were watching him. Finally, drawing a breath, he walked stiffly across the street, up the Slades' walk and onto their porch. Bobby and I tiptoed to the front of Mr. Salvucci's house and crouched behind the car in his driveway.

Father rang the doorbell but no one answered. He rang again with his ear cocked, then inserted his hand through a tear in the screen and knocked. He waited, at attention, with clouds of breath swirling around his head.

The door opened and I saw someone indistinctly behind the screen. It occurred to me then that I had never actually seen Mrs. Slade. I had formed a picture of a sullen, disheveled woman who looked like the European refugees in newspaper photographs. She did not come onto the porch. I strained to see around Father, but there was only the dark screen.

Suddenly another figure caught my eye. Will Slade, in only a shirt and overalls, was edging along the side of the house toward the front. In one hand, nearly out of my view, he held a shotgun. He was struggling to keep the weapon concealed behind his leg, and his movements resembled those of a wounded soldier.

Bobby grabbed my arm but we were both too scared to think. In any case we had no time, for Will turned the corner and raised the shotgun at Father. Neither of them spoke. Father, who had probably done no more than introduce himself to Mrs. Slade, backed slowly off the porch. At the same time Will climbed onto the end of the porch and advanced sideways toward the door, never faltering, never dropping the twin barrels as he stepped flawlessly over the loose boards. He stopped in front of his mother, who remained only partly visible. With his left elbow jammed against his hip, he propped up the gun barrel so that it pointed right at Father's abdomen. Will's face hardened in a cast of simple-minded, bloodless determination. No one could have doubted the consequence of a rash act by Father.

Not that Father could have acted at all. He stood there motionless; even the clouds of breath seemed to have died out. For the first time, he looked small and a little silly in his long overcoat and symmetrically positioned fedora, like the Fuller Brush man calling in a shantytown. It was probably fortunate that I could not see his face and compare it to Will's.

The confrontation ended when Mrs. Slade said something through the screen. Will didn't move, but Father showed them his palms and backed down the walk. At the end of their yard he turned and walked rigidly away. Will continued to aim the shotgun at him until he had crossed to our side of the street. After Will went inside, Bobby and I raced home through the back yards.

In the living room Mother was reading and ignoring Father, who stood in the doorway, still in shock, with his coat and hat on. When Bobby and I bounded in through the kitchen and halted in front of him, he entered the room, grim-faced, immediately aware that we knew everything, and sank into his favorite armchair. Unable to predict his reaction, I hesitated to speak, but when Bobby started blurting out the story I could no longer hold myself in. We clamored at each other to give Mother the details, and I shoved him aside to demonstrate how Will Slade had moved along the house with the shotgun. She glared, open-mouthed, from us to Father. All the while Father sat like an iceberg, looking at no one.

I expected Mother to respond with one of her funny-sounding Yiddish expressions, but she only caught Bobby and me by the arms and scrutinized our faces as if to make absolutely sure we were not harmed. She looked severely at Father. Then she went to the telephone.

"I'm calling Joe Miller."

"No!" Father suddenly exploded. "Put it down!"

Mother pressed the receiver button before the operator answered. "What! she cried. "These people are crazy. You're lucky they didn't kill you. Can we let a kid like that run around with a gun?"

"The last thing they need is Joe Miller again. Besides, he's almost sixty and he hasn't used a gun in years. Somebody might get hurt." Father gazed blankly for a moment, and I knew he was seeing the hard face of Will Slade. "I'll talk to Joe on Monday."

Mother shook a finger at Bobby and me. "You don't go anywhere near those kids, understand? Not here, not at school, nowhere. Regardless of what your father thinks, they're a bunch of maniacs."

Father continued to brood in his chair. When I fetched the broom and started to repeat my imitation of Will Slade, Mother said, "Enough, already. I don't want to hear any more." She headed for the kitchen. Bobby and I went to our bedroom, where we reenacted the incident many times and discoursed on the Slades and the war in general.

* * *

During Christmas vacation Mother spent hours on the phone deploring the barbarians in our midst. Bobby and I, riding our new bikes around Devencrest, joyously regaled our own friends. We polished the details of the story and adorned it with speculation and the observations of successive listeners ("Sure the gun was loaded; they don't have the brains to bluff like that." "They all carry guns where they come from.") We waited for Sheriff Miller to come with a posse and disarm the Slades, but he never showed up. He told Father that they had broken no law and he wasn't planning to tangle with that she-devil until they did.

Father never again mentioned the Slades. In the spring, when the ice melted and he resumed his daily walks, he kept a respectful distance from their house. More and more he craved solitude, submerging himself in thoughts he wouldn't reveal. At any moment he might slide away from us into his own world and become utterly inept at household tasks. He seemed wracked by some relentless confusion.

One day he called in sick to work, although he showed no signs of illness. When Bobby and I left for school, he was slouched in his armchair, wearing pajamas and slippers and gazing blankly out the window. When we came home, he was still undressed in the same position, and Mother was completely exasperated.

"Do you want to lose your Job?" she scolded.

"I ought to be in Europe," he replied vaguely.

Usually he performed his dress and grooming rituals as before, but without the same conviction and sometimes with an adolescent testiness. I often hesitated to approach him; or, seeing him in a relaxed mood, I would say ridiculous things about his favorite political leaders just to make him angry. But he never took the bait: he only became morose. I felt guilty and betrayed. An invisible wall had descended between us.

The community lived with the Slades, Coyles, Cragos, and others, whose names we never learned, until the men returned from the war. Then, one by one, these families vanished overnight. Even their next-door neighbors had no inkling of their departure until they began hauling their belongings out to their trucks. I remember Mrs. Cavanaugh, with Bullseye irrascibly in tow, scurrying down the street and flinging her arms around Mother:

"Rose, they're going! Praise God! They're going!"

No one knew for sure where the families went. The only thing I ever heard was that all of them moved to Fall River to work in the textile mills.

Two decades later, Father had passed away, Bobby and I were living in suburbs of Boston, and Mother had taken an apartment near me. One day, when I was visiting her, we opened our old photo albums. In the Ayer section there were some pictures of the Armistice Day parade of 1945, and in one of them a thin, plain woman stood in a crowd with three boys, two by her side and a little one supported on her hip. With her free hand she was pointing to someone in the parade. Bobby or I must have been turned loose with a camera, for only a child would have wasted film on random pictures of a crowd.

"Aren't those the Slades?" I asked.

Mother had to look closely at the small figures. "Those are the boys. Sure, that must be her, too. I never met her, you know."

It was 1965. Malcolm X, always properly groomed and attired, had just been slain in New York and ragged, long-haired protestors were burning draft cards. I wished that Father could have lived through it all.

THE POET AND HIS STATEMENT

Although I had seen him before, I didn't recognize Sam Berenberg when he spoke to me in the coin-op laundromat near the University. It was a noisy, dimly lit place, acrid-smelling from soap, but many students congregated there in the evenings or on Saturday morning before the heat of the Southwest made the dampness uncomfortable. It was 1969 and I was a sophomore. On Thursdays I used to read humanities assignments in the laundromat while I waited. Occasionally some of the locals---the few who didn't have their own facilities---brought in loads of wash.

One evening the voice of Sam Berenberg rose above the din of machines. He had begun to lecture his wife on the importance of following instructions. The washers called for a single packet of soap; she insisted on adding two.

"What does it say, Ester? You can read? Please read the words on the lid," With his fat, spotted hands he made as if to convey the words to her eyes and her eyes to the words. He spoke with a New York accent, which, oddly enough, may have contributed to my failure to recognize him. He wore a rumpled gray suit, too heavy for spring in the Southwest, a wide tie skewed at the neck, and a pair of old black brogues. He and his wife were both short and rat with comically large features. They appeared to be in their fifties. A few students glanced up from their books and stared at them.

"You remember the last time, your good shirt?" his wife retorted. "It came out like it went in." She spoke in a shrill but gentle cackle, wagging her finger as if in affectionate reproach to a grandchild. Not until I grew accustomed to the pitch of her voice did I hear the similarity of their accents. Her half-gray, dark hair was tied in a bun. She bulged in all directions through a yellow summer dress and wore blue canvas shoes. "Can you read the words, Ester?"

"Of course I can read, But I know what I know."

"You don't know nothing. You put in two packs, you'll mess up the machine. You wanna mess up the machine and have to pay, go ahead." He flung up his arms and turned away.

"I'm putting it in."

"Sure, put in three, four, why don't you? Look, ask this gentleman here."

He meant me. I was sitting in a writing chair with a humanities book trying to remember where I had seen these people.

"Sir," he began, "you are obviously an intelligent fellow. Can you explain to my poor wife that the machine clearly says one pack of soap?"

"What are you doing?" cried his wife. "He's busy."

"I can see he's busy. He's probably a student. He's reading...what is that you're reading, if I may?"

"Western philosophy."

"Ah, very interesting. What period, if I may?"

"Renaissance."

"Yes, I know that period. Whom are you reading?"

"Erasmus."

"Rastus?"

"Erasmus!"

"Erasmus, yes. It's noisy in here."

I held up the paperback, and he leaned backward to see it better. He nodded gravely, appearing to be deeply impressed.

"An important thinker," he said. "Ah, but I wonder, would you be kind enough to explain to my wife... by the way, my name is Berenberg. Sam Berenberg. My wife, Ester. We're actually from New York, but she has an asthmatic condition that has become worse. She was advised to resettle here."

I introduced myself, and their faces lit up.

"Jewish, eh?" said Sam too loudly. "I had a feeling you were Jewish. You're from the East?"

"From Phoenix. When I was a boy we lived in Chicago."

"Chicago's not so bad."

We had acquired an audience. The audacity of the guy amused me, although I preferred not to have my religious background proclaimed to a room full of Gentiles.

"So you're a student here," he went on. "Very nice. I attended the Vietnam teach-in last month. Also the debate between William Buckley and Sidney Lens. You know, the labor man in the peace movement. Did you see it?"

Now I recalled where I had seen him: the Sunday Evening Series. The SES was a weekly program of cultural and political events sponsored by a local citizens' group. They held them in the University's main auditorium because of the seating capacity, but usually only townspeople showed up. Several months ago Sam Berenberg had taken on none other than Governor George Wallace, a rash act that he probably wished to forget. But before I could dwell on that incident he had already launched into an analysis of the Buckley-Lens debate, another SES event. As we chatted, Ester Berenberg quietly slipped two packets of soap into the washer and started it.

"I agree with you completely," Sam declared expansively, as if I had asked him to broadcast my opinions to the whole room. "Buckley is witty and very clever but without heart. You know what I'm saying? He lacks heart." Sam's loud voice and boisterous gestures had by now made him the center of frowning attention.

"Sam read his book," Ester put in.

He addressed her irritably: "What! I read six pages. That's all I needed."

"Where do you live in town?" she asked.

I told her about the rooming house a block away.

"Ah, convenient for school. And you go home for the summer?"

"Ester," Sam broke in, "what are you prying? We're discussing political matters."

I noticed a grimace and a head shaking among the students. Just then, a bit of froth emerged from the top of Ester's washing machine.

"My God!" cried Sam. "What did you do?"

"It's nothing. Nothing's wrong."

"What are you talking? It's overflowing!"

"Sam, it's one bubble. Don't get so excited."

"One bubble she says." He appealed to me and to the other students, who dropped their heads. He whirled around and clutched his thin, gray hair. "You know what those things cost? How do you turn it off? We gotta turn it off before it overflows!"

I went over and lifted the lid. The machine stopped.

"Oi! Look at that!" cried Sam at the billowing, popping mass of suds.

"They'll clear out in the rinse cycle," I said.

"You see," said Ester triumphantly.

"Ach!" Sam wailed. "A simple washing machine she can't use."

* * *

We left the laundromat together with our baskets. The Berenbergs went to their car, a rusted ten-year-old heap from the ostentatious fin era. It still bore New York plates. They drove off along the wide street lined with old, well kept stucco houses and orange trees.

Like many students from out of town I thought of the city in terms of the campus area and everything else. The first contained all I needed--- stores, restaurants, places of entertainment. The second had a downtown business district, a poor Chicano section, scattered working-class and middle-class areas, and pockets of wealthy ranch homes on the outskirts behind forests of saguaro and desert scrub. The Berenbergs had driven out of sight into the flat distance. I wondered why they would bring their laundry all the way to the campus area.

Also, I recalled Sam's confrontation of George Wallace. The governor had come to deliver his states' rights message, and the house was packed. There were placards, arguments, and one fist fight outside the auditorium. In the middle of Wallace's speech two students in the balcony unfurled a long banner that read: "Liberty and justice for all. Segregation is un-American." Afterwards, during the question-and-answer period, Sam marched to the microphone at the front of the aisle.

"You call it states' rights," he bellowed, shaking his finger at Wallace on the stage. "It's racism! You're not fooling anyone. So you hate liberals? Let me tell you something about liberals."

He barked out a long, incoherent monologue on the contributions of Franklin Roosevelt, Norman Thomas, Eugene Debs, and other progressives. His passion obscured his accent. When he paused to wipe his mouth the moderator asked if he would please state his question. This brought a roar of laughter.

"Yes, I have a question," Sam shot back, and he proceeded into a diatribe against bigots and warmongers.

The laughter of the audience turned to hooting and catcalls until Sam was forced back to his seat. He thumped his heavy body down, crimson and writhing with indignation. Ester, sitting beside him, tried frantically to calm him, but he tore away from her touch. Wallace responded with a restrained quip that he probably saved for hecklers. Amid the laughter Sam jumped to his feet again, but now the moderator ignored him and took the next question. I had to laugh too, although I squirmed at the same time.

* * *

The following Thursday I happened to be in the laundromat at exactly the same hour. So were the Berenbergs. They entered as I was emptying my clothes into a washer.

"You're still reading this Rasmussen?" said Sam.

"No. Montaigne now." I showed him a paperback of Montaigne's essays.

"Montaigne...Montaigne...," Sam held the book at arm's length and scrutinized the cover. "Very nice. A French name, isn't it? From the Renaissance, of course."

"Yes. He came after Erasmus."

"Ah, I see. So what we have is a progression of thought." He moved his hand in steps to indicate a progression.

"You're doing it wrong," Ester cackled. "Didn't your mama teach you to separate darks from lights? In the wash we don't integrate." She chuckled and began dividing my clothes between two washers, although there was barely enough for one.

"Ester, for Pete's sake, what are you doing? They're his clothes."

"They'll discolor."

"Stop, will you. He'll go broke with your help."

This made her stop. "Oh, I'm sorry," she said contritely. "I forgot." She started to retrieve the clothes from one of the washers, but I assured her it was better her way and I appreciated the advice.

"Listen," said Sam, "we were wondering if you'd come over for dinner, eh? Would that be convenient? We could discuss more about the Renaissance."

"You like corned beef, New England style?" Ester added excitedly. "I bet you don't get that away from home."

The invitation caught me off guard. An evening with the Berenbergs and a boiled dinner held very little appeal.

"Well, I have an exam."

Their faces fell, but Sam quickly recovered. "Oh, we didn't mean tonight. And not Friday or Saturday. You probably got dates. What about Sunday night? We could eat and go to the SES. This week they got a travelogue on Brazil. Should be very nice."

Their eyes implored me.

"I guess Sunday will be okay. But I won't be able to make SES. I have a paper to write."

They broke into wide grins. Sam patted my arm affectionately.

"Also," he said, "I'd like to show you some of my own writings. It's not much, but you could give me your opinion as an educated person."

"He's a poet," Ester explained delightedly. "He writes lovely poems."

Sam waved his hand at her. "Lovely, she says. They're poems, that's all. I try to say what's on my mind."

"The newspaper always prints them. In New York they never printed his poems but here they love 'em."

Sam shot her a look of annoyance but she continued: "Have you seen them in the paper?"

"No, I don't read it much."

"I agree," said Sam. "The paper is trash. Militaristic, rich man's trash. I never read it either."

"But they must have a literary person on the staff," said Ester. "They always print his poems."

I wondered what I had gotten myself into.

* * *

The Berenbergs rented a small furnished adobe house in a working-class neighborhood of similar dwellings. The owner had elected desert landscaping: A few decrepit barrel cacti and prickly pear and a dead palm stood in the front yard. Sam, in the same gray suit that he wore to the laundromat, was watching for me from the living-room window as I pulled into their unpaved driveway. He called to Ester, and they came onto the stoop to greet me.

"Come in, come in," he bade me, shaking my hand and patting my shoulder. "Glad you could make it."

I handed Ester a bottle of rose.

"Ooh, for me? How fancy!"

"Let me see," said Sam. He took the bottle and examined the label like an instruction sheet. "Robert Mondavi. Napa Valley, California. Must be a fine brand. Tell me," he asked, "do you feel an important difference exists between American and European wines? I'm speaking mainly of French, you know."

"Don't ask me. I'm under age. A friend of mine bought it."

He laughed. "Very good, Here, Ester, some glasses please." He gave her the bottle and showed me an armchair in the living room.

"Shouldn't we chill it, Sam?" she asked.

The question bothered him. "Chill? Sure, chill it. You like it chilled?" he asked me.

For a moment none of us knew what to do with the wine. I suggested that she refrigerate it and serve it for dinner.

"We only have the two Shabbas glasses," she reminded him.

He waved his arms at her. "Go look in the cabinet, You'll find something."

She scurried into the kitchen. When she was gone Sam rubbed his hands and sat down in the other armchair. The upholstery on the sofa and chairs was a faded tan, threadbare and permanently stained in places. From a tack above the sofa hung a tiny pen-and-ink drawing of a full-bearded Jew in prayer. The wood floor had been recently waxed, every surface polished, and the white curtains, though yellow with age, looked freshly cleaned. A portable TV rested on a table, and an evaporative cooler---the Southwest's inexpensive alternative to air conditioning---hummed in the window.

Sam drew my attention to a folder of newspaper clippings on the coffee table. That is, he opened and closed the folder and moved it around, but he asked about my schoolwork.

"So can you give some idea of this Monsieur Montaigne? Where would you put him in the progression of western thought?"

I mentioned something about Montaigne's religious convictions and his influence on the personal essay.

"You boys want a Seven-Up?" Ester called from the kitchen.

Sam threw an impatient glance at her. Then, remembering his manners, he repeated her offer. I declined.

"Well, you seem to have learned your lessons very well," he said. "It's important to know about the great thinkers. It gives you a better understanding of life."

"Sam wanted to show his poems," Ester called.

"Ester, what are you interrupting? We're talking about Montaigne." He dropped the folder and sank back in his chair.

Acknowledging the inevitable, I inquired about his poems. He made various belittling gestures, then picked up the folder again and removed the clippings.

"They're not so much. You know, I get an idea, I jot it down. The editor---whoever he is---seems to like them. See, he puts them on the editorial page. But, you know, it is hard to tell if they're any good and I thought you could give me an unbiased opinion. As an educated person, I mean."

"I'll try but I'm no expert on poetry."

Brushing aside my shortcomings, he handed me the clippings. Each contained the letters-to-the-editor section, in the center of which, enclosed by a rectangular border, was one of his poems. In some cases an artist had supplied a little graphic, such as a suspension bridge to accompany a poem on bridges.

The poems were about twenty lines long. They all rhymed, either in couplet or quatrain, and the verses scanned meticulously. Each poem had a pleasant urban theme---summer evenings at a concert, a park on a sunny day, a stroll through city streets---but at the end something always happened to spoil the picture. Pink-faced children with shiny shoes trampled the flowers in the park. The strolling narrator came to a building which he was forbidden to enter. There were no flourishes of rhetoric or novel uses of language. Sam told me he had written them in New York, and I surmised that they appealed to a small-town editor because of their dreary comment on big-city life. But I didn't mention that.

"They're nice," I said. "I'll bet a lot of people enjoy them."

Ester scurried into the room. "You see. He doesn't listen when I tell him." Then she returned to the kitchen.

Sam shrugged, smiled, murmured, and squirmed in his chair. My words were apparently just what he wanted to hear.

"It's my way of making a statement," he said. "So you think they have merit?"

I told him yes and reminded him that the editor obviously agreed.

"It's very kind of you to say this. But let me show you one more. This one I wrote here." He gave me three sheets of white paper on which he had handwritten a longer poem. His writing was a jumble of forward and backward strokes sloping downward across the page. "Could you give me your opinion on this one? It's different."

It was indeed, at least in regard to theme. The poem contained perhaps a dozen quatrains, each of which described successive periods of warfare, especially the weapons of war. It began with clubs and spears and proceeded through swords, bows and arrows, guns, cannon, gas, and various kinds of bombs. The last stanzas mentioned fragmentation bombs and napalm and the effects of the latter on human flesh. Words like "soulless" and "profane" stood out. No one familiar with recent news stories could have mistaken the meaning of the poem. The historical part seemed incidental. The poem was Sam's statement against the war in Vietnam.

"Strong stuff," I said.

"You like it?"

"I agree with the sentiment."

"That I figured. You're a smart boy. But do you think I should send it?"

"Why not?"

He leaned close to me and spoke quietly: "You must know the general feeling here. Look at these letters."

He spread out the newspaper pages again and pointed out several letters to the editor. I'd never paid much attention to the local paper, and now the vehemence of its readers amazed me. Some of them could barely render an English sentence, but their anger toward demonstrators, draft-card burners, and muddle-headed professors sublimed from the pages.

"I've been struggling with the decision," said Sam. "You must know there's a lot of anti-Semitism out here. Not at the University, thank God, but..." He extended his arm to indicate the rest of the city.

"It's ready," called Ester. She carried some dishes from the kitchen to the dining ell.

"Just a minute!" Sam barked at her. To me he said, "Would you really advise I send it?"

"Sure." I vaguely understood what he meant by linking pro-war opinion with anti-Semitism, but his apprehension struck me as silly.

Ester came over to fetch us. "You like the war poem?" she asked.

"Yes. I think he should send it in."

"There, what did I tell you? Nothing to be so scared about. Now come eat."

We gathered in unmatched chairs around a table covered with white oilcloth. Ester had set the plate of corned beef in front of Sam. In a bowl the pungent cabbage, turnips, and potatoes steamed. There was a basket of commercial bread and the incompletely chilled rose. Sam recited the traditional Hebrew blessing, I caught him looking at me from under his brows as if to gauge my convictions.

While he cut the meat, Ester and I took helpings of bread and vegetables. She smiled approvingly at the size of my portions. Then she realized there was no way to open the wine bottle.

"We don't have a corkscrew?" Sam upbraided her.

"I didn't expect. For Manischewitz you don't need one."

She returned to the kitchen. "We got Seven-Up, prune juice, and ice water."

We all agreed on ice water.

"So do you think Nixon can end the war?" said Sam.

He talked at great length about the war. The Republicans wouldn't end it because they favored the wealthy and too many people were getting rich off the war. Chemical companies, construction companies, the arms industry. The little people were pawns for the high and mighty. He feverishly washed down his food as additional ideas occurred to him.

"We had a bumper sticker that read: 'War is good business. Invest your son.' Of course I took it off when we came out here, but I thought it was very clever. Invest your son." He laughed in a humorless way, and this caused him to choke. His face turned red until he dislodged the particle of food. Ester, who had endured his speech in silent distress, cautioned him, but he dismissed her with a wave and bit off a massive chunk of bread.

"You were bar mitzvahed?" he asked with his mouthfull.

"Yes."

"Here or in Chicago?"

"In Phoenix."

This seemed to disappoint him. "Yes, I know they have synagogues out here. One day we drove to that temple on the east side, and all we saw were Cadillacs. So I said, 'Who needs such a congregation?' and we came home. We hold our own service for Shabbas. Who needs to hear about their business and their kids in..."

College, I assumed he was going to say. But his voice trailed off and he bit into his bread again as if he suddenly remembered who I was. Or changed his mind about embarrassing me. As he rampaged through his food, a flash of intuition alerted me. Here was a bitter, troubled man. This champion of the people resented the people, resented me. Had the war affected him so deeply or was it ordinary jealousy, the result of their meager circumstances?

"Sam, cut some more meat," said Ester.

"Oh, none for me, thanks," I said. "It was delicious."

"I got a chocolate cake for dessert."

Sam rushed through the last of his plate as she began clearing the table. When she brought in the cake, I expressed my admiration and she replied, "From scratch I made it, nothing too good for our fine guest." And the subject of conversation was changed.

"Tell us about your family," she said.

I told them about our home in Phoenix, where my father worked for an electronics firm and my mother taught school. My brother would be going to college next year, and my two sisters were in junior high.

"Four children! What a big family. And you didn't miss Chicago?"

"Not for long. We fell in love with the Southwest."

"Ach, I wish we could say the same. It's hard to make the adjustment. Anyway, it's been wonderful for my asthma."

She asked more questions about my family, and eventually I mentioned that all of us were avid equestrians and had owned horses for years. This evoked a happy memory in Ester.

"When I was a girl I used to ride. We lived upstate in New York, and my sister and I were allowed to ride a man's horses on his farm. Remember, Sam, I told you about Tempest. He was a beautiful appaloosa. You know, with the spotted behind."

"Do you still ride?" I asked absurdly.

"Oh my, no. Not with these." She patted her wide hips. "Still, it might be fun to ride out here someday."

"Why don't you come with me? I know a stable that rents horses, and the desert is very pretty in the spring." Of course they would never accept.

She laughed. "Hear that, Sam? Wouldn't that be romantic?" Despite her levity she sounded more enthusiastic than I'd expected.

Sam mumbled and grumbled as if he'd been jostled in his sleep.

"He doesn't ride," she said.

"He can learn?"

"Hear that, Sam? You wanna learn?"

He flapped his hand at her. "A regular Dale Evans. Sorry, I'm not Hoy Rogers."

"We could get out and see the desert. You wanted to write a poem about the desert."

"From a car I can see the desert."

Ester shrugged. "No adventure in him. But it was nice of you to suggest."

I was glad to have made the offer and relieved that they declined.

* * *

In the weeks ahead I noticed the Berenbergs more often in the campus area. Perhaps they had been around before but had escaped my attention. They went to SES every Sunday. Occasionally they sat in the Student Union lounge with the campus newspaper. I saw Sam alone in the coffee shop. He sat in a booth drumming his fingers and twisting around at everyone who walked in. At the bookstore he took paperbacks off the shelf, read the covers, and replaced them. He watched and listened to the students like a spy. I managed to avoid them at all times, fearing they would seize upon my Jewish background to hoist themselves into my life.

One day my landlady handed me a sealed note that Sam had left with her. Written in his hodgepodge downhill script, it read: "I'm sorry to impose upon your kind nature but my wife has been begging to ride horses. Could we arrange a time? Whatever is convenient for you will suit us."

Just what I needed. A ride on the desert with two overweight, middle-aged New Yorkers. Still, I owed them for the meal, so I called the number on the note. Ester answered in a high-spirited cackle:

"You see, I persuaded him. He thinks I'm crazy but when you mentioned riding on the desert it sounded wonderful. Like maybe just what we need."

"Are you sure Sam can manage it?"

"Oh, he'll do it. And you shouldn't worry, he's built strong. But if you have schoolwork we wouldn't impose."

"How about Sunday afternoon?"

"That's fine with us. You won't forget, now. I really think Sam will enjoy this. He needs to get accustomed to the outdoor life here,"

In the background I heard, "Enough already, enough,"

When I arrived on Sunday I found them in very different moods. Ester had dressed gaily for the occasion in a bright pink blouse and straw hat. Somehow she had packed herself into light blue cotton slacks. She was all chatter and absent-minded motion, starting toward the door, then scurrying into the bedroom for sunglasses and camera, stuffing them into her purse, then deciding to leave the purse, with its forgotten contents, at home.

Sam for once had abandoned his gray suit. He wore a white short-sleeved shirt, already stained under the arms, and an old pair of brown Bermuda shorts. He had on his brogues with dark soaks pulled half way up his albino calves. He muttered impatiently at Ester as she bustled distractedly around the house. His face had a pained look, as if he were already feeling the effects of the saddle.

At the car Ester opened the door herself, pushed the front seat forward, and climbed in back.

"You men sit up front and talk," she said, "Sam, cheer up!"

"Cheer up? Am I miserable? I'm looking forward."

We drove northeast to the edge of town. In the distance rose the majestic southern Rockies, serene and beckoning under a pure blue sky. The spring sunshine was pleasantly warm and dry. The car churned up dust as we traveled over dirt roads leading to the stables.

"What a sight!" Ester exclaimed as the desert basin came into view. "So many plants. It's silly but before we moved here I thought the desert would look like the Sahara."

"The Sahara?" Sam mumbled." How could it look like the Sahara? The Sahara's in Africa." He sat with his shoulders pressed against the seat.

"The mountains really are purple," she went on. "Just like in the song." And she began singing and humming "America The Beautiful."

The owners of the stable had gone for the day and left the place in the care of their hired man, a leathery, humorless fellow whom I'd never liked. He and a friend, dressed in cowboy hats, denim, and boots, were leaning over the corral fence, smoking and ogling two teenage girls, who were jumping their horses. The men glanced at us indifferently as we drove up. I asked the hired man if the three horses tied nearby were the ones I had reserved and he answered "Yeah" without moving his elbows from the rail.

"Ooh! Such fine ones!" Ester squealed. She boldly stroked the face and mane of a handsome roan mare.

"They're so big," said Sam. "What if a person fell from such a horse? Are you sure they're ours? Maybe there's a mistake."

"The guy says they're ours," I said.

"Wait. Better let me check."

He went over to the hired man and began asking questions in his garrulous, gesticulating manner. The man regarded him as if he were a lunatic.

"You never been on a horse? Christ! Nobody told me nothing."

"I'm sorry to make trouble for you. I know you're a busy man. But maybe a smaller one the first time."

The man tossed his cigarette away and glared at Sam as if he mistook his excessive tactfulness for sarcasm. He stomped away to the stable but suddenly turned around.

"How many o' you never rode before?"

"Just me," Sam called. I'm very sorry to put you..." But the man had already disappeared into the stable.

Minutes later he emerged with an aged swaybacked mare in tow. The horse was smaller than the others by several hands.

"Thank you," Sam told him. "It's very kind of you.

"I'm sure this one will do fine."

"Don't you lather her, y'hear?"

"No, I wouldn't."

He left to rejoin his friend. Don't lather her. I thought, imagining the dumpy Berenbergs streaking across the desert like Apache braves. Sam's lips were trembling, and he turned his face away.

"Never mind," said Ester. "It's nothing. Let's go."

I helped them into their saddles and gave Sam a short lesson on how to control his horse. He preferred to grip the reins and saddle horn with both hands. We started along the dirt trail to the desert road, myself in the lead and Sam in the rear, looking like our vassal on his emaciated little horse. It plodded ahead, following the familiar path independently of his signals.

We walked our horses abreast along the unpaved desert road. No other humans were in sight, and our horses' hooves and our voices were the only sounds abroad. On both sides the rugged, tortuous vegetation stood motionless as if awed by these strange intruders. On some of the saguaros clusters of yellow and white flowers bedecked the tips of the arms, providing tiny points of contrast with the humble greens and browns. Ester, in her pink blouse, could have been spotted from the mountain tops.

She actually looked quite dignified atop her horse. Beneath her straw hat she seemed less round-shouldered and more poised as she grasped the reins confidently in one hand while the other hung loosely at her side. She kept her knees slightly bent and her canvas shoes balanced firmly at the balls of her feet in the stirrups. She looked more relaxed in the saddle than in her own living room. After a while she wanted to know the names of the cacti. She nodded and smiled as I answered her questions, and when she was silent her bearing resembled that of a touring queen. Sam maintained his tight grip on the saddle horn and watched his horse mistrustfully. Now and then his face worked bitterly as if he were still avenging himself on the hired man.

I decided to take them to a spot I knew, and we headed for the looming ragged face of the mountains. In the foothills we guided our horses through an arroyo past great patches of stones and boulders borne by the floods of previous rainy seasons. We arrived at a little grove of paloverdes in the midst of which an ancient assembly of dust-covered sittable rooks overlooked a magnificent desert panorama. Every variety of cactus was there---prickly pear, spaghetti-like ocotillo, pincushion cholla, with saguaros towering like parents in a crowd of children. A section of the mountain jutted out in the distance, providing an awesome backdrop, shade-mottled below and dark-banded with pine forest at higher elevations. A small white razor-edged cloud hesitated to pass over the top, as if it sensed danger in the valley.

"You think there could be rattlesnakes here?" Sam wanted to know. "Or those tarantulas? I've heard they hide under rooks."

I assured him that I had never encountered any venomous wildlife.

"But still it could happen," he said.

We tied our horses to a paloverde and found places on the rocks. Ester sat down on the dusty surface without heed of her garments.

"What a lovely sight! I've never seen such a thing. Sam, sit here and look."

"I'm looking. It's very nice."

He searched through the rooks. Finding nothing alarming, he eased his heavy body onto a low flat boulder. He tried to wipe the dust off his shoes.

Ester pointed to the sky. "See that bird, Sam. What is it? An eagle, you think? Look at him glide so graceful. I bet he has a nest on the mountain."

"It could be an eagle. They got eagles here."

We sat a while in the sun. The scenery made no impression on Sam. He asked a few technical questions about the terrain and the climate, and he commented that the cacti were interesting. Ester must have sensed that her efforts to generate some enthusiasm in him had failed. She drifted into her own private thoughts. Her silence allowed Sam to return to his favorite subject:

"Did you see the poll in the newspaper last week?"

He meant the campus newspaper. They had polled the student body on the war and found about equal numbers for and against with an unbelievable twenty percent undecided. This at the end of the nineteen-sixties.

"So few against," he said. "We've been here six months and all they had was one little teach-in. The students talk like the war wasn't an issue. They talk about parties and cars. What kind of school is this?"

He was partly correct. As in most college towns the campus was indeed the oasis of enlightenment, but there was plenty of dry, complacent sand in the oasis. Still, I had the feeling of being personally accused.

"In New York it was different. I know because I lived in Manhattan all my life. For the last twenty years I worked behind the counter in a delicatessen right between Columbia and City College. The students used to come over for lunch, and I'd fix them sandwiches. They'd sit in the booths with their long hair and beads and their crazy clothes and they'd talk about everything. Lately the war but before that intellectual stuff. They'd argue about this and that for hours. When I was young it was the Depression and I had to find work.

I stared at some insects on the ground. Ester, who had apparently heard this before, sighed and gazed blankly at the mountain.

"There was a kid who came in a lot. Marty his name was. His father's an acquaintance of mine---Ester, you remember Aaron with the gassy stomach---a real parasite. All day he spends at the broker's watching the numbers. So while the father was out grubbing for bucks the son was organizing a big antiwar demonstration for Central Park. Folk singers, showbiz people, politicians, everybody. Marty was one of the leaders while his father was getting rich off his stocks in weapons companies. A smart, good looking boy like yourself. He and his friends planned the whole thing while they ate my sandwiches, and I asked myself why does God give such a son to such a miser."

"Sam, maybe he doesn't want to hear this," said Ester.

"Well, I was just saying I was surprised to read that poll. You students shouldn't be so concerned about parties."

Me? I thought. What have I done?

"Whew! It's getting hot," said Ester, rising to her feet. "Such a lovely view, though."

We remounted our horses and started down the bajada, steering circuitously through a dense growth of scrub and cacti. I rode in front, and Ester brought up the rear. Suddenly she cried out:

"Oh! I'm stuck!"

She meant stuck with needles. Her horse had stumbled as it tried to negotiate a sharp downhill turn and pressed her against a cholla. A dozen straw-colored spines had dislodged from the cactus into her thigh.

"Help! Oh, help!" Sam shouted. He slid off his horse and scrambled twenty yards back to assist her. "Gewalt! Dear God! What is?"

He ran forward to meet me. I had dismounted and climbed up the little rise. Grasping my shirt sleeve, he almost pulled me to the ground.

"Quick! Come quick! Look!"

By now Ester had realized that the spines, though frightening to behold, actually produced very little pain.

"They're poisonous?" Sam demanded. He searched her face for signs of crisis. "They're infectious?"

"Don't worry," I said. "They're not poisonous and she probably won't be infected." I plucked out the spines one at a time.

"It's all right, Sam," she told him. "It doesn't hurt so much."

He tore at his hair. "How can you be sure they're not poisonous? I think we should see a doctor. A doctor! What am I saying? Where is a doctor out here?" He swept his arm contemptuously at the desert basin.

Ester dismounted and walked around a mesquite bush, limping a little. See, Sam, I'm alright. Really, you're making such a fuss over nothing. A couple of pin pricks is all." Her shrill cackle and the merriment in her face made me think she was flattered by his sudden concern.

"Look how she limps. Do you have first aid in the car?"

He made her ride in front of him in case she might topple from the horse. As we rode out to the main road and back to the stable, she kept repeating her assurances and he kept insisting on some form of medical treatment. They continued bickering most of the way home.

* * *

Three weeks passed. During that time I saw the Berenbergs only once. I was walking by the main auditorium one Sunday night as the SES crowd was entering. A travelogue on Finland was featured, and the turnout was sparse. Sam and Ester had just climbed the steps to the little auditorium plaza. She had her arm in his, and he, in his wrinkled suit, walked erect and soberly, his white shirted paunch protruding from his unbuttoned jacket. As I approached on the sidewalk, he happened to turn, and I thought he noticed me. But he pretended to greet an elderly couple, and I quickened my pace.

By chance I saw his latest poem in the local paper. It was a short one, written in three quatrains, describing his trip to the desert. The heat and dryness, the mountains and the cacti were all there. The last three lines of the third quatrain went something like this: So splendid to behold/ A garden full of peace/ In God's all-loving fold. His New York poems, though similarly structured, had expressed his feelings in a cathartic sort of way. This one contained as much feeling as a Christmas card. It bore no statement.

Hoping to avoid the Berenbergs, I had begun doing laundry on Saturday mornings. One Saturday, as I prepared to leave, my landlady knocked.

"That man is here again, and he seems awfully upset about something,"

On the front porch I found Sam pacing back and forth, gesticulating and muttering half audibly to himself. He grabbed me by the arm.

"Come," he instructed me, his stern manner brooking no argument. "Come...come..." as he steered me down the walk to his car. He drove off toward his home. At the first intersection he barreled right through a stop sign. When I gasped he became even more flustered.

"The poem...wait...you'll see..." He passed his hand over his mouth and cleared his throat violently.

"The desert poem? Yes, I read it."

"No, no. The war poem. They printed it two days ago. You told me to send it but you were wrong. You should open your eyes and see what's going on around you,"

When we arrived I saw the reason for his agitation. Someone had spray-painted black swastikas on the front of his house, one on each side of the door. A third had been sprayed crudely on the dead palm in the front yard.

"Jesus!" I whispered.

He shoved out his hand toward the house as if to force me to accept the evidence.

"Where's Ester?"

"Inside lying down. Her asthma...when she saw."

"Who did it?"

"How do I know? They came in the night. It's their retribution against someone who speaks his mind. These superpatriots and cowboys! Come."

We hurried from the car to the house. Up close the swastikas fascinated me. They gleamed in the morning sun. Little rivulets of black paint had run down from the horizontal bars. For an instant I felt exposed, as if someone were watching us, and I looked up and down the street. Sam unlocked the door.

"Come in quick," he said.

For some reason his panicky state produced in me a determination to take a different view.

"It might have been kids," I said, "High-school kids who don't know what it means. Not Nazis."

"High-school kids? Tell me, where do high-school kids get such ideas? Not Nazis, you say. Yes Nazis. People who think like Nazis." He was hissing and jabbing his finger at my chest. "They're everywhere out here. You should have heard them cheer for Wallace."

"I was there."

"You were there? At the SES? Well, you saw what they did. They came right onto the campus and wouldn't let me speak. And you students are too busy with parties to care."

There was no chance of reasoning with him. "I'll help you clean it up," I said, and we went in to check on Ester.

She was sitting on the edge of the bed weeping mutely and struggling for breath, her head tilted in her hand. An open bottle of pills had been tipped over on the dresser. Sam sat down beside her, and she took his hand and folded it tightly in hers.

"Do you want to go to the hospital?" he asked.

She shook her head, closed her eyes, and made an effort to overcome the congestion. To me she made little helpless gestures.

"We won't stay," she whispered to Sam.

"Nonsense! Of course we'll stay. What, some highschool kids are gonna run us out?"

"Kids?" she repeated meekly. She turned her eyes, stricken and searching, up to his. Then she stroked his face and kissed his hand.

I went out to the front yard. I noticed that one swastika had been drawn clockwise and the other counter clockwise. Some Nazis. As I wondered how to remove them, a man came across the street on foot.

"What happened here?" he asked.

"We don't know. The Berenbergs found it this morning."

"Berenbergs? Never met them. They Jewish?"

He was a good-looking man, somewhat younger than Sam and neatly dressed in casual clothes. A pipe stuck out of his shirt pocket. He examined one of the swastikas with his fingers.

"That'll come off with paint remover. S'pose they're pretty shook up."

Just then I saw Sam looking out the window from behind the curtains. His wide eyes were fixed on his neighbor.

"I'm Bill Henderson," the man told me. "S'pose I shoulda got acquainted long ago. You reckon they got any paint remover?"

"I doubt it."

"I got some. They call the police? Probably won't do no good."

He crossed the street to his garage. Sam continued to watch him from the window. When he returned, Sam watched him eradicate the swastikas, leaning close to the glass to keep him in view. The one on the tree had been drawn so poorly that it could hardly be recognized. Henderson sawed it off.

"I see they're from New York," he said, indicating their license plates. "Always wanted to see New York. Not live there, of course."

He told me about his family, his job in a hardware store ("I'm the guy that answers the questions."), and his camping trips around the state. All the while Sam stared out at him.

"Best be going to work now," said Henderson. "Probably just a dumb prank but we'll keep an eye out anyway."

After he drove away Sam came warily onto the stoop. He frowned at Henderson's work. "What did he say?" he asked.

I repeated what Henderson had told me. "He's a friendly sort," I said.

"Come inside." Sam narrowed his eyes at the house across the street. "He told you about their teenage boy? Maybe that's why he doesn't want the police."

"Oh no, Sam. Henderson doesn't know who did it."

"How do you know? You said yourself high-school kids."

"He's a nice guy."

Sam wasn't listening. We went inside, and he glared out the living-room window. He spat at Henderson's house. "Kids!" he muttered. "Everything today---kids. You can keep your kids."

The ugliness of his mood startled me. He looked at me as if I had betrayed him. Then he turned abruptly and went in to Ester. I saw no hope of changing his mind. I slipped out the door and walked the long distance home.

* * *

Two weeks later, on my way to the campus, I noticed Ester folding clothes in the laundromat. I stopped to chat. She looked weary, and her face was full of lines I had not seen before. She smiled weakly at me.

"How've you been?" I asked.

"Oh, getting along."

"Where's Sam?"

"Home." She kept folding her clothes. It was just before finals, and the students in the room were buried in books. "He refuses to leave the house unguarded."

"Have you been bothered again?"

She shook her head. "He wouldn't even go with me to thank Mr. Henderson. He wanted to buy a gun, but I told him definitely no. So he sits by the window with my rolling pin."

"And you still don't know who did it?"

"No. It might have been a prank or some nut who read the poem. Who knows? Whatever it was, we can't stay here or Sam'll crack up. I think we'll go back to New York."

"What about your asthma?"

"Ach, I'll survive." She smiled affectionately at me.

Her eyes softened and she touched my cheek. "Your mama and papa are so lucky. If we could have had children, so much would be different.

It's always been the big hole in our lives." She flapped her hand at me. "Ach! Time to go."

I carried her basket to her car, and she gave me a parting hug. I held the door for her.

"That ride in the desert," she said. "I'll never forget it."

"I'll come over after finals," I said.

And she drove away.

After my last exam I went to visit them, but no one was home. I tried once again, without success, before leaving town for the summer. By the time I returned in September another family had moved into their house. A jumprope and a tricycle had been left in the driveway.

YOU'RE WEIRD, IRENE

I hate to admit it but Mom is right about Irene. The girl's mind is totally messed up. If my parents find out what she got me into today, they'll ground me for the rest of Christmas vacation.

Irene's in my eighth-grade class but we're only sometime-friends. I wish we were close friends because she's the most popular girl in school. She's even been on dates with boys, and I know she's been kissed a million times. She sort of lets you know.

This afternoon Irene calls and wants me to go downtown with her to buy Christmas presents.

She goes, "Pam, you've got to come with me. I mean, the bus is boring. And I have a surprise for you."

"What is it?"

"You'll see."

A trip downtown is no problem for Irene. She gets permission to go anywhere. Me, I never know what my parents will say. But Mom's helping at the church boutique and Dad doesn't know Irene. He's stringing Christmas lights on the roof.

I ask him if I can go and he thinks about it for a minute. Finally he goes, "Okay, I guess, but take this in case of emergency." He hands me down a ten-dollar bill and I go inside to tell Irene. When I leave the house Dad checks to see that I'm wearing my winter coat. We wave to each other and he calls out, "Be home before dark."

Irene's already at the bus stop. She looks mad about something, but she always looks that way when she's alone. As soon as she sees me, she puts on a big grin. She's wearing blue eye shadow, which I'm not allowed to wear till I'm fourteen.

I go, "What's the big surprise?"

"Wait till we get on the bus."

When the bus comes Irene leads me all the way to the back seat. The rest of the bus is empty. She goes, "Are you ready?" and I go, "Yeah, what is it?"

She opens her purse and takes out two cigarettes. I about have a hernia, I'm so scared.

"Oh, my God! Where did you get them?"

"My mom's boy friend gave them to me."

Irene puts one cigarette in my hand and the other in her mouth. She takes out some matches and tries to light one. When it crumples in half she cusses at it.

She lights the next one, touches it to her cigarette, and puffs away. Pretty soon the air is full of smoke. I hold my breath as long as I can.

Irene hands me the matches. "Try it. They taste really great."

I'm thinking about that cancer movie we saw in health class, but I don't want to sound dumb.

"Come on. Everybody's doing it."

I duck my head so the bus driver won't see me in the mirror. Irene lights a match for me.

"Inhale."

I inhale and it doesn't feel like anything. "Through your mouth, not your nose."

"Okay."

I'm not so scared the second time. I suck in a mouthful of smoke and inhale through my mouth and suddenly I'm gagging and coughing like I breathed in mashed potatoes. My eyes are watering and I'm about ready to pass out.

The bus driver stops the bus. He goes, "You all right back there?"

I panic and crush the cigarette on the floor---with my hand. God! I mean pain. But Irene doesn't care anything about the driver. She stares right back at him. She takes another puff and blows out the smoke in a long trail. The guy makes a disgusted face and keeps on driving.

Irene and I don't talk for a while. I feel like an idiot and I hope she won't tell anyone how I acted.

When she finishes her cigarette she digs in her purse again. I notice a picture of a man and a girl hugging each other. The man is lifting the girl off her feet, and she has her arms real tight around his neck. It's probably Irene a couple of years ago, before we met. She and the man both have reddish blond hair.

"Is that your dad?" I know her parents are divorced. She covers up the picture and pulls out a handful of bills. "See, ten bucks. Babysitting money."

I'm still thinking about the picture, and it takes me a minute to remember that she's lying about the money. Irene used to babysit but nobody asks her anymore because she let her boyfriends come over and got caught. I don't call her on it, though. She gets mad when you call her on things.

"What are you going to buy with it?"

"Something at The Chocolate Shoppe."

"For Joey?"

"Yeah! He'll love it."

Joey is Irene's latest boyfriend. He's a chocolate freak. At school he dumps his lunch in the trash and buys Heath Bars and King Dons. He bums the money off his friends.

"You really like Joey, don't you?"

"Oh man! He is major motion."

She winks at me in a sly way, like I'm supposed to understand something. I only wish I did.

* * *

Downtown everything is decorated with cascading lights and red and green banners and wreaths. A million people are rushing along Jefferson Street with their shopping bags. Santa Clauses and Salvation Army people are clanging bells.

At The Chocolate Shoppe we have to take a number and wait. God! You would not believe the stuff they have. There's a chocolate Rudolph that has a red gumdrop nose and stands higher than my knee. It costs $75.

There are chocolate Christmas trees and Santa Clauses and white, pink, and brown snowmen.

Irene thinks about a big chocolate camel. "Nah, that's dumb. I'll get him a variety."

When they call her number she goes along the bins of filled chocolates. Four French mints, four peanut butter cremes, four cherry-filled, and so on. She buys about two dozen. The guy puts them in a bag and we leave.

I don't have anything to buy, so we cross the street to wait for our bus. After a couple of minutes Irene starts to get bored. She goes, "Let's walk around."

I'm thinking we ought to wait but I don't want to sound babyish, and it's all so neat downtown with the color and people and bells ringing. I'm not even cold. We walk along Jefferson Street until we come to the government building. Then Irene opens the bag of chocolates.

"What the heck? He won't miss a few."

She gives me one and we sink our teeth into sweet, rich heaven. Mine is a peanut butter creme. God! Is it delicious! I could eat a whole box of them. Irene must be thinking the same thing because she gives me two more, a fudge-filled and a French mint.

We sit there on the wide steps, massively pigging out and wiping chocolate off our mouths. People look at us as they walk by. We eat one of each kind and we agree that the fudge-filled are best but the cherry-filled are sick.

"Hey, you better save some for Joey."

"True." Irene stuffs the bag into her pocket. It's only half full now.

We get up to go and suddenly a car screeches to a halt in front of us. This old woman---like she must be a hundred years old---is crossing the street toward our side. She's nowhere near a crosswalk and she doesn't even look at the car that almost hit her. I mean, I'm talking weird! She's wearing this torn-up, man's overcoat, almost down to her ankles, and tennis shoes with broken laces. Her hair is scraggly and greasy and her face is smudged. The way she's chewing her lips, I can tell she doesn't have any teeth. She's got an old cloth shopping bag that's empty and ripped under the handle.

Irene whispers to me: "Is she for real?"

The woman walks with a limp and she has to pull herself onto the sidewalk. She goes right past us like we're invisible.

We start giggling and then Irene gets this bright idea:

"Let's follow her."

"What! Are you crazy?"

"Let's see where she lives. I bet she lives downtown somewhere." Irene laughs like it's just a game but she doesn't get this excited over games.

I go, "This is weird," and then, like a dummy, I go along. It seems like nothing can happen to me if I'm with Irene. We start following the woman but we stay a short distance behind her so nobody will notice.

The woman limps at the same pace all the way through the shopping district. She doesn't stop to look at the decorations in the stores. She doesn't even stop for traffic lights. A few people look at her but she doesn't look at anybody.

I go, "Is she retarded or what?"

Irene's not paying attention to me. She's watching the woman's back like a spy.

At one intersection there's a cop directing traffic. People are crowded on the corner waiting to cross, but the woman goes right through everyone into the street. A driver blares his horn at her, and the cop yells, "Where the hell ya goin', lady?"

She keeps on walking like she never heard him. Some of the people laugh and some stand on their toes to see her. The cop shakes his head and grumbles to himself. When he lets us go Irene and I run to catch up with the woman.

We come to the edge of downtown, right before the freeway. The stores here are old and their windows are all grimy. There's a big warehouse with trucks backed up to a platform. Some workmen are standing around and one man on the platform shouts, "How ya doin', Granny?" and the others laugh. The woman just passes them by.

I grab Irene's arm. "We better go back."

"No!" She jerks away from me. "Come on. They won't do anything."

"What's got into you?"

Irene's eyes are glued to the woman. She pulls me forward, in front of the workmen, and one of them whistles at us. I don't even dare to look sideways, but Irene cusses at them under her breath. She goes, "I'm not afraid of those losers."

We catch up with the woman again. She turns down an alley, and I mean this place is unbelievable. There's trash everywhere and a stink of grease and soot. An old wreck of a car is toppled over with its hood up and its tires missing. A dog is roaming through the paper and cans and bottles.

The three of us are the only people in the alley. Irene and I follow the woman past the backs of stores: Ross Electrical Supply, Fabric City, Plastic Home Products. We step around a dead cat in the road.

The woman stops at a trash can that's overflowing onto the ground. She sets her bag down and starts to rummage in the trash can.

I go, "Barf me out!" and Irene goes, "Not so loud!"

The woman picks out empty cartons and metal junk and drops them on the ground. Then she finds a small cardboard box. She shakes it next to her ear, opens it, closes it again, and puts it in her bag. She leans way over inside the trash can, and we can hear her banging things around. She lifts up something yellow that looks like a comb and puts that in her bag, too. Then she starts over again at the next can.

I go, "What's she doing?" but Irene doesn't answer. She's watching the woman and her mouth is twitching in a way I never noticed before.

The whole alley is lined with trash cans. The woman hunts through all of them. She pulls out all kinds of things---wire, cloth, pieces of wrapping paper---and puts them in her shopping bag. Irene and I stay out of sight behind building walls and telephone poles. 'At the end of the alley the woman's bag is full, and it bumps against her leg as she limps along.

I go, "Thank God! She's heading back."

The woman circles the block and we're on Jefferson Street again. This time we don't have to pass the workmen. When we get to the shopping district I go, "That was fun, wasn't it?" and I walk toward a bus, but Irene goes, "I want to find out where she lives."

"What if she sees us and calls the cops? What if she has a gun in her bag?"

"Oh, don't be such a wimp."

Irene pulls me by the arm again. We follow the woman all the way through the shopping district. At least we're still on Jefferson Street, which is the bus route, and I'm thinking about a quick getaway if anything happens. At the end of the shopping district the woman turns the corner and crosses the street toward an abandoned two-story apartment house. I look at the place and I go. "No way!"

I mean, this building is total scum. The bricks are black. Every single window is broken; some are just plain gone. There are steps going up to a wooden porch and the porch is caved in on one side like it was rammed by a truck. Every few seconds the front door swings open and bangs shut in the wind.

Under the porch there's another flight of steps. The woman hobbles down them to the basement entrance.

Irene goes, "Do you believe that place?" and I go, "We better catch the bus here," but Irene is already crossing the street like the building was some kind of castle.

She goes, "Let's peek in the basement window."

"Then can we go?"

"Yeah, yeah. Come on."

There's an empty lot on one side of the building and a paint store on the other. A few cars are passing by and nobody scary is around. So I follow Irene across the street.

We peek in the first basement window but there's nothing to see. The ground outside is covered with glass and wood and rusty nails. The bang of the front door makes me jump.

Irene runs on to the next window and kneels down. Suddenly she waves at me to hurry. "Look! There she is."

I squat down and we watch the woman inside the room. We can see pretty well because most of the window is broken out. The woman is taking her things out of the bag and setting them on a little table under the window. This table and one chair are the only furniture in the room. In one corner there's a mattress and a messy blanket.

I go, "Is that where she lives?" and Irene goes, "She must freeze her butt off."

The woman has this philodendron in a pot. She sets it on the table and breaks off a couple of brown leaves. Then she starts fastening her little things onto the plant. She uses bits of wire to tie on colored cloth and red wrapping paper and the yellow comb. She fishes some yarn out of her bag, breaks it on the edge of the table, and hangs pieces of it on the leaves. Then she sits in the chair and gazes at the plant. Irene and I look at each other but we don't say a word.

The woman sits there a while and then we can see her face changing. It looks like she's got all the troubles in the whole world. Her face crinkles up and she starts to cry. She wipes away her tears but they keep coming down and flowing into her toothless mouth. She bites her knuckles and we can hear scraping noises in her throat.

I'm scared and I don't know what to do. I get up and head toward the street. I'm hoping Irene will follow me.

She goes, "Pam! Wait!"

She runs after me but suddenly she changes her mind. She dashes down the steps to the basement.

"Irene! Don't!"

This time I do not follow her. I run back to the basement window. Irene comes into the room where the woman is sitting and crying. She tiptoes up behind her and touches her hair. After a while the woman quiets down but I can't tell if she knows Irene is there.

Irene takes the bag of chocolates out of her coat pocket. She looks at the woman and she looks down into the bag. Then, one by one, she sets all the chocolates in a neat row under the philodendron. She wads up the bag, stuffs it in her pocket, and tiptoes out of the room. We meet again in front of the building.

I go, "What about Joey?" but she doesn't answer. We run across the street to catch the bus.

It's getting dark now. Lots of people are on the bus with brightly wrapped packages. Some little kid up front is singing "Frosty the Snowman" so loud that the whole bus can hear. People are smiling at him and his mother is trying to make him pipe down. We pass the convention center, where they have the big Christmas tree. It's loaded with a million colored ornaments and long strings of lights.

The whole trip Irene looks out the window. She clutches her purse to her stomach with both hands. I can tell she doesn't want to talk.

Just before we reach our stop, when there's nobody left on the bus, she turns to me. She says in a cold voice:

"I cried like that once."

I make a dumb little smile because I don't know what to say. Irene looks at me in a mean way, like she's jealous of me, and I'm thinking this is the end of whatever friendship we had. But when we get off the bus she suddenly goes, "Just kidding," and she laughs out loud. I am totally confused.

We head off in different directions, and she twirls and skips down the street. She keeps shouting things to me:

"Merry Christmas, Pam! Happy New Year, Pam! Happy Easter, Pam! You're a cool dude!"

I wave back but I don't say anything. I'm going: Weird, Irene, you are weird!

SIT-SPINS

It's Christmas morning and I'm thinking over the plan I thought up yesterday. I'll talk about it in a minute, after I explain about Tony, my son.

Tony's sixteen and all he does lately is sit. He sits on his bed and reads comic books---Garfield, Beetle Bailey. He sits in front of the TV and watches junk. At the hamburger place he sits by himself and eats junk.

Every day I try something else. I say, "Tony, let's throw the football." He says nah and keeps on watching the tube.

"Want to go skating?" I ask him.

He squints at the sitcoms like they're important matters and I shouldn't bother him. The laugh tracks go on and on but Tony don't laugh. He just sits.

"I can't figure it. He's a healthy kid. He don't drink or use drugs. I admit he's no Einstein but he's no dummy either. And he likes to work. In the summer he used to mow lawns and in the winter he shoveled drive ways. He had a paper route for years. Now he won't even help me around the apartment.

Last week I said to him, "Let's get a tree."

He said, "For Pete's sake, Dad, I'm watching a movie."

I said, "We always look for a tree together. Come on or the place'll close."

He said, "I'll help you decorate it."

I drove over to the lot where the Boy Scouts sell Christmas trees and I bought a nice one, tall and fat. It cost me a day's pay but, what the hell, it 1s Christmas. When I got home, Tony was in his room with the door locked.

"Let's decorate it together, like always," I said to him.

He said, "Yeah, I'll be out."

I sawed off the bottom of the trunk. I put the tree in the stand and added water. I wrapped the lights around and hung the bulbs and tinsel on. Then I stuck the angel on top. After I finished, Tony came out of his room all riled up.

"Why didn't you wait?" he said. "I was going to help."

It hurts because we used to be pals. We went fishing together, rode bikes, drove a hundred miles to see a base ball game. In the winter we went ice skating even though I'm not so good at it. Tony was real good and he loved it. He was only ten and he could do sit-spins and all kinds of jumps. He had talent. I got him some lessons and started moonlighting to pay for them. Mrs. Flynn came in to sit while I was out at night. But Tony'd get soared when I was gone. He couldn't sleep. When I came home around midnight, he'd run out of his room and hug me. Then he refused to go to his lessons, said he hated the instructor and just wanted to skate for fun. So I let him quit, which was a mistake because he hardly ever skated after that.

I sometimes think he could have been a speed skater or a figure skater like those guys in the Olympics. Probably not hookey since he's not a real tough kid.

Before this year Tony had lots of friends. When he was in middle school, he and his pals'd come over to the gas station for Cokes and they'd watch me working under the lift. Tony'd tell them, "That's the muffler" and "That's the gear box." They'd argue about whether a Porsche could beat a Ferrari. Tony knew all the numbers---r.p.m., engine displacement, acceleration. He'd give them all the dope on sports cars and then he'd look over at me and we'd wink at each other.

Now his friends drive in to use the self-service pumps. They're packed in four to a seat, sometimes with girls. When I look at them, they turn away. One time I thought they were laughing at me. Tony's never with them anymore.

Since Christmas vacation started, Tony's been home all day long. The other day I said, "why don't you call up that Mayfield kid? I saw him today at the gas station."

Tony was reading a Garfield book.

I said, "If you invite him over, we can get a pizza. Maybe the two of you can go skating at the rink."

He said, "Forget it. All Mayfield wants to do is show off his car. He's the biggest dork around."

"Dork?" I said. "What's a dork?"

He gave me a disgusted look, like I'm too dumb to know anything.

Actually I'm not so dumb. I'm a pretty decent mechanic. I started working at the gas station after I got out of the Army and I've been working there ever since. I'm the only full-time mechanic except for Carl, who owns the place. But people think if you fix cars, you're a nobody. Like Mrs. Weatherbee, the old lady that lives in one or the big houses near us. She owns a Ford that's almost an antique, and one day she brought it in steaming like a Turkish bath. It was just a blown freeze plug, but I had to pull the engine to get at it. Two bucks for the part, a hundred for labor. That's fair, I swear to God, but try telling it to that stingy old dame.

"I want to see the proprietor!" she said.

The proprietor. Like she didn't know Carl's name.

"He's on vacation," I told her.

"I'll have the Consumer Bureau investigate this. I'll write the Company."

I had to be polite.

"You're all alike," she said, and she went away in a huff.

People like that give me a pain.

A few weeks ago I came home from the grocery store and Tony was sitting in a new place---the chair by the telephone table. He was slouched down and pouting, like he used to do when he didn't get his way. I took an apple out of the grocery bag and tossed it at him easy.

"Think fast," I said. It hit him in the chest and made him jump.

"Cut it out!" he hollered. He slammed the apple on the floor.

"Hey, sorry," I said, but he stomped away to his room.

Then I saw this paper on the telephone table. It was a notice about a Christmas dance at the high school. There was a little silhouette drawing or a boy and girl dancing under mistletoe. I saw Tony's doodles on the paper, and someone's phone number was written down. I wondered if I should say anything. The apple on the floor was split open, so. I tossed it in the trash. Better leave him alone, I figured.

Laura died right after Tony was born. It was some kind of complication that shocked everybody. The doctor explained it to me, but I couldn't understand those crazy words. I cried all week, couldn't eat, sleep, nothing. If Mrs. Flynn hadn't been around, I don't know what would have happened. She lived in the apartment below us and when I brought Tony home from the hospital, she came upstairs and introduced herself. She took care of us both, then showed me how to do things myself. When Tony was growing up, she helped me a lot, watching him during the day and making his supper I had to work late. On holidays she loved to surprise us with cookies and preserves, and she always made Tony a sweater for Christmas. I tried to pay her---all she had was Social Security---but she wouldn't take a dime. She was a good woman, rest her soul.

I know what Tony wants for Christmas---a car. All the kids have cars nowadays. I told him about this fifteen year-old Plymouth we could get for four hundred. It runs okay but it needs a muffler and the water pump is cracked. The body needs work. I told him we could fix it up together, make it look great, and he'd learn a lot. He said after all the work it'd still be a fifteen-year-old car. He said the other kids have cars that are only a few years old. Some kids even have new oars.

"Where do they get the money?" I asked him.

"From their parents," he said.

"Tell you what," I said. "You make the honor roll and I'll buy you a Cadillac for Christmas."

I shouldn't have said that. It was a mean joke and it made him mad. In school Tony gets C's and D's. Once in a while, if likes a teacher, he'll pull a B. I'm always after him to study more because I want him to go to college. Maybe he won't be a doctor or a lawyer, but he could start his own business and really go places. Nowadays you have to go to college to be somebody. If I'd gone to college, I might be designing cars instead of fixing them.

* * *

Today is Christmas and I've got this plan. I'm in the living room waiting for Tony to get up.

He finally comes in around ten o'clock. He looks under the tree, where we put the two presents.

I say, "Merry Christmas, son."

He says, "Yeah, merry Christmas."

He hands me my present and starts to open his. I got him this board game called Axis and Allies. The girl in the store told me all the kids are buying it, especially the teenagers. It's supposed to help a kid learn geography.

Tony looks at it and gives me a little smile. He says, "Thanks."

My present from him is a red flannel shirt that looks nice and warm. I say, "Well, now, this is a beauty! And it's just my size."

He says, "You didn't change much from last year." Last year he gave me a shirt too.

Tony goes into the kitchen for breakfast, but I say, "Wait. Grab a couple or doughnuts and let's take a ride." I give him my car keys. "Here, you drive.

"He says, "What is this?"

"You'll see." We put on our jackets. I grab the doughnut box and we go out to the car. "Take the freeway south."

"Where are we going?"

"Someplace."

He's acting real peeved. "You gonna tell me or what?"

"Hey, loosen up," I say. "It's Christmas."

We ride along for a while without talking. We pass some girls in a VW, and Tony looks over at them. He looks at them again in the mirror.

I say, "Why don't you call up a girl over the vacation, make a date or something?"

He don't answer.

I say, "What about Cassie, that girl you used to like?"

"Are you kidding? I'd never call her."

"You used to be friends."

"I'd never call her! Never! She thinks she's too good for anyone. Just because her father's a doctor she thinks...Oh forget it."

He bites off a hunk of doughnut and quits talking.

We go another five miles on the freeway and I make him pull off. We ride along a country road for a few miles.

"Slow down here," I tell him. I'm watching for this pond I know about.

Pretty soon I see it. I tell Tony to turn onto a dirt road that circles the pond. He bumps the car over the ruts in the road.

"Hey, take it easy," I say.

We stop near the frozen pond and get out. He says, "Where are we, for Pete's sake?"

"Just a place I remember. Up the road is the biggest auto parts dump in the state. You can get any part you want there."

"So?"

"Come here. I got a surprise."

I open the trunk and hand him the box inside. It's all gift-wrapped in red and green. "Open it," I say. He opens it and takes out the figure skates I bought yesterday. His eyes get huge and he makes a low whistling sound.

"Merry Christmas again," I say. "What do you think?"

He takes off a blade guard and runs his finger over the blade and toe rake. The blades are side-honed for the best grip.

"Fantastic!" he says.

"Put 'em on. I got mine here too."

I take my old ones out of a bag and we sit down on a log to change. It's cold and quiet around us, & the sky is pale blue. There's a light sprinkle of snow on the hard ground. All around the pond are bare woods, and I can smell something faint. Or maybe I'm just not smelling anything for a change. Tony laces up slowly. He's getting the feel of his skates.

He says, "What about that sign?"

There's a sign near the pond that says NO SKATING. I throw a rook up and it thuds on the ice and slides a little. I step onto the edge and then go out farther.

"It's solid," I say. "It's been below freezing all week."

"But it's illegal."

"So we'll go to jail together."

He looks all around. There's nobody in sight.

"How do they feel?" I ask him.

"Pretty good."

"So come on."

Tony skates onto the ice. We move out toward the middle of the pond. The ice is smooth except for a few rough spots.

I'm not much of a skater. I'm about as graceful as a dog walking on his hind legs. Mainly I don't want to fall and break something. But Tony starts to warm up. In a few minutes he's got his old style back. He sails over the ice in long sweeps from one side of the pond to the other. He goes faster and faster and then he does a jump with a full turn. He comes roaring up to me and makes a racing stop that sprays ice up to my chin.

"Not bad," I say. "Can you still do a sit-spin?"

He tries it but loses his balance. He keeps trying and on the fourth or fifth try he does a real steady spin. When he comes up to me again, I clap for him. He makes a little bow and says, "Thank you, thank you." We skate together slowly with our hands in our jacket pockets. Tony stays with me as I shuffle around the pond.

"Funny place to spend Christmas," I say.

"I like it out here," he says.

A car passes along the paved road, too far away to hear. Some blackbirds fly over the pond into the woods, where we can't see them. It's cold out but the sun is warm and we're moving all the time. Tony turns on the speed again. He whips around the whole pond before I go a quarter of the distance.

"Come on, Dad, open 'er up," he says.

"Uh-uh, not me."

"Come on. You can do it."

He skates backwards in front of me. I try to go faster and for a minute I'm really making time. Then I come to a rough spot and lurch forward. I go sprawling like a runner sliding into second base. Tony comes over quick but I'm not really hurt. He helps me up. I laugh a little and brush the ice off.

"Nice move, Dad," he says.

I put my arm around him. "You know, I think I lost the edge."

We go around the pond again easy. Then Tony does a couple of jumps with half-turns, skating backwards when he lands. He skates by himself for a while. Then he pulls alongside me.

"What are we having for dinner?" he asks.

"Same as every Christmas. Ham with Mrs. Flynn's orange sauce."

"All right!" He skates out to the middle of the pond again.

"Do you remember Mrs. Flynn?" I call to him.

"Sure I remember her," he calls back. "Her kitchen was the best place in the whole world."

Tony swings his leg and goes into a sit-spin. He keeps his arms and right leg out like a Russian dancer. He goes faster and faster until he's just a blur of color. His down skate is whirring so loud, it sounds like he's drilling through the ice. Then he slows down and rises. He comes to a stop with his arms raised above his head.

I skate up to him and we slap the high fives. Suddenly we're hugging each other the way we always did, only now his chin hangs over my shoulder. He's not even embarrassed. I feel like making a speech but I can't put the words together.

"Let's get that ham started," he says, and we skate toward the car.

While we're changing into our shoes, Tony says, "Remember that old Plymouth you told me about? Is it still for sale?"

"Could be."

"How much body work does it need?"

"Mostly it needs repainting. That and a couple of dents you'd have to pound out."

Tony wipes his runners off on his jacket. He turns them so they flash in the sun. He says, "I was thinking. I still got two hundred saved from that paper route. If you can put in the rest, I'll get a restaurant job and pay you back."

"I'll call the guy tonight."

We pack up our skates and drive back over the dirt road. This time Tony practically creeps over the frozen ruts. He's got a new look in his eye. I bet he don't even know he's smiling.

THE KNOW-IT-ALL

It was nearly that time again---the New Year's Eve party. For twelve months I had dreaded the dismal event. As the old year tapered down through the days after Christmas, I became more sullen and desperate, like a man abandoned to abject ruin. I remonstrated with my wife:

"We're too old for these flings. We'll stay too late, and the food and drink will make us ill. And you know what I think of the crowd. Plainly and simply, their intellectual onanism is egregious!"

"Whatever do you mean?" she replied. "Really, you must try to be more sociable this year. And dear Charlotte will be coming."

I shuddered violently. "Let's beg off. Tell them I'm indisposed. With so many coming we won't be missed."

"We can't do that. We have obligations. Do you want to spend New Year's watching the mess in Times Square?"

"I just want to go to bed."

"We have obligations. You can wear your Christmas tie."

Of course she was right. One can't ignore one's friends. Yet what pleasure could I find in a gathering of my colleagues, fellow academics, the least redeemable bores in human society? First we'd brandish our intellects over recondite topics while eating and drinking ourselves into states of dyspepsia. After midnight we'd sprawl about the living room, flatulent and mesmerized by the glowing hearth. The talk would degenerate into tedious jokes and muddled embellishments of the banal. Better to curl up with a book and nod off in my own bed.

But I must be honest. There was a more compelling reason for my resistance: Charlotte Roon would be there. Charlotte Roon, PhD., LL.D., L.H.D., author of heralded biographies and historical treatises, student of the human personality, gourmet cook, art critic, book critic, fluent in five languages, into tennis, into fashion, into travel from the Northwest Territories to Eastern Africa. Tall, erect, beak-nosed Charlotte Roon, ceaseless bearer of enlightenment.

I remembered the party two years ago when she first joined our group. She had recently moved into the area after a chilling experience. Her husband, also a learned individual, had finally succeeded in committing suicide after two failed attempts. The reason for his persistence no one knew.

At the party the guests had been frivolously trying to outdo one another with appropriate quotations of poetry. Around eleven o'clock I jettisoned all caution, lifted my glass, and blurted;

"As Whittier put it, 'One hour to madness and joy!'"

A surprised silence. People stared oddly in my direction as I halted, my glass poised before me.

"Whitman," said Charlotte Roon.

"Pardon?"

"Whitman wrote it; Whittier could never have written it."

"Have I mentioned that I am a professor of English with a specialty in nineteenth century American literature?"

With the laughter ringing in my ears I retreated to a dark corner, where my trembling lip and gnashing stomach would not be detected. The house of our hosts was illuminated by a few candles and the glow from the fireplace. Aromas of bayberry and exotic hors d 'oeuvres mingled in the air. The company had fragmented into little groups discussing common interests. From my hidden vantage I glowered at Charlotte Roon as she sailed hither and thither, wine glass in hand, bestowing her morsels of erudition like a thin-faced rain goddess bringing relief to parched domains. "Charlotte," somebody importuned, "you must meet the Harrisons. They were in Greece last summer, too." Then another: "Charlotte, can you recommend a white wine for the Cocquilles Saint Jacques?" And: "Charlotte, in your book on states of mind didn't you confirm Jung's concept of synchronistic phenomena?"

How they loved her, these scholarly fools! How they doted on this insufferable omniscient and her endless articles and books. Observing her black silk pajama suit against the background of the fireplace, I tried to bring about a telekinesis of the flames so as to purge the room of her presence. I had planned to drop reminders of my own forthcoming book on the origins of nineteenth-century American romanticism, but the subject seemed pallid beside the brilliant cornucopia of Charlotte Roon. My two-year endeavor might have elicited a few indulgent murmurs. Or, worse, the blasted woman might have pointed out some glaring error.

A year later I blundered again. Our discussions at the party ranged from philosophy to classical music to cybernetics and finally alighted upon art. I am not entirely unfamiliar with this topic, having shown several of my watercolors at local exhibitions.

"I've always felt that pop art was directly traceable to the French Dadas," Charlotte declared.

Mistaking her comment for humor, I responded with some forgettable quip about dadas and mamas.

"I had the impression we were speaking seriously," she intoned.

A colleague took me aside and gently elaborated on the Dadaist movement of the nineteen-twenties.

"Anyone could have made such an error," he assured me.

I retired furtively to a basement TV room. There I remained until the wee hours. At midnight I gazed at the great luminous New York apple descending like a slow guillotine.

Throughout the succeeding year I dreamed of avenging myself I even composed a little ode:

> Charlotte Roon,
> O learned prune,
> With head ballooned
> You cant simoons.
> Your dirge will soon
> Proclaim my boon.

But apart from soothing my pride these musings were ineffectual. Charlotte Roon would be there again, swathed in admiration, while I sulked in some nether region of the house. Then, on the day of the party, I was struck by inspiration. A colleague in Agricultural Chemistry had given me a new phosphorus poison to solve a rodent problem in our home. It was unlikely that any analysis for the substance had been developed.

A delightful idea took possession of me. Yes, I would definitely find a way. I stopped complaining and even bought some champagne for the party.

That evening the conversation gushed and sparkled like moonlit fountains. Charlotte, as usual, was the glittering center of attention. I kept aloof, however, for my mind was riveted to a single purpose. I awaited the most advantageous moment.

After the midnight eruption the company gradually settled into weary, bloated states. Everywhere people lay belching, dozing, muttering incomprehensible things. By two o'clock only Charlotte and I could manage some coherence. As she approached me with her glass of champagne, I fingered my jacket pocket and felt the vial inside.

She sat cross-legged beside me and criticized the tartness of the liver plate. She didn't know that my wife had spent hours trying to get it right. When she reached for the last of the salmon squares, I deftly poured the powder into her glass.

She sipped her drink and turned to me. "I just finished your book on the origins of romanticism. It was marvelous! I'm reviewing it for the Times."

"You...you're...?"

"Why, that chapter on the Hindu seers... I had no idea what an influence they had. I was spellbound!"

I leaned toward her, chin upon my knuckles. Oh, dear perspicacious Charlotte!

Suddenly she started. Her eyes bulged and she caught at her throat. Rising clumsily, she staggered toward the bathroom.

My God! What had I done. I hurried after her. We stumbled over guests, who grunted irascibly in their stupor. What should I do? I clutched my head as if to wring out an answer. Then I remembered the universal antidote. Two parts charcoal from burned toast, one part tannic acid from tea, one part magnesia. Darting into the kitchen, I found some bread and dropped it into the toaster. I fumbled through the cupboards until I found the instant tea. The Phillips would be in the bathroom if they had any.

Charlotte was kneeling above the commode trying to rid herself of the noxious fluid. I sprung the medicine chest and gratefully snatched the blue bottle. In the kitchen an eon passed while the bread cooked. It popped up too light. I turned the dial to its maximum and waited again, pacing the floor, shielding my ears from the tortured moans in the bathroom. When the toast popped, I scraped the carbon into a glass, added the tea and milk of magnesia, stirred, and raced back to the bathroom. Charlotte was supine on the floor, croaking and rolling witlessly from side to side. On my knees I raised up her head.

"Dear lady, take this."

Her writhing was unmanageable, her face hideously contorted. I couldn't pour the liquid into her mouth.

"Forgive me," I wailed. "I've wronged you. I've maligned you worse than Hester Prim."

Suddenly her thrashing halted. Clutching my lapels, she slowly and arduously pulled herself up.

"P...P...P..." she sputtered.

"What is it, Charlotte? Can you drink this?"

"Pr...Pr...Pr..."

She collapsed in my arms. I felt her pulse grow weaker, and in another minute it ceased. I lowered her gently to the floor, wondering what she had wanted to tell me. Undoubtedly some further comment on my book. Prodigious effort, perhaps. Or: probing account.

LAST SLIDE, PLEASE

Thank you, thank you, ladies and gentlemen, for your enthusiastic welcome. It is always an immense pleasure to address my colleagues at the International Conference on Exceptional Biology. Indeed, we have much to discuss, and I find it abominable that I must devote so much time to my own troubles. But my last hope of justice lies in your learned hands, and I must appeal to your scientific integrity and commitment as the forces of darkness encircle my laboratory. Yes, thank you again, thank you; your applause buoys my spirits. I know I can count on you, but if there still be any doubters, let me now set the record straight. Let me review the astonishing discoveries which have sucked me into the present political maelstrom. May I have the first slide, please?

Here we see the apparatus used by my research team. Besides the common in vitro fertilization equipment you can see the highly sophisticated instruments which are needed to monitor the mutagenic agents. My people have worked tirelessly for a decade to develop our equipment and protocols. Because of their devoted efforts we are now able to maintain our embryos in precise chemical environments---an absolute necessity for practical genetic alteration.

We grow the embryos in nutrient broth in Petri dishes. Then, as they enter the fetal stage, we transfer them to loosely covered holding jars. The next five slides show a progression of fetal stages after treatment of the broth with Agent 116, which alters genes for eye development. As we advance slowly through the slides, you will notice the aberrant form of the fetal eyes---perfectly round, contracted, and lidless, much like those of a fish. We were greatly encouraged by this early success.

The next few slides illustrate results with other mutagenic agents. Here is a two month-old fetus, and the enlarged fingers and toes are obvious. And on the next one you can see the rearranged sex organs. After that, yes, here we have severe asymmetry of the facial features---we called this one "Picasso." We become deeply attached to our in-vitro progeny, and we hate to electrocute them at the end of the experiment.

Our next breakthrough was the result of an accident. The fellow using the apparatus before me failed to clean it properly, and I inadvertently added two agents at once to the Petri dish. The unexpected development of the fetus amazed us until my guilty colleague confessed and we realized what had happened. In the next slide, which was taken only a day after transfer to the holding jar, you can see the sudden acceleration of growth. The little guy is half out of the jar. I had to make a swift decision, and I chose to allow him to grow a bit longer. I transferred him to a larger container. The next slide shows his maximum length, about 60 centimeters, before he gave up the ghost. I conferred with my research team. There were arguments about how to proceed, but all of us were determined to explore this new avenue of serendipity.

But at this point our program was derailed by external events. As word of our achievements spread, an insidious opposition arose among various loud, gullible zealots in our community. Students, religious demagogues, and professional agitators allied themselves against us. There were demonstrations and attempts to enter our building. My research people were harassed as they came and went, and our management was compelled to hire a security force and install surveillance cameras. I underwent long, trying interviews and press conferences, and finally I had to order a temporary halt to our work. We were bitter and depressed. But eventually the shrill voices found other targets, and we hastened back to the lab.

We decided to test combinations of agents, varying concentrations and other parameters, and see what popped up. And here I must beg your indulgence, ladies and gentlemen, as a scientist's vanity, so long submerged in details, rises to the surface. For what popped up was the fruition of my many years of painstaking toil.

My experiments revealed that I could alter two genetic traits at once: bone size and musculature. Also, the proper ratio of agents profoundly stimulated the gene affecting growth rate. The data are incomplete but it is possible that another gene, governing disposition, also joined the game. On the next slide I've listed the agents and the probable genes affected. And on the following slide, my friends, I give you---Cyclone!

Isn't he magnificent! No one actually saw him alive; this photo was taken by a surveillance camera. We found him one morning, shriveled up on the laboratory floor, and we all guessed what had happened. Cyclone had given birth to himself, so to speak, somehow climbing out of his jar in the night. His movements caused the lights to go on and the camera to capture him.

Just look at him, will you! A giant of a man, perfectly proportioned and superhumanly powerful. As yet we have no explanation for the enlarged upper canines and the hair on his tongue. Also his obvious crouch has us baffled. But see the fire in his eyes, the flared nostrils. Can't you tell his hormones are flowing!

We were thankful that he burst forth at night and expired quickly. The next slide will show you what Cyclone accomplished in his brief hours of life, before his hyperactive gene for growth carried him over the cliff to his demise. He began by gulping whole bottles of nutrient broth to sustain himself. He used up our whole supply. Enraged over the lack of food, he threw a tantrum, and you can see the overturned incubator, the gaping hole in the wall, and the uprooted lab bench. Notice also the smashed glass and twisted equipment, the ceiling lights ripped from their moorings, the shredded books and papers. The empty cages here contained four rabbits. Cyclone devoured them all without a trace. Thank God he didn't get to our sensitive instruments. We keep them locked in a special closet.

It took us a week to restore order. We conferred again and swore an oath of secrecy, all of us dreading the consequences of loose lips. We roped off our section of the building and turned away visitors with phony excuses. Yet somehow the story leaked out. Again the furor went up, and again the angry mob besieged us. I have a slide here of one obnoxious loudmouth just after he scaled the wall around our building and was caught by guards. Look at his long, filthy hair and twisted features. You can almost smell him, can't you? He is a member of People Insisting on

Safe Science, and you can see his vulgar "PISSed off!" tee shirt. This is the quality of our opposition, ladies and gentlemen. Yes, I hear your cries of outrage and I share your revulsion at these wild monsters.

So we endured another round of inquiries, more bashing by cynical journalists and politicians, and nagging legal challenges. And then the unkindest cut: Our government funding was stopped.

At first we were disheartened, but our common sense of purpose and our astonishing progress led us to rally. My team voted unanimously to provide our own funds. We exhausted our savings to buy chemicals and equipment. We worked sixteen hour days, hoping to produce a result that would silence our critics. I cannot adequately express my love and admiration for my co-workers. They are the martyrs of progressive civilization, their courage and fortitude... ah, forgive me, ladies and gentlemen. I cannot speak of these splendid visionaries without tears. Yes, thank you, thank you so much. Your applause sustains me. And I must also acknowledge the indefatigable efforts of my friends here who are helping me navigate the legal shoals. They have found me the finest attorneys and have raised the bail money which I needed to attend this excellent colloquium. Yes, yes, give them your earnest applause! Thank you so much. I am sure you will all stand by us. And now let me attempt to conclude this talk on a positive note.

The next slide illustrates some of our achievements in the weeks after our decision to carry on. We believe we have activated genes affecting intelligence, creativity, immune responses, and general tranquility. Of course, we don't know which way these traits will go, but the mere fact that we've zeroed in on the pertinent genes gives us enormous hope. Indeed, the horizon is glowing with possibilities. Our species is on the verge of perfection, of truly celestial ascension. Just observe these fetuses, fully viable in their jars, each one labeled with its mutagenic agent and altered gene. We had planned to let the little tykes develop and show their stuff; in fact, that's all we asked.

But the armies of atavism would not allow it. They vowed to keep up their violence until they had shut us down and hauled us off to the pillory. Every day they marched with their angry signs, assaulted us with obscenities, threw rocks and explosives over the wall. We increased our security force and demanded help from the authorities, but for every defender we added, our enemies enlisted ten. A showdown was clearly coming.

Matters finally boiled over when the most radical members of P.I.S.S. whipped the mob into a drunken frenzy. All morning they flung themselves in waves at our guards, and I knew they would eventually overwhelm us. I was terribly frustrated. Years of toil were about to be trampled into dust. I envisioned my co-workers bloodied and cast aside. No, these things must not come to pass!

I sent my people home with an armed escort. Then I locked myself in the laboratory and covered the door pane. My thoughts may not have been charitable but they were focused.

By noon, a fertilized egg was floating in a Petri dish, and I added the first of the agents. An hour later I transferred the embryo to a holding jar. I fed it a fine brew of delicately seasoned nutrients, and soon the bath water became the baby. The next slide, taken by surveillance camera, shows my impatient little pet flopping out of his jar. Can you see the intensity in his eyes and the rudimentary, but impressive, muscle development? I kept on feeding him with larger and larger flasks and bottles. In the next four slides you can see his rapid growth; here he has surpassed me in height and weight. His only purpose, of course, was to nourish his burgeoning body.

The demonstrators had overcome the security force. I heard them rampaging through the corridors, smashing glass and equipment. I tossed my new Cyclone an empty bottle and slipped out the door. His deafening roar made me cringe as I fled. A final photograph was taken shortly after the "PISSed off!" leaders burst into my lab. Ha!

They didn't know the meaning of their own slogan.

May I have the last slide, please?

WINKEN, BLINKEN AND NOD

Bad thoughts go through my head a lot. Sometimes terrible nightmares come that leave me shaking in the dark. I can't always tell what was real and what was dream. I'll maybe see something, like hate in a man's eyes or a bloody knife, and my mind'll chew on it and reshape it and one day it'll bust into my head like a monster. Alls I can do then is find myself a bottle and calm my nerves. But sometimes I drink too much and make things worse.

I'm the janitor at the wax museum. It's a lousy job but, like they say, it's a marriage of convenience. I work here because no one else will hire me, and the curator keeps me on because no one else in his right mind'd work in this creepy place. I've been fixing to quit for years, and after last night I just might do it. One thing's sure: I ain't going back there any time soon.

The museum has ten display rooms, plus the big lobby, the curator's office, the johns, and the gift shop out front. Every day I come on at six p.m., when the staff people are all going home. The place gets lonely then and noises and echoes start up. The woodwork crackles and mice scamper around. By the time I finish cleaning the johns it's almost dark. The museum has what the curator calls "oblique lighting" and, let me tell you, it's spooky. The shadows seem to come alive.

I go on to sweep the lobby, dust shelves in the gift shop, and run the vacuum in the curator's office. Then I always stop at the janitor's closet, where I keep a bottle hid. I take a couple of long snorts because the display room floors are next and that's when my nerves start acting up.

Each display room has a different theme, like the presidents or the Civil War or the famous murderers. Some of the wolks, which is what I call the wax folks, are fine and handsome, but others give me a chill. In the Dawn of Man room the stumpy cavemen stare at me with cruel, animal eyes. Next door, the Roman emperor's watching gladiators fight with maces, and next to that is the devil judge in his red robe from the Spanish Inquisition. In the Civil War room a soldier is bleeding and moaning because his leg's blowed off. Then comes a samurai screaming and waving his sword, and savages dancing around shrunken heads, and that wild-eyed female ax murderer. They're not real, I keep telling myself. But they were real. And I know their spirits live in the museum. They follow me all the way through the place and fill my head with awful pictures.

The worst room of all is the French Revolution room. It's got this guillotine up on a platform. The curator says it's the real McCoy, sent over from France in the nineteenth century. The blade is pulled up, ready to fall, and some poor sucker is on his knees with his head through the hole. An executioner in a black mask is all set to let go the rope. In my mind I can see the head popping off and rolling down the wooden chute into the bucket on the floor. There's two wax heads in the bucket with their eyes open. I looked in once and saw them, and I had nightmares for a month.

Last night something happened that must have been a dream, but I can't shake it. Seems I drank too much in the janitor's closet and got real sleepy. I shut the door, sat down on the soft mop, and dozed off. Way later, there was a loud crash that woke me up. Jeez, I wondered, did I dream that or what? My head was killing me, and bloody thoughts were making me shiver. Finally I opened the door, looked at the clock, and saw it was after midnight. What the hell, I figured, forget the rest and go home.

Then heard voices. At night you can hear lots of sounds but not voices. Nobody but me is supposed to be in the museum after dark. I was crapping my pants thinking about them wolks coming to life.

I peeked around the corner and heard the voices coming from the French Revolution room across the lobby. Just then someone looked out of the room. He was a tall young man and he was wearing a white lab coat. I felt relieved to see a human being and not a wolk staggering toward me, but then I wondered what this dude was up to. Seemed like he was checking to see if anyone was around.

I tiptoed across the lobby and peeked into the French Revolution room. Two men were standing at the rail in front of the guillotine, and a third man, the tall one who looked out the door, was on the platform pulling up the blade. Now I knew what woke me up.

One of the men at the rail was an older, gray-haired fella with glasses. He was also wearing a lab coat, and he had a notebook in his hand. Next to him was another young man. This one was wearing a blue and white sweatshirt, which are the colors of the college up the street. It hit me that the old fella was maybe a professor and the young ones were his students. On the floor was an empty gunnysack, a stainless steel basin with white towels in it, a bucket of water, a detergent bottle, and two big sponges. In a corner of the room the executioner was propped against the wall and his victim was laying underneath him.

The tall man on the platform gave the rope a tug, and the blade moved up and down a little. "It's heavier than it looks," he said. "Damn fine piece of work."

Then the professor and the young man in the sweatshirt started talking. When the young man turned his head, I saw his face was pale as death.

"You can change your mind, Ted," the professor told him.

"It's what I want," this Ted fella answered. His voice was so weak, I could hardly hear.

The tall man on the platform wound the rope around one leg of the guillotine. Then he jumped down, fetched a chair, and took it up on the platform with him. He stood on it and ran his finger along the blade. "Hoo-wee! She's still plenty sharp," he said.

"Are you sure it's the best way?" the professor asked Ted.

"The chemotherapy isn't working," he answered. "I'm in constant pain. This way, at least, I'll be making a contribution."

"A major contribution," said the professor.

The tall man jumped down again, lifted the stainless steel basin and water bucket onto the platform, and tossed up the detergent, sponges, and gunnysack. He leaped back up and poured some of the detergent into the water. Then he looked impatiently at his watch.

"All right," the professor said in a gruff voice. "There's no reason why we shouldn't go through with it. Let's review the objective, now. We need to find out whether you know it's off, even for an instant. You should concentrate heavily on the objective right up to the final moment. Then, if you know it's off, blink once. You probably won't have enough strength to do more than that."

"I say he should wink," said the tall man. "That way, we'll be sure."

The professor thought it over. "No. That may be impossible. One blink is best."

"I understand," Ted rasped.

The professor helped him under the rail, and then both men in white coats helped him onto the platform. The professor pulled off the wooden chute and set it aside. He climbed onto the platform, moved the chair in front of the guillotine, and sat down with the basin in his lap. Meanwhile the tall man unwound the rope and gave it a couple of tugs.

"Right through here," he said as he raised the wooden bar with his free hand. Ted got down on his knees.

"Are you concentrating?" asked the professor.

"Yes," came a whisper.

"Remember, now, a single blink."

My stomach started to heave, and I ran like hell across the lobby and out the door. I can't remember if I heard the crash or just imagined it. You couldn't have heard it, I keep telling myself. You was asleep and drunk and it was all a bad dream. Nothing in that place is real.

IS JHENG THE WAY?

They were still arriving at the Great Hall of Culture as the suns went down and the twilight passed through its malachite stage. In groups of three or four they came from dozens of places: whiskered, bug-eyed quadrupeds from Andromeda, transparent sylphids from the Planet oflce, finned amphibs from beyond the rigorously mapped zones. In the sweltering dusk a saucer from the Sulfide Belt spun down, and its tentacled, foul-smelling passengers oozed self-consciously across the field toward the big stone edifice. Many more ships, each unique in appearance and markings, landed before darkness was complete.

At the foot of the wide steps a towering sign flashed sequentially in the five accepted languages of the known universe:

WELCOME DELEGATES

FIRST INTERGALACTIC PEACE CONFERENCE
IS JHENG THE WAY?

In a corner of the sign the temperature and humidity were inconspicuously displayed: 311 degrees absolute; 96%. Boranians considered it their finest weather.

Inside the auditorium Malik and his assistant, Qoti, sat at the moderator's table on stage. Malik was terribly nervous; his scales and lower arms quivered as he watched the entering procession. Qoti, maintaining her usual calm demeanor, patted him unobtrusively and spoke reassuring words. At last she went over to test the translation microphones and check the cups of fluids on the speakers' tables. She also spent a moment with the bolo crew and spoke with the engineers in the transmission room. Then she sat down again beside her boss.

"Did they try the signals?" he asked.

"We're beaming all the way to the Virgo cluster. Every sector is on board." Malik scanned the auditorium. "Do you think the turnout might be too big?"

"Stop worrying! It's going to work fine."

He put all his hands together in a quick prayer and stepped to the podium. "Citizens of the universe," he began, "my name is Malik Adze and I'll be your moderator this evening." He paused until the few latecomers had a chance to adjust their headphones. "On behalf of our sponsors I'd like to welcome you to Planet Borane. As you have undoubtedly gathered, nothing beats a bisolar planet in offering a warm welcome."

Flutey sighs rang out from the sylphids. The delegates were miserable in the hot room, and none of them appreciated the humor. Eyeing the holovision cameras, Malik decided to omit the jokes and get to the point.

"The theme of our conference is, as you know, the role of Jheng. Is it a fad? Is it just one more system of beliefs? Or can it possibly be that elusive structure that will end our many hostilities and bind us all together in peace and harmony?"

Malik paused again as three giant bicephalics entered the auditorium. The six heads spent a long time arguing where to sit and finally chose a spot in the very center of the room. The feathered occupants of those seats scattered in alarm.

"To debate these questions," Malik continued, "we have enlisted two highly distinguished speakers, whom I'd like to introduce now." He placed a 3x5 card on the lectern. "Academician Ohn Fyre comes to us from the Small Magellanic Clouds and will, of course, uphold the pro-Jheng side. Academician Fyre has written the definitive treatise on Jheng and has published dozens of articles on its application in numerous environments. Just to mention a few of his papers: 'Jheng and Timelessness,' 'Jheng as the Key to Life-ability,' 'Endings Begin with Jheng,' and, the most widely read essay in the last star-period, 'Jheng and Your Sex Life.'"

Malik rattled all his upper digits as the small, egg-shaped Fyre ascended the stage. Half the audience applauded along with him, rattling, thumping, or squealing, as befit their species. The other half amused themselves with derisive comments or remained stonily silent. Seating himself at one of the speakers' tables, Fyre nodded impatiently to acknowledge the applause. His eyestalks, fitted with lollipop spectacles, rotated warily in a semicircle. He appeared to sense trouble.

Malik turned up the second card. "To articulate the opposing view, we have the renowned historian and cultural analyst, Niobia III, from the Milky Way." Some in the audience erupted prematurely in a variety of sounds, and Malik had to raise all his arms for quiet. "Niobia III has authored best-selling monographs on everything from the rewards of stress to the perils of leisure. She has won six Nova awards for her insightful commentary and her no-compromise approach to a long list of social problems. Her soon-to-be-published book---if she will permit me to whet your appetites---has the title Clawing Your Way to Truth. I give you now: Niobia III."

From the front row a crimson, sharp-beaked avioid, six feet from crest to tail, flew into the air and swooped to the other speaker's table. Alighting upon the seat back, she folded her winged arms and gave herself a quick, two-shot preening. An indescribable blend of admiring noises rose up from her supporters. Across the stage, Academician Fyre's eyestalks listed backward as he watched his opponent's talons curl into the fabric of the chair.

"Without further ado," said Malik, "let us begin the debate. We have already agreed that Academician Pyre will go first."

Fyre waddled to the podium and climbed onto the wooden block to reach the microphone. "I want to thank Malik for his splendid work in arranging this conference," he began in his rapid voice, which seemed to be racing to keep up with his many thoughts. "And I'd like to assure him that the radiant heat of Borane is not a problem for Jhengists. We've learned to take the heat wherever we go." Fyre's oval body shook as he cackled at his own wit. His admirers, brimming with affection, forgot their sweaty distress and sent up a gleeful din of squeals, bassoon-like honks, and short, loud wheezing noises. Malik and Qoti exchanged crafty looks as though anticipating a lively evening.

"I should like to begin by stating three premises which I think we can all accept," Fyre went on. "Number one: All aspects of the presently known universe can be interpreted in terms of planes. Two: Time is irrelevant. And three: psychohistorical mechanisms have been studied with ambiguous analytical approaches, but the ambiguity stems solely from the models we employ." Fyre's eyestalks rotated from side to side. No disagreement was expressed.

"Very good," he said. "And now let me invite you to follow a simple trail of logic. Keeping in mind these three premises..."

A frightening squawk shattered the air. "Assumptions!" cried Niobia III from her perch.

"Well, I think the term premises..."

"Assumptions!"

Fyre's lips compressed. "'If we assume these premises,' he mocked, "the path is straightforward to our first useful conclusion. Since the total life form mass of the known universe has decreased over the last hundred star periods, it is clear why our aggregate mind power (which I'll define in a moment) can no longer accept hypernatural phenomena, much less put parameters on them."

Niobia III flung up her winged arms and uttered a deafening, metal-on-metal shriek. "Irrelevant! Immaterial! Illogical!" she screamed, rattling the teeth in Fyre's domelike head. Her supporters turned the words into a wrathful chant, which inspired an equally furious clamor from the opposition. The heat-crazed delegates waved signs and made obscene gestures at each other. In the center of the crowd the giant bicephalics pounded on a group of quadrupeds while braying like foghorns.

Malik and Qoti suppressed their smiles. But when a clique of flame-breathing arthropods began menacing the Sulfide group, Malik rushed to the microphone and appealed for order. Academician Fyre was kicking the lectern in exasperation. Slit-like orifices opened all over his body, and traces of a caustic yellow vapor seeped out. Malik brought him a cup of fluid, then signaled feverishly to a cameraman, who dollied in as Fyre poured the oily drink into his wide maw.

"My reasoning is flawless!" Fyre bellowed, and a roar went up from his followers. "Can you not grasp the simplest thread of logic?" he shouted at Niobia III, now preening herself in a brazen show of indifference.

"Please," Malik beseeched the delegates, "let's save the comments for the Q and A."

At last the audience settled down, and he returned to his seat. "It's happening too fast," he whispered to Qoti. "I didn't think the heat would get to them so soon."

Academician Fyre wiped the steam off his glasses, slid them back on, and composed himself. "Let us for simplicity divide the known universe into two categories of history, which I shall refer to merely as Jheng-favored and Jheng-disfavored. I'm not implying any preference here, only drawing a hypothetical distinction for the purpose of constructing a useful model."

"Rubbish!" someone called from the audience.

"A useful model," Fyre repeated with emphasis.

"Simulation models can't be trusted," crowed Niobia III. "We want hard data."

"If I may be allowed to speak!" Fyre demanded.

"You're wasting your breath."

"He's wasting our time," shouted the heckler.

A storm of outraged voices rumbled and swelled and was swiftly met by an opposing crescendo. Signs began to wave again. Objects were hurled with increasing vigor.

"If you care nothing for truth..." Fyre taunted, but a roar of derisive laughter silenced him. When he again attempted to speak, a soft, fruity missile smote the top of his head.

"Niobia! Niobia! Niobia!" chanted her supporters, who were immediately challenged by "Fyre and Jheng! Fyre and Jheng!"

"Can you control your pack of troglodytes?" Fyre cried to Niobia III.

"Your own puny-minded lemmings started it. Puny minds in puny bodies. I've laid eggs bigger than you."

Niobia III flounced and flapped on her perch. Fyre was luminous white with rage. Pandemonium had broken out among the suffocating delegates, who assaulted one another with fists, fangs, claws, and tentacles. Signs came down on heads. Truculent growls and shrieks filled the air, and desperate sounds of pain rose and fell. The sylphids and other less robust lifeforms retreated frantically toward the exits.

The holo crew did their best to record it all, but eventually two of them were knocked off their mobile units. Malik and Qoti rushed to take their places. Malik dollied up and down the aisles, recording as much as possible, while Qoti, instructed through earphones from the transmission room, focused on the melee on stage.

Niobia III was swooping back and forth over Fyre's head. Her steely talons had crushed his glasses, and she was trying to grab his eyestalks. Blind and terrified, Fyre emitted plumes of corrosive yellow vapor in all directions as he searched futilely for his tormentor. Suddenly his luck improved: A jet of vapor seared off Niobia's tail feathers, and she veered clumsily away from the stage and over the delegates' heads. Fyre's supporters flung books, clothes, footwear, and headphones at her. She sailed out of control from one end of the hall to the other, Qoti capturing her ragged flight while Malik honed in on the upturned, hate-blackened faces. Finally she swung back toward the stage, where the bewildered Fyre was still looking for her. A frightful collision ensued. Fyre actually exploded, and a vast cloud of yellow poison drifted out from the stage. Niobia III seemed to dissolve. The delegates lumbered, galloped, fluttered, and oozed toward the exits, smothering and trampling one another as they fled. Broken, bleeding figures writhed in the aisles. Malik and Qoti recorded gasps and rattles up to the last second, then raced out of the building.

"Well, the sponsors ought to be pleased with that," Qoti remarked as they rested on the stone steps.

"I just hope we didn't lose it too soon," said Malik.

Qoti laughed. "You know what, my dear? You worry too much." She massaged his upper scales affectionately until he began to relax. "The transmission room figured we got an 80% share," she told him. He purred at the news.

The night air was warm and humid, pleasant to the two Boranians. Malik lit his pipe. Bodies of every description were sprawled on the steps, and a column of battered delegates struggled across the field toward their ships. In the distance the wail of medical vehicles grew louder.

Qoti smiled at the flashing sign above them. "So, Malik, what do you think? Is Jheng the way?"

"Tonight it was, if that 80% holds up. But our ratings might be even higher for the next conference."

"Did they choose a topic?"

"We're doing 'Miscegenation: How Far Do We Take It?'"

Qoti's eyes lit up as she imagined the scene. "That'll be fantastic! The sponsors must be drooling."

Malik leaned back and puffed confidently on his pipe. He traced invisible numbers on the stone: 80, 85, 90. But suddenly he clouded over. "I just hope we don't lose it as soon as the fun starts."

HELLO... ZACK?

Hello...Zack? Listen, on this motorcycle thing, I just wanted to say that when I heard about it on the TV news I cried. I really did. I wept. You know, grown-ups aren't supposed to cry? Don't believe it, Zack. I went through two handkerchiefs. I got so upset that an innocent Joe, minding his own business, could have this happen to him, and I said to my son---he's sixteen now and he's been wanting to buy this Suzuki from his friend---I told him "See that!" And I tell you, he argued with me at first but he's thinking about it now, so at this point I don't know what he'll do. I told him it's his decision; I can't live his life for him. But he's got to face the facts.

Hi, Zack, nice to talk to you. Say, I have a comment on that motorcycle incident. Seems like it's on everybody's mind tonight. I kind of agree with the lady who wondered why they can't enclose those overpasses in fencing or something, so you wouldn't have these kinds of problems. When I lived in Dayton we had a screened-in overpass, you know, totally screened-in from one end to the other, and nothing like this ever happened. Course you know if a kid---and I'm assuming it was kids---if a kid wants to cause trouble he's going to find a way to do it, and if you block him one way he's going to find another way, but still the cost of screens is nothing compared to a human being. Don't you agree or am I way off base?

Zack, I'm surprised at you, picking the American League. Where's their pitching, Zack? Tell me how you win a game without pitching. Sure, I know about Wilson and McFadden, but look at what they've been facing all year. Every time they pitch against a hitting team they get clobbered.

They're overrated, Zack. They're the darlings of the media. Oh, and let me say one thing about the motorcycle thing. When they catch the kids that did it, I hope they throw away the key. You know what I mean? They'll be in court one day and the next day they'll be out doing it again. You'll get some of them fancy civil liberties lawyers down there, and them punks'll get off scot-free. Makes me madder'n HE double toothpicks every time I think about it. An honest citizen is at the mercy of every kook and crook in the state. But who's gonna listen to me, huh?

Zack, how are you tonight? I'd like to add my two cents to the great debate, if you don't mind. Now don't misunderstand me, I don't condone what those kids did---if they were kids, and that seems to be the consensus here tonight. But that motorcycle rider wasn't wearing a helmet, and it's just possible that if he had a helmet he might not have been hurt so badly. What is it they're saying? He lost an eye? Both eyes. Well, that's tragic, no doubt about it, but the fact remains if you don't obey the law---and that new helmet law they passed last year is very specific. Of course, they don't enforce those things. I realize the police have enough to do, especially in that part of town, and don't get me wrong, they're not all bad people down there, but you can't expect good enforcement of these safety-type laws. Every one of us is responsible to see that they're enforced, and I wonder, since it was pointed out that he was coming from a big party, I wonder if someone at that party couldn't have suggested that he wear a helmet and maybe loaned him one or something. I don't know, what do you think?

Zack, honey, I just wanted to relate an incident that happened to my sister in Pittsburgh. She lives near a freeway there, and one day she was driving home and she spotted some kids on one of those overpasses. You know, they were just horsing around where they shouldn't be. So she turned off at the next exit and got the police to check up on them. Now I'm not saying they were dropping bricks---matter of fact, she never did find out if they were causing trouble---but they might have been, and her quick action might have prevented a tragedy like we had here. It's too bad some motorist didn't take action when he saw those kids up there. But then it was night, wasn't it, and maybe you couldn't see them. But we still need to be more responsible about reporting potential crimes whenever we see them happening. Anyway, that's my feeling on the matter.

Zack, two things. First of all, I'd like to take umbrage with the gentleman about the American League pitching. I believe that Wilson and McFadden rate with anybody the National League can field. The only problem is the designated-hitter rule, so those guys may have to hit for themselves and, of course, who can tell if they can hit? But on this motorcycle business I agree with that other caller. It ought to be pointed out that these incidents are exactly the sort of thing you can expect in that part of town. You know, they say idle hands make trouble or mischief or something? Well, whatever they make, it's not good. And you have those folks down there sitting around on their rear ends all day and they need something to relieve the boredom, so they go out and commit murder and rape. It's too bad the government sees fit in its wisdom to harbor these people and coddle them with welfare checks. Right, I understand you have to break for a commercial, and I just wanted to say I enjoy your show, I listen every night, and I'm picking the American League!

Okay... Zack... I'm on? Okay, let me turn down my radio. I was going to say something else, but I can't let what that last caller said pass unchallenged. Those folks down there, as he refers to them, are mostly law-abiding citizens. Just because you have a couple of bad apples doesn't mean you have to throw the baby out with the bath water. A lot of them work hard to keep food on their table, and it certainly isn't their fault if the economy's in a recession. Besides, there's plenty of crime to go around all over this city, including the north side, where that rich kid murdered his mother with a tire iron last spring. So let's not point fingers at someone else's glass house.

Zack, I may be pretty unsophisticated, but the debate here tonight strikes me as pretty negative. I mean, sure we all agree that what those kids did was wrong and they ought to be punished, but when there's so much trouble in the world, why dwell on it so much? We need to look on the positive side of things. First there's all this nuclear talk and the economy's going sour, and now this thing right here in our own city. And what do all these negative nay-sayers propose for solutions? You know what I think? They enjoy themselves with all their nay-saying and griping about the world. We've got to get back to simple truths, if you know what I mean. The simple truths.

Zack, I think I can clear up some of the confusion in people's minds. You know how that motorcycle rider was coming from a party? Well, at work we've got a secretary whose roommate thinks she was at that same party. The gal can't be sure because the picture they showed in the paper was apparently an old one and didn't show his long hair and beard. Also, you couldn't tell from the picture if his hair was blond or red; the guy she remembers had red hair. But the important thing is that according to her he was drinking like a sailor all evening, and when he drove off he was weaving all over the road. She can't understand how those kids could have hit him. And you know, when you consider the damage these drunk drivers cause, it's hard to sympathize with the guy. If indeed it was him.

Hey, Zacharias, how's it going, man? Lots of heavy stuff tonight, eh? Seriously though, I've been listening to your show for the last hour and, with all due respect, your callers are really missing the point on this motorcycle case. I mean, one woman says we ought to put up screens and some guy says we ought to hang the kids that did it and someone else thinks we should all be more vigilant, but nobody understands the truth of what happened. Fact is, Zackie baby, that dude got hit by a brick because it was his destiny to get hit. It was written, as the Arabs say. Nothing can change a man's destiny, Zackie, not screens or helmets or anything. So I suggest we all say a prayer for the poor dude and hope the rest of his life brings him better luck. More than that we cannot do.

Oh, and Zackie, I'd love to help you out with the baseball problem, but I'm afraid that one's beyond my humble capabilities. Yeah, too lofty a realm for this poor guru.

THE REAL WORLD

The early settlers of the Great Smoky Mountains left behind many disturbing tales, some of which have risen like the mist into legend and myth. I heard one of them from Sarah Bell, a clerk at the Heritage Crafts store in Gatlinburg. Sarah's ancestors had come to the Smokies in the 1820s, and she herself had lived there all of her twenty-eight years. She was a pretty, robust, unfashionably dressed woman, an easy talker with a broad knowledge of the area. She had graduated from the same college which had just appointed me assistant professor of chemistry.

One day I visited the crafts store to look at musical instruments. Sarah and I took an instant liking to each other, and we spent an hour playing hammered dulcimers. We began dating. Sarah loved to hike in the mountains, which to me were almost a foreign country. She led me up and down rocky trails and told me about her backpacking trips, encounters with animals, and scary, but spiritually healing, nights in the forest. Once, while we sat by a stream, she told me an eerie tale handed down from her pioneer ancestors, the great-grandparents of her great-grandparents.

They had come with their two daughters and built a cabin in a remote part of the forest. They lived off their crops, a few chickens and hogs, and a cow. The parents were fanatically religious, but their angry piety brought them disaster and an ungodly retribution. Their older daughter, Mary, became pregnant after a liaison with a Cherokee boy. To hide the family's shame, her parents imprisoned her in the attic, where she languished in a sickly condition. Finally she gave birth. But as soon as she fell asleep, her parents took the baby into the woods and left it to die. When Mary awoke to their treachery, she forced herself up, bleeding and emaciated, and staggered over the landscape in a frantic search. Two days later she was found dead with the lifeless body of the child in her arms. The parents placed them in the same coffin and buried them near the cabin in what eventually became the family cemetery. The sparse settler community was told that Mary had died of a fever.

On the night of the burial the younger daughter awoke in the attic room and saw a vision of her dead sister. Mary's ghost demanded milk for the baby and warned her sister not to inform their parents. The frightened girl crept down the ladder and hid a bowl of milk on the hearth. The ghost made her do this every night, and in the mornings, before anyone noticed, the girl put away the empty bowl. But one night her father caught her and forced an explanation. When she told him of the ghost, he flew into a rage, accused her of conjuring, and chased her out of the cabin. She ran to her sister's grave and cowered by the headstone. He pounced on her there, but before he could deliver his blows they were both shocked into breathless silence. They heard the unmistakable cries of a hungry infant rising mercilessly from the grave.

After that, a bowl of milk was set out regularly. Whenever it was forgotten, someone received a shimmering visitation by the dead mother. The secret was kept from generation to generation, and the tradition of the milk went on until the twentieth century, when the cabin was finally abandoned.

"So what do you think?" Sarah asked me.

"Just another Appalachian ghost story. I've heard lots of them."

My reaction seemed to displease her, so I tried to show more interest. "Have you ever seen the place?"

"My mother took me there when I was a child. The cabin was still standing. She told me about the ghost, and I was so scared that we had to leave. Even today I sometimes have nightmares about it."

"Surely you don't believe the story."

"I don't know. A lot of honest people in my family have sworn that Mary appeared in that cabin. They couldn't all have been crazy."

"Sarah, for Pete's sake! Are you living in the real world?"

She turned away, embarrassed, and I apologized. I considered her a bright, level headed woman, and we were heading toward a serious relationship. Her admission to superstitious fear surprised and disappointed me. As a scientist I felt obligated to demonstrate the limits of natural law.

"Will you take me to the cabin?" I asked.

"Are you serious?"

"Of course. I bet it will help you sleep."

"I'm not sure I can still find it. It's been twenty years."

"Let's give it a shot anyway. I know you love an adventure, and you must be curious about the place."

"Yes, but I've never gone near it. Maybe we don't know as much about the world as we think." Her words sounded like a challenge.

"Then let's find out what we don't know. Let's get our bedrolls and spend a night in the cabin. This ghost should be put out of her misery."

We shared a laugh, then decided to go that very day.

* * *

It was late afternoon when we arrived at the trailhead with our backpacks and bedrolls. The trail through the valley took us into a section of forest spared by twentieth century logging companies. Interspersed among the myriad weeds, shrubs, and young trees were giant maples and poplars, over twenty feet around the base. They towered above the forest like primitive gods holding the secrets of life and death on their unreachable limbs.

"They probably rose out of the ground with our ghost," Sarah remarked with a little nervous laughter.

A mist, spawned by an earlier rain, bore a faint odor of volatiles from plants and decaying matter. Sarah led me off the trail many times to search for the cabin, but we kept running into barriers or pinning ourselves to thorny shrubbery. Our arms and legs accumulated scratches and insect bites. Once, Sarah recoiled as a banded copperhead wound arrogantly across our path. When we moved on, my eyes were darting wildly in every direction.

"I hope we find the place before dark," she said.

"Maybe this was a bad idea. Do you want to go back?"

"No. You were right. It's time I settled this matter. I don't like to think of my ancestors as a bunch of nutcases."

"If we're lucky we'll figure out what was bothering them."

Her determination boosted my confidence. As the daylight waned we pushed on with greater urgency. Our hike had become a mission, and every bend in the trail held new hope of success. We let ourselves fall into the stealthy embrace of night.

Suddenly Sarah put up her hands. "Wait! I think it's around here." We took out our flashlights and aimed them down a broad, gentle slope. Again we abandoned the faintly moonlit trail. After picking our way through tall rhododendron bushes, we emerged into a dark theater of huge trees. The steadily mounting clamor of katydids, tree frogs, and cicadas reached a peak, as if nature were giving us a last warning.

"Yes, I remember this," Sarah said. "The cabin is here somewhere."

We swept our beams over the ground, moved a few steps, and repeated the process.

"What's that?" I cried.

Two eyes, at the level of my shoulders, reflected back from a rhododendron thicket. When Sarah gasped, the eyes disappeared. We heard a soft crash and the sound of an animal scuttling away.

"A raccoon?" she guessed. "It must have jumped from a branch and run."

"Scared the hell out of me."

We both laughed at ourselves.

"Look! That might be the cabin," she said.

We advanced toward the shadowy structure, about twenty yards away. I happened to glance behind us and noticed that the raccoon, or whatever it was, had decided to watch us from a safe distance.

"Yes, this is it," Sarah said. "And the graveyard is just beyond those trees."

We stood before the doorless entrance to the black ruin. Its walls resembled a rail fence, so wide were the gaps between logs. An empty window gazed at us as if we had disrupted its drugged sleep. The roof sagged like a hammock, and much of the chimney had crumbled.

The two small rooms of the cabin were completely empty. Our flashlights illuminated a thick layer of ash and dust on the floor, especially around the cold, barren hearth. The density of the surrounding forest would have reduced all wind and rain to their mildest terms, and one could easily imagine the dust to have lain undisturbed for decades. A mouse scampered across the floor and out its private portal. Other than that, only the intricate cobwebs, like remains of some ancient artwork, testified to the presence of life.

"Do you want to stay?" Sarah asked.

"Definitely. Just think how many people lived here. Is it okay with you?"

"I'm fine. Of course, that could change if our ghost shows up."

I climbed a wobbly ladder and peered into the attic, where the children had slept. My light beam struck the hovering trees through gaps in the roof A choking closeness gripped me. Did I fear this room, where the ghost had first appeared? No, I decided, old campfire tales would not affect me. I held my breath and spent a minute upstairs inspecting nothing in particular.

"I'm hungry," Sarah called.

She took sandwiches and a canteen from her backpack, and we had a late dinner. At first every noise startled us. But after a while the seamless shrill of insects imparted a reassuring rhythm. We sat close and enjoyed a tender hour. We kept one of the flashlights on because the darkness was nearly total.

Eventually we opened our bedrolls and prepared to sleep. I felt a pleasant agitation, as if I were starting a new experiment. I wondered of the mere contemplation of death and graveyards might induce nocturnal visions in susceptible people.

Sometime later I awoke to find Sarah tossing and turning in her bedroll.

"Uncomfortable?" I asked.

"I can't sleep. I'm too wound up."

"We can talk some more if it'll help."

"I don't want to keep you up. Don't worry. I'll fall asleep."

Her good humor had dried up and she sounded testy. Hoping to soothe her nerves, I yawned loudly and tried to sound calm and unconcerned. Then, as I began to drift off again, she suddenly sat up, jolting me awake.

"What is it?" I asked.

"She's here," Sarah whispered.

"The ghost?" I said facetiously. "Where?" I swept my flashlight over the room.

"I think I saw her."

"There's nothing."

"Listen."

Then I realized that the deafening insect choir had softened, as if all the members closest to the cabin had finished their parts. A nearly imperceptible breeze had invaded the cabin, bringing with it a musty odor, quite alien to the forest.

Sarah began fumbling in her backpack. She pulled out a bowl and a second canteen.

"I brought this just in case," she said. She poured milk into the bowl and placed it inside the stone fireplace. "I think we'd better go."

"Wait. Let me look around."

I checked the attic and searched outside the cabin. Nothing seemed out of the ordinary except the insects and the unfamiliar odor. When I returned, Sarah had tied up her bedroll and zipped her backpack.

"There's no one here," I said.

She shook her head. "I saw her. I can feel her."

"You're upset. The mind can invent all sorts of..."

"No. Trust me. Mary is watching us."

"Okay, okay. I won't argue. But let's do one thing before we leave. Come with me to the graveyard. See for yourself that no baby is crying in the ground. At least we can lay that part of the story to rest."

Sarah was flustered but, when I took her hands, she settled down. I could tell that she didn't want to disappoint me, and I gave her a reassuring hug.

"Are you up to it?"

"Okay," she said, "but stay close."

With our flashlights we fought through the bramble to a stand of old poplars. Sarah found some half-buried stone slabs, which might have been markers. Their earthen mantle wrapped them so firmly that we couldn't tear it away.

"I'm sure this is the cemetery," she said.

"And what do you hear?"

The graves yielded up only silence. Her downcast eyes acknowledged the obvious.

"Satisfied?" I asked.

"Well, you know how stories change."

"Yes, they do. And we're always hoping there's more to the world than we can see. You know what I think? Ghosts appear only to people who believe in them."

She smiled at my teasing. "I suppose you're right. I must have dozed off and started to dream."

"Do you still want to go?"

"No. I'll stay if you like."

"Let's finish off this ghost once and for all."

I enjoyed a feeling of triumph as we made our way back to the cabin. Sarah reopened her bedroll and went over to get the bowl.

"Oh, my God! Look!" she cried.

I stared incredulously at the fireplace. The bowl was empty.

"She was here," Sarah said.

"Now, take it easy. There's got to be a reason for this." I wracked my brain feverishly. "Wait! It was the raccoon, of course. It followed us, hoping for a handout, and probably couldn't believe its luck." I laughed out loud, but my glee only irritated Sarah.

She studied the hearth closely with her flashlight. "Do you see any tracks?"

I knelt beside her. Our own footprints were clearly etched in the dust, but no trace of another intruder was present. Inside the fireplace, close to the bowl, the dust was completely undisturbed. This silent testimony left me shaken.

"Well?" Sarah demanded.

"How the hell do I know? Let's just get out of here."

She said nothing more---which was fine with me---as I led the way back to the real world.

PELE

They bought in Victorian Village, of course, one of those sprawling, early twentieth-century palaces. Gingerbread all over, rows of dormers on the third story, vast porches, even a balcony and a Queen Anne tower. Acres of parquet inside and twelve foot ceilings. Rococo trim that must have been carved by a madman. They paid a ridiculous price, but they simply couldn't let it go. ("Mediocrity is our national hallmark," Charles is forever deploring. "Live by the bland and you perish by it.") They moved in last fall with their basenji.

What the Van Slykes didn't know---what no one knows, for that matter---is that houses in Victorian Village come with horrid problems. Outwardly they're all character and distinction, just the thing for lovers of the outré, but they're awfully old and cancers migrate through their bowels. The Van Slykes' was no exception. They saw the blemishes on the surface, of course, the broken balustrade on the porch, the gutted driveway that kept their Audis at bay. But how could they tell that half the roof was rotten or that a clan of roaches lived under the kitchen floor? We'll get to the cellar in a moment; the plumbing is best forgotten.

No doubt you've heard of Courtney and her famous whims. She redid the parlor in glass! Glass and ceramic, top to bottom. First she turned the west wall into a mirror. ("Creates an expanse," she says; never mind that the room is already a football field.) She raided art shops all over the state and brought back Chinese porcelain lamps and vases and a whole glass menagerie of little swans, alligators, and prancing horses. Then it was off to London, where she bought an antique French chandelier at

Sotheby's---enormous thing, supposedly hung in some marquis' castle. She refers to the parlor as Silicon Valley East. It's become a legend in the neighborhood. Kids on the street call it the Fortress of Solitude, although none of them has ever seen it.

Charles and Courtney would never dream of children, you know. "Only a head planted ostrich would bring children into a world like this," she argues. Charles rolls his eyes at the oriental vases: "Can you imagine kids in here?" He works for one of those genetic engineering firms, looking for some bug that'll fix nitrogen and live on the roots of wheat. Claims it's the mouse trap that'll have the Third World groveling at his doorstep. "Sub-Saharan Africa will finally get off the world's case," as he puts it. Courtney's an interior designer.

They bought a spider. Another of her impulses, no doubt. They were on a cruise to the lower Caribbean, had a stopover in St. Vincent, north of that place we invaded. They found this little souvenir shop in the village. Proprietor had a whole shelf full of spiders in Parana pine cages. Understand this wasn't an ordinary spider but an avicularian. South American version of our tarantula but larger, big as a dinner plate. A black and yellow thing with hair all over it. From Brazil, the Amazon basin.

They smuggled him in without any trouble. Simply stuck his cage in the suitcase with their other souvenirs, mostly balsa carvings and spiny seashells. Customs man never batted an eye. Once they got home, they let him out and he never went back to the cage. Fell in love with Silicon Valley, all those urns and vases. Charles said he raced back and forth on the coffee table, dancing for joy, according to him. They didn't have the heart to lock him up.

Yodel, their basenji, had big problems. Nothing can frighten a basenji, they say, but this dog was so freaked, he ran all the way to the attic. Charles had to go fetch him. They tried everything to allay his fear, but it was no use. As soon as they brought him anywhere near the spider, he'd leap out of their arms and flee upstairs. They swore they heard him bark, although no one believed it. Basenjis can yodel but they can't bark.

Eventually they solved the problem by putting the dog outside during the day and the spider in the cellar at night. It worked fine and they got an unexpected benefit: Their roach problem suddenly disappeared.

Charles, you know, is very athletic and keeps a huge trunk of sports equipment in the cellar. One morning he was leaving on a fishing trip, and he went down very early to get his gear. He found the spider asleep on a soccer ball. Deeply moved, he rushed upstairs, woke Courtney, and made her come down to see. It was simply precious, according to her. They stood there holding hands and gazing at him. When he awoke, Charles held out his arm, and the spider tripped up to his shoulder. That's when they started calling him Pelé. They were just delighted.

Their friends were dying to see him, so the Van Slykes threw a big wine-and cheese affair. Pelé had the run of the house and he loved it. Played hide-and-seek the whole evening. Things were a bit tense at first, what with no one sitting down and the food going untouched. Charles kept pointing him out: "There he is!" and everyone would snap around. But aside from Joan and Candace, who left with headaches, the guests all developed some rapport. They gathered around while Charles fed him anchovies on his lap. Courtney carried him about in her cleavage.

The neighbors had their own opinion. Mothers wouldn't let their kids anywhere near the place, and the kids all had nightmares. Someone tried a lawsuit, and three houses went up for sale. The only one who dared approach the house was the paperboy, a curious teenager. Every day on his route he'd peek in the diamond-shaped windows of the parlor. He told people he'd seen "the monster" on a vase, but it was probably the oriental design in league with his imagination.

One day the Jehovah's Witnesses were doing Victorian Village. A tall, stout woman called at the Van Slykes' with a little girl, about seven or eight. Courtney was home alone and wanted company, so she let them in.

The woman sat with her daughter on the sofa and went through her monologue about the perfect world to come and religion without priests, and so on. While she spoke her daughter gazed languidly around the room. The glass animals in the étagère caught her fancy. She rose to have a better look, but her mother retrieved her quickly and made her sit.

"Oh, it's all right," Courtney insisted. She led the child across the room and placed a swan in her hand. "Isn't he fascinating! If you hold him up just right, you can see colors in him. Be very careful, now."

The girl peered at the strange reflections in the swan. Courtney returned to the mother, who opened her Bible to Revelations. "Have you thought about God's plan for the future?"

Courtney explained that she and Charles were still in the process of defining their lives and weren't quite ready to commit to a particular religious form. "We don't rule out any," she added. "Even the cults are a possibility."

"Oh, we're not a cult." That woman started to laugh, but just then there was a crash of glass. She looked incredulously at her child, who for some reason had thrown the swan up to the ceiling, from which it fell in two pieces.

"Eugenia!" shouted the woman.

The girl was standing utterly rigid, glaring at the étagère. Every trace of color had gone from her face. Her mother sprang across the room and grabbed her arm, but in the next instant she saw the reason for her daughter's outburst. On the middle shelf, half hidden behind a fat delft crocus pot, was Pelé like a bashful schoolboy, not knowing whether to advance or retreat. With a gasp the mother swept the child off the floor into her sturdy arms.

Courtney rushed over. "Oh, you don't have to be afraid. Come on, Pelé." She cupped her hands, and he scampered on board. "See, he won't hurt you." She held him out to the child, who was now in a tight fetal position on her mother's breast. The mother backed away to the sofa.

"Beast... bottomless pit..." she hissed. Her eyes were fixed on Pelé. She had one arm around the child, while she groped behind her with the other.

"Don't be afraid," Courtney pleaded. "He doesn't bite or sting or anything."

The woman found the Bible and held it up resolutely in front of her. She backed toward the door, while Courtney stood there bewildered. The woman somehow got the door open with the hand that held her daughter. She never lowered the Bible as she backed outside, down the walk, and down the street.

Did you know Elizabeth Tibbet, that mousy British girl? Used to flutter on the fringe at parties. She visited the Van Slykes in April, that week we had all the rain. She'd been in England for months tending her sick mother and hadn't seen the house.

Elizabeth was always an oddball, very quiet but extravagantly nervous. She would have been invisible if not for her studious fidgeting. One day she'd be tugging strands of hair, the next chewing on a hangnail or rubbing at her neck. People often made bets on what she'd be doing to herself. She was a small, rather plain woman, early thirties, never married. Endlessly into self-improvement. Enhance Your Self-Esteem, Productive Relationships, Positive Prayer, Dealing with Stress, wherever there was a course or a workshop, there was Elizabeth by herself in the back of the room, zealously scribbling notes and picking at her body surfaces. No one knew what all those sessions did for her, but she couldn't live without them.

When she arrived at the Van Slykes' it was late in the afternoon and another rainstorm was just ending. Elizabeth folded up her umbrella, removed her plastic rain hood and raincoat, and stripped a pair of rubber boots from her tan oxfords. Charles and Courtney noted wryly that she had walked only ten paces from her car.

They showed her the house and all their things, laying emphasis on their new Stourbridge glass collection. Then they sat around the coffee table in the parlor. Elizabeth told them about her stay in England and her mother's unexpected recovery. She seemed her usual anxiously pleasant self, clearing her throat every few seconds, explaining that she must not have swallowed something properly.

"So what are you doing these days?" Charles asked.

"I'm taking that series of assertiveness-training workshops at the library."

"How wonderful!" Courtney exclaimed. "Tell us all about it."

"Well, I've only just started. I think they'll be very helpful to me. And there's something else..." Elizabeth blushed and cleared her throat twice. "You see, there's a man taking the workshops, and we've been on a date."

"How wonderful!" Courtney repeated. "Tell us everything."

"Well, his name is Leonard and he's very scholarly. He's written a book..." Elizabeth paused a moment and blinked at the large porcelain vase near Charles's armchair. Two of Pelé's legs protruded over the rim. "... a book on comparative linguistics."

"Really!" Charles and Courtney exclaimed at once.

"Tell us about your date," said Charles.

Elizabeth glanced at the vase again. Four of Pelé's legs and part of his head were now visible. "We had dinner at La Gondola... uh... is there something in that vase?"

"Oh," said Charles, "it's Pelé, our spider. Would you like to meet him?" He reached over to the vase, and Pelé ran up his arm. Elizabeth wheezed and sprang backward on the sofa as if she had imploded.

"Don't panic!" Charles admonished her. "He's perfectly harmless. Try not to act afraid or he'll pick up the vibrations and become terribly self-conscious." Indeed, Pelé had withdrawn behind Charles's neck and was feeling around his ear with a foreleg.

"Oh, you big baby," Courtney crooned at him. "Come out and say hello to Elizabeth."

Pelé climbed slowly onto Charles's shoulder and faced Elizabeth.

"He can hardly see you," said Charles. "They have eight eyes but they're very myopic."

"But he knows you're here," said Courtney reassuringly.

Elizabeth tucked her dress in tightly around her knees. She did this several times in rapid succession. She had stopped clearing her throat now; in fact, she made no sound at all while Charles and Courtney tweaked Pelé's legs, trying to induce him to be more sociable.

"He's really very friendly when he gets to know you," said Courtney. "You're not afraid, are you?"

Elizabeth shook her head jerkily.

"He'll spend a few minutes checking you out," said Charles. "Don't pay any attention to him."

Elizabeth tucked in her dress again. "Tell us about Leonard," said Courtney. "He's...book...tall."

"A book on linguistics. Sounds heavy."

"Yes," Elizabeth exhaled.

"And he's taking the assertiveness-training course. How nice."

Just then, Pelé scampered down the back of Charles's armchair, ran across the carpet, climbed up the wall, and approached the chandelier upside-down, as daintily as a trapeze artist. The chandelier hung nine feet above the coffee table, between Elizabeth and the Van Slykes.

"Oh, God," said Courtney, "he's going to show off."

Pelé detached himself onto the unlit chandelier, which swayed very slightly for a second. He raced around the perimeter, causing the crystal pendants to clink softly against each other.

"He can't resist an audience," Charles groaned.

Pelé continued his circular race, accompanied by a sound resembling wind chimes in a gathering storm. At last he seemed to grow bored and lumbered out of sight into the center of the chandelier. The tinkling died out.

"Do you think it might lead somewhere?" Courtney asked.

"What did you say?" Elizabeth whispered.

"Leonard, I mean."

"Leonard? Oh, yes... no... He says I bottle up my feelings."

"What!" Charles cried.

"I bottle up, repress, you know." Elizabeth shot a glance at the chandelier.

"That's nonsense. You don't bottle up your feelings."

"Well," said Courtney, "I've often felt that she's not assertive enough. Like the time she was on that bus tour and got left in the restroom."

"What's that got to do with assertiveness?"

"She was afraid to ask the driver to wait."

"Rubbish! Everyone's a shrink nowadays."

Soft clinking sounds emerged from the chandelier. Elizabeth's eyes flashed up and down like semaphore lamps.

"Just because someone is quiet doesn't mean they bottle up their feelings," Charles insisted.

"Still," said Courtney, "assertiveness-training will do her good. It's unthinkable that a modem woman... Oh, he's jumping again."

Like an empty parachute, Pelé swooped toward the coffee table, landing clumsily on the fleshy leaves of a jade plant. He scampered onto the glass tabletop, as though about to take a bow. Elizabeth began to pant very rapidly, and some immense pressure appeared to be rising inside her, demanding to be let loose. She screamed long and loud and almost joyously. Never losing her pitch, she vaulted over the sofa, ran out of the room and through the kitchen, and barricaded herself behind the first door she saw. Pelé raced after her, with Charles and Courtney close behind.

"He didn't mean to scare you," Charles called. "He was just doing his jungle thing."

Elizabeth had fled behind the door to the cellar. Courtney tried to open it, but Elizabeth was pulling with long untapped reserves of strength.

"Please open it, Elizabeth. He's feeling awfully hurt."

"HELP!" Elizabeth screamed. "OH PLEASE HELP!"

Suddenly the doorknob popped out, and she tumbled backward down the stairs. She managed to grab the railing half way to the bottom, but now she was horrified by a new discovery. You remember, it had been raining in torrents the whole week. The Van Slykes' cellar, unknown to them, contained over three feet of water. In addition to the water, an utterly nauseating odor filled the darkness, as if the sealed remains of a hundred photophobes had been flushed out.

Courtney opened the door and gagged: "Oh, God, it's vile!" She staggered away. Charles put a handkerchief to his nose, flipped on the light, and stared in disbelief. Pelé, perhaps thinking it was bedtime, crept down a few stairs and stopped short. Something was clearly wrong.

So this was the picture: Elizabeth was near the bottom of the stairs with the noxious pool at her rear; Charles and Courtney were at the top, yelping and thrashing in a feckless tizzy; and Pelé was perched on the edge of a stair half way between, feeling out blindly in all directions.

Elizabeth gripped the railing with one hand and pressed the other against the plaster wall. She closed her eyes, tilted her head back, and began to mouth some incantation. The Van Slykes couldn't hear, but it must have been something she learned in one of her courses. Positive thinking, maybe, or productive prayer. While she was silently murmuring, Pelé crawled up the wall and hoisted himself onto the railing.

"Elizabeth..." Courtney squeaked.

When Elizabeth opened her eyes, Pelé was no longer before her, and for an instant she was relieved. Then she felt a hairy tickle on her hand. She let out another piercing scream and somehow, in jerking back her hand, flung the poor creature into the swamp. She leaped up the steps, plowed through the Van Slykes like a fullback, and fled into the parlor. She was totally insensate. "You're out of your flipping tree! You ought to be locked up! You're a bloody menace!" She glared around wildly at the glass menagerie, as if the swans and alligators might spring to life.

In the kitchen Courtney was sobbing. "Pelé! Oh, Charles, he's drowning. Do something!"

But Charles wouldn't budge. The stench from the cellar was overpowering. Suddenly he and Courtney must have had the same thought, and they rushed to the front door just ahead of Elizabeth. They looked at her accusingly.

"You've murdered him," Courtney rasped.

"He only wanted to be friendly," muttered Charles.

Elizabeth looked from one to the other. She tried to speak, but the words would not come. She began to shake. Her breathing soared to a crescendo.

"Out of my way!" she bellowed.

Shoving them aside, she stalked toward the cellar, plunged down the stairs, pulled off her shoes at the water line, and waded into the morass. "Lunatics! Psychotics! Belong in a Transylvanian booby hatch!" She was up to her hips, churning through the dim cavern. Wood and paper debris floated around her. A variety of balls and Charles's fishing hat were bobbing up and down. Finally she spotted Pelé. The poor thing was exhausted; trying to find his soccer ball, they guessed.

Elizabeth approached warily, making absolutely certain he had stopped moving. The soccer ball happened to float by, and she lifted him up with it. Then she made her way back with the ball at arm's length. Dripping a plague, she squeezed into her shoes and tramped up the steps. Pelé was draped over the ball like boiled spinach.

"Here!" She thrust the ball at the Van Slykes. "Give him mouth-to-mouth, you bloody perverts!" She slipped and stumbled through the parqueted dining room and stormed out the front door.

Pelé thank heaven, survived. Charles's swift application of a hair dryer and Courtney's diligent, if anxious, massage brought him around in a few minutes. He remained disoriented for some time, though, unable to stand on all eight legs. The Van Slykes kept a vigil well into the night, Charles cradling him in his hands and Courtney fondling his abdomen. By morning he had fully recovered.

The only lasting effect seemed to be his fear of the cellar. Even after they had it pumped out and fumigated, they still couldn't get him down there. Whenever they opened the door, he'd race off to the parlor and hide in one of the urns. Since Yodel couldn't sleep with him around, they finally took Pelé upstairs to their own bedroom and let him settle in at the foot of their bed. He made the adjustment nicely and, as far as we can tell, he's slept there ever since.

THE LAST ORDEAL OF JAMES WILLOUGHBY

Opinions differed about James Willoughby. To some he was a brilliant naturalist, a meticulous observer of plants and animals in the Great Smoky Mountains. He discovered more species of salamanders than all his contemporaries combined. He published studies on the hibernation behavior of bats, the life cycles of aquatic insects, and the recovery of ramp (a.k.a. wild leek) populations. His works were required reading in advanced biology courses.

But to those who had actually met him, Willoughby was a hopeless fruitcake. He showed up at conferences in tattered denim and mud-caked hiking boots. He was often heard talking to himself, even debating himself. Though physically attractive and robust, he was socially awkward, sometimes ducking behind doors to avoid his colleagues. He had no friends or family and spent most of his time in the woods, as far from humanity as he could get.

Probably because of his odd behavior, doubts about his scientific credibility arose in certain quarters. Attempts to reproduce his work yielded inconclusive results. There was talk of a committee to investigate his research. Then one day, as if to escape his detractors, he set out on a mountain trail and never returned.

Willoughby remained in oblivion for over a decade. His name suddenly resurfaced when some hikers discovered an uninhabited cave in a remote area of the Smokies and found a stack of mildewed notebooks marked J.W. The hikers spent two days reading. Then, astonished and confused, they emptied their backpacks, crammed in the notebooks, scrambled down the mountain, and headed to the nearest police station. Soon the old controversies about James Willoughby were reignited.

The fate of Willoughby himself remains unknown, although many who have studied his strange legacy have formed their own opinions. A condensation of the events he recorded is presented here.

FROM THE JOURNALS OF JAMES WILLOUGHBY

May 22---Cataloguing saprophytes at the higher elevations

This morning I had the most astounding encounter of my life. It occurred on the periphery of a heath bald (elev. approx. 5000 ft.). I had awakened just before dawn and emerged from my tent into a silken mist. Falling away behind me was the chattering spruce forest; ahead lay the most formidable bald I have ever seen---no trees anywhere, their places taken by a towering, impenetrable jungle of steel-branched rhododendron and laurel, wrapping the mountain peak like a hood.

Movement in a rhododendron bush caught my eye. Some animal, about the size of a young child, seemed to be nestled in a matrix of long, shiny leaves and pink blooms. Thinking it to be a cat or a bear cub, I kept still as the mist began its gradual rise. Now I thought my eyes were playing tricks. Reclining lazily within the twisted branches was a naked, motley-colored, flaccid, misshapen creature, entirely beyond my experience or imagination. It seemed perfectly content as it chewed on a cluster of petals. I crept closer. A breeze rolling over the mountain brought me a fragrant, patchouli-like aroma, evidently ascribable to the unnatural being.

It sat there like a large, fat toddler fascinated with a colorful plaything. Its squat head seemed to have partly melted into a puddle of jowls. Two peaceful, lidless eyes and two gnarled structures, possibly ears, adorned its forehead, but I saw neither nose nor hair. Teeth and tongue revealed themselves when the creature's jaw descended in an apparent yawn.

Its two arms and two legs were roughly humanoid in shape but possessed a startling elasticity. The arms stretched out leisurely to half-again their length and dainty fingers picked off flowers, while the flabby torso never moved. The color of the creature's skin varied from albino white above the chest to beige in the mid-section to a deep orange in the lower extremities. The texture of its skin brought to mind a plucked chicken.

This was clearly no terrestrial form of life. I had stumbled upon a dwarfish, aromatic alien.

Protruding from its chest was a most peculiar appendage, attached at its center and resembling an upside-down conch. At first I took it for an ornament because of its metallic sheen, but when the creature batted it idly, it twirled like a lopsided propeller. I saw that it was actually a body part. Its purpose eluded me completely.

I kept watch throughout the morning. Shortly after noon, a second alien, an exact copy of the first, crawled out of the dense foliage. The two of them babbled fervently in a language as inscrutable as the voices of an aviary. Their fragrant aroma intensified. I sensed that they were happy to see each other. After yielding its place in the bush, the first creature disappeared into the thicket. The second arranged itself in their snug little alcove and began chewing a pink blossom. Had I not witnessed the exchange, I would never have guessed it had taken place.

Who are these sweet-smelling Lilliputians and how many inhabit the bald? I saw no more though I watched until dark.

June 5:

After two weeks I have learned a few things about the aliens. First, they station themselves at regular intervals around the bald. In a single day I have counted forty-four. There may be a whole population deep within the bushes. Second, I can now see small variations in their anatomy, reminiscent of the slight differences one finds in identical twins. Could they all be from the same brood? Or have they achieved a remarkable degree of genetic control?

Their skin, which is always fully exposed, seems to be their olfactory organ. Their fragrant scent arises from the shiny appendage on their breast. I would love to examine this conch-shaped organ more closely. If it hasn't a role in mating, I cannot imagine a use for it.

I am still probing for access to the heart of the bald. The massive interwoven shrubs refuse to be violated. After a few yards of pulling, squeezing, and twisting, I am too exhausted to go on. If only I could transform myself into one of these wee elastic creatures.

August 10:

Today I finally penetrated to the center of the bald---the fruit of two months of excruciating labor. I have carved out an above-ground tunnel beneath the lowest branches. Access is still difficult, but assured. And my efforts were richly rewarded.

A whole colony of them dwells on a grassy field, the last shrub-free half-acre of the original bald. Approximately two hundred aliens were there; an exact count was impossible. I could not tell differences in gender, but there was a range of sizes: infants and children seemed to be present. Scattered about the field were numerous ceramic-like fragments. I am only guessing but they could be the remains of the vehicle that brought these creatures here.

I found the aliens in a state of extreme torpor. They lay supine in the shade of bushes and hardly stirred. The heat and drought must torment them. Their skin looked dry and scaly, and their limbs had lost their amazing elasticity. Even when I approached within arm's length they were too lethargic to respond.

A new scent---much like hickory smoke---emanated from their breasts. Inhaling this essence, I felt an overwhelming thirst myself. A single urgent thought possessed me.

Returning to my campsite, I took my canteen and stewpot down to the spring, filled them with water, and struggled back up the hill. I crawled through my tunnel and quietly set the pot beside one heat-stricken creature. When he lunged for it, the pot overturned. He vainly tried to save the water, finally burying his jowly face in the sedge and emitting agonized yelps. I hurried back to the spring, refilled the pot, and this time managed to pour some of the water over his parched body. Judging from the sounds he made, it gave him enormous relief.

I went down and up the hill all day fetching water. As word spread throughout the colony, they all dragged themselves across the field for refreshment. By evening they were able to walk and chatter. I tried to communicate with them, but they responded neither to words nor to gestures. When I touched one of them, the whole crowd waddled in terror into the bushes.

They allow me to penetrate their fortress, accept my aid, then shun my attempts to befriend them. They react as instinctively as animals, yet their intelligence cannot be doubted. Have these creatures traveled light years only to keep aloof? Why won't they trust me?

I've lost my canteen, probably in the tunnel. If it doesn't turn up tomorrow, I'll have to buy another one in town, which means six days wasted. Best to save that errand for the future.

August 20:

Flowers and leaves are their food of choice. They also like beetles, which are slow enough for them to catch. They eat partridgeberries and mushrooms if I set them out. So far I have detected no waste products; their metabolic systems must be extremely efficient.

They use fragments of their spaceship(?) as bowls to collect rain. They bathe two or three times a day, apparently out of urgent necessity.

The children spar and roll in the grass. The adults spend most of their time in the bushes, idly chewing leaves or playing some kind of game with rocks and ceramic chips. Occasionally two adults will separate from the larger group and perform a fascinating dance in which their bodies elongate, intertwine, and quiver amid bursts of squealing and twittering. A strong lilac scent billows up from their breast organs. If I am close enough to inhale it, the most pleasant sensations permeate my body.

October 26:

Since finding the colony I have been troubled by bouts of vertigo. These occur every ten days or so and always catch me unprepared. To avoid fainting I must sit on the ground and focus my eyes intently on an object. Minutes later the ordeal ends, leaving me shaken and confused.

Today I experienced such an attack. Had it not delayed me, I might have prevented a catastrophe, which I shall describe here.

Every day I patrol the entire perimeter of the bald. My rounds begin at dawn and end in mid-afternoon. Having checked all the alien sentries, I crawl through my tunnel to the edge of the field. I spy on the colony until convinced that no new disasters---like last month's incident with the hawk and the infant---have befallen them.

This morning, on the north trail, I began to feel dizzy and immediately lowered myself to the ground. I tried unsuccessfully to focus on something. The distant hills became a spinning blur of autumn color. I lost consciousness. Ten minutes later I awoke, still dazed and wondering what was happening to me.

When I reached the 38th sentry, he was enjoying a catnap, as they frequently do in their tedious posts. Suddenly he snapped awake, and a searing ammoniacal odor filled the air. A volley of angry barking erupted in the woods. I saw that a poacher and his dog had ascended to the edge of the trees and positioned themselves a few yards in front of the alien. The man leveled a shotgun from behind a spruce tree.

Jolted from my own worries, I hurled myself at the protruding gun barrel. The astonished poacher struggled with me for the weapon. It discharged between us with a blast that slammed us both to the ground. We faced each other in a moment of shock and paralysis. With my ragged hair and the hellfire that must have burned in my eyes, I was surely the very portrait of madness. The man scrambled to his feet and fled back through the woods with his dog. I pursued them down the steep slope although in my state of wild alarm I had no idea what to do with them. That issue was abruptly taken out of my hands. They both tumbled onto an outcropping of rock and slid off into bottomless space. The man's scream of terror froze my heart.

Back on the bald I saw that the alien was gone. The shotgun was nowhere in sight. A trail of milky fluid, resembling the hemolymph of an insect and smelling like ammonia led into the bushes. Nearby I found the shiny scent-organ, ripped from the little one's breast by the buckshot. More of the noisome fluid seeped from its mangled wound. This organ is a remarkable composite. Though it gleams like polished steel, it is more porous and elastic than human flesh. I have preserved it in an airtight plastic container.

The incident with the poacher must not be repeated. I'm not sorry for the man; his kind brings wanton violence to the mountains. I grieve for the helpless sentry, lying dead somewhere or in mortal agony. Here and now I swear an oath to protect the colony from further harm.

November 28:

I have learned how they overwinter. They hibernate in parts of their spaceship, which they cover with mounds of earth and dead leaves. They erect these mounds beneath the bushes.

I myself will spend the winter in an abandoned bat cave on the south face. When the snows come, I must be available if needed.

December 31:

I have developed a theory about the aliens. Their ancestors landed here at least two centuries ago, and the blasts from their ships destroyed the trees on several peaks. Thus were created the balds, which are known to be that old but whose origin has always been a mystery. Survivors of the journey and the landing joined up in the forest. There they lived for years, encountering the Cherokee and the early settlers with results as violent as human nature. (What a shame that we humans, who should be their greeters and hosts, student and teachers, ambassadors of our planet, are feared and distrusted by them.) As new shrubbery covered the balds, the little ones retreated to these safe havens. In all my explorations I have never found signs of these creatures elsewhere. This may be the last surviving colony.

They still face many dangers. When their skin dries out, they become vulnerable to insects. Flies and mosquitoes feast on their white upper bodies, leaving painful blue welts. Every day of summer I must check their rain bowls. I don't know how to protect the children from birds of prey (two infants carried off). And of course there is always the threat of human intrusion. The sound of an airplane causes them no alarm; I have to scare them into the bushes. This problem concerns me greatly.

Did this colony choose to remain on Earth or were they stranded by their brothers? Are they scouts for a larger invasion? What happened to their tools and weapons? Surely a race that achieved space travel must have possessed technological wonders; yet these creatures cannot even produce fire. I think their earthly stay, their confinement on the bald, and possibly inbreeding have caused their minds and bodies to deteriorate over the centuries. Only their scent-organs, marvelous broadcasters of their emotions, remain healthy.

They rebuff all my attempts to communicate. My fellow humans would likely be offended by such discourtesy and treat them as unwelcome immigrants. Cruel men would be spurred on to savagery by their awkwardness and timidity. I must shield the little ones from these perils.

Second Year

January 6:

Another day of light snow. I made it through the tunnel and found their winter cocoons undisturbed. Even their slight movements have ceased. I cannot tell if they're alive, but I maintain hope. I must hike to the cave while the trails are still open.

January 8:

Heavy snow. I cannot leave the cave. Thank God I have plenty of food and firewood. I spent the day reading Muir and Thoreau. The snowy vista is breathtaking. I hope that someday the little ones can appreciate the beauty of this planet.

I had intended to add some poems to my chapbook, but it's gone. It must be lying under snow at the campsite. A pity, for the mountains and my ruminations on the colony inspire me.

(The chapbook, canteen, Swiss Army knife, cans of food---all missing in the last six months. I must keep better track of my things.)

The dizzy spells are milder and less frequent now. My head is clear. The pure, icy air restores my health and invigorates me. But I sorely miss the fragrance of my little ones.

April3:

They are stirring! The first sleepyheads have risen from their long winter nap and are nibbling dandelions and buttercups. I made sure their rain bowls were full.

Apri 10:

I counted as carefully as possible: 206. All but four survived. I rejoice!
I anoint myself with their essence.

June 20:

Another baby was killed by a hawk. I didn't see it happen but the bird
must have dropped the child from the air. The grieving mother bleated and
slapped the ground as she clutched the gored remains. Her agony lasted all
day and into the night. Eventually several of them dug a hole, buried the
child, and crowded around the mother. The whole colony gazed up at the
midnight sky and gabbled a somber chant that rose and fell discordantly
for over an hour. Though it was gibberish to my ears, I imagined they were
singing about a homeland that had only become a legend.

As they mourned, a piney smell arose from their congregation and
spread above the field. When it reached my nostrils, a heavy sorrow weighed
upon my heart and sapped all my energy. Later, quite bemused and listless,
I made my exit. Their effusions overpower me like an addiction. They may
be causing my dizzy spells. When I inhale these aromas, I feel emotionally
bonded to the colony. Their problems become my obsessions. It has always
been my rule to observe the natural world without influencing it; now I
cannot resist the impulse to intervene. When the little ones need me, I
hasten to their rescue.

July 17:

Today I used my hatchet to cut two slender trees near the bald. Hard
work. I dragged them uphill and, one by one, maneuvered them through
the tunnel. I am determined to build shelters for the children. If they can
learn to play inside them, they should be less vulnerable to the birds. I
plan to add three or four trees per day.

August 7:

A setback. While cutting I was overcome by dizziness. I twisted my
ankle and fell into a chasm, where I lay unconscious for an hour or so.

My vision is still blurred, and it is hard to write. I will have to pace myself more intelligently.

August 8:

Better today except for my ankle, which is sore and will not support my weight. One tree harvested, but I couldn't get it uphill. My little ones are okay.

August 22:

Four trees today. I must go further downhill to find the right size. Another dizzy spell, just before supper, and I couldn't eat anything.

October 10:

First shelter finished. It is simply a log roof supported on several clusters of logs. I camouflaged it with rhododendron branches. As soon as I withdrew, they all waddled out from the bushes to investigate. They chattered and squealed, and the children tussled playfully under the roof. I think they understand its purpose. I tried again to communicate but was totally ignored.

December 6:

I took a chance and left them during their hibernation period. I descended the mountain and rode a bus to the library in Raleigh. Several books on Appalachian history contained anecdotes about goblins and strange woodland odors. To uninformed persons this would be typical mountain folklore, but I am sure it supports my theories.

While in town I had a close call. A spell of vertigo, the worst yet, hit me and I passed out. I woke up on a gurney in an emergency room. A doctor and an ambulance driver were talking about me. The doctor asked me questions but I didn't answer. They're not to be trusted. They'd find a way to keep me down and helpless.

My head was throbbing. The doctor probed around my skull, shined a light in my eyes and ears, then went to get someone else. The driver followed him out. I forced myself onto my feet and staggered out of the hospital. Somehow I found my way to the bus station.

I will never abandon my darlings.

Third Year

July 8:

My health continues to ebb. The vertigo leaves me clammy and nauseous, with headaches and double vision. I have no appetite and am nothing but skin and bones. Some days I can hardly move. Yet I do not falter when the little ones need me. I've built them shelters, maintained their water supply during drought, found netting to stop the insects, caught trout in the vain hope of strengthening their bodies with protein. I've guarded their beds in winter and scattered their sentries whenever a poacher or hiker ventured too close. Today another crisis befell the colony. The outcome is still in doubt.

This afternoon they were all in the field. The children were tumbling in and out of the shelters. Suddenly I heard distant engines. The airplane from the south has become a regular menace. It flies over the bald on alternate weeks. Every time it passes I must shoo my angels under cover.

I leaped into the open, shouting and waving my arms. Fleeing from my commotion, one group waddled toward the corner abutting the precipice. A nest of wasps awaited them. The angry villains shot out of the ground and hailed down upon my little ones, mutilating their torsos into purple, suppurating lumps. Fifty victims bleated and writhed in the grass. The ammoniacal stench---their alarm bell---flooded the air. I hobbled across the field, flung netting over them, and took the wrath of the wasps upon myself. My face and arms accumulated a dozen painful stings. The swarming devils chased me back to the tunnel, where I finally eluded them.

Ignoring my own distress, I crawled through and lurched down to the spring. A patch of bee balm grows there. I stuffed the minty weeds into my shirt and pants, clawed my way uphill, and struggled back to the field. For hours I applied poultices to my suffering dear ones. It was futile. All fifty of them died in hideous torment.

I wept and shouted my rage: "Why did this happen? I only wanted to protect them. They cannot survive without me."

Ten yards away the colony gathered to watch. I heard an under current of gurgling voices. Their expressions never change, and I couldn't assess their reactions. I smelled nothing, as if their scent-organs were being suppressed to hide their feelings. Exhausted and ill, I stumbled through them. They retreated before my step, then followed me as far as the tunnel.

"Do you understand what I've done for you?" I cried. "I am your savior!"

They only stared. Their faces remained immobile. Not a trace of odor came my way.

July 12:

Today was the first time in four days that I've seen the colony. The disaster with the wasps left me sick at heart as well as in body. I could not stand on my feet. The vertigo would not abate.

This morning I felt well enough to negotiate the tunnel. They have buried the dead, probably at night to escape the wasps. I noticed freshly turned earth near the precipice.

Within the burial ground is a flat, table-sized surface of rock, which I had overlooked until now. It is surrounded by laurel and is safely removed from the wasp nest. There I was surprised to find all the articles I have missed over the years---my canteen, Swiss Army knife, magnifying glass, wool socks, many open and rusted food cans. My chapbook was there with half its pages torn out. A shotgun, most likely the poacher's, had been dissected.

In addition there were tools and implements which looked like relics from the pioneer days, along with Indian arrows and beaded jewelry. Although this discovery supports my theories, it left me mortified. I had forgotten that the little ones are intelligent beings. They have been studying me while I, in my egregious vanity, believed I was studying them. They and their ancestors have been gathering data on humans for perhaps two centuries.

As I sifted through their cache, lidless eyes stared out from the bushes. I heard no sound, caught no scent. They were all around me.

One of them waddled into view, making low, rasping sounds. He held the round edge of his scent-organ, and for some reason this made me think: The time has come. Now we will communicate.

I sat on my haunches. He began to chant the mournful gibberish which I have heard on sad occasions. The others took up the chorus, too. They all stepped out of the bushes, and I was completely surrounded by tremors of sound, escalating to a crescendo. Their leader pointed the tapered end of his scent-organ at me. A jet of liquid shot into my face. I fell backward, blinded, and began coughing and fighting for breath. I thought the caustic oil would dissolve my eyes and lungs. They kept up their dreadful chant as I rolled witlessly on the ground. Then they quit. I could hardly see and I had to strain for every breath. The little ones had disappeared into the bushes. I got to my feet and made for the tunnel.

I have no idea what day it is. My life is ebbing away. When I returned to the colony, they rushed at me, pointing their scent-organs, and I had to flee. They still blame me for the wasp attack. Even after my long devotion to their community, they won't accept me back. I am crushed. I don't want to live. But if I must die on this evil mountain, I will not die alone.

Thus ended Willoughby's journals. Unfortunately they gave no hint about the location of his mountain. Many adventurous souls have searched for it without conclusive results. One hiking party did find some clues, but its members disagreed about their significance. They found ceramic fragments on what might have been a heath bald. The site had been ravaged by fire, and the verdure was in various stages of recovery. One fellow ventured that Willoughby, in his half blind, vengeful state, had cremated the aliens and possibly immolated himself at the same time. He insisted that the ceramic shards supported Willoughby's account. But another man argued that lightning fires were well-documented in the Smokies, and no remains of any creature, let alone aliens, had been discovered. Also, if the aliens had stolen Willoughby's equipment---and even his book of poems---why hadn't they taken his journals?

Questions persisted. What if the aliens had escaped the fire and fled to other parts of the wilderness? What if Willoughby's eccentric mind had finally snapped and he'd created a colossal fantasy? The vertigo that plagued him may have been a symptom of his madness. Or was it a symptom of his addiction to the alien scents?

Local historians and naturalists still tell the story of James Willoughby around campfires. They speak of the marvelous scent-organ, supposedly preserved by Willoughby, as if it were the Holy Grail. Hardy adventurers have scoured the hills for it, or for any definitive answers. But the ancient mists of the Great Smoky Mountains know how to keep their secrets.

THE PASSAGE

On September 10, 1993 Raymond P. Walcott, a fertilizer salesman who had once been a mid-level executive, was struck by lightning near his home in Detroit. A curious crowd gathered around him as soon as the rain stopped. Nobody knew quite what to do, and one woman suggested it might be dangerous to touch an electrocuted person. A pre-med student and a nurse's aide did manage to examine him, at least, before an ambulance took him away.

That evening, the student visited Raymond in the hospital. Lucinda, Raymond's wife of twenty-two years, was also present.

"Boy! I'd have sworn you bought it," the student recalled. "You had no pulse and your eyeballs were rolled back. The aide stuck a mirror under your nose---nothing. One joker said to forget 911 and call a priest."

"But he survived," Lucinda said, patting her husband's pale hand. He came back from the dead."

After the student left, Raymond told her to shut the door and come closer. "What you said," he whispered. "Do you think it could happen? Coming back from the dead, I mean."

"Well, I don't know," she said, a little puzzled. "A lot of people are talking about it nowadays."

"I think I did it."

"Oh, Raymond, really..."

"I'm serious. You heard the guy. Those people were positive I was dead. Maybe I was. Ever since I woke up I've been remembering things that went through my head. It was fantastic!"

"What went through your head? When?"

"When I was lying there, dead or whatever. I remember light, the brightest light I ever saw, all colors of the rainbow. And music, the most beautiful music, lifting me up in a kind of spiral and filling me with peace and hope. All through it I felt close to some great loving power. I couldn't see it, but it guided me toward a long upward passage, where I was going to be cleansed or prepared in some way. I trusted the power to lead me safely through it. I was absolutely sure that everlasting joy was waiting on the other side, but then... I came back."

Lucinda listened with growing enthusiasm as Raymond described the experience again and again. She asked many questions, and each time he was able to refine certain details and add others. The inspirational music, for example, ranged beyond the capacities of earthly strings and winds. And the mysterious passageway evolved into a fragrant trail, canopied with flowers, where Raymond heard encouraging voices and felt the embrace of unseen arms. Then he remembered seeing a face---was it his grandfather? The vision had lasted only a moment. Yes, he decided, it was his grandfather, and the old man greeted him with a "Hiya, tiger!" as he had in life. With Lucinda prodding him, Raymond searched his memory, and his recollections grew like a jigsaw puzzle.

At home Lucinda filled up a notepad with her husband's account. When Raymond was released the next day, she told him about her terrific idea.

"You must share this experience with the world," she said. "You've got to write a book."

"I was thinking the same thing," he said, "but a book? How can I write a book?"

"Of course you can. I took down everything you told me, so you wouldn't forget."

"Actually I've remembered even more."

They enlisted the help of an unemployed freelance writer, who cackled and chain smoked as he hunched over his keyboard. In three months they completed "The Ecstasy Without the Agony." A publisher snapped it up, and it sold 100,000 copies almost overnight. The book jacket asserted that a young doctor, a registered nurse, and a priest had witnessed not just the near death, but the clinical death, of Raymond P. Walcott. The publisher promised that Raymond had experienced more than vague sensations and predictable dreams; he would astonish the reader with his journey through the most vivid and exalting sights and sounds.

To give perspective to the extraordinary event, Raymond (that is, his ghost writer) devoted the opening chapters to an autobiography. He showed how numerous incidents, which had once convinced him of his "hopeless addiction to reckless impulses," were actually "guideposts on his strenuous, if unwitting, voyage toward that shattering bolt of enlightenment." He discussed, among other things, his childhood experiment with firecrackers in his mother's ceramic vases, his bout with dementia after swallowing hallucinogens in college, and his brief infatuation with a shaman, who ran off with his life savings. Even his short-lived rise up the corporate ladder, followed by the sudden removal of the ladder after his disastrous business initiatives, loomed as a milestone on his path of destiny. "If I have learned one thing from life," he wrote at the end of chapter five, "it is that failure and success are both relative, intertwined, and ultimately but an overture to the grand operatic triumph awaiting us."

"That's brilliant!" Lucinda gushed.

"You don't think it's overstated?"

"Certainly not. It's exactly what people want to hear."

Raymond went on the talk-show circuit, and then speaking invitations began flowing in. He joyously quit his job at the fertilizer factory and traveled with Lucinda all over the country. In city after city they found auditoriums packed with breathless admirers.

They upgraded their lifestyle in different ways. A couple of nice shirts and a new car satisfied Raymond, who sometimes worried about the jinx of overconfidence. Lucinda, less impeded by such concerns, bought four complete wardrobes at Bergdorf's and jewelry at Tiffany's. She fell in love with an exquisite diamond brooch and wore it everywhere because, as she explained to Raymond, "people relate to symbols." Unable to staunch the flow of money, they eventually purchased a large home in fashionable Grosse Pointe and two similar vacation homes on the Upper Peninsula and the Florida coast. Raymond overcame his superstitions and bought a European sports car. They donated a sizeable sum to a California school involved in psychic research.

Soon, however, a rash of imitators sprouted up. A stockyard worker in Chicago claimed to have fallen into a vat of lard and seen the twelve apostles. Two elderly spinsters in Kansas were swept away by a tornado and heard a choir of angels led by Archangel Michael himself. The Walcotts never commented publicly on these reports except to suggest that people exercise caution, as a rule, in what they believe.

To keep ahead of the competition, Lucinda made plans to produce a video. Actors young and middle-aged auditioned to play Raymond in different phases of his life. A special effects team was brought in. A composer provided a score, and musicians were hired to play real instruments. ("Not those tacky synthesizers," Lucinda insisted.) It worked. The video, at $39.95 plus shipping, topped the charts and established the Walcotts' preeminence in the field.

But eventually the competition came snapping at their heels again. The "lord of lard," as the Walcotts called him, paid a football star introduce his video. The "twister sisters" created a website. The Walcotts' speaking invitations fell off, and their names began to fade from the public eye.

"There's only one thing to do," Lucinda decided. "We need a fresh new experience."

"Like what?" Raymond muttered as he polished the hubcaps on his Ferrari.

"Let's put our minds to it." Lucinda strolled out to the rolling lawn behind their house. Soon she came running back.

"I've got it!" she cried. "Lightning will strike you again. We'll have a sequel, but this time you'll go through the passage to the other side. I mean, if you can, of course."

"Are you crazy?"

"No! It can't miss."

"Even if I could do it, who would believe it?"

"They'll believe the miracle of it. Don't you see?"

"But what if...?"

"Quit worrying. You'll be fine. And they're predicting thunderstorms for tomorrow."

The next day, Raymond stood on his vast lawn as the sky blackened and the first raindrops tickled his neck. He bowed his head and shut his eyes tight.

"Lord, help me to remember what it was like. I know that something incredible happened. It must have. I'm not smart enough to make it up."

His eyes popped open as thunder rumbled across the boiling sky. He turned toward a grove of fruit trees, where Lucinda, in a yellow slicker, watched him through the viewfinder of a video camera.

"If I've changed a few details," he prayed softly, "my intention was not to deceive, but only to overcome people's instinctive doubts, excite their imagination, and guide them toward belief. The world turns on salesmanship, you know."

A terrible crash of thunder shook his bowels. Lightning zigzaged hotly, and rain battered his shoulders.

"Hang in there!" Lucinda shouted.

"It's not working. Let's forget it."

"We can't. Too many people are depending on us. If they stop believing in you, it's back to selling fertilizer."

Raymond groaned. Another bone-rattling thunderclap made him yelp. He was drenched now, and the lawn around him had become a roaring lake.

"Try not to slouch," Lucinda cried.

"Dear Lord," Raymond prayed, "I know you're out there. I know you might not be completely pleased with our crusade. But how many thousands have come into your fold since we started..."

Lightning struck a fencepost to Raymond's left. Sparks flew up wrathfully, and the air smelled like a doused campfire. The next blast of thunder knocked him to his knees. He thrashed wildly toward Lucinda, but just before he reached her flowered sanctuary, the whole earth seemed to burst into flame. Raymond slipped, smacked his chin on the ground, and was momentarily disoriented. When he recovered himself, he groped his way to his wife, who lay face-down in four inches of water. Diamonds from her brooch formed a halo around her head.

"Lucinda, can you hear me?" he cried. "Are you in the passage?"

PUBLISH OR PERISH

Professor Edward Sutherland arrived at Barlowe Hall in a testy mood. Having lugged a briefcase full of books, lecture notes, and exam papers the entire length of the hilly campus and having accelerated his pace when he realized it was already past 8:00 a.m., he burst into the old brick building in a panting, sweaty state and pushed his way through a few student stragglers into the lecture hall. Wheezing, he bustled down the aisle to the front of the room. One hundred students suppressed laughter as they looked down at him, and he was keenly aware of his paunchy, bald figure and dripping red face, so unseemly in a domain of youth and fitness. For a moment he imagined they were about to pass judgment on him instead of the other way around.

Without delay he opened his briefcase and handed out stacks of exams. Their distribution took ten minutes; it was almost 8:15.

"You may ignore the last question," he announced, "or if you can work it in, I'll count it as extra credit."

Feeling absolved, he drew a deep breath and inserted his heavy body into a writing chair beside the demonstration table. He wiped his face with a soiled handkerchief and loosened his tie. His head throbbed painfully. He cursed the invisible powers who scheduled a microbiology class at the farthest possible distance from the Biological Sciences building.

He rubbed his aching eyes. Never again! he vowed. This time I mean it. I'll never take another drink.

He watched the students as they scribbled busily and strained to recall their lessons. Four weeks into the spring quarter and he knew none of them by name. That was the way with these large undergraduate courses. Their anonymity made him feel foolish, as if his efforts counted for nothing. Three times a week, as he lectured before this faceless audience, he thought he might as well be talking to the fish in the sea. On the other hand, after June he'd never see any of these kids again, so why bother learning their names?

A young woman in the front row stood up, tossed her hair back, and approached him with her test paper. Here we go, he thought.

"When you say 'Describe the Euglena,' do you want a picture or just words?"

"Whatever you think appropriate," he replied with a thin smile.

"Should we mention its photosynthetic ability?"

"Only if it applies."

She gave him a look and went to her seat. He understood their tricks. He was happy to add to her confusion.

No sooner had she sat down than a big dour fellow in shabby denim tramped down the aisle. He tossed his paper onto the writing arm of Sutherland's chair.

"In number three," he mumbled, "do you mean classes of virus like animal and bacterial or like pox and herpes and stuff like that?"

"It says 'general categories."

The fellow scrutinized the exam paper. "Oh, yeah," he said, and climbed back to his seat.

Sutherland sighed. "Stuff like that." Even after ten years of disillusionment and decline, the irreverence of "stuff like that" infuriated him. Couldn't they show a little respect for a hundred years of brilliant human achievement even if they viewed as a laughing stock? He hated this course. They stuck you with it when they figured you were washed up.

Halfway through the hour, Sutherland's gaze fell upon a very beautiful woman several rows up. She seemed a bit older than the others, and her appearance was strikingly different. In a tide of denims and preppy knits she wore a white, calf-length dress and a long beaded necklace. Her lips were painted dark red and her black hair was short and gracefully marcelled. Sutherland, who was not a keen observer of feminine fashion, was nevertheless reminded of old family photographs of his mother and aunts. He wondered how she could have escaped his attention this long.

As he watched he noticed that she was copying answers from the fellow beside her, who was either unaware or indifferent. Sutherland could easily see the movement of her eyes as they swung left, gathered in their harvest, and transported it to her own paper. He saw her do this several times.

Suddenly she glanced up and their eyes met. She was obviously shaken. Then, recovering quickly, she pretended to be deep in thought. But she continued to peer down at him, warily at first, then disdainfully.

The last thing Sutherland wanted was trouble. If I accuse her, he thought, she'll deny it and make a scene. He pretended to interest himself in various objects around the room. Now and then he peeked at her.

God! She's pretty, he thought.

She stood up, collected her books, and descended toward the demonstration table. He massaged his eyes to avoid looking at her. Opening them a few seconds later, he was startled to find her gone. Her exam paper lay on the table.

How did she leave so fast? he wondered. She couldn't possibly have returned up the aisle. The side doors? They would have made sounds. Must have had a mental lapse, he decided.

He read the name on her paper: Donna Lapurge. She had finished less than half the test.

At the end of the hour Sutherland packed the papers into his briefcase and began the long trek across campus. On the way he passed Mirror Pond, a little man-made body of water in the midst of a neatly landscaped garden. This was a place where students and faculty members came in the afternoon to relax and meditate and chat on the high-backed stone benches. The shrubs and trees were in their first April growth. The day was sunny and already heating up. Across the pond Donna Lapurge huddled by herself in the comer of a stone bench. Her knuckles were pressed into her cheeks, and she stared intently at the water. Sutherland observed her just long enough to form an impression that something weightier than a poor exam grade afflicted her.

Reaching his laboratory in the Biological Sciences building, Sutherland inadvertently banged his briefcase against a cart of flasks in the corridor. The sterilized liquids sloshed around, and he had to catch some pipets before they rolled off. His clumsiness caused two passing graduate students to snicker. As they turned the comer, one of them said something and they both laughed. Sutherland heard the words "off the wagon" and guessed that the fellow had made a pun linking the flask cart with their favorite item of gossip---his drinking problem. He shook his fist after them. The years of such disrespect had still not inured him to it.

He walked through his laboratory to the tiny adjoining office and locked up the exam papers. The latest issue of the Journal of Bacteriology lay on his desk. He opened it, found an article that sounded interesting, and read the first paragraph. With a yawn he placed the journal on a shelf

"I'll read it this afternoon," he told himself.

He gazed out at his laboratory. The work benches stood fallow, the incubator cold and dry. A layer of dust coated the jars of chemicals and plastic microscope covers.

Facing him was an old poster of a bikini-clad model emerging from the ocean. His last graduate student had left it behind. The eyes of the proud, sinewy temptress glared sideways at him. The corner of her mouth curled up mockingly.

"You made your tenure and gave up," she said to him. "You haven't published anything in ten years. You betrayed the University."

He always made the same excuses. "When Ellen divorced me, I couldn't go on. The experiments failed. The grant proposals were rejected."

"But that's not all, is it?"

He looked away.

"Tell me the real reason."

"I don't have the talent," he hissed at her.

"And how did you make your tenure?"

"Ellen... and the Dean. They were... He figured he owed me. They left together years ago."

"Mediocrity," she taunted. "At the University we cannot tolerate mediocrity. It's a betrayal of trust."

"I'm a good teacher. Isn't that enough?"

"You haven't published. You betrayed the University."

The woman in the poster laughed at him.

Toward noon he considered what to do for lunch. His colleagues never invited him out anymore. On a whim he decided to buy a sandwich from the vending machine and eat it at Mirror Pond. He thought about Donna Lapurge. She would be long gone, of course.

He ascended the western slope of the campus with his sandwich and Coke. It was hot out and Sutherland perspired in his suit and tie. He passed crowds of students in tee shirts and shorts. It was futile, he knew, but he hurried in hopes of seeing her there. At the steps leading down to the little pond he paused to catch his breath and wipe his brow. Then he cautiously rounded a clump of bushes.

His heart leaped! She was sitting on the same stone bench, her head tilted sideways into one corner, eyes gazing at the water. Her necklace sparkled in the sun. She kept her hands in her lap, paying no attention to the people strolling by. Had she been like this for three hours? Again Sutherland sensed that something oppressed her.

He lowered himself onto a bench on the opposite side of the pond. Unraveling his sandwich, he held it with both hands in front of his belly. His eyes remained fixed on her. He raised the bread to his mouth and slowly bit off a massive chunk. His damp red cheek bulged as he chewed.

She sat there motionless. Her white dress reached below her knees. She was lovely, and Sutherland wondered why none of the young men stopped to talk to her. He hardly tasted his sandwich. When he finished it, he idly swirled his can of pop.

Suddenly Donna Lapurge sat up straight. She seemed alarmed, as if she had no idea where she was. She collected the books and notebooks beside her. Then, noticing Sutherland, she became flustered and spilled her things on the ground. She gathered them up hastily and hurried away. Sutherland watched her vanish in the shrubbery.

She didn't come to the next lecture. Sutherland looked for her and was disappointed.

She's embarrassed about the exam, he thought.

At noon he went again to Mirror Pond with his lunch. She was sitting cross legged on the other side, twirling a stick in the water. He dropped heavily onto a stone bench, removed his sandwich wrapper, and bit greedily. She glanced up smiling, as if she'd been waiting for him. He tried to return the greeting, but his mouth was full of food.

Suddenly he heard a frightened gasp from someone on the bench with him. He jumped up but no one was there. No one was even close. A dozen yards away two professors were strolling on the footpath, intent upon their conversation. Surely they hadn't made the sound. Could it have been an echo? Whirling around, he saw that Donna had disappeared.

"What the hell is going on?" he whispered.

He tossed away his lunch and hurried back to his office.

Sutherland was elated when she entered the lecture hall. She took a seat in the rear. During the lecture he looked at her several times, but she was clearly daydreaming. Once their eyes met for an instant, and he looked away. At the end of the lecture Sutherland left the room perplexed.

They all hate the course, he thought, but at least the others go through the motions. Why come just to snooze?

At lunch hour they met again on opposite sides of the pond. They smiled at each other. Sutherland felt certain she expected to see him. The idea was titillating.

A pattern emerged. Donna came to the morning lecture and daydreamed. At noon they met on opposite sides of the pond. They greeted each other, and he ate his lunch. Sutherland anticipated their silent rendezvous all morning. On rainy days, when he had to eat indoors, he sulked.

He bought a toupee. He went on a diet and walked for thirty minutes in the evening. He resisted the temptation of his liquor cabinet. His old research projects surfaced in his mind.

I'll write a protocol for that viral mutant study, he resolved, and I'll get into genetic engineering. He fished out ten-year-old journals with his published articles and reread his works. He was seized with a passion to start.

But everything was so difficult. In his soul lurked despair that whatever he did would fail. He faltered and slid back. After a week of abstinence he drank himself to sleep. But the next day, after seeing Donna, he was filled with new determination to alter his destiny, to rise above his modest gifts.

On the day of the second exam Sutherland arrived at Barlowe Hall in good spirits. He had put aside the fact that in four weeks Donna Lapurge had not demonstrated a particle of interest in microbiology. She had the weekend to prepare, he reasoned. The exam was easy. If she had taken in anything, even by osmosis, she ought to redeem herself.

She entered the top of the room a minute before the bell. She paused and looked over the class, but avoided looking at Sutherland. Finally she sat next to a fellow whom Sutherland recognized as the only student who seemed interested in the subject. He asked questions and took voluminous notes.

Sutherland's heart sank. He knew what she intended. He also knew that he couldn't deal with it. He handed a paper to the last straggler, then sat in his chair at the front and scanned the room for problems. There were none. He closed his eyes and prayed.

When he looked up again, he saw her cheating. With the concentration of a surgeon she abstracted the answers of her neighbor as soon as he wrote them down. She seemed completely unconcerned about the risk. He was outraged.

He rose and paced back and forth, hoping to scare her. She ignored him. She didn't even try to disguise her crime.

Students came down to him with questions. He dealt with them brusquely. He was flushed and perspiring. He imagined himself confronting her, demanding her paper. But the thought of losing her rendered him impotent.

Why should I care if she cheats? he remonstrated. What difference will it make to anyone?

Then something happened that bewildered him. The fellow beside Donna leaned back and casually rested his arm on the back of her chair. He seemed to be thinking about one of the questions. A minute later he placed his elbow on the writing arm of his own chair and leaned his chin on his hand. These movements, so natural and innocuous, brought his head so close to hers that they must have been in contact, yet the fellow seemed unaware of her presence. He moved around her periphery exactly as if she were not there!

Sutherland rubbed his eyes. What's wrong with me? he thought. Am I hallucinating? I haven't had a drink for days.

He peered up at them. Again they violated each other's space like two independent receptions on a television screen. He looked at the floor. Feeling dizzy, he gripped the arm of his chair. A boy came down and asked him to clarify an exam question. Sutherland blurted out the whole answer.

After that a queue formed in front of him and, one by one, the students returned happily to their seats.

At last the hour ended. Sutherland fled into the sunlight. He stalked to his laboratory by a route that avoided the Mirror Pond area.

For a week he lunched in his office. He was relieved that Donna stayed away from his class. Then he found a note on his desk. Written in ornate feminine script, it read: "Come today." He was positive his office had been locked.

He bustled wheezily up to the pond at noon. She was sitting on the ground against a dogwood tree, gazing at the blue sky. Azaleas and tulips framed her white dress, the same dress she always wore. The beauty and gracefulness of her figure so enraptured him that he set his lunch aside and sat like a worshipper on the bench. And then Donna Lapurge began to sing.

Her voice floated sweetly, almost palpably, over the pond. It filled the air, seeming to emanate from the trees and rise from the flower beds. She sang an Elizabethan love song:

> Come live with me and be my love
> And we will all the pleasures prove
> That hills and valleys, dales and fields,
> Woods or steepy mountain yields.
>
> The shepherd swains shall dance and sing
> For thy delight each May morning;
> If these delights they mind may move,
> Come live with me and be my love.

The melody enveloped and caressed him, absorbing his senses and addling his perception. He experienced only her. He felt himself transported to her side but without any awareness of movement. Or had she come to him? He gazed at her face and felt a joyous stream of tears on his cheeks. "What is happening to me?" he whispered.

It didn't matter, for he was fully prepared to yield. He loved her beyond reason and will.

Suddenly she was gone---vanished---and he sat alone on his bench. People strolled by undistracted. Birds chirped in the bushes and squirrels raced about. The same water, the same landscape; nothing had happened. "This is madness," he murmured. "I need help."

* * *

At the Department of Parapsychology the noted Professor George Saeger's private secretary announced the arrival of Edward Sutherland over her intercom.

"Yes, show him in," the noted voice responded.

Sutherland was ushered into an office three times larger than his own, with oak furniture, a carpet, paneling, and paintings of European harbors and landscapes. There were bookcases filled with scholarly journals and a small library of books on parapsychology and related subjects, some authored by Saeger himself.

Saeger, tall, broad shouldered, graying handsomely, rose from his polished desk. The two men shook hands and introduced themselves.

"Please sit down," said Saeger. "You're in micro, eh?"

"That's right." Sutherland already regretted coming here. This tidy, ornate office made his look like a Dumpster. Although he had doubts about Saeger's profession, the man's reputation intimidated him. But the only alternative---admitting lunacy---was worse.

"I've been knocking my head against these grant proposals," said Saeger. "I swear, I must spend eighty percent of my time filling them out. But you're aware of the problem, I'm sure."

Sutherland smiled weakly. He suspected he was being sized up as a failure, as someone who could never win a research grant. On the desk he noticed reprinted articles from the Journal of Psychic Research with Saeger as the lead author.

"Well, how can I help you?" Saeger asked.

Sutherland took a deep breath. "I think I've seen a ghost."

"Really." Saeger made a wry face.

"At Mirror Pond."

Saeger's face straightened out and his eyes became intense. "Yes, go on." Sutherland told his tale. He had expected amused disbelief, if not outright derision, and was surprised by his host's serious reaction. "Can you describe the woman?"

"Slender. Exquisite face. Short, black hair.

"What about her clothes?"

"A white dress." Sutherland thought a moment. "Yes, she always wears that same white dress."

"Is it something the other women wear around campus?"

"Why, no. It's one of those roaring-Twenties flapper styles."

Saeger folded his hands under his chin. He seemed to be weighing a decision. Then he went to his file cabinet and hunted through a drawer. He pulled out a photocopy of a newspaper article.

"Have a look," he said.

Sutherland's eyes widened. "It's her!"

"You might like to read the story. I'll leave it with you while I give this proposal to my secretary." Saeger gathered up his papers. "Publish or perish," he quipped as he left the room.

The headline on the photocopy had appeared on the front page of the local newspaper. The date was May 12, 1928. SLAIN CO-ED FOUND IN MIRROR POND, read the oversized print. The story described an affair between a student of medieval music, Donna Lapurge, and a Professor Jameson of the Mathematics Department. Jameson was accused of clubbing the woman to death with a hammer and dumping her body into Mirror Pond.

Saeger returned with amusement on his face. "Well, what do you think?" Sutherland turned palms up.

"Don't believe in ghosts, eh?"

"Do you?"

"Well, in this profession one comes across certain phenomena that are, shall we say, nebulous."

"This has happened before, hasn't it? Otherwise you wouldn't have searched for the article."

"Yes, it has. At least twice, in fact. She appeared to two members of the faculty in the same way you've described. Both men came to see me about it. They caught Miss Lapurge cheating in class and were later regaled by her at Mirror Pond. I did some historical work and found the murder story."

"Who were they?"

"Nobody important. One man left to teach high school after failing to get his book published. The other got involved in radical politics. Tried to incite the students against University policies."

"What happened to him?"

"He was found dead."

"Dead? How?"

"You don't remember? It was about five years ago. Coincidentally he was found near Mirror Pond." Saeger shuffled some papers on his desk. For the first time he avoided Sutherland's eyes, and Sutherland sensed he was being devious.

"What happened to Jameson?"

"He was executed. In the electric chair."

"Oh, God!"

"You feel sorry for him? I don't. He caught the girl cheating, she offered her body in return for his silence, and he agreed. Later he did her in to keep her silent. No, I don't feel sorry for Jameson. He was a murderer and he betrayed the University. Electrocution is just what he deserved."

A fragment of a recollection flickered and died in Sutherland's head. "Unfortunately these things seldom come without loose ends. We may never learn why she chose you. Perhaps you have something in common with the others," Saeger added with a hint of disdain.

Neither man spoke for a while.

"I wonder if you could tell me something," Saeger finally said. "Please be assured that I will hold it in the strictest confidence and will not make light of it. Could you tell me how you feel about this apparition, that is, not about seeing a ghost but about Miss Lapurge herself?"

"I think at first I was charmed by her. When she sang to me, I fell in love."

"I see." Saeger seemed to be making another calculation. "And you will seek her again?"

"Seek? It seems I can't avoid her."

Saeger laughed and stood up, ending the interview. "She'll probably get tired of you and look for someone else to haunt. I'd keep it quiet, though, or we could end up looking like a pair of wackos."

"I'm not going to publicize it."

"Good. Let me know if anything else happens."

They shook hands and went out to the anteroom, where the secretary was typing busily. Just then, a young man entered with a sheaf of papers.

"Ah, Hodges," said Saeger. "Finally got it done?"

"Yes, sir." He handed over the papers.

"It's about time, isn't it?"

"I'm sorry it took so long. It won't happen again."

"I think we'll send it to the Journal of Psychic Research or maybe Parallel Science Quarterly. What do you think?"

Sutherland smiled politely and slipped out the door. "Yes, yes, Professor Saeger," he muttered, "we're all impressed with your glorious record of publications."

Sutherland existed in a state of anxious despair. He dressed himself, ate, drifted through his academic routines, and went to sleep, all without premeditation. He walked around campus in a desultory manner, hands in his pockets, eyes on the ground. He kept hearing a single question: Why do you go on living?

The only flame to brighten his life had been extinguished. Was it possible to love a ghost? Could there be any real communication? On the other hand, if he were to die and enter her realm, what would he find?

In his office he pondered these questions until his scientific curiosity was aroused. Here, after all, was virgin territory. He might be the only mortal with access to the spirit world. He ought to be planning his analysis, prodding and measuring this ghost, finding answers like Pasteur and Koch. But no ideas were coming to him.

"I'm a failure!" He pounded his desk.

The woman in the poster smirked at him as she climbed out of the water. "You fell behind and got flabby," she taunted. "The University cannot tolerate this betrayal."

I must see Donna again, he decided. I must go back to the pond.

He wasn't sure why. Part of him wanted to analyze Donna, part only to be mesmerized by her.

In the closing days of the spring quarter he took his lunch to the pond. He waited, scanning the benches and shrubs, but she never appeared. He tried to conjure her up with a mental effort. This also failed. She's left me, he thought.

One day, he noticed that he was being watched. He had definitely glimpsed the face of Saeger's graduate student, Hodges, behind a clump of evergreens. When he stood up, Hodges fled. Bewildered, Sutherland headed back to his office, turning a few times to check behind him.

Sutherland's heart leaped when he saw the note on his desk. The single word "Midnight" was written in the same ornate script he had seen before. The note resolved his confusion. He realized how much he yearned for Donna. If he could not bring about their physical union, he would be content to lie peacefully in her sight. His ideas of scientific analysis now struck him as repugnant. This spirit had been sent to give him solace, not to be jabbed and sliced like a laboratory animal.

That evening he enjoyed a leisurely dinner at an off-campus restaurant, then strolled about the area watching the crowds and reading idly in a bookstore. He felt a joyful anticipation. With the midnight tryst Donna surely had a plan for him. She must know his simple desires and would requite them in her own eerie way.

A few minutes before midnight, he arrived at his favorite bench beside the pond. The sky was luminescent with a full moon and stars, and the air was warm and balmy. There was no one else in sight, and the only sound was a faint rustling in the bushes.

The bell in the Student Union tolled midnight. Sutherland noticed a silent churning in the middle of the pond. The water's motion rose, moonlit, into the air, a wispy plasma struggling for form, billowing toward him. As it moved, it took the shape of a woman, naked, her head smashed on one side, her face contorted in wrath. She pointed a finger at him.

"Betrayal," her voice rasped.

He wanted to run but he could not stand. His ankles and wrists were manacled to the stone bench, which had become a wired armchair of oak. When he understood his plight, he gasped in terror. His body jerked taut and he collapsed.

Minutes later, a tall figure emerged from the bushes and moved warily toward the slumped form on the bench.

"Sutherland?" whispered Professor Saeger. He looked closely. "My God! It's happened again."

Saeger scanned the pond, the grounds, the sky to no avail. Then he pulled back the sleeve of the dead man's shirt. He noted the black splotch on the wrist. There were similar marks on the other wrist and on both legs above the ankles. Kneeling, Saeger withdrew a small metric ruler from his coat and carefully measured the diameter of each burn mark. When he looked again at the wide-eyed, gaping countenance, he recoiled.

"Incredible!" In high spirits he hurried away from the pond.

At the Department of Parapsychology he bounded upstairs to his office. He fumbled through his desk until he found paper and pen. He took a series of deep breaths. At last his trembling hand dispensed a barely legible scrawl:

[To the Journal of Psychic Research]

A previous communication from this laboratory described the possible sighting of a female apparition of the Naiadal (fresh water) subgroup. Our speculation that the apparition caused the death by electrocution of a human perceptor has since been challenged by other research teams, who have contended that fatality in human perceptors cannot be induced by the alteration and manipulation of terrestrial objects by phantasmal entities. The present report provides evidence that contravenes these assertions and substantiates the transformation of a stone bench...

GARDENS OF PARADISE

The usual mob had come to see us off. They waved their little flags in time to the band music. They elbowed and shoved each other for a better view. When street vendors arrived with syn-dogs and nutri-chips, the good citizens of the dome fought like jungle beasts for a place in line. Civility tends to flee our big occasions.

The mayor and members of the Perpetuity Council were on the stand with us, gleaming in their medals and red, white and blue sashes. The patriotic colors extended from their breasts to the sound shell, to the whole heliport and back down the boulevard toward the downtown area, where thousands more watched the ceremony on giant screens. WE LOVE OUR HORIZONS UNLIMITED HEROES! cried banners from the rooftops. GOD KEEP US STRONG AND PURE.

And preferably sane, I hoped. They were pelting each other with syn-food now, using the public holiday to cast out their private terror. I wished the mayor would quit socializing and get started. Beyond the sanitary locks our helijet waited to fly us out to Beagle IV.

At last His Honor strode to the podium. "Fellow survivors," he proclaimed, "on this glorious morning we assemble to reaffirm our unshakable trust in our most merciful God and to ask His blessings upon our three valiant saviors. May their mission be crowned with unparalleled success!"

For the last ninety years or so, he had begun every Embarkation Day ceremony with the same lines. And as they had done on every one of those occasions the people responded with thunderous cheers. He then yielded the podium to the Bishop, who recited a long prayer for our guidance and protection in the septic environment. The people stood with their heads bowed, their eyes tightly shut, and their fists clenched, as if trying with all their might to help God make the right decision.

After the amen, the mayor gave his speech. He started with his annually updated opener: "Eight score and eighteen years ago, after we survived the Pandemic Era, the catastrophic plagues, the unkillable microbes, whose spores still ride the winds of the septic world, when the voice of God called us into the desert and taught us how to build and pave this mighty fortress, our beloved and pristine city-dome..."

I glanced at the rapt faces. The people remembered what had caused the Pandemic Era: age-retarding herbal extracts---a.k.a. ARHEX's, Methusalehs, gray chasers, boost juice---the ultimate drugs, and the extreme overpopulation to which they had led. And every citizen knew that I had been a pioneer in ARHEX research. But they gazed up at me with love and devotion. They would not hear of my role in the near extinction of the human race, and the tactful mayor would never refer to that historical detail. Why should he? With all males vasectomized, overpopulation was no longer a threat. The only concern now was to find ever more potent ARHEX's.

"... the man who, with his brilliant, devoted colleagues at the Futures Institute, has given us the blessings of youth and vitality, who continues to risk his life by traveling twenty thousand kilometers a year in the dismal world of germs..."

The crowd was already screaming.

"... Professor Ernest Kruger!"

I stepped to the podium and embraced the mayor. He was at his puffed-up best, and the people were almost out of control. I waited for them to settle down and then told them what they wanted to hear: Since last year's mission, four new extracts on the market, all isolated from Pacific island plants which were now grown hydroponically within the dome; age-retardation index 10-12%; safe and effective for men and women both; compatible with the whole range of syn-food.

The crowd went wild. "Kru-ger! Kru-ger! Kru-ger!"

When they stopped yelling, I introduced the other two members of the Horizons Unlimited team. Colonel Jack Doyle, a charismatic ex-soldier known to all, received a fresh wave of cheers. Doyle was our security officer. He cut a fine athletic figure in his white, skintight polyalkyl protective suit and boots. His flame-pistol jutted out of its holster, and I remembered the time he ashed a wild pig that had torn down our lab tent. He could hack out paths through intractable jungle, never losing his sense of direction. Doyle was a strict rules-and-regulations type, a bit ludicrous perhaps, except on contaminated, unpredictable islands.

Robert Bigelow, a pale, stringy, highly intelligent fellow, avoided the limelight, and his accomplishments were not widely known. I had taken him on reluctantly after my senior assistant lapsed into T-depression and injected himself with chloroform. The man's death had left my research team frightened, suspicious, and withdrawn; not one had volunteered to go in his place.

Then Bigelow came over from Modification with an impressive résumé: one hundred and ten years in artificial flavors and essences, including work on flavors 95-109, which were used in everything; after that, sixty years in pseudosoil technology. By incorporating flavor capsules into his soil ingredients he had grown the first hydroponic vegetables with any taste. Then, in a stunning tour de force, he had hybridized two island herbs and produced an extract 5% more potent than those of the parent species.

When I told all this to the crowd, they cheered Bigelow feverishly. What I didn't say was that he had earned the nickname "Weed" for excessive cultivation and frequent use of hydroponic Cannabis and that he spent his leisure time composing insufferably long ballads about the moon, the stars, and some heavenly gardens of Paradise. Nor did I mention that he lacked jungle experience, indeed had never even left the dome.

Bigelow knew how to use our analyzers. He wanted to make the trip, was eager, as he put it, to "bring something to fruition." He had promised to leave his weed at home. I had qualms, and I knew that Doyle didn't trust him, but I had to admit one thing: The guy got results.

Which was what I told the crowd. It was all they wanted to hear.

* * *

CI175-19W/10-80N was a gloomy island that was really a tight ring of islets fringed by coral beaches and enclosing a lagoon. From Beagle IV, our laboratory ship, the jungle seemed like a dark green shroud hiding deadly secrets. It gave me a chill. But the big coral islands had yielded the richest harvest of ARHEX's, and I had surveyed the others in previous years. This one---the most remote of all---could not be left out.

Our thin, white protective suits, gloves, and boots were made of microporous, detergent-active polyalkyl fiber. Our helmets, hermetically zipped to the neckline, contained a disinfecting air filter and a tiny sound-enhancer. We couldn't smell anything but we could hear each other clearly; distant sounds were partly muffled but audible.

We loaded the analyzers, cartridges of nutri-flux, disinfectant canisters, and camping equipment into the landing craft. The plastic hood protected us from any noxious droplets of seawater as Doyle drove us in. The moment we hit the beach, he handed out disinfectant and we sprayed our suits, boots, and helmets.

A horseshoe crab came tripping over the coarse, white sand. When Bigelow tried to catch it, Doyle grabbed his arm.

"Uh-uh, Weed-boy! We don't touch anything that moves."

"Polyalkyl is antiseptic," Bigelow retorted. "You forgot your lessons."

"We don't touch anything that moves."

The two men glowered through their visors. They had taken an instant dislike to one another. On the Beagle, Doyle had dogged Bigelow relentlessly, as if he expected him to unzip his helmet and sneak a puff of something. Bigelow had fought back with sarcasm. I was appalled at their lack of professionalism.

"Both of you, levelize!" I told them. "Loss of composure means loss of resistance."

They mumbled apologies and went on scowling. Actually the colonel's sharp warning pleased me. Bigelow might need a forceful reminder of the hazards around us.

He turned away from Doyle and spread his arms. "This is the first time I've touched earth since the dome was built," he rejoiced.

"Earth? This is just limestone," I said. "The organic crud is in there." The jungle was bordered with cacao trees, iridescent in the burning sun.

"It's beautiful. I haven't seen a real tree in 178 years. Oh, look!"

A flock of birds rose up and swirled around the treetops. Lorikeets, I guessed, observing their multicolored feathers. Our helmets muffled their harsh squawking. Just as suddenly they disappeared into the glistening leaves, and Bigelow waved his arms to scare them up again.

"Let's get started," I said.

We shouldered our gear and headed into the wet jungle. Doyle led the way up and down muddy slopes thick with trees, vines, and pulpy vegetation. Rats scampered out of our path. In a mangrove bog a huge snake crawled under the maze of exposed roots. The shrieking of birds, though muted, continued to ring in my ears as we plodded through a hot, sticky, insect-ridden valley. At every turn Bigelow stopped to look and listen, and I had to keep urging him forward.

Near the center of the islet we paused to rest and consult the field guide. Our suits were soaked with sweat. Many of the small, round-leaf ARHEX plants were growing here, but none of them were new. We already raised these species hydroponically.

Bigelow knelt and almost caressed the muddy floor of the jungle. "Soil," he murmured, "real, organic soil. It must be full of mysteries."

"Which is why we don't allow it in the dome," I reminded him. "Let's move on to the lagoon."

Frangipani trees, in white and yellow bloom, formed a little grove near the sandy beach of the lagoon. Bigelow examined the flowers, actually brushing the intakes of his helmet against their petals. "I can't smell them," he lamented, and fingered the hermetic zipper on his chest, as if to remove his helmet. He changed his mind when Doyle rushed up, barking "Uh-uh! Stop right there!" Bigelow flung up his arms in a mocking gesture.

"This looks like a good place to start," I said, raising my voice deliberately.

Some delicate, round-leaf plants had caught my attention. I took Bigelow aside and placed the field guide in his hands. After studying the plants, we agreed that they were new.

We attached cartridges of nutri-flux and had an early dinner. Doyle went to work inflating the plastic tents, arranging the analyzers, and disinfecting everything in his usual thorough way. Bigelow and I began to collect plant specimens. In less than an hour he found six new species.

"Good job," I told him. "We'll be busy tonight."

"Where's the colonel going?"

Doyle, having set up camp, was heading into the bush.

"We won't see much of him from now on. His idea of security is a broad overview without distractions. Don't worry, though. We'll never be out of his sight."

I meant this both as reassurance and admonition.

* * *

That evening, Bigelow and I began our analyses in the lab tent. We had found a total of nine new plants. Thanks to miniaturization, automation, and high-performance equipment, we were able to run all the extractions, separate the components, make chemical tests, predict biological activities, and start incubating model cells with possible age-retardants. With several dozen microplates in the incubator, we retired to the transparent sleeping tent. We zipped ourselves in, turned on the plasma lamp, fumigated, started the air purifier, and took of our helmets. A fusion of night sounds drowned out the hum of the air purifier. Somewhere at the edge of the jungle Doyle would have set up a sleeping bubble for his own use.

Bigelow lay back on his air mattress, hands behind his head. "Listen to that," he whispered. "It's a symphony."

"Cacophony, you mean."

"There must be a thousand creatures out there. The simulations at the museum don't do it justice."

"Nonsense. They're precise to three decahertz."

"They reproduce the sound but not the music."

Robert Bigelow's pale, delicate face reflected the lamplight, and his soft gaze seemed to span another world. I wondered if he was strolling through his gardens of Paradise. Would he become an obstacle on this mission, as Doyle evidently feared? Damn, I thought, save me from poets.

"Let's get some sleep," I said. "We'll try the other side of the lagoon tomorrow."

I turned off the lamp and fell asleep in minutes. Later I awoke to find Bigelow writing in a notepad under a minilamp.

"You better get some rest," I told him.

He was totally preoccupied and didn't answer. To his consternation I snatched away the notepad. He had written:

My hopes are grandly met. This brightly colored, melodic isle puts all my senses on edge. I cannot sleep. I tingle with anticipation of new surprises.

In the jungle I am strong and vigorous, no longer afraid of death. My fear and depression have vanished in the steam.

"'No longer afraid of death'? What do you mean?"

I asked him. "I was outlining a poem, sir. May I have the notepad?"

I looked at the blackness around us. The jungle noise had resolved itself into cheerless avian belches and a background of insect whining. "You're not planning some grand poetic exit, I hope."

"No," he muttered, turning away in displeasure.

"And this depression," I persisted. "You mustn't let that become a problem here." I was thinking of my late assistant, whose place Bigelow had taken.

"It's not a problem here. I was depressed in the dome."

"Oh? Why don't you find someone and mate up for a few weeks? It works better than weed."

"Yes, sir."

I gave him back the notepad. "You'll be getting the Medal of Valor for this trip, you know. And on Survivors Day you'll be invited to the Perpetuity Council's gala."

He looked at me and stifled a laugh.

"What's so funny? It works for Doyle."

"I'm not Doyle, sir, and neither are you."

We stared at each other, and I knew then that something unpleasant was going to happen. For an instant I felt sorry for Bigelow. "Turn off the lamp," I said. "We'll need to be alert tomorrow."

In the darkness he murmured a final word: "I don't intend to be depressed again, sir."

* * *

Early in the morning we checked the cell cultures, recorded thirty-six failures, and marked twenty compounds for further testing. Better than average, I thought. Once again these poisonous islands might grant us a blessing.

Doyle joined us, and we all fortified ourselves with nutri-flux. Doyle checked our suits, boots, and helmets for tightness and made sure we sprayed. Then he slipped back into the trees.

Bigelow and I collected more of the potentially useful plants and stored then in plastic bags. In my laboratory aboard the Beagle they would have to be extracted again for the second round of tests. Finally, seeds (and only seeds!) of the most promising plants would be decontaminated and brought into the dome.

We set out with the field guide. The other side of the lagoon appeared to be a broader land area---a thicker, less hospitable jungle. We paused on the narrow beach. The hot, viscous air made our suits and helmets a torment. My boots felt like lead weights. Flies and armies of lagoon insects swooped down on us, while seabirds nagged incessantly overhead. The dark portals of the jungle made me shudder.

"Look!" Bigelow cried, lurching ahead. His boots left craters in the sand as he staggered toward a row of shrubs. "Azaleas, aren't they? I've seen them in books. And look at the size of these ferns!" He whirled from one plant to the next, laughing and fondling their blooms.

"If you can tear yourself away, we have work to do," I reminded him.

"These flowers are luxuriant. Imagine how the dome would look with flowers! We had rose and lilac seeds once, but we didn't preserve them. Professor, you could have brought back seeds..."

"Our job is ARHEX plants, not flowers. Would you waste greenhouse space on flowers?" I looked at him in dismay, and he compressed his lips. "Come on, let's finish this damn survey and get the hell out of here."

For half an hour we collected samples of beachfront vegetation. The sun rose to its murderous peak. Our bodies were limp, and I had morbid fantasies of flinging myself into the lagoon. Seeking relief, we began to forage in the jungle. By this time my brain was so addled that I never objected when Bigelow quietly widened his range.

Suddenly Doyle burst out of the trees. "That weed-head's gone! He found a trail and started exploring it. I followed him a while, but then I heard a noise, a soft droning sound that I couldn't identify. Bigelow heard it too and ducked into some bushes about twenty yards ahead of me. We both kept still and listened. The noise seemed far off, but I wasn't sure.

When it finally stopped, I realized he'd disappeared. Come with me, if you will, sir. There's something I want to show you."

He led me to a small grove, where no ferns or shrubs were present. A pit, lined with gray and white smudges, descended a few feet into the ground, and charred fragments of branches lay about. Doyle used a rock to scrape a little earth from the pit wall.

"Ashes," he informed me. "Sir, this island is inhabited."

I was stunned. "Outpeople? My God! The jokes were true."

In the old days we had tossed around theories that isolated communities might have survived in the septic world. Their people might have developed hardy immune systems or simply found a lucky refuge, untouched by the windborne spores. The theories had evolved into outpeople jokes. (If survivors live in the city-dome, where do outpeople live? Doom-city.)

"Damn! Where the hell is Bigelow?" I muttered.

"This way, sir. See the web?"

He picked the shreds of a broken spider's web off a low branch. I would have missed it completely. Again I was grateful for the man's ingenuity in these treacherous dungholes.

We pushed our way into the steamy, vine-laden depth of the jungle. The possibility of encountering outpeople worried me. How degraded might a lone band of humans become on a remote island in the septic environment? Doyle, of course, had his flame-pistol, but there might be more than wild pigs to deal with.

We moved on warily. Every few yards Doyle paused to examine a bent branch or the faint arc of a bootprint. Then we heard the droning noise. One moment it sounded like voices, the next like the hum of an air purifier. Distorted by my helmet and the rampant vegetation, it seemed ominous, as though our presence had aroused some kind of mobilization. I crouched beside Doyle, who had frozen intense concentration. Levelize! I told myself. Don't let your imagination destroy your composure.

"Sir," he whispered, "you better get back to camp."

"What do you think it is?"

He shook his head and listened again. "I don't know, but right now you need to get the samples to the boat. I'll find Bigelow."

"I can't just leave you here." My protest was feeble. Doyle had taken over command.

"Our first priority is the samples. Please go. If I don't find him soon, I'll join you."

That weed-head Bigelow will get us all killed, I thought. I almost insisted on leaving him to the outs. But I needed his help with the analyses, and Doyle, who considered me a brave professional, would have been shocked. With the scent of action, his soldierly adrenaline was flowing.

"Good luck, Colonel," I said, and slipped away.

* * *

Minutes later I was groping fecklessly through the bush and repeating aloud, "I am not lost. The lagoon is straight ahead." But everywhere I turned, the vegetation seemed to increase in density. Birds screeched and cackled above me, as if amused by my helplessness. Voracious insects collided with my visor. Breathless, I leaned against a fruited banyan tree and drank a cartridge of ultrafiltered water. "I am not lost…"

The droning was getting louder, closer. There was no longer any doubt: It was a chorus of human voices. Primitive, repetitive chanting, accompanied by the slow beating of a drum, apparently some ritual of the outpeople. I guessed that they had begun on a neighboring island and crossed over to ours.

Again I twisted through the jungle labyrinth, swatting pulpy foliage out of my face, trying desperately to avoid a fatal tear in my suit. Where the hell was the damn lagoon? As my apprehension mounted, my progress diminished, and I lost all sense of direction. The monotonous chanting seemed to come from everywhere.

Then I burst into a clearing, and thirty feet ahead of me Bigelow was sitting on the ground, talking to a dark-skinned, half-naked woman. His helmet rested in his lap. Beside them were another pit, a pile of logs, and a large coral trough filled with boiling water and a mash of flowers and leaves. Great hideous masks were arranged around the pit. At my sudden intrusion Bigelow leaped to his feet, and the young woman backed away.

"Have you lost your mind?" I stalked up to him and jammed the helmet onto his head. When I tried to close the zipper, he pulled away and started toward the woman. She fled into the jungle.

"Lee-Tai, don't go!" he cried.

I wrapped my arms around him, and we toppled to the ground. "Stop fighting me!" I shouted. "You'll tear our suits."

"She's friendly, sir."

"She's filthy."

I recoiled at my own state of mind. Get your composure back, I told myself I stood up and tightened my intakes. Bigelow sat on the ground, simmering.

"Who was she?" I asked. He wouldn't answer, and I had to repeat the question.

"An attendant of some kind," he muttered.

"Do you hear that chanting? Is it coming this way?"

"It probably is, sir." At last he picked himself up and pointed to the boiling mash. "Something is going to happen here. She was preparing the trough for a ceremony, I think. The flowers have a fragrant smell. She tried to explain but I couldn't understand."

"Well, whatever's going on is irrelevant to us. We have to find the lagoon and get off this island."

"I'm not going, sir."

"What!"

My shock was blunted by the sudden realization that the chanting procession of outpeople had almost reached us. I yanked Bigelow into the bushes.

In minutes the paunchy leader of the parade emerged solemnly into the clearing. His brown face and massive body were painted in white streaks, and a necklace of large animal teeth swayed with his ponderous steps. He gripped a long staff decorated with tufts of colored feathers. I took him to be a medicine man or shaman.

The rest of the outs, still moaning their woebegone chorus, filed in behind him. Two burly men carried a bed of branches on their shoulders. Upon this crude bier the corpse of a gray-haired man was partly visible under a pall of palm leaves. Several women followed the pallbearers, then children of various ages. All except the children were painted and ornamented, though less garishly than the shaman. Last of all, the drummer appeared, thumping his hide-covered instrument.

The bier was set down across the pit, which the pallbearers then filled with logs from the woodpile. When the crowd had arranged itself around the pit, an old, fat woman, looking forlorn and tearful, stepped forward, and the shaman placed his hands on her head, lifted his face to the sky, and called out a long, solemn prayer. The bereaved woman was then comforted by other mourners.

At the shaman's signal the group of children approached the dead man and tossed flowers, woodcarvings, and bits of colored coral onto the bier. All the outs began singing again, a more festive chant this time, with swaying and hand-clapping. Steam billowed up from the boiling trough, apparently masking the smell of death with aromatic volatiles.

The children fascinated me. I hadn't seen a child since the early days of the city dome. I watched them as they peeked out from behind the adults, imitated the swaying and clapping, touched one another playfully, and confided secrets. The youngest ones played with straw dolls, occasionally turning their attention to the ceremony and regarding the huge shaman with innocent awe.

Bigelow was captivated. His eyes glistened and he murmured little sounds of delight. He laughed and clapped his hands when the smallest child, a sweet-faced girl clad only in mud, jumped up and down in imitation of her mother. I kept an eye on him, fearing he would do something insane.

It was hard to believe that people so primitive had developed superior immune systems. But it was only a little less improbable that the island had escaped the plagues. We had always assumed that the windborne spores had overspread the globe. If this island had been spared, were there other sanctuaries?

Why hadn't the outs discovered their ARHEX plants? Or had they tried them, realized the danger of protracted life on a small island, and forbidden their use?

I was drowning in questions. On the one hand, my old scientific curiosity, ages in hibernation, was lumbering out of its cave, hungry for answers; on the other, I began to doubt my own wisdom, as an ancient general might have done after leading his army to ruin. The children looked so pretty. I wanted to touch them, give them gifts, understand their secrets.

Bigelow was utterly entranced. Before I could stop him, he removed his helmet and wandered out of our concealment. I lunged for him, stumbled, and both of us were now exposed. The ceremony halted. Mothers seized their children. The shaman and the whole party of outs retreated to the edge of the clearing.

At that moment the woman, Lee-Tai, arrived with half a dozen spear-wielding men. Bigelow, as if lost in a weed-induced reverie, started toward her but was instantly confronted by a row of spearpoints. One of the outs, who seemed to be the chief, let out a ferocious scream and leaped forward.

"Wait!" Bigelow cried, throwing up his arms.

The chief paused for a second, then raised his spear again. In that posture he was engulfed in a blinding, roaring plume of white fire. The man simply evaporated. A moment later the fireball vanished, and a few particles of ash drifted to the ground.

Colonel Doyle stepped out of the bush.

Before his flame-pistol the horrified outs faltered back toward the shaman and the others.

"No!" Bigelow howled. "Murderer!"

Insanely he flung his helmet above the outs, who cringed beneath the shrubs. He rushed at Doyle and tried to wrench off his helmet. The colonel spun him around, fastened a headlock on him, and, motioning for me to follow, dragged the flailing, moaning Bigelow into the trees. We had not gone far when Bigelow managed to break free. Doyle and I tried to stop him, but in his desperation he eluded us and plunged again into the clearing. He was met by the outs, who must have sensed weakness. First one, then another spear ripped his torso, and he toppled to the ground. One overwrought man bellowed defiantly at us. His brothers, eyeing the flame-pistol, rushed to hold him back.

But Doyle was no longer a threat. He had come to a rigid halt, and I could almost feel his shock and anguish. He had failed to protect us. The mission might be lost. The colonel had never experienced such a calamity.

I eased the pistol from his hand. "It's not your fault!" I shouted. "This is what he wanted all along."

Doyle gazed uncomprehendingly through his visor. I turned him around, pushed him toward the jungle, and kept driving him forward until he began to gather his wits and move ahead on his own. Thankfully the outs chose not to follow us.

By some remarkable instinct Doyle found a way to the lagoon. Speechless and still confused, we circled the inner beach to our campsite. We gathered the samples, left the equipment, and fled sullenly to the outer shore. I wasn't thinking about Bigelow, the outs, or even the horrible fireball. I kept seeing the face of the little muddy girl, the smooth, dainty bodies of the children, their eyes full of innocence and curiosity. A foolish part of me longed to return.

At dusk we arrived at the outer shore. As we rode the waves out to Beagle IV, Doyle finally broke the tense silence.

"I suppose you'll have to tell the Council how he was killed."

I shrugged. "He got careless, allowed his suit to be penetrated, and died."

I saw no point in staining the colonel's reputation, and the truth about Bigelow would only distress people.

"And the outs? Will you put that in your report?"

"There are too many unknowns about them. Our citizens are doing all right in the dome, and they'll probably perish outside it. We shouldn't put ideas in their heads."

My answers satisfied Doyle, but they failed to comfort me. I gazed back at the surf, rolling silently onto the beach. The jungle was illuminated in an auburn sunset. Flocks of birds played around the treetops, while a hawk sailed in and out of view. As the island receded, my thoughts drifted ten thousand kilometers to a mob of pitiful, frightened souls. What would they do if I brought them flowers?

Printed in the United States
By Bookmasters